D1021912

STILL LIFE

STILL LIFE

Zoë Wicomb

THE
NEW
PRESS

NEW YORK
LONDON

Requests for permission to reproduce selections from this book
should be made through our website: https://thenewpress.com/contact.

Originally published in South Africa by Umuzi, an imprint of
Penguin Random House South Africa (Pty) Ltd. 2020
Published in the United States by The New Press, New York, 2020
Distributed by Two Rivers Distribution

LIBRARY OF CONGRESS CATALOGING-IN-PUBLICATION DATA

Names: Wicomb, Zoë, author.
Title: Still life / Zoe Wicomb.
Description: New York : The New Press, 2020. | "Originally published in
South Africa by Umuzi, an imprint of Penguin Random House South Africa
(Pty) Ltd. 2020" | Summary: "A novel that tells the story of an author
struggling to write a biography of long-forgotten Scottish poet Thomas
Pringle, whose only legacy is in South Africa where he is dubbed the
"Father of South African Poetry."—Provided by publisher.
Identifiers: LCCN 2020030731 | ISBN 9781620976104 (hardback)
ISBN 9781620976111 (ebook)
Classification: LCC PR9369.3.W53 S75 2020 | DDC 823/.914—dc23
LC record available at https://lccn.loc.gov/2020030731

The New Press publishes books that promote and enrich public
discussion and understanding of the issues vital to our democracy
and to a more equitable world. These books are made possible
by the enthusiasm of our readers; the support of a committed
group of donors, large and small; the collaboration of our many
partners in the independent media and the not-for-profit sector;
booksellers, who often hand-sell New Press books;
librarians; and above all by our authors.

www.thenewpress.com

Book design by Fahiema Hallam
This book was set in Adobe Caslon Pro

Printed in the United States of America

2   4   6   8   10   9   7   5   3   1

For Milo McClure

I

I do not think this a task that I could, or even should, take on. The responsibility is simply too heavy to shoulder; besides, the obligation is of a dubious nature. Thus I try to keep my head averted from these powdery phantoms that stir and falter in the dark. But they remain, pleading wordlessly – or so it seems.

What kind of makeshift shelter is this? Wind rattles the reeds that pass for rafters and the corroded sheets of corrugated iron lift creakily and fall, lift and fall, so that shafts of light snap at the spectral figures flailing, writhing in their am-dram poses. I resist the use of a torch, but cannot stop myself from peering inside when the light allows. Which is taken for encouragement – they are not as comatose as they once appeared to be – so that their rustling sounds rise above the wind sigh. I cannot tell how many there are, but there is no mistaking that these feverish forms are fixed on coming into being, on finding language, on making their demands on me.

One of them whispers: It is not so unusual, neither novel nor extraordinary, not so much to ask; it has been done before.

I listen in silence to their strange and various accents, to the voices growing louder, cacophonous in their clamour to be heard. The slight, bent form in the corner rocks to and fro, declaims in a dazed, rasping voice so that I catch only fragments: Poppy, or charms … one short sleep past … the round earth's corners. Over and over, growing fainter until it fades away.

After all, says the larger, older woman, the boldest, the most insistent of the lot, we do not have to be invented, no need to think of yourself as a god, a creator. Good Christian souls, all of us, prematurely cut off but, of course, blessed with eternal life all the same, so only a small matter of giving us another chance, of allowing us our fair share of years.

She stumbles to her knees, strains forward, and if her form is wobbly, a strong, vegetal whiff of desire rises from it, a greed for life, for recovering time – those bitter years of duress, salted bondage and subjugation gone for good, finished and done with. Her palms scrape, slap against each other as she reaches for the possibilities of a new life, a new century, a world shaken up in so many ways, so much more forgiving than the unjust, punitive world of yore. This is exactly what she had dreamt of, what she craves – a fresh start, her just deserts. She will not be held back.

Looks like some kind of punishment, this eternal life bestowed by your God, I venture, but there is no uptake. They are not interested in argument; their focus is on filling out, on coming into being, and they are not above pleading.

The woman speaks as if I had not spoken. Oh, we have our different desires, as you must know, she says, but we are bound together all the same. The bond of love.

Love! I roll my eyes, squirm.

The men seem more circumspect; they too shrink visibly at the word, which keeps them quiet for a while. I ignore the young man whose hand is up like a schoolboy's waiting for permission to speak.

Bonded indeed. As if I've not heard that kind of talk before, the justifying cant of politicians and ordinary folk alike, even as they pursue their selfish interests.

What do I know beyond what the history books say? Does the woman think me omniscient? Her words leave me impotent, tongue-tied. Frankly, I have no idea what to do; I do not know how to proceed. I who have freely admitted failure, who have given up on the business of writing, who have comforted myself with the promise of carefree, indolent days, albeit under dark northern skies. Who would not rather watch clouds tumbling through the heavens? Slouching in a deck chair with a woollen rug (from childhood, the dun tartan of overnight train journeys) over her knees, cherishing the slivers of stingy sunlight? For fighting slow time, there is a garden in which to hoe, to shake earth free from the roots of weeds, and watch worms writhe into the humus. I would rather drum my fingers and wait for forget-me-nots to spread into a blue haze and tulip spears to unfold their slow promise of red, and battle with indomitable slugs.

Why should I return to the fray and struggle with the stories of these creatures? Why invite judgment of my abilities? Whilst these figures imagine a new era of millennial harmony, it is I who will have to rise to unexpected challenges and fend off the slurs reserved for upstarts of my ilk.

I note that the young man, giving up, has dropped his supplicating arm, but no such luck with the woman. Come, come, she breathes, prodding a finger at her breastbone, Mary here, Mary Prince.

As if I don't know her name. Her voice grows stronger as she remonstrates: Get over yourself. It's not about you at all. So very little we ask of you, nothing more than allowing us to be, setting us free. She shakes her head as I grimace at the word. You don't like my language? The way I speak? Well, that's nothing new to me; I'm used to my island's tropical tongue being mocked. But look, you're free to improvise, to correct, and use your own fancy words. Here we are, emaciated, and …

Whilst she falters, the young man slips in: In the words of another poet, dusted to mildew.

Oh shush, Mary says impatiently, and rudely points at me. It is you, oh yes, there is no question, it is *you* who have sought us out, peered at us through the cracks. Look, there is room for you to dress us up or down, but we want out, we've had enough of being trapped in this derelict pondok of history.

She stretches her arms up, slowly, testing as it were their materiality, their flexibility, then rises to one knee, placing a foot on the ground. Nothing can hold us back now, she declares. Think of us as ready-mades, and that is an advantage not to be sniffed at. So there you are: a shoulder to the writing wheel, a pen filled with black ink, and Bob's your uncle.

Unbelievable. Where does the woman, barely risen from dust and mildew, get her confidence? Clearly, she is one to be watched, one not past elbowing the others out of the way and taking over. If only she knew that I could house them in little more than another pondok – of another order, yes, but the house of fiction within my means, with its rusted tin roof, may be no less leaky.

The older man, the pale, slight poet rocking to and fro, should know better, should know that having a ready-made subject does not guarantee a work.

If they are my responsibility, I have no idea how to proceed. If I stamp my feet in frustration, insist that I will not be bullied by phantoms, it is also the case that my idyll of battling with garden slugs and nursing tulips slain by vernal gusts grows dimmer by the second. Foolish, foolish me. I should have crept away, not have peeped, listened in, or spoken. Before I can say humpty-dumpty I find myself tied to this desk, a Procrustean bed, with no more than a bag of sweets for comfort. Beside me a mound of wrappers grows. No question of kidding myself that an epiphany will rise out of the crackle of cellophane and foil; rather, an unsightly crop of spots has appeared across my forehead. Sweet Jesus, am I to be propelled backwards, awkward and pimply, into adolescence? Whilst these my subjects bully and bluster their way out of history?

Let me start with the poet in the corner, muttering about poppies and charms, he of the eternally boyish looks and slight frame, a pair of crutches tucked neatly under his arm as he rises to his knees. Pure trouble, even as he averts his eyes in modesty, so that I push back my chair and grope for the stash of fortifying chocolate sweeties in the drawer.

I favour the dark variety, at least seventy per cent cocoa solids, ones filled with keen, candied ginger, sharp enough to kick-start things. It is also, if not mainly, for the lovely silver and gold foil wrappings – the luxurious treasures of a child of the bundu – that I buy them at all. Perhaps I ought to drop the actual sweet straight into the bin, given that I eat only out of the habit of husbanding resources, of waste-not-want-not frugality. But as far as achievements go, that would not be so staggering, so why deprive myself? It is the wrapper that brings lasting joy and makes the mouth water. The extra, outer cover of cellophane is for delaying gratification; for holding up to the light, for seeing the world momentarily through pink, blue or green before scrunching it up. Then the quarry: silver or gold foil, metallic paper I hold down with the left thumb, firmly rub with the right index finger until the rectangle is returned to an original, pristine state. Ta-dah! Voilà! Ecco! There! Now the perfectly smooth foil can be folded meticulously into a solid strip, a band to be wrapped around my finger like a wedding ring. When I tire of touching of smoothing of tightening of stroking, the band drops on to my desk where it leisurely lets go, uncoils somewhat, but holds on to the memory of having once been a perfect circle. There! The rings settle into the intimacy of a growing pile on my left, may even hook into each other. Call it procrastination, but it does no harm; in my book this counts as an achievement, could be the precursor to who knows what.

I ignore the hm-hm of Mary clearing her throat, her scornful hiss of Sugar!, ignore the impatient shuffles and mutters of the others. Being a dab hand at foil rings is of no interest to them. Better than sitting on my hands, I reckon, for it is a start of sorts. Look, I am at my desk, once more like the child learning to form her letters, filling her page with wobbly ABCs. And here is material proof of my presence: strips of curved foil each bearing the shape of a band, a ring, something accomplished with my hands. Perhaps I should start by filling a page with his name, the poet's, which would be to name the project. Then wait for the letters to stir, in the manner of the mound on my desk, coils of silver foil easing their shoulders, unfurling their sugary history.

The woman stirs. My history is one of salt, she hisses; as for sugar plantations … I wave her into silence with new, gingered strength, but she leans forward, elbow comfortably on her raised knee. Just start at the beginning, she pleads, no need for anything fancy. Our stories are connected, so I'll fill in the gaps.

A history, then, of our man the poet, who binds together these phantom creatures and in whose interest they have gathered here. 'His story', as we feminists of the 1970s called it, scorning etymology, dismissing the history of the word, and not caring about being thought ignorant of Latin. Years before that, when the nineteenth century was new, our young poet, the punctilious scholar busily copying documents in Edinburgh's Old General Register House, would have bristled with irritation at such sloppy ways, but och see, if he can't mellow over the centuries what would be the point of living on and on and on? Even if it is only in what he still fondly thinks of as the colony, whereas in his beloved Scotland he has long since been forgotten. (In truth, he never made much of a mark even when he lived there; or rather, such mark as he had made in *Blackwood's'* treacherous literary circles is best forgotten.) His story it may be, but all will be thrown up in the air as others throw in their tuppenny's worth, as events arrive in who knows which way, out of order, not unlike my shiny sweet wrappers hooking up higgledy-piggledy with others, and how should I presume the wherewithal to straighten things out?

Strange, thinking of him now as my subject. (How a queen must clutch her throat and shudder at the thought of subjects, even as she goes on to tilt her head, and wave, and pat her pearls and smile graciously, regally, at those very entities.) Be gracious, I upbraid myself, sans pearls. So I salute my subject, the poet with weak lungs, and tilt my head at the keyboard. Now, to lunge into his story, the story of a dead white man. Of which there are so very many, quite enough really, and there's the rub, but Mary, ever the meddler, interrupts in a voice grown stronger that that can be dealt with later; indeed, that the man would agree to deal with the problem himself. He wants out as much as I do, she says confidently. Then louder, proudly: He is, has always been, the Father of South African Poetry.

I note the twitch as he raises his head, holds it as if listening for an air to creep upon the waters of time. And I have to lean in to hear as he rasps, *But ... not ... known ... in Scotland.*

Oh yes, unmistakably the voice of one who has never wanted for ambition, who became even more fired up once he came to believe in a brave new world free of slavery. No need to fret, Mary soothes, addressing the man, helping him up. We're here for you. Over her shoulder she says, Together we'll turn the story into a devil-may-care whistling of women, and she winks at me. Which I find only mildly encouraging.

History/His story: anachronistic it may be, and now mellowed, but all the same, the poet senses a way out in the insertion of that superfluous 's' in hisstory. He is not ungrateful. Mary and the young man have kindly, heroically taken on the project of restoring him to the wider world, by which he means Great Britain, but where after all would they have been without him? Indebted, they are his, have in a sense, in their different ways, been made by him, and it is *his* story, one of which he has every reason to be proud, so there must be a way of wading boldly through the centuries to arrive at it, shape it and present it to the world.

A memorable start it was too. No schoolboy could forget the auspicious year of his birth. Even there on the Scottish Borders, on the banks of the Tweed, all the way across the Cheviots, the tenor of his life was set by the whiff of liberty, equality, fraternity that drifted over from Europe, settling like a fine mist around his cradle. Seventeen eighty-nine, the year of revolution, a year in which to foresee the end of slavery and fine-tune the limited enlightenment of his land, usher it into the bright light of liberty for all. History, his story, made, then unmade and now to be remade, and he sees that in this woman's reluctant hands it will become inseparable from theirs, the stories of the other ghostly figures in whose making he had had a hand; and thus, with these allies by his side, a story to be packaged anew, cast in yet another light.

Inseparable for sure, Mary interjects in a voice grown firm. She hauls the young man from the shadows into which he has retreated and presents him, as if for inspection, whilst she speechifies as if I'm not there. We, in our love and gratitude, have founded this project and assigned to this available writer the task of restoring Mr P, a great poet and humanitarian, Father of South African Poetry, to the wider world. Holding her collaborator firmly by the hand she asks if 1789 is not also the year of Sara Baartman's birth. Like Mr P, her remains, too, have been taken home to the Eastern Cape. Should there not be room in their project for that unfortunate South African woman, rudely displayed on European stages? She no doubt would want to account for herself.

But the young man shakes his head firmly. Mr P, he says, would certainly have rescued poor Saartjie in London, clothed her, yes, but she came later, once he was dead. Besides, she has no need of us. Back home she has been remade in many forms, fought over, tossed hither and thither, clothed and unclothed as in a French farce. What that unfortunate woman needs more than anything is to be left alone, to rest in her warm Eastern Cape grave – although he imagines that she'd rather be wrapped in Parisian couture than her new shroud of native kudu skin. But he holds up a cautionary hand: No further dust-ups; we have quite enough on our plate. Rather, the young man fancies, 1789 was the year of the infant Mr P sopping on the issues of emancipation posed by the great Jeremy Bentham: The question is not, Can they reason? nor Can they talk? but, Can they suffer?

Mary stamps her foot. Well, I certainly can and always could do all of those, so let's not bother with questions so clearly directed at animals.

Mary may have appointed herself as chief agent, but with all the clamouring for a place in his story he, the poet, the subject of this narrative, will have to keep an eye on her. Keenly as he remembers the unfortunate natives of the Cape Colony, his story cannot accommodate all the abused of those unenlightened times. Now, to proceed. There may be confusion over who has chosen whom, but he is happy to submit to the eeny-meeny-miny-mo of being a subject. Being in the lady writer's hands, he must wait for her to name him. An author with a good track record, a man of steady outputs, of sound reputation and at least a whiff of celebrity, would have been preferable, but beggars cannot choose. For all her dithering, they will have to make do, for at least she is familiar with the terrain. If only she were younger, more energetic, less hesitant – although it may be the mark of the times rather than of her age, race, sex. No choice then but to keep faith, to believe that she'll manage. Besides, the indomitable Mary will be there to keep an eye on things.

He fears there'll be some fanciful feminising, but is in no position to quibble. What will this female author make of him? Of the great cause of liberty? And of the question of slavery that centuries ago he had identified as a poisoned bowl which taints with leprosy the White Man's soul and his civilizing mission? Above all, will she do justice to his poetry? He cannot expect passion to rise out of her prose, but he will settle for kindness, for tolerance of what has cruelly been dubbed the familiar trot of his iambic tetrameters. Justice and kindness are all he requires. And, of course, for the schoolchildren of the Cheviots to recognise his verse, recognise him as the champion of freedom. He notes that the lady writer's brow furrows suspiciously, uncertainly. Perhaps justice and kindness cannot always be coaxed into partnership, so he may have to settle for kindness. Is it for her too an act of faith, as her hands hover over the new-fangled keyboard? Och, how she dithers, how she tries his patience; nevertheless, there is no hiding from her. She suspects him of dissembling, that kindness, justice, tolerance are not all that he requires, that he wants the attention of Edinburgh and London. Her frowning asks if it is not enough to be the Father of South African Poetry. Well, no, and it is not so much to ask: he wants to be more than a colonial poet, wants to be *known* for God's sake, in England and Scotland. (Our man has never cared about Wales and Ireland, Mary whispers.) He must try to think in contemporary terms, but why had Scotland cut him down? Persona non grata for defending natives at the Cape Colony and slaves in the West Indies, understandable perhaps in the bad old times when enrichment from the colonies was the order of the day, but it smarts to have been dismissed as a mere rhymster, a man with a bee in his bunnet and an axe to grind. No doubt he was too innovative, ahead of his time, combining as he did the roles of poet and activist when it was perhaps expected of him to choose between the two. Now, in another century, time has taken the sting from the bee, and the axe could surely be buried. Might a new generation of Scots living in comfort and security, and with their social consciences now keenly honed, not make allowances for both? Might weapons not be laid down with the birth of a new society and room made for the rehabilitation of a colonial struggle poet? Can his roots on the Scottish Borders not now be acknowledged? Has he not made history? He has in any case written many a poem celebrating that land itself, quite free of social comment, surely acceptable to these moderns?

He has in mind a genteel dinner table in Auld Reekie's New Town, under ornately moulded ceilings, with starched napery and gleaming Caithness crystal – and *not* for auld lang syne. How splendid and dignified that would be, with dear Margaret by his side. Except, modest Margaret in sensible shoes would not want a resurrection of that kind, would frown upon the fanciness. He will have to hold his own in this new world. With the shadow of Mr Hyde scuttling through dark, dank passageways and Hogg's demons prancing in silhouette on Arthur's Seat – midst all that doubling – could there not be a place for the neglected poet at such a twenty-first century literary table? Oh he'd even be prepared to put up with doing the honours at Burns Night, much as he deplored in the past the man's folksy language, or his willingness to seek his fortune in Jamaica, willing, for heaven's sake, to manage slaves on a sugar plantation. Perhaps it is best not to judge. That was after all a couple of years before the Revolution. And is it not often the task of the poet, as indeed it was in his own case, to travel to the very spring of abomination, if only to discover for himself the workings of injustice, and subsequently take on the fight for righteousness? Fortunately the man's poetry and his abominable freemasons had saved the day, so that young Rabbie Burns, spared the journey to Jamaica and the ignominious life of a slaver, is highly revered at home. So why not he? This then is the grand project devised by Mary and the dear boy, his loyal protégés: the colonial poet brought home – on the wings of his verse against oppression.

Strictly speaking, on the wings of the woman writer's prose. (She has perversely dismissed his polite term, lady writer.) If he frets about what she'll do, how she will proceed, and from which angle, he is also resigned to the fact that it cannot be purely his story, not with all the others clamouring for being, clamouring for control. Whatever happens, some unknown beast will necessarily come yawning and blinking out of the attempt, but he is ready, is game for it, as they say. Invariably there will be a-slipping and a-sliding between third and first persons, elastic conjugations, role-switching perhaps between male and female, subject and author – this century it would seem is without limits – so all he can hope for is that the multi-faced monster will be of friendly mien, free at least of malice. He has had quite enough of neck-wrenching, of having turned first this cheek then that to the men of the master classes, be they political or literary. Practised in forbearance, and having survived so many constructions in the colony, both in life and in death – well, if this turns out to be yet another pooh-poohing, would that a final death follow. But thanks to the faithful protégés who have taken up the cudgels he is ready to give it a go, even in this baffling new world. The question, however, arises: what then is his role? The slipperiness of being a subject; for instance, will he as a white man be expected to step aside? What to do about this talk of a dead white man that he does not understand? He has prided himself on his dealings with all manner of men, but had never before come across the category of white man. He is somewhat tickled that a woman of her kind – 'of colour', as they say – has taken on the task (how the world has changed) and, of course, the idea of vengefulness cannot entirely be ruled out. Will he have to gird his loins for the new and unexpected ways in which to be dwarfed? Och, faith, he admonishes himself, the doubting Thomas must be cast out. Perhaps they could come to some kind of agreement, a contract of sorts.

These my subjects do not know of the actual contract, the one that Belinda alludes to with ever so delicate a smile. After that first book – which in retrospect seemed almost soothing to write compared with the terror that now besets me, the terror of expectations – I am quite simply paralysed. My agent, Belinda Montague, honey blonde, absurdly young, painfully, fashionably thin, beautifully shod, and one who slides unnervingly between being chirpy and matter-of-fact, sends by Royal Mail old-fashioned arty postcards, which is to say something from the Impressionists, knowing that I pretend not to read her emails. She avoids the word I, and always ends with: So-o-o looking forward to the typescript. Do send first chapters. Happy to read and advise.

Nowadays I barely check the picture, and after a cursory scan, toss the card into the recycle bin. For some months Belinda has been pretending that I do not mean what I say. Of course you won't give up on the novel, she states. A carefree signature it was and now the contract holds, no matter what I decide. By way of encouraging me to do the right thing, she warns that I'd have to return the generous advance for the two-book deal. She does not mind my not replying. Predictably, the invitations to meet never include the legendary literary lunch. Does that institution no longer exist?

Belinda is committed to the genre of life-writing, a term she finds more appropriate than memoir. You have such rich experiences, just get them down on the page, she says. Aim for the artless. And try not to be arch; it's not nice.

I, who have been incapable of beating out as much as a word, am not above taking advice. Belinda is right about my abominable tendency to be arch, and rather than fret about the word *nice* I should pay heed, for she may well turn out to be the one to save me from this motley group of phantoms.

Belinda may not have in mind my day as a supply teacher in a comprehensive school – how else am I supposed to live? – but my fingers fly across the keyboard as I imagine a recording of the morning's experience, one that, as she recommends, is simply to be transferred to the screen. Easier to start with the end, when after a morning of colourful abuse from teenagers, I nipped into the head teacher's office to announce that I'd had enough and was walking out in spite of my promise to stay until half-term. (See then, dear Belinda, how practised I am in breaking contracts. I'll have to find a new way of keeping the wolf from the door.) The event meticulously recast into the third person, there are nevertheless a couple of persistent 'I's that still have to be replaced. In no time at all I also knock off a beginning to the piece, recount the day as accurately as possible. If I've achieved the desired artlessness, there is nothing to be done about its failure as a short story.

Belinda's reply comes within two days, in tiny, spidery writing on a picture postcard of mud-coloured Gauguin girls: Absolutely bloody marvellous. Don't even mention a wolf at the door – it's a brilliant story, just waiting to be developed. Perhaps turn into first person and then a little toning down? We NEED novels of this kind. See, you were made for better things than teaching ignorant teenagers. Why not come up to London for lunch and we'll go through your plan. Can't wait. Xxx

Her first x is always capitalised. So finally, the fabled literary lunch, the invitation to drop by, as if Scotland were a stone's throw away and the journey indeed *up* to London. Mind you, no mention of the train fare. The word 'plan' makes me snigger. If only I had one, or even believed in the efficacy of having a plan. And if I were to have such a thing, it certainly would have nothing to do with uncouth kids in a classroom. I happen to believe in education and therefore cannot promote stories of failure. What can Belinda possibly mean by a novel when I've sent her what must pass for a short story? I have told her, admittedly over a year ago, explained in detail that the next novel was to be about the Father of South African Poetry, Defender of a Free Press, Arch-enemy of the Cape Governor, Lord Charles Somerset, and as an Abolitionist, an enemy of all slavers: Thomas Pringle.

There, I've written his name – THOMAS PRINGLE – which surely has broken the spell.

But first a few more words about Belinda. Which may or may not be a delaying tactic: there is, as far as I can see, no reliable way of telling. Belinda is a feminist who believes in the category of women's writing, which is to say women's lives; believes in its value. She is not actually an editor. Belinda is an agent who believes her role to include that of editing, by which she means helping an author to shape a narrative. She demonstrates what she is after, what is required, by editing a page or ten – ever so lightly, she promises. She does not care for semicolons, and irony persistently ducks out of her ken. She has questioned me on unreliable characters and even insisted on the removal of what she calls an inconsistency.

Irony, I explain, but oh no, too obscure; readers would not get what you call irony, she insists. In other words, I am in her hands, although not in the way she imagines. But all things considered, including her slight frame, they are strong, supportive hands and I am indeed sorry to let her down in this way, especially since I've turned out to be her discovery. A puzzling term used by more than one reviewer, puzzling since I had, like anyone else, simply sent my first manuscript to Belinda, whom I had found in the *Writers' and Artists' Yearbook*. It was well after I signed up with her that she declared her belief that a novel should be a happy collaboration between writer, agent and editor. Vigilance therefore is the name of the game: there is no question of letting her loose on an unfinished manuscript.

A thumbnail sketch: Belinda is well dressed, usually in reliable linen, ever so lightly made up and often in fabulous red shoes; she speaks chummily (that's when she slides down in her chair and waggles an exquisitely shod foot) about all women needing just a touch of eyeliner, a mere stain of lipstick. Then she crosses her lovely legs and puts her palms together thoughtfully. I know that she is preparing an assault when her fingertips are brought to rest ever so lightly on her top lip whilst staring fixedly ahead. ('Ever so lightly' is a favourite phrase of hers, her signature aesthetic; it is also a contagious term.) I fear that Belinda has too clear an idea of what women like myself ought to write. I fear that she believes readers to expect a true story, that she will have nothing other than could be read as Real Life; she has the capacity to turn my most fantastical tale into such a story, believes in the power, the necessity, of the authentic first person. Once, when we chatted about eating habits and dress sizes, she referred to my weight problems as a child. I have never been fat, I said, and she smiled knowingly, as if she had caught me out, as if I had forgotten a confession made in writing. Is that, I wonder, what drives me to the non-real, the magical? Even when my subjects are historical figures? And why do I now tease her with this nonsense about my day as a supply teacher? A shame about the lunch, but I do not want to see her in person. I shamelessly promise in writing to pursue the redemptive comprehensive-school novel, an updated, female version of *To Sir, with Love*, and Belinda, appeased, promises that we'll have lunch next time, over the next chapter.

Perhaps I should give it a whirl; perhaps it will be less difficult to beat out a true story, although I will have to be on guard. Being a supply teacher for five weeks at St Mungo's Hill Comprehensive

School is not the whole story; hidden in it is another that has nothing to do with the ebullient racism of teenagers from the council estate fondly known as Muggers' Hill, one that cannot be injected with redemptive elements. It is the story about Annie that may try to intrude; a story infused with shame that cannot be exorcised through writing, one that needs to be forgotten.

To Miss, with Love, I cackle wryly to myself – a matter of getting a move on. I really would hate to lose Belinda. Where would I find another agent? Who would put up with my dilly-dallying, shilly-shallying ways? Who would have a ditherer like me? I can after all not be discovered a second time. And there is the real possibility that Belinda will tire of jollying me along, will run out of encouraging words.

The slight poet, looking over my shoulder, feels his pectorals expand. Thomas Pringle. He has been named. Which, in this dismal state of affairs, must count as progress, he supposes. The stuff about Belinda and being a schoolmistress is an unhelpful digression and also a painful reminder of Harington House, although this lady writer's Scottish Comprehensive School for the unruly lower orders is, of course, not to be compared with the 1820s Academy for Young Gentlemen that he established in Cape Town. But such nonsense will hopefully run its course. Now for a course of action, and for a while at least the others will have to step aside. Let him imagine for a moment that in this making he is she, she is he, that together they form a fleet set of hands that learn to fly in unison over the keyboard, pounding new life into the dormant material. It is a matter of pride: he refuses to remain a wraith, a spectral figure with hissing lungs. Unbelievable that he should have no choice but to wait in limbo for this woman to pull the strings at her will.

(I, on the other hand, reject the role of puppeteer; that is not it at all, I protest. I imagine him standing behind me, barely a silhouette, with hands resting on my shoulders, the masseur prodding and kneading with gentle reminders, with meaningful pressure on the taut muscles of my mutinous flesh. My fingers, despite the exercise of folding silver wrappers, are stiff and arthritic. As befits a ghost he is, after all, the one who commands, Remember me, and I, the shirker, will hesitate. See how he snatches at the least opportunity, his vanity irrepressible. See how he nurses a fond idea of coming into being at the Edinburgh Festival, bowing to applause, then stepping out of the Book Festival's gloomy yurt into the gentle light of the modern, affluent Paris of the North.)

Would that the great John Fairbairn were restored to be his interlocutor, to tell of the heady days when together they brought civilisation to the beautiful, benighted Cape with the very first *South African Journal* and their fiery editorials in the *Commercial Advertiser*. Were it not for his untimely death, cruelly cut down after a mere forty-six years, he, Thomas, would have written his own Life and avoided this dependency on a woman. An account by Fairbairn would have been the next best thing. Fairbairn would have wrought the truth from the documents, the records and copious notes produced over the years for that very purpose, but och, his dear friend ever was a busy man who, with the many demands of the colony, could not always get round to things. And now, what a merry-go-round, having to start from scratch, and that with a strange woman whose reluctance is palpable. For a man of his stature it is hard to countenance that on this limen of the living he, Thomas Pringle, is being lined up for scrutiny.

Anyone with a South African education knows his story, or ought to know. But it may help to rehearse with objectivity the bare bones of that history and clarify his relationship with Mary and the young man, Hinza. Many a dictation has found its own momentum in the mind of the scribe, so this woman writer may well run with it, find her own voice, as they say.

He clears his throat, nods at her, and she dutifully scribbles as he dictates the sketch in the third person:

Born on the Borders, the poet Thomas Pringle was educated in Thurso and thereafter at Edinburgh University. In that city he led a distinguished literary life, befriended by the luminaries of the time.

The extended Pringle family suffered difficulties, and assisted passages offered by the Colonial Office spurred him in 1820 to lead a party of Scots emigrants to the Cape Province. Once the family was settled as farmers in the Eastern Cape, Thomas and his wife Margaret went to Cape Town where with his bosom friend, John Fairbairn, he championed freedom of the press, started an academy for young gentlemen, and developed the National Library. Thomas keenly felt for the oppressed indigenous peoples. Their cause, he believed, would also be served through poetry that exposed their plight, but his progressive views fell foul of the autocratic governor, Lord Charles Somerset, whose persecution drove him out of the colony to London, where he alerted the world to the true nature of slavery at the Cape and exposed the conditions of the benighted native peoples of that land. The native boy, Hinza Marossi, whom he had rescued, was given permission to accompany the Pringles to London, but sadly he did not survive the inclement climate. As secretary for the Anti-Slavery Society, Thomas signed the Abolition Act in August 1833; he had earlier facilitated the writing of *The History of Mary Prince*, the first female slave narrative published in England, for which he was roundly reviled. He died in 1834 whilst preparing for his return to the Cape, but his reputation as the Father of South African Poetry endures.

This, in short, is the story that needs to be fleshed out. The time has come to challenge nineteenth-century class bias and pernicious Toryism, all of which were responsible for thwarting Pringle's ambitions and keeping him out of the annals of history.

(I do, of course, know this much, but knowing also of the ambiguities, uncertainties, the alleged duplicities and repackaging of that life, I am not keen to meddle and offer judgement. No doubt there will be apologetics and smokescreens, let alone the residual beliefs of the times, for which I do not have the stomach. For the moment, however, I must listen without interruption to the voice, into which has crept an unmistakable whine.)

Cut down in my prime, Pringle complains, there was no time to convert our people to humanitarianism and the ways of Christian compassion for the natives. Certainly there was not enough time to hone my poetic skills. So short a life, so little achieved; nevertheless, there is enough to remember with pride: an admiring letter from none other than the great Coleridge himself, commending 'the most perfect lyric poem in our language'; the support of Scott, Sir Walter no less, and also of James Hogg the Ettrick Shepherd whose death is lamented by the great Wordsworth; and my very own signature on the Act of the Emancipation of Slaves, a signature that my dearest Margaret held to her lips. But what did my countrymen across the border care? Not a fig. Rather, they would have me pilloried for my very commitment to freedom. I remember every vituperative word, the slanders are etched in my mind, and really I was powerless against the influential MacQueen of *The Glasgow Courier*, who called me a liar and advised that I be taken by the neck and with a good rattan or a Mauritius oxwhip be lashed through the streets of London. All for exposing the illegal slave trade in Mauritius. And such calumny published in *Blackwood's*, the very journal established and once edited by me! Can anyone blame me for wanting to return to the world and recover my reputation in my beloved Scotland? In this new era, I would surely be guaranteed a hearing.

Yes, my time has come, he declaims, the time to gather stones together in the land that will embrace the poet and activist and allow me to belong to more than one country. Poetry has ever dissolved boundaries. If that makes me a vain man, so be it. In the words of Ecclesiastes, all is vanity, a striving after the wind, and nothing to be gained under the sun, yet I have seen with my own eyes all the oppressions practised under the sun, and have spoken out. If only there had been time left to roam the Eastern Cape and learn to sing in clearer voice of the koppies and vleis, the gold and violet sunsets, the stark thorn trees silhouetted in evening light, the honeyed mimosa. Pringle's voice grows peevish: A longer life, and I would have managed to forge a suitable voice for the African veld. How churlish that I now should be reviled for resorting to English literary conventions, when there had simply not been time to attune the ear to the trill of the bokmakierie or the roar of lions! He beats his hollow chest – I am above all a poet – wheezes, and collapses into a coughing fit.

Mary stumbles, reaches over with nursing arms to pat his back and enfold him. No one, she consoles, pursing her full lips, no one under the sun escapes vanity; every one of us strives after the wind, and that, God's own truth, is the end of it. So let's get the project off the ground, get Mr P's Life written, and as a matter of urgency fix up a contract with the writer. She, Mary, has after all in the past come a cropper in that respect. Uncivil perhaps to mention it now to one who has been her benefactor, who arranged for her history to be told, and she does of course not apportion blame, but a contract then might well have ensured that her own story be accurately written down.

Pringle withdraws from her embrace and clears his throat to continue. If only he'd been spared for a decade or two to see things through. A few years back at the Cape to keep an eye on the letter of the law, wipe out the persistence of slavery in its various guises, for sadly their fellow Europeans could not be trusted. With the Whigs in power, he and Fairbairn would have turned the colony into a beacon of truth and light with which to instil compassion and humanitarian values in the hearts of white men. Besides, as Fairbairn pointed out, to civilise and convert the natives into friendly customers would have been more profitable than to exterminate or reduce them to slavery.

Hinza, shaking his head, staggers to his feet, makes as if to speak, but Mary roughly pushes him back, gesturing vigorously, so that he sighs, slides down with his head in his hands and mutters, All astride the wind. None of which appears to be registered by the poet, who continues after yet another clearing of the throat.

Once Abolition was achieved, he would have returned to the Cape and settled for an appointment as resident magistrate in the new district on the Cafferland border, or even a modest post at the Kat River Mission, Dr Philip's haven for Hottentots. In that heat and clear air his lungs would have healed, and allowed him to plan the next phase of moral and intellectual development for natives. But even the Whigs denied him, could not countenance him as Magistrate. Such are politicians: nothing is to be expected on the grounds of merit; his humble origins never to be forgotten, in spite of all his achievements. No, that office was kept for applicants of another caste, in spite of his high connections. And then, God's inscrutable will – even with a ticket in his hand, the coffers packed, the sails of the Sherburne all but set as a fair wind swept east-north-east – to strike him down. Cruelly cut off when there was still so much to do.

And now this opportunity: a chance to resist fate and make known his life's work. Let it not be forgotten that he had resisted injustice all his life. Had he not taken on the arrogance of the Cape Governor, Lord Somerset and his Reign of Terror? Or the Scottish Tories? (slavers really, for those who benefit from slavery are no less than that). Besides, he has been made and remade so many times, in a hayrick of words heaped upon each other, the tattered old stories raked over, heaped in both glory and scorn, his precious verse laid out for scrutiny. The time has come to take control. There have been no concessions, none for a man on crutches, a man with poor lungs, and for that he feels gratitude of sorts. He has long since forgiven the malice of his own people, but it should be known that they were mistaken in overlooking him. He, Thomas Pringle, is yet a man of the Cheviots and the Eildon Hills. Oh, for a ramble along Linton Loch in the rising light of February, the wind keen and the rain fresh, and there by the brae … there stands Nanny Potts, her hands on her hips, dear Pottsie waiting, scolding – the gypsies will come and take you away if you don't eat your kale … the alphabet again, in best copperplate this time … do stop teasing your wee brother, or the gypsies … dear Nanny Potts … and the Paps of Eildon veiled in the rain …

Mary Prince is shaken by Mr P's retreat into a childhood of which she knows nothing. She must focus, gather herself, remember the times in London when he stood firm for freedom. It is not easy to enter the wavering world of the past, but enter it she must. Mary rocks to and fro, hums a hallelujah, then mutters to herself in a low, throaty voice:

All night this house tosses on a dark sea, sways like a ship on fluid foundations. A black house, or one that turns black as night falls, as we lay ourselves down to rest. Women in the attic room and men in the parlour below, black as the kind night itself. We are bundled in bedrolls, arranged top to tail in rows. Not a slave ship at all, I say over and over. No, peaceful, benign, were it not for the past that presses its demons upon us in the dark, clamps its claws around our throats so that the women around me gargle their terror, scream, thrash wildly, strangling themselves in their bedclothes. How often I have to light a candle and soothe or scold them into silence. Heavens above, what namby-pamby sugar lumps these young women are; they would melt in the softest of English rain.

Cut out the feartie, as Mr P often says to me. Straighten those backbones, I scold. How on earth have you lot managed to escape from your masters? I am in charge. I give them no more than an hour to gather themselves. There is no sense in endless kindness, because mark you me, I say sternly, freedom is not for namby-pambies. Your bodies may have been abused and broken, may also be practised in recovery, but your minds have not been exercised in the ways that a new kind of living will demand of you. Now freed, do not imagine that you should rest on your oars, or go about banking on others. You will have to act of your own accord, make decisions, choices, and it takes strength to do so. No bed of roses, this kind of freedom, so cast the demons out once and for all. Have we not always found solace in the night when under kind black skies we sank, exhausted, into the oblivion of sleep? Besides, you know that here we are all protected. Safe in the house of Pringle.

The women weep; they moan about flames of hell. What I would not do for a decent night's sleep! To hasten their recovery, to exorcise the demons – God will forgive me – I rush about the room with a lit candle in each hand and thrust the flickering flames up into dark

28

corners. I mutter in a low, growling, voodoo voice the mumbo-jumbo that Mam chanted, even as she urged us to embrace blue-eyed God and the Christ-child Jesus. But I cannot keep it up; I see again, hear again Mammy's deranged jabbering as she arrives on the boat to rake the salt at Turk's Island, raving, and not as much as recognising me, her own honeychild. The candles have, thank God, been blown out in the rushing about, and I say, See, the light has gobbled up the demons. I press my hands over my ears and swallow the sound of Mam's mad shrieks. No point in dwelling over the bitterness of that deeper past.

Spare a thought for others, I remonstrate. Our benefactors, wrenched out of the soft, plump arms of sleep by your bloodcurdling cries – they must be tossing and turning in their beds, wondering about the wisdom of taking in strange runaways. Really, I am tired of soothing; my days of being nursemaid are well and truly over. The younger girls still snuffle around for mothers; they look at me hungrily, would nuzzle into my breasts and clutch at my skirts if I were to give them an inch. There is no point in beating about the bush, no point in delaying their recovery, their independence. I am nobody's bloody mother, I say as brutally as I can, slapping at my dugs; there is no milky bosom, no heart here to mother anyone. So pull yourselves together, brace yourselves for this new bittersweet life of freedom. Let us not blacken this house in vain.

We do not usually have so many stray people in the house, but there has been a fire at the Friends' Meeting House in Islington. We have our suspicions about that fire, by no means the first. There are many respectable citizens who so believe in the rights of slave owners that they'd stoop to anything. The Pringles have taken in the female runaways, packed them into this small house like the hold of a slave ship.

We must all do what we can for these poor souls, Mrs P said, looking pointedly at me. You'll have your attic to yourself again, Mary. The Society will place them with good abolitionist families as soon as they can, but for now you are responsible for these women. She does not think me unkind, but she knows how I value this precious little space with a bed of my own and the yellow patchwork cover I have stitched myself. Along the top edge, in the centre, I have sewn a large square, admittedly out of kilter with the rest. It is the whole of Daniel's best grey handkerchief he gave me as keepsake, visible all day long, and at night I draw it up and bury my face in its story. Now with my cot pushed right up against the wall for space, I have folded away the cover, fearful that others may touch my heart so boldly laid out.

Often I trail my fingers along the perimeter of the walls, savouring the safety of a private space. Mrs P does not, of course, have a room to herself. She spends all night with a husband, and I wonder if she does not at times wish to explore the full measure of a bed, fling out her arms and settle where she will, hum a tune to herself, or light a candle and turn the pages of the good book as and when she pleases. That would be freedom indeed, to have had enough of the comfort of another body in bed. Not that I ever desired such freedom. Even Captain Abbott, a kind enough man, who came for a good number of years to my hut, would leave well before the night was over. Not until Daniel did I have the comfort and joy of a whole night with a husband, a free man, of waking up together in the light, even though there were some who said that a marriage could not be lawful without the blessing of the English Church. Which is, of course, a piece of nonsense, given that that church does not allow the marriage of slaves. Now I will never know whether after years of marriage I would desire the freedom of a bed of my own. I will never know if Daniel thinks I ought to have taken the risk of returning, but I know in my arthritic bones that if I were to return, the Woods' punishment for speaking of their cruelty would be to sell me off to a far-flung place; that return to the island would never be a return to Daniel. Oh, the scales have wavered between freedom and love, but it is not that I have chosen freedom over love, or chosen, as my wicked enemies have accused, licentiousness over being with one husband. Love untested over the years will remain, steadfast, unwavering; rather, I chose between freedom and bondage, freely chose that over which I had control. Daniel would certainly have been snatched from me the very moment I laid my eyes on him. I shut my ears to the rumour, no doubt broadcast by the Woods, that he has found a new woman. With freedom secured here by Mr P, love is not a risk I could allow myself to take. Or should I have risked returning?

The women fall into fitful sleep after the demons have been driven out, but the demon in my heart beats against my ribcage, so that I slip out of the house into the icy night. With Mrs P's handed-down coat draped hastily over my nightgown I hobble as fast as I can to the Heath. St Anthony's fire flares in my gammy left leg, but the pounding of my heart is the only remedy for driving out thought. Had I miscalculated? Misread the wavering beam of the scales? Am I indeed a wicked selfish woman unworthy of the good Moravians who married us? I stumble as fast as I can across the Heath, circle it, over and over until my lungs burn and I can run no more. Falling down against a tree trunk, I wait for my breath to return and my burning leg to cool.

I do not know what to make of my years. The categories of young and old mean nothing to me, but here in London, in my heart, I feel for the first time the thrust of Spring's spears, the delicate, lime scent of newborn leaf that sends the blood pumping in a heady rhythm. Mrs Pringle says that I am still young, that this is my second life granted by God. In which I grow in health and strength, especially since I avoid the white stuff to which slavers are addicted. Taking neither sugar nor the demon salt has calmed my rheumatism, so that distanced from greed and desire, my blood is freshened, fizzing with health. These tongue-tricking, white substances show nothing of their histories, the grubbiness with which they come to be in the world, hence I will have no truck with them. The herbalist in Highbury agrees that abstaining will soothe my rheumatic joints, and already I feel the pain subsiding. Mrs P says that freedom and, above all, belief flush the body out and cleanse the temple of God. I am grateful to Mrs P for not ever alluding to Daniel. Unlike others, she has not questioned my decision to remain in London. I will never forget her bashful eyes when she asked me to strip off my clothes, down to my naked flesh. The fire had been stoked and the curtains drawn. I am ashamed to say, she explained, that whilst I have no doubts at all, it is expected of me to confirm that I have seen on your body the evidence of ill-treatment and cruelty inflicted by your owners. Your history, so carefully written down by Miss Strickland, is thought to be a story of fantasy. She planted her feet firmly and ran her fingers over the welts and criss-crossed scars. I know my owners by each scar, I started, but she put a finger across her lips, hush now, then called briskly for Miss Strickland to witness the welted flesh.

The shame is of course not hers. No, shame belongs unquestioningly to Mr P's enemies, who insist that he has maliciously published a sheaf of lies that is my story, that it is false and wrong to show slavery in such a vicious light.

Mary starts with a shudder. Hallelujah, she all but shouts. Bugger the Whigs and Tories, and to hell with their magistrates. Come now, Mr P, Nanny Potts is dead as a dormouse, and we've to get your history written. We'll all go to your Eastern Cape, and our writer must come along to see for herself the state of affairs. Paint the region red, so we will.

Hush now Mary, Pringle remonstrates, but he flings out his arms all the same. Now that would be recompense, to go with you and Hinza on a trip to the Kat River. He had always had that in mind for the boy who would follow in his footsteps, follow a life of Christian humanitarianism in Africa. He reaches for Mary's hand; he hopes that she'll have some influence with the woman writer, for who knows what Missy has in mind for her marionette? And indeed the woman shakes her head, says that a trip will have to wait, that there is groundwork to be done right there.

How long he has waited for this moment of recovery, of his life's work brought to attention, especially in his beloved Scotland. Vainglorious? No, that's not it at all. Rather, it's a matter of history which belongs to everyone, and in which he undoubtedly has had a humble role to play. Only, he could not have imagined his new maker to be like this, of this ilk. Och, the world has changed for sure and he must give her a chance, hope for the best. He must take this woman, who has after all agreed to tell the story, at face value. Is this not an opportunity to look afresh at those colliding worlds? Now, on this border where life and death jostle, he could stand the world on its head and cry, Hurrah, cry out loud that God is distant, but man is near! Phew! How thorny they turned out to be, those paths he trod, or rather, on his wooden crutches, flew along with the impatience of youth. Now, as he feels his hands fully shaped, feels the strength of his own fingers as they fall on her shoulders (attempting to guide her?), he believes that he could give it a whirl.

He can, of course, only hope, clutch at straws, but hope floods his being, infuses the blood that pulses in his veins. A whip crack – let's get going! – sounds in the air. But first, there are boundaries to be set. Oh, he hopes that she will not start with that old tale about dear Nurse Potts dropping him as a three-year-old and then concealing his hip injury. The poor woman has suffered enough over that; and he certainly has never held a grudge against her; in the absence of a mother, she has come close to being one, has done her best. Besides, where has that story come from, and who knows if it is true? He may have once believed it, but the memory of a three-year-old cannot be relied on.

And pray God that she does not vulgarly pry into his marriage bed, that she spare Margaret who, like the tumbleweed that the dear woman loved to watch spinning across the barren plain, would at such intrusion somersault over and over in her grave. There has been distasteful lingering over Margaret's lack of dowry, as if there were nothing else to say about her. Why on earth would anyone imagine that he, who had never been wealthy, would enrich himself through marriage? He could only be grateful that a woman with Margaret's attributes had accepted him. Not that her piety did not irk, to begin with at least, but as for the 'unfortunate marriage', as theirs was branded, well, he could not have wished for better. A good, sensible woman, above reproach, whose unsuitability, it would seem, lay in the word 'spinster', as the grown men with their child-wives called her. For sure, Margaret was a good nine years older than he, but any sensible man would regard that as a blessing, and her motherly care could hardly be seen as a defect. He had much to learn from Margaret, and not only from her experience of farming that came in so handy on the foreign Cape frontier. Again he sees her dear face lifted at an angle, quizzically, lit with the beauty of reason, as she thor-·oughly considered his postulations, and gently led him to their flaws. Margaret, raised on a Scottish farm, devoid of airs and graces, how well and without a word of complaint she adapted to the African wilds. How appreciatively she listened to the nocturnal serenade of beasts; lulled to sleep by the roar of lions and the elephant's trumpet, and daunted only by slithering snakes and spiders. And how eminently suitable without her dowry. He must insist on her being accurately drawn, but can that ever be the case? He fears not, thus he is prepared to fall to his knees, to beg for Margaret to be spared. No, that is not enough: he is prepared to fade back into oblivion, rather than have the dear, diffident woman's life raked over. And so he arrives at the first clause of the contract.

Can this woman be trusted with the task, this story that is neither fish nor fowl, neither fact nor fiction? He fears that the writing machine that cuts and pastes might spawn all kinds of fanciful ideas, that the times will throw new light on things, that held up against new instruments of thought ... oh, that is the risk that must be taken. For that he must gird his loins. But, all things considered, he is game for another take, a take of another kind. Call him needy, vain, and craving the attention of those who scorned him – a shabby confession it may be, though surely a justifiable sin – but he wants to be restored to his rightful place; a man of both the north and the south, a man traversing the hemispheres. Surely the desire to be known and acknowledged at home is not a vain striving after the wind.

Alas, his fickle friend Hogg and the great Sir Walter both gone – but Scotland remains the magical name that thrills to the heart like electric flame. Faith, that is what is required. Even if this lady, or rather woman writer has no understanding of frontier life, still, he will have faith. Dead white man he may be in her book, but now, dusted down, he feels himself growing stronger by the minute. If anything, his lust for living is fanned by her palpable scepticism.

Dare in commendam – he commends himself into her hands.

With his fingertips resting on my shoulders, I believe that we now have a contract of sorts. But what can that possibly mean, where the notions of truth and compassion that he demands are involved? Otherwise, he has given me *carte blanche* – no, I dissemble, for what choice does he have? There will inevitably be a struggle over past events and the long evening shadows that they cast over our story, his and mine. Again, I dissemble; my version will prevail, and there's the rub.

Not only am I attracted to his inbetweenness, but there is more to unearth, there are the others spinning about his orbit, clamouring to be heard, to put in their ha'pennies' worth. Except for the filmy figure that emerges and reveals herself as Margaret, the long-suffering wife, who has no desire to join the fray, who has been dragged in against her will, but who now, determined, on her way out, and without opening her eyes, remonstrates in a barely audible brogue, urging all to let be, to let bygones be bygones, to lay down all pens. As for Thomas's reputation, she asks, what might that turn out to mean? A reckoning, a calculation? In this new light, the likelihood is that the books won't balance. Pray desist, she whispers; it cannae be done. A chill breeze announces her departure.

A pity, since this tale could do with more sensible female voices. Thus I am further paralysed, no, stricken by this conflicting demand to desist. I must somehow buck up. I reach for more sweets, tear off the wrappers. My fingers try to smooth out the silver foil, but I fumble. Alas, I am unwell, unable, and must in sooth justify delay, must lie down and claim *morbus sonticus.*

Whilst the others keep their distance, there is no way of hiding from Mary, who eyes me and my bag of sweets with distaste. The old toff's trick of big words, foreign words, ey? she sneers. As if I've not done my time in courts of law, the Court of the King's Bench, no less. Her hands are on her hips. Look, this won't do; this can't be what all your learning boils down to, she carps. Is there not help to be found in a book? This is the time to act. See how Scotland is fast changing, with people now talking about the true horror of slavery, so what better time to introduce Mr P, reviled as he was then, as a new national hero? For God's sake, pull yourself together, quit the brooding over where, when and how. Tell it as it is, she says, sounding like Belinda. Or consult a book, *do* something.

I may as well be sent to catch a falling star.

Mary's impatience strikes a chord, brings home the obstacles. In Hinza's words, we are all astride the wind. I am not up to it. Fear and cowardice, and distaste for pulling people up, for holding them to account. Who am I to judge? I cannot claim to be a woman true and fair.

Perhaps there *is* help to be found in a book.

II

Women can't write; women can't paint.
(And the swarthy ones will ever whine about being overlooked.)

I do not know where this new voice comes from, but I sense a solution, even if it is in the form of a question: *Who's afraid of Nicholas Greene?*

Am I? There is the convenience of a ready-made character, strange and unsuitable as he may seem, stepping off the page, stepping with a gallant bow to the rescue. The idea scrambles through the briars of history and gingerly worms its way into the chaos of this unfledged story. Too much thinking about the pros and cons will only bring further inertia so, uncertain as I may be, I have no choice but to amble with it. Thus I place our project in the hands of Sir Nicholas Greene, once upon a time a poet, now knight, critic, Litt.D., professor and famously immortal, although he too requires some dusting down.

Who has recruited whom? It turns out he's been there all along – strangely at ease, above clamouring, keeping an imperious distance in the background, waiting quietly, knowing that I would eventually have to call upon him. Now languid and lounging knowingly in a chair, he does not see himself as party to the other phantoms. And rightly so: he is of a different order.

My plan is met with scepticism. Thomas is puzzled, disappointed. Greene, he broods, Sir Nicholas Greene, can't say I've heard of him. Has anyone heard of him? I simply don't trust these titled, entitled types. Where does he hail from?

Mary shakes her head. A truly dead white man, she complains.

Mary's misgivings are not unfounded, but what can I do? Far from being omnipotent, I have no choice; I have to take whoever comes along, and Nick has entered the ring, has confidently, wordlessly made himself available, presented himself, so to speak. I have a feeling that he can save the day. Why, I do not know. What I do know is that he brings new problems, that he is not trustworthy, not above malice, but we'll have to give it a go.

Of course, they do not know Nick Greene, who really, fully came into being in the early twentieth century; besides, not many nowadays remember him at all. Sir Nicholas Greene – he of the slouched hat and black doublet, and tall tales of gadding about with Kit Marlowe; he whose ancestor has bequeathed to us the name of the Royal Borough of Greenwich, the home of new, imperial time; he the famed poet turned critic, now grown portly, who has lived through the centuries and proven his prowess with the tricks of time. If his poetry was never up to scratch, so be it, but I will put my foot down so that this tale will at least not be told in rhyming couplets, following the man's admiration for Addison.

Hinza – Thomas's son, as he declares himself to Greene, and who has thus far been silent – is the only one to perk up at the idea; he does not disapprove. Ahead of the others, he is an avid reader of fiction and a fan of modernism; he knows of Nicholas Greene's previous incarnations, is mildly amused that I've recruited him, and thinks it piquant to have an agent of that ilk. It may well help that he is a poet, albeit an indifferent one, Hinza ventures. He giggles at the thought of collaborating with the snobbish old man and urges Mary to forbear. Is a renowned, canonised and titled white man not exactly what they need? Mr Pringle, for that matter, is nowadays unknown; he needs plenty of help to get the project off the ground.

Nicholas listens to their arguments dispassionately. Without moving a facial muscle, and with a barely discernible nod, he agrees to step in. Still smarting at having been dropped in the distant past, he too looks forward to a revival. Unlikely agent he may be, but he can be counted on to defend me against the helpful Belinda. Agent is not a term that pleases Sir Nicholas, but unable to think of another appellation, I explain its modern usage, reassure him that there is no connection with Belinda's role as literary agent, or for that matter with the spies of his Elizabethan days. I go with my hunch that an immortal literary figure is just the man for the job. Mary complains that there's no knowing with whom they'll end up if I keep passing the buck. Think of it rather as the baton, Hinza suggests.

Sir Nicholas, who is in original dress of doublet and slouched hat, uncovers his head and bows ceremoniously; he pledges to do his best. Which is to say that he bows me out. I insist that there has to be a transitional period, that he needs to be eased into the job, into the confidence of his collaborators, which is how Mary and Hinza are to be viewed. Indeed, he agrees. He remembers clearly the turbulent times after the Peterloo scuffles – 1819 was it? –when the Foreign Secretary set up the migration scheme to South Africa for starving commoners. No doubt his collaborators will fill him in on how it all worked out at the Cape Colony. Mary stares at him in consternation. The Pringles were certainly not starving commoners, she says. Nicholas replies by raising an eyebrow.

This set-up is not ideal, but I feel immense relief at the get-out, at admitting that I had bitten off more than I can chew. There is only a little groundwork to do before retreating.

—

How had I alighted upon Nick Greene?

The trigger was the famous tree at Eildon, Thomas Pringle's house in the Eastern Cape, or rather the site of his old beehive house, a stone's throw from the tree. He had built it with his own hands, it is told, but that, of course, is what many a master says even as he packs off two servants for yet more barrowfuls of stones. Still, there the famous old wittegat tree was when I recently visited, gnarled and bent with its burden of literary history.

All of two hundred years ago, Thomas, the young, enthusiastic immigrant, fresh from the Scottish Borders, sat under the umbrella of its youthful branches. In the dappled light, waiting for the muse, he imagined the wittegat as a northern species, the tree of Zeus, whose commands could be heard through a rustle of oak leaves. And indeed, fluttering on cue through the branches of the tree, now called an umbra by the settler, were magnificent birds that swooped and dived and flashed the bright yellow of their undercarriages, so that the poet reached for his pen. Surveying the land, the Baviaansriver mountains, he conjured up his beloved Cheviots, watched the landscapes slide like screens into each other, so that words tumbled onto the page – the craggy glens and the Scottish dells, where Cape fig-marigolds translated themselves into tufts of primrose.

Ja-nee, zo werk 't heimwee mos, his new Boer neighbours declared.

On my visit to Eildon, the young occupants explained that any landscape gardener would recommend getting rid of the wittegat tree, or better still, move it some metres over to the right, where it would serve the picturesque vista more purposefully, but no, mindful of their responsibility to preserve the past, they would have none of that. Pringle's old beehive hut had, of course, been demolished hundreds of years ago, they exaggerated; this decent modern house had been built in its stead, but the tree, oh no the tree, the woman holding up her right palm in a stop sign repeated, now *that* is sacrosanct. An inspiration it was to our forefather, the great Father of South African Poetry, she said, nodding reverently at the wizened wittegat that swayed and creaked in the afternoon wind. Not a word could he write, she explained, except by sitting under its branches where the muse came in a rustle and a flash of yellow wings.

It is no mean task keeping Nicholas to the matter in hand. I prompt him with The Oak Tree that featured in his youthful 'Visit to a Nobleman in the Country', but no, he is well acquainted with the generic role of trees and their symbolism, he says; there is no need to genuflect to specific exemplars. As for Pringle's wittegat, that's a name he need not wrap around his English tongue. A tree is a tree is a tree … but then, scrolling back in time as is his wont, into age-old memory, he sniggers afresh at his noble patron of bygone years, at Orlando and his lordship's inspirational oak tree on the hill, rendered into a poem. He who had been plain old Nick the Poet at the time could not resist a malicious dig at those whose class commanded everything; he would, of course, not admit that for all his derision, Nick the copycat, ever deferential, had lingered under the very oak tree, waiting for inspiration. Now, after centuries' reflection, he should perhaps not have billed Orlando's 'Oak Tree' as the pretentious verbiage that it undoubtedly was; he should have been generous; it had been in his interest to be kind, to call the poem a masterpiece; he had after all enjoyed a handsome stipend from his lordship. Besides, aeons later, it was he who carried off for publication Orlando's revised 'The Oak Tree' in the breast pocket of his modern grey morning suit. And what did the ungrateful author do? Left it lying unburied under its parent oak to outlive Sir Nicholas's entire oeuvre, to endure whilst he, Nicholas, was summarily dismissed from the narrative.

And what had all that business of high and low art, of canonising and demonising, amounted to? Sweet nothing, as new generations have repeatedly turned things on their heads, changed the goalposts, lowered the thresholds, skewed everything, even admitting women to the canon, for heaven's sake. In fact, nothing irks Nick more than the fact that he owes his very life to a woman writer, and to add insult to injury, one who scorned the great gift of life, who cared not a fig for longevity, who strode insolently into the Ouse, her pockets of finest cashmere laden with rough stones.

Sir Nicholas sighs, plants his palms on his plump thighs. His muse forever fled, and having had to make do with a knighthood instead, the truth is that he can only be grateful for this Pringle commission, even if it involves a motley crowd: a dour, holier-than-thou Scotsman who looks as if he has already had enough of this new world; and the nigger upstarts – a saucy slave woman, and a badly dressed Bushman who turns out to be the Scotsman's son. Small wonder the man wrote in scandalous praise of miscegenation. Altogether beneath Sir Nicholas, of course, but he'll see what he can do, he who has waded comfortably through the centuries, adapting to place and time. These days, he understands, such people are not to be overlooked, which reminds him that he had better mind his ps and qs, the word 'nigger' for some reason no longer being usable.

You mean the N-word, says the provocative Hinza, who finds him amusing, encourages tales from his illustrious past, and asks Mary to forbear. Did the man not hang about in the same alley as Shakespeare in his pointed shoes? he asks, upon which Sir Nick nods vigorously; he is more than happy to tell of the playwright heeding his advice on the novel ways in which the sonnet's volta could be deployed.

Greene does not come free of trouble. Committed to short cuts, he sees no sense in going all the way to Southern Africa in search of the wittegat tree. Just as Mary predicted, he lacks respect; he waves away my reasons with an arrogant flip of the hand. Verisimilitude and all that, yes, of course, but four short years that our subject spent causing trouble at the Cape, he snorts, that's nothing at all when you're centuries old like myself; besides, did Pringle not write his *Narrative* and the African poems here in London, or at least revise them substantially? Which surely means according to the troposphere of this enlightened city. For colonial detail, he, Sir Nicholas, has these forward natives to fill him in. He refuses to remember that the West Indies, where Mary hails from, is quite a different kettle of fish. The north, he insists, this green and pleasant land, will have to do: an oak tree can stand in for the wittegat, much as Pringle himself imagined. A pity though that he, Nicholas, no longer has access to landscaped estates where the project could be tackled in comfort. Poets are not as welcome, not cultivated by gentry as they used to be in the times of Will and Kit and latterly the great Addison. Gone are those halcyon days when poets wrote for Gloire, he sighs, and were accordingly revered.

Thomas desists from saying, I told you so. The man holds the indecent views of his times, and does not come free of trouble, he ventures, but I shush him, beg for his patience. This era is after all not short on indecent views.

Thomas breathes with difficulty, sinks back with exhaustion. This return, re-entry, revival, resurrection – call it what you will – turns out not all it's cracked up to be. It is the case that he, a poet above all else, has difficulty answering the writer woman's questions; the discourse of these times floors him. He fears that her customs and manners are too alien, that she underestimates him and fails to appreciate the mores, the intricacies of colonial times. For all Mary and Hinza's detailed explanations of reinstating him (he fears for his dissolution, even at the Cape) and alerting Scotland to his achievements, her sympathies seem to waver.

Pringle knows only too well that ghost writing is not without difficulties, but respect is surely the first requirement. Catherine Richardson was certainly appreciative of his contribution to her *Scenes and Occurrences in Albany and Cafferland*. As was Thompson for the sterling work he did on the man's *Travels and Adventures*, really at the expense of his own *Narrative of a Residence*. (Has the woman even read it?) Admittedly, something different is required here, but he surely deserves respect. The woman's questioning shows that she has no feeling for the idea of home; she believes it to be a notion that has turned itself inside out, a worn garment in need of mending. The faith he has mustered in her is fast waning. Besides, the situation now is unclear. This agent Greene she has roped in, well, Thomas doesn't know what to make of him, although for all their political differences and the man's irritating patrician mantle, they may after all have more in common.

Above all, he must stand his ground. Thomas is a man from the Scottish Borders, comfortable on borderlands, which is not to say that he has a foot planted on each side; rather, he appreciates a place-lessness of sorts, where a self need not be irrevocably fixed, but can incline this way or that, learn something new from the other side. Such is the beauty of borders. Hence his belief – unpopular as this notion may have been at home – that there was something to be gained from the Union with England, whilst his patriotism remained steadfast, a belief that sustained him at the Cape where the inhospitable land allocated to his party placed them on the border of the colony. Of course they were disappointed, but a man from the Borders rises to the challenge of occupying the frontier and being responsible for keeping native others at bay. It was clear that Lord Charles Somerset, having placed the English in the relatively comfortable and safe environs of Albany, used the Scottish settlement along the Baviaans River, where baboons howled mockingly, as a buffer. Hardy the Scots undoubtedly were, but how dispiriting to be given the wild territory, subjected to continuous raids by natives: the San who thought it theirs and who lurked in the wilds; the Xhosa, expelled from the area, who would not accept the settlement; and the ghosts of rebel Boers, killed by the British in righteous defence of Hottentots, although they should perhaps not have been so contemptuous of those first Dutch settlers.

Thomas brushes aside the woman's question about colonial names for native peoples. As if he hadn't dealt with that in the *Narrative*; besides, no one at the time regarded naming. With challenges of survival, there simply was no time to think of rights. The place was what it was: beleaguered, contested perhaps, but all they had in which to prove themselves. A far cry from the three Eildon Paps that had nurtured his youth, from the mossy banks and verdant valley of the Tweed, but it was his duty to adapt and shape a new world for his people. The frontier was the place where the doughty Scots would defend the colony, where they indeed made their mark on the history of that new country. Shuttling between skirmish and peace, he could imagine a future of settler and indigene one day burying their differences, but first there was the urgent business of survival in the unfamiliar heat of the Eastern Cape, occupying more worlds than one, where his border sympathies spun dizzily across the divide. What choice had he but to turn a blind eye to the rivals who laid counter-claims to the land? It was not a question of brushing aside their grievances. That, surely, was the business of the Colonial Office, which had come to arrangements with the various peoples; in any case, in those days such questions did not arise. How unjust, then, that he should now give an account of himself. He can barely bring himself to recall the writer woman's method of questioning, an interrogation that he hopes this Greene fellow will not pursue. As inquisitor she ought to have been more open to the ambiguities of freedom, but no, madam remained stern, po-faced, and relentless in her clipped questions.

A vast, empty tract of land, did you say?

Did he say that? Well, yes, officially it was, and inhospitable to boot. There was so much to think of, so much to overcome in that wild and dangerous settlement; there were no roads to markets, no means of irrigation, and space for cultivation was hopelessly inadequate.

And raids by the San and amaXhosa – who did you think they were? How did you imagine they came to be there? You asked the landdrost for military protection against them..

Yes, and he kindly sent us ten armed Hottentots, themselves indigenous people, who were happy to protect us. Why would we not then have thought of the marauders as common thieves?

Then you demanded more land?

With no water, and rough terrain that resisted cultivation, it became clear that the only means of survival was stock farming. For pastures we needed land, so yes, we asked for more. The British government had not given the emigration scheme enough thought; we were misled, and the Eastern Cape was a far cry from the Garden of Eden that the Foreign Secretary had promised. But there was no shortage of land in that vast country. Boundaries in the colony were after all always provisional, moveable. No one would have called us greedy, especially with my brother William planning to join us later. Our boundaries had of necessity to shift, down along the Cheviot, to include Kloppers Kraal, Elands Kloof and Kaffir Kraal.

And the Boers you displaced?

They presented no problem at all. The Slagtersnek lot were foolish rebels who treated the natives abominably, in fact, insisted on their right to kill disobedient Hottentot servants, so the British had no choice.

Slagter refers to butchery …

A matter of justice it was, to execute the ringleader Bezuidenhout, and drive the rebels off the land. I certainly had no qualms settling on a farm that had been occupied by a Boer rebel …

And previously occupied by the indigenous San. Your great cause, they say, was the emancipation of indigenous people and slaves at the Cape. How was that to be reconciled with the colonial project?

Bringing the Word of God to the colony should be seen as the first step towards the emancipation of native people, and the Word at the same time ought to liberate Europeans from the bitter and baleful draught that is slavery. Themselves debased …

Thomas could not read the expression that flitted across the writer woman's face before she turned away without hearing him out. Distaste perhaps? Certainly incivility. He will not be judged in this way, according to positions taken in another century. That is not fair. No, he would rather sink back into oblivion …

It seems that she has left Sir Nicholas to take up the cudgels, and he represents a new set of problems that Thomas is equally loath to tackle. But he'll bide his time, see how the man manages, or whether the writer woman will summon the courage to return – for, whether she admits it or not, it is a matter of courage.

A border may not be the ideal place for a man on crutches. There is limited room for physical movement, so it calls upon the imagination to produce a space for finding his feet, his balance, for leaning this way and that. The woman has a point. Thomas was not entirely insensible to the ambiguities of the colonial project; he tried to fold the alien worlds into each other, superimpose one upon another, juggle the competing points of view and find a position in which to settle. Also, as a non-believer, the woman cannot appreciate the counter claims of the Faith, the requirement of the gospel to civilise unbelievers. He has not reckoned on being upbraided, of all being held up for scrutiny. She has come equipped with magnifying glass and tweezers, as if he were an insect; worst of all, it turns out that even in the land where he had for years been revered as the Father of Poetry, he is now being questioned. Is she aware of the irony? He has worked tirelessly for the freedom of slaves and indigenous peoples, and this is what it has come to. Mary and Hinza mean well, but they have no idea what they have taken on, of the cruel hostility he now will have to brave.

It was on the journey back to Britain, on the brig *Mary*, that matters presented themselves differently. Defeated really, driven out by Somerset, and sad as he was to leave the Cape, Thomas found that as the waters parted before the bow the fog lifted somewhat and the colonial project seemed as a dark tangle of ideas, a cacophonous mayhem of bleats and roars from which the ship retreated. Tossed on the swell, with the dear child Hinza tugging at his sleeve, brimming with questions, both he and Margaret stumbled on the deck, unsure not only about where they were going, but also of what they'd left behind. Had they not always been scrupulous about steering clear of slaves, of paying the Hottentot servants? Had it not taken patience to train that lazy, feckless race, barely capable of instruction? Had they not taken in the devastated Bastaard families as workers and tenant farmers, mixed-race men who had been disowned by their own European fathers? Had he not demanded that Somerset improve the lot of settlers, as well as the conditions for natives and slaves?

Conflicting demands, Margaret soothed, of the poet compelled to attend to matters of unjust governance. No wonder he was both spiritually drained and, thanks to Governor Somerset, financially ruined.

Thomas naturally fought for compensation in London. Here, humanitarianism had taken root and flourished amongst intellectuals, and thus he found the mantle of activist that the vile autocrat had conferred upon him to be of suitable cloth. Had his actions not, in fact, been driven by philanthropy? In London, the native problem could be reassessed, and the wider question of slavery be addressed in rewarding calm.

Och, the world has changed for sure. The comfortable cushion of beliefs has been thrown up in the air to explode into a flurry of feathers, a scatter of questions that can no more be gathered together.

If the idea of settlement had been sold to the Scots as occupation of empty land, it was one that neither he nor others had thought of questioning. Instead they hoped to erase the history of the terrain, to save it from being what it was through renaming. Trekking through the wilds to their allocated farms, in the absence of roads they had to cross the Baviaans River twenty-seven times. A place of rock it was, sheer slabs of stone all along the river with outcrops like malevolent growths, ridges to hinder progress, relieved only by wading here and there through pools of shallow water. How would the thistle seed they had brought along take root in such rock? Cleansing its history, he named the valley Cheviotdale. Like any homemakers who lay out familiar belongings, making a new place their own, they renamed all within sight, all according to the Borders they occupied back home. Who could have lived in a place called Kaffir Kraal, branding themselves as unbelievers and usurpers? Names like Glen-Lynden or Glen Douglas were pleasing to all.

Thomas is prepared to beat his chest and shout to the world *mea culpa*, prepared for the woman to represent him on her own terms. But what he has not been prepared for is the infectious vitriol of questions. He sees his own boy Hinza, the apple of his eye, tilting his head, wavering. That it should come to this! Such is his love, that if the boy should question the halcyon days of the beehive hut, he would give up, fade out, for restoring his reputation is nothing in the face of losing Hinza's love.

Nicholas's line of questioning may be of a different order, but it is even more irksome, not least because the man, fortified by his knighthood, languidly adopts the position of the upper classes. His aim seems to be to exonerate Charles Somerset. And perversely, by way of defending the tyrant, insists that Thomas was not a radical, and that he first fell out with the governor over an article about the unfair treatment and neglect of the British settlers in Albany, rather than about the colony's treatment of slaves and indigenes. And published in London too. Unkind, and an error on Lord Charles's part, to call you a Whig and an arrant dissenter, the man drawls, for you were, of course, nothing of the kind.

Mary and Hinza look up in alarm as Thomas reels with confusion. Had he too, he wonders, in that place and time, thought it unkind and an error? Were those his thoughts? His words? Is he expected to rise to the bait? He cannot trust himself to speak as, quivering with rage, Thomas remembers Somerset summoning him to interview. The man's haughty eye, the domineering arrogance, accusing him, Pringle, of ingratitude … how dare he … and Thomas lurches, reaches for the table in order to steady himself.

This is not what he had in mind at all. The air in his lungs compresses; he grows faint, cannot breathe. I can't go on, he whispers,

49

falling into Mary's waiting arms. Mary, in a touching pietà, sinks with thighs spread to receive the head against her shoulder and Hinza, holding the man's feet, finally looks up to announce: Mr Thomas Pringle has had enough. He has no wish to defend himself against such cynical questioning. He will not be back.

Nicholas nods, tiptoes out of the room, and the door clicks shut.

Call her demanding if you like, but one would have thought that with this new life her hands and feet might have recovered from working the buckra households or the salt pans of the Turks Islands. Mary chooses not to regard the old scars on her body, but look at these hands, rough claws that will not let bygones be bygones. At least she is nowadays shod like any lady, her deformed hands gloved in winter, and thus there is no need to dwell on old injuries, old tales. On summers' nights when she strides through the long grass in Victoria Park and carries aloft her shoes, allowing her toes to plough into leaf-silk greenness, she imagines these feet to be young and slender, the black skin smooth above the rising paleness of her soles. Then no thought of their salt history hinders her passage through the vegetal green, when freedom from a vicious master, a greedy mistress, once again holds the tingling newness of summer grass. Not for Mary these namby-pamby moderns who nurture the prosthetic pain of subjugation and enslavement, which is to say their ancestors' pain. She will cleave to this revival, even if freedom in this new century turns out to be a many-faced, treacherous business. And so she says to Hinza that Mr P would not deny them this further chance of being. They must proceed without him.

Free or not, but ready for yet another life, Mary Prince does not need Nicholas Greene to make a pass at her – if you can call it that. Old as Methuselah, she is past coupling, past the very thought of men. She's had more than her fair share of them fumbling in the dark, whether welcome joukery-pawkery or the nasty weight of a master fallen drunkenly upon her. The idea of it! There is no decency in the man. With his bad breath and crocodile skin he cannot entice any woman, so in the belief that she doesn't count he alights upon her.

Nicholas imagines that she'd be grateful for being so crudely accosted. Leaning forward in his chair, he idly lifts her skirts with his walking stick and wheezes, Come on old chickie, you must miss the tumbles in them ole cotton fields back home. I have a good mind to tup you right here by the hearth and give you the time of your life.

As if he could. Mary has no difficulty snatching his stick and pushing the old devil deep down into his chair, holding the stick for a menacing few seconds over his head. Filthy dog. But she will not demean herself by cursing him.

There was a comely nigger girl, Nicholas pants, in Lord Orlando's house, whom one may well think of as an example of gracious black womanhood. Always ready to please and not so quick to take offence. Ah yes, black Grace Robinson who showed all her teeth at once in a broad grin. Well, she may have prevaricated, scratching and biting like a wild Afric cat, but really she loved being tumbled in that dark crypt. It was no mean feat, taming and turning her into a grinning Christian lassie.

Mary says as quietly as she can that he has clearly lost his mind. If there were a crypt in her house, that is where he'd find himself, alone and tied up, but since there isn't, she'll have not another word of such talk, and Hinza had better not know of his slipping up so badly. We'll start again tomorrow, she says sternly, helping him out of the chair. At nine a.m. sharp. Upon which she shows him the door.

Only then does she laugh out loud. With her story written in a book – the very first account in Britain of a black woman's life as a slave, she'll let him know – and read over the years, she is immune to human badness, to his type; she cannot be harmed.

So won't your book do? Why are you not satisfied? Nick wants to know. Why bother with Thomas Pringle's story?

The man is a fool, asks foolish questions because he lacks the imagination to see things from their point of view. Sir Nick – perhaps more could be squeezed out of that mean soul if his title were used –

has difficulty thinking it a worthwhile project. He believes that if Mr P has not garnered a reputation with his poems, he is best left to oblivion. Mary explains that there was much more to Mr P than his poems; that he struggled between his vocation as a poet and his social conscience; that he was a radical who defended slaves and the oppressed native people in the colonies. Here in London he not only rescued her and published stories of the oppressed, largely out of his own pocket, but he also canvassed and raised money for repatriating Stuurman, the last chief of the Khoesan people, from Australia, where he had been transported by Governor Somerset for his resistance to colonial law.

Unfortunately too late. That Hottentot convict died just before he was released and sent home, Nick drawls. Typical, really, of all Pringle's misfired projects.

The man is intent on nastiness. Mary points out that that was hardly the fault of the good Mr P who campaigned with all his might.

No, no, no Ma-ry, Nick says in his careful voice, as if she has difficulty in understanding English. Do you not know? This much I've discovered, that in the colony itself your man Pringle made it perfectly clear, in fact he was vociferous about not being a radical, claiming that it was slanderous of Lord Charles Somerset – a very fine governor, mind – to brand him as such. And as for taking you into his home, has it occurred to you that it may not have been primarily for your protection?

More slowly, pausing between each whip of a word, he lashes out: You were their servant, simply tricked back into a benign kind of slavery – and who knows what else, he winks lewdly.

Mary fixes him with her eyes. It is hardly clever to trot out the views aired at the time by the vile MacQueen in his *Glasgow Courier*, intent on harming both her and Mr P. She shouldn't deign to reply, but the man's libellous words are etched in her memory, words that so pained the Pringles: 'Servants are not removed from the washing tub into the parlour without an object'. Such were the filthy minds of slavers who attribute to decent people their own lewdness, and Nicholas cannot be excluded from that class.

Still, Sir Nick laughs indulgently, imagine thinking things would be better here in England! How on earth did you black numbskulls on the islands come to believe that the damp English air could cure your rheumatism? A cropper you came there, hey!

We-ell, Mary stalls. Why should she explain? She tries not to laugh. Any fool ought to see through a story like that, but no, then it suited people to believe that slaves were dumb victims of old wives' tales and superstition, above all incapable of subterfuge, and it clearly still suits Nick to do so. How could the masters have imagined slaves did not know that once they reached English shores, where slavery was illegal, they'd be free? Certainly they knew nothing of how dreadful the climate actually was, but it suited nicely to enthuse about the English air curing rheumatism, a good enough word to stand in for bondage. Besides, the Woods, humble folk before their ill-gotten riches, were keen to display their new wealth and chattels in the old country. Slurping their sugared tea with pinkies aloft, they could laugh all they wished at the stupidity of black people wanting to come along in the belief that their rheumatism would be cured; the slaves themselves knew what they were after. Mary had argued back and forth with her new husband Daniel, for a freed man cannot always put himself back in the shoes of the bonded, but he came to agree that going to London was a risk worth taking, and that she would then be able to return to be a proper free wife.

Nicholas cannot think of a riposte, so he adopts a haughty silence. The man lacks a sense of the equivocal – a fine word that Hinza has explained to her. Which may or may not be the effect of having been born out of writing, although it could be said that she too was born out of writing, but what Mary means is that unlike her he had no existence whatsoever before his appearance in a book. So she ignores his jeer about rheumatism and the London cure, and returns to the topic of the Pringles.

Things were not as simple as that, she says. True, she was the

Pringles' servant, but at her own behest. First and foremost, Mr P, an honourable man if ever there were one, took her into his home for her own protection against the Woods, who owned her. It was Mary's idea that she earn her keep by doing household chores. With Hinza so often ill, Mrs P by no means strong, Miss Susan, her sister that is, earning her living as a schoolmistress, and Mr P at the Anti-Slavery office most days, they sure needed someone to help in the house – of course in Africa, where servants were plentiful, they had got used to the idea of help – and for that she, Mary, earned some money as well. When the Pringles went to Edinburgh for a whole month, it was she who kept the house in order. What self-respecting person would sponge on her benefactors without entering a sensible contract like that? And please note that the terms of the contract were entirely set up by her, Mary. But if he, and she adds pointedly, Sir Nicholas, if he wishes to call her a slave, so be it, but please, he must not imagine himself to be her master. Mary plants herself before him to say: My understanding is that you agreed with Hinza and me to get the book on Mr P written, that you are willing in return for a chance of tasting a new century. But if you can't do it on our terms, well, we'll have to think again.

Nick is, in fact, all lusty façade. Mary has noted how easily he is winded, how easily he tires. My dear woman, hold your horses! I'm simply checking all possibilities; I am of course at your service, he protests. Visibly pained by his own abasing words, he seems to gasp for breath, and she can only hope that he'll perk up enough to carry on. There is a job to be done. She suspects that he has misgivings, kept under his hat, of course, because they, his collaborators, are proving to be more difficult than he imagined. She has caught him sitting with his hands on his knees, staring abstractedly into the fire and exclaiming out loud: Life, life, life! Which makes Hinza titter unkindly.

How derivative, Hinza says under his breath; no doubt our laureate would prefer to languish on a mossy hill under Orlando's oak tree.

Hinza's job is to trawl through the material they have gathered and present it to Sir Nicholas – interpret it, really, since the man, whose idea of the contemporary is to fall in with Tory ideas, will look at things in such a queer light. Which is to say that he'll not accept everything they present, thus Mary must gird her loins for the final showdown when points of view will have to be negotiated. Besides, the old man has embarked on his own research, so who knows what he'll come up with? All to be balanced against the advantage of having the Life of Mr P written with the authority and kudos of a titled and literary white man.

Hinza says that they need not worry, that there are plenty of enlightened readers who will find meaning between the lines, or who will uncover the palimpsest that is their first-hand account. Full of fancy words, is Hinza, but Mary begs to differ. She would rather not rely on so-called clever readers, who may well be subject to outlandish fashions in reading. Surely the equivocal, too, could be told in a straightforward fashion: first, look ye here; then, look ye there …

Sir Nicholas's old Gladstone bag is as capacious as his belly. It bulges with papers, documents and notes, but he is not ready to pass anything over to them. Premature, he insists. The most he will do is read out aloud a paragraph or so. He does love the declamatory style, but so does Mary, so she keeps her promise of kicking Hinza's shins when he laughs out loud. Hinza claims that the bag is stuffed with the old man's entire oeuvre, including fragments that he plagiarised from Orlando. Well, Mary doesn't know about that, and frankly she shan't be worrying her head about those noble types – Mr P was right about that class of parasite – or indeed about Old Nick's earlier outputs. All she asks is that he make progress on the project, which seems to be going in fits and starts. Without her badgering it would surely grind to a halt, because right now she has a suspicion that Hinza's interest too has waned. Nowadays that one is deep, distracted, falls into unsmiling reverie; she shall have to find the right circumstances in which to corral him back into getting Mr P's Life on paper. The truth is that without Hinza, the bona fide African, she simply couldn't manage the project. Although Mary too is of African ancestry, she reminds him. Albeit ancestors who were happy to sell their people to slavers, as the narrative of Louis Asa-Asa shows, she adds; but that seems to cut no ice with the laddie, who says that slavery comes in many forms, a truth that she cannot dispute.

This morning Nicholas arrives in a crabby mood. He will have neither coffee nor tea, nor a comfortable suck on his pipe. He has done some research on his own and wants to discuss the gypsy question. Not again, Mary sighs; their project has nothing to do with those travelling people. The poor gypsies are best left alone in their caravans.

Don't get me wrong, Nick says, unlike his modern critics, I happen to think that the young Pringle's condemnation of gypsies pouring into Scotland shows sense and insight. Who, after all, were these people, what business had they coming from India or Egypt or wherever Gypsyland may be to lower the tone in the Borders? If you ask me, the Union had enough on its plate, dealing with the native savagery of the Highlanders, Nick wheezes.

Mary too has little truck with people who do not understand the value of soap and water and an easily found scrubbing board, but Hinza turns on her. Whoa, he says, holding up an admonishing hand and fixing her with his slanted eyes. (She could swear the boy has Bushman blood.) I thought we'd decided to focus on Mr P's years in Africa and then the short period in London, Hinza says. You can't take Nicholas's word and side against persecuted people; besides, there's no reason to include Mr P's youthful views about gypsies, which he would surely have revised in maturity.

It is only fair, Sir Nick says, tapping his good foot, to show that the young Thomas had interesting ideas about ensuring Scotland's commitment to decency and enlightenment. And it wasn't his fault that the gypsy incomers failed to appreciate the virtues of progress. Admirable, the way he took them on, and sensible, for in the newish union with England he saw clearly how Scotland could adapt to a more civilised way of life. Civilising the deceitful and disorderly race rather than tolerating their savage ways and being swamped by them was undoubtedly the correct route to follow.

Hinza is outraged. Oh please, spare me the bigotry. Do think of the arithmetic of being swamped by a handful of indigent people. How about allowing your Christian soul to dwell on the word 'indigent'? It simply isn't fair to rake up the gypsy article; besides, we know nothing of how that came to be written, the context in which such contentious views came about. I won't have such insensitive representation of Mr P.

Sir Nick laughs his falsetto laugh. Me insensitive! These modern macadamised roads packed with tar may not allow for sensitivity, but let me tell you that once upon a time I could find my way about London purely through the feel of the cobbles. Even now I can sense the bump of a pea through any mattress, a mark of princely sensitivity. There can be no arguing with the printed word, dear boy, he drawls. Your man Pringle took advantage of his position at *Blackwood's* and himself published his diatribe against gypsies. It's there in black and white. No evidence to be found there of his compassion or of identifying with the dirty hopeless peoples of the world.

Hopeless peoples of the world! Hinza shouts, banging his fists on the table. And who might they be? There are groups of disadvantaged, downtrodden people in different situations who do not give up hope, in spite of being bullied by the over-fed.

Mary puts down her knitting needles, but before she as much as opens her mouth, Hinza storms out, slamming the door loudly so that the windows rattle in their casements and a horrible draught cuts across the room. She stokes the fire with a few lumps of coal and the last of the logs, biding her time. The boy will be back; he is not usually given to fits of rage.

No need to worry about him, Nick says. He'll be off to meet the older gentleman with whom he spends much time these days. It would seem that our boy has a penchant for the older pansies. Which makes one wonder about Pringle …

No, Mary interrupts, absolutely not. Stop right there and keep your dirty speculations to yourself.

But my dear, a Christian woman, a lady like yourself is surely outraged. I presume that you know about young Hinza preferring the company of older men of, shall we say, dubious persuasion.

Mary will not admit that she knows nothing of Hinza's private life; besides, old Nick is not the most trustworthy of informants. What I do know from my long years of forced labour, years of feeding British sensitivity and British prosperity, she says slowly – fairly gulping at the words that come from she knows not where – what I do know is that there can be no harm in that which is freely chosen and does not harm others. And picking up her work once more, she fixes on the needles that click ferociously, taking on a life of their own.

Nick raises a comic eyebrow and says that he knows what he knows, that the fair sex is not always capable of discerning harm, and that there are at least questions to be asked. Upon which, catching her angry eye, he hastily gathers his coat and cane, and leaves. As always, she is relieved to see the back of him.

For the first time in this new era, Mary feels distinctly unwell. Her joints swell as if she's been gorging on sugar and salt, and listlessness engulfs her, a feeling that usually can be nipped in the bud. There is no question of holding back. It is something that has to be cleared up. The newspapers these days are full of it. Relentlessly, with lurid details, one case after the other, even in the holy church, crops up to collective gasps of disbelief. But her eyes prick; she doesn't have the stomach for it, and instead knots her head-wrap tightly, ready to go out. Mary says over her shoulder to Hinza that there is some matter to be discussed when she returns. He looks up from his book, nods okay as if he has no care in the world, and she wonders why she's allowed Nick to plant such terrible suspicions in her mind.

Courage, Mary, she upbraids herself. No sooner has she shut the door and taken five paces down the path – the bloody weeds, already popped up again between the stone slabs – than she turns back and bursts through the door to confront the boy. No lies please, she blurts, no beating about the bush, no sparing of feelings, just tell me straight: your relationship with Mr Pringle. Did he do it? To you? Is that why …?

Hinza looks at her blankly for a while. Then his face contorts with something she does not understand as he bellows. It? It? What are you talking about? How could you, how dare you, Mary Prince? Spit out your 'it', go on, spell out what it stands for!

She stands with her back to the door, not knowing what to say, except she needs to know the truth.

Hinza wags his finger and shouts, Come on, say your 'it' out loud so that you can hear yourself.

Incapable, she shakes her head, and they stare at each other in silence.

Your 'it' is sex, sexual abuse, is it not? Hinza finally says in a quiet voice. You should be ashamed of yourself. That is what they said about you, Mary, when Mr P took you in and defended you against slavers. You ought to know that the man was not capable of such behaviour. You ought to hang your filthy head in shame.

Upon which he storms out, slamming the door. This their comedy of errors, of comings and goings, of opening and shutting doors. Mary resists running after him. It is best to speak when he has calmed down.

Mary delays supper of slow-cooked lambs' hearts and black-eyed peas, spiced island food that she prepared specially for Hinza. When he finally returns late that evening, she says that she is truly sorry, explains that she simply wanted to be reassured; but Hinza says no, that she wants to pry into his private life, that he knows Nick spies on him, that the pop psychology of attributing his friendships to childhood abuse is stupid and disgusting.

I am entitled to a private life, Hinza says. And so are you. You never speak of your husband, Mr Jones. Does he even exist, one might ask. In the story of your life, that which you offered the whole world, you barely say anything of him, and rightly so. There are things, Mary, we do not wish to broadcast, or even whisper about, and not because there is anything bad or evil to be hidden; rather, we need to keep some things to ourselves. That is what private selves are about. I have no doubt that Mr P felt much the same and asked no questions of your private life.

Mary rises to enfold the boy in her arms. You are wise, and I am a sorry, foolish old person, she says, that I freely admit. Having given in for a short moment, he wriggles out of her embrace, but they sit down companionably on the sofa with a consoling bottle of ale. For some time now she's been of the opinion that brown ale soothes the joints and keeps the heart beating at a good old pace. And tomorrow she'll tackle the weeds once again.

Mary is secretly proud of the ways in which Hinza has taken to new-fangled modernity. From the internet he's printed out a picture which he holds aloft.

How vain you were, Mary, posing for a photograph with your people, he teases.

My people? She has no idea what he is talking about.

Look, here's a portrait of you in a fancy frock, or is it a nightdress, with your owners, the Woods, and Hinza falls about laughing. Grinning like a proud monkey, you are, whilst the Woods show you off; and how grand they are, posing with their chattel.

Mary wrestles the paper from him, and pores over the picture. The young black woman in white with a black apron and slave's cap is not in the least like her, and it is not true that she's grinning. Who are these people? she asks.

At least the slave woman is not the roly-poly Aunt Jemima so favoured by white people; at least she is young and slim, if ugly. The woman's lips are pursed, her head is held at an angle, defiantly, angrily; she refuses to be a willing, serene sitter. She appears to not care two hoots for the white baby she holds diffidently, holds out really, in her left arm, at a distance. But then, neither does the mother, a hatched-faced woman with hair dressed as flaps over her ears, who leans in towards her husband, away from the slave and the baby. These people are not the Woods, but they do bear an uncanny resemblance to them. No wonder the image had been widely circulated as that of Mary with her owners, in spite of the fact that the woman looks nothing like her. Besides, if *The Times*, reporting on the libel case brought by Wood against Mr P, referred to Mary as a negress of very ordinary features, well, that could not be said about the unattractive woman in the picture.

This slave woman, Mary observes, is more knowing than she, Mary, ever was; the woman knows how to give her people short shrift, although there is an ugly bitterness about her mouth that is certainly not enviable. The poor girl has no hope, no belief in her ability to escape; no doubt she remained a slave. Mary sees that that is the function of photographing yourself with your human chattel: fixing the woman in her subservient role. She may lean forever away from them, but her feet are planted in their field, forever enslaved. No hope there, just anger that will get her nowhere new. These people have nothing to do with Mary, so she scrunches the paper and tosses it into the fire.

Mary asks Hinza to pass over her well-thumbed book, *The History of Mary Prince*, which is always at hand. Don't laugh, she admonishes, holding it aloft. I've not had good luck with likenesses. See how this image on the cover also looks nothing at all like me. Imagine, me as a woman with parted lips, and kneeling on one knee, my hands clasped and held up in supplication! Adorned with a chain as if it were jewellery – well fuck that, if you'll pardon my French. I would never have approved such a cover. And the indecency of my chest on display! AM I NOT A WOMAN AND A SISTER? the streamer asks, as if the proof lies in my bare breasts. Well, I do know that I am not a banner; I don't speak in slogans, and I would never have asked such a stupid bloody question. I'm Mary Prince, and a fair sight better, healthier looking than that tragic person. A ridiculous picture, it fair spoils my book – no wonder no one nowadays recognises me.

Perhaps you're not recognised because with your appetite you've turned into roly-poly Aunt Jemima after all, Hinza teases, so that she cuffs his ears.

As if I don't cook purely for your benefit, she says. The boy has the lean body of a hunter-gatherer and her plans to fatten him come to nothing.

Nicholas Greene wanders through central London, marvelling at postmodernity, all glass and chrome, and ingeniously inserted into monumental old granite. Not a patch, of course, on the fretwork and friezes of the past on which it so impertinently imposes. He needs to find his way to one of the many houses where Pringle lived and where he'll meet the others. Mary and Hinza are adamant that he should visit these places. They also think it necessary that he go to the site of the Anti-Slavery Office at Aldermanbury – these days surely a Mc-Donalds – where Pringle worked as secretary. Mary boasts of his signature on the 1833 Act of Emancipation as only an illiterate would, but really, who has heard of him? Every schoolboy knows of Wilberforce or Granville Sharp or Wedgwood, but where is Pringle's name to be found? The man had swopped his African idyll for colourful slaves, a poor exchange for the picturesque land of purple mountains and chrome-winged birds rustling in the wittegat tree. The poet converted to activist – agitprop, or whatever the man had in mind – there is clearly a story behind it. Nick doesn't get it, but uncover the hidden story, that he will. He does wonder why Hinza splits his sides at the mention of wittegat; no doubt a simple ploy to lord it over him with so-called native knowledge.

Nicholas cannot find his way about this modern London; he has forever lacked a sense of direction. Truly, he was made for country estates, where one could always find one's way back to a magnificent house centred in the landscape, where chimney stacks beckon with curls of wood smoke and where a pair of pert hills, or a kidney-shaped copse, serves as landmark. Now he is hopelessly lost, cannot find an Underground station, but just as he thinks he ought to ask someone for directions, he is stopped in his tracks. For there, on a vast sheet of plate glass in an art gallery, is announced none other than 'The Oak Tree'.

Shaking his hoary head at the wily tricks of time, Nick enters the pristine white space, conscious that his morning suit is somewhat shabby and that his beloved slouch hat may be seen as an affectation. It turns out that the exhibit has nothing to do with *the* Oak Tree but rather is a tree in another guise, reincarnated in an art gallery, and as the leaflet explains, itself a reincarnation or repetition of a work born in the twentieth century, although he understands the artist to be still very much alive. There, boldly on a plain glass shelf protruding from a white wall, sits a glass of water, all clear and transparent, declaring itself none other than an Oak Tree. Not even transubstantiated, Nick gathers from the leaflet – that nonsense dreamt up by a religious fanatic – no, says the artist, forever no; it IS an oak tree. Period, as they say in the no-longer-new world. Forget the realm of symbols and metaphors.

Nick cannot believe the brass neck of the artist. What would his dear patron have thought of this, he who floundered so shamefully in the world of metaphors? And Orlando's voice rings in his ear, clear as a bell: *Such simplicity … such clarity, as he scored out yet again a line about the sky, not blue after all, but like the veils which a thousand Madonnas had let fall from their hair …* Clear and simple for sure, old Nick concedes. What on earth would milord/milady Orlando have made of this glass of water of an oak tree? He laughs out loud, only to be admonished by a loud throat-clearing to his left.

And who should be leaning, if you please, in a far corner against the dazzling white wall, but sooty Hinza himself, dressed from top to toe in black, undoubtedly, perversely flaunting his blackness, and evidently finding Nick's laughter a disturbance. He steps forward, sketchpad in hand, with an exaggerated swagger. He offers his right hand, which Nick is obliged to take. A cheeky Hottentot, or is it Bushman, who would do well to get rid of the heathenish name of Hinza.

So, who *is* afraid of Sir Nicholas Greene? Hinza, for one, in spite of his bravado, of claiming to find the man amusing, although strictly speaking he's thinking of the young version of Nick Greene, the poet. Knowing Nick's origins, he knows that younger man to be already mendacious, malicious, a name-dropper, above all a copycat, and thus quite capable of slicing off his head, declaring: Ah, a Moor – or perhaps a Bushman – head! Macabre, the obsession that civilised people have ever had with severed heads and skulls. Mr P promised Sir Walter Scott both a Bushman and a Caffre skull, and indeed sent two San skulls to the Edinburgh solicitor, George Combe. Of course, dear Mr P could not have known that that authority on phrenology would use the gift to promote his scientific racism and argue the case for the San being sub-human, closer to the lower animals.

Copycat Nick will surely hang his, Hinza's, head up in the rafters to dry and shrivel, an object to lunge at from time to time, for the man will not hesitate to plagiarise Orlando. But here he is sans sword, disarmed by an oak tree grown from a glass of water on a shelf, so Hinza feels himself for the moment to be safe. Besides, having arrived earlier, he has a wee advantage over the old man.

Nicholas, visibly out of his depth, smiles sardonically at Hinza. Sketching a tree, I see. I had no idea that you embraced the no-longer-fine arts. What might be the point of sketching a glass of water on a shelf?

We-ell, Hinza improvises, as a contemporary artist I have nothing against pastiche. All in the captions, he says, holding up his sketchpad. See, one with, This is NOT an Oak Tree, and another saying, This IS an Oak Tree.

You didn't say you were an artist. Nick looks him up and down.

And you didn't ask what I do. Given this second chance, that's exactly how I spend my time. Not even Mary expects me to be the missionary that Mr P once had in mind for me.

So, an artist from Afric, and a proponent of postmodern balderdash to boot, he smiles – how very often Nicholas finds himself these days shaking his head in disbelief! Really, he would have liked to see the effrontery of the oak-tree artist stop at least here in the gallery, rather than endlessly reproduced.

Och, it's old hat really. Centuries ago people in Africa etched their visions into rock – the hunting of antelope or eland, figures with both human and animal features, even the arrival of idle hands-on-hips Europeans; but also abstract, geometric forms. All from the artists' entry into the spirit world, and ultimately not so very different from calling a glass of water an oak tree. But we're late, he says, gathering his belongings. We should make our way to the house in Islington. Aldermanbury will have to wait for another day. Just as well I am here to guide you, make sure you don't get lost. When, I wonder, will the black man's burden end?

Nicholas gives him a considered look and shakes his head at the young man's impudence.

Stepping out of the Underground station, Nick marvels afresh at this London he could never have imagined. Amazed at the newsvendors, fruit sellers, young women, or are they men, in hoodies trying to flog all manner of things, including mechanical puppies that snap at your ankles, and outlandish vegetables that look like the devil's own organ. And such various peoples of swarthy complexions! He congratulates himself on not using the N-word; soon he will rid himself of the habit, soon be in a position to admonish others, he chuckles to himself.

True, this is quite new to me, he complains, a shock to the system; I may need a guide after all. Who could have imagined a London so … so different and sprawling in every direction? This is all horribly new. And so very many foreigners, with tribal markings too, or so he discerns from the tattoos adorning the very many exposed bodies. Please remind me why we're here.

Hinza explains that history has come full circle. All those voyages of discovery, the scramble for wealth and for Christian converts in the new worlds, claiming those lands and peoples for Europe, well, here is the outcome. The chickens have come home to roost in Greatest Britain: your subjects come from far and wide to pay their respects, to return the compliment of settling in their countries. Your turn to be hosts, to show civility.

Nicholas does not find it amusing.

Islington is not a bad area at all, gentrified for some time now, Hinza says. The artists were first to move in, but now it's where the wealthy have their little townhouses, so out of the reach of artists. In Mr Pringle's day it was respectable enough, a newly built village with rows of houses facing squares of private gardens. So, you don't know why we've come here today? Well, things must be meticulously re-searched; an authentic account can only be given if you experience for yourself where and how Mr Pringle lived. Perhaps being here will imbue you with some feeling for your subject, and so help to bring him to life. If you were to sit at his desk in a striped cravat and hold his pen, you could for a moment become the poet, if perhaps not the activist, but with perseverance that may well come; we must keep faith, he teases. If only you could leaf through Mr P's papers, fling open the window as he had done, enter his being, so to speak, absorb his views, and so render him all the more faithfully. Hinza ignores Nick's guffaw. Sadly, this place has not been preserved as a monu-ment to him, nothing to keep his memory alive. Let's have a look at the house from across the square. All those years ago when we ar-rived at Claremont Square, Mr P, Ma'am and myself, 1831 it was—

So you say Pringle is a well-known poet in Africa? Nicholas inter-rupts as they approach the enclosed gardens.

Certainly, people may not have heard of him here, nor in his native Scotland, but way down in South Africa he is still celebrated as Abo-litionist, Defender of a Free Press, and above all the Father of South African Poetry. Although nowadays I believe, in certain leftier-than-thou circles, his humanitarianism is questioned and he is dismissed as a colonial poet. Understandably, earlier, indigenous poetry has become better known since the demise of apartheid, and Mr P's epithet will have to expand to Father of Colonial South African Poetry. Still, he is well known – every schoolboy and girl has come across the much-anthologised poem 'Afar in the Desert'. You'll see what a fine poem it is, but just in case you wonder: I was *not* the silent Bushboy by the poet's side as he galloped alone through the empty land. That is the work of misguided critics and sloppy readers who confused Mr Pringle's boys. As you can imagine, I was never silent, and Mr P would never have portrayed me as such.

Nicholas pretends not to listen as he scrutinises, on the railings that fence off the square, a Council notice about recycling. Uh-hum, 1830s, he says when Hinza has done. Indeed, your man Pringle is quite unknown to me. With whom did he associate in London? Can't say I came across him in my heyday; he clearly did not pass muster in the top literary circles where more pressing aesthetic matters than slaves in faraway places were being discussed.

Hinza's suspicions are confirmed. The man has not as much as read the works they've recommended. He takes out of his canvas bag the tattered, loose-leaf volume of Pringle's African poems, miraculously come to light in the vault of the Charing Cross antiquarian bookseller who took an interest in the young man's desire for an old edition. Hinza imagines that the poet himself collated this work, that Mr P's own hands smoothed the pages. Reluctantly he places it in Nicholas's hands. This was the poet's personal copy, he claims, so please do be very careful. I'm prepared to part with it while you order a new volume. Then he adds, Enjoy. Mr Coleridge certainly did.

Enjoy? and again, Enjoy? Sir Nicholas queries. What kind of comment, or rather, injunction is that? Does that pass for polite discourse? The imperative mood, young man, must be used with caution. Well, I may or I may not enjoy this verse but, whatever the case, it will have nothing to do with your command. Or with that foolish Sammy Coleridge. And he makes as if to walk off.

No, please stay. Hinza takes his arm. Mary should be here soon; we've arranged to meet at this house that means so much to her.

Nick has reservations about Mary's involvement. Women, he knows, have contrary ideas, will mess things up with their limited knowledge and skills, but Hinza has been adamant. It is after all largely her idea, he argued, and although Mary is not much concerned with the poet, they share the other interests that so occupied the man. Now Hinza takes out of his bag a pink notebook. What you need to get across is how torn Mr P was. Listen to this, from his letter to a friend. Mr P hoped, and he reads aloud, *'to write something that may not dishonour Scotland. At present however I almost feel criminal in giving up any part of my heart or time to poetry … sensible of the vast importance of the task I have undertaken and I will not flinch from it'*. He refers, of course, to his work as secretary of the Anti-Slavery Society and his personal defence of many a slave seeking help. Can you imagine how difficult the man must have found it, negotiating the demands of art and politics, having to lay off the muse whilst he diverted his energies to the cause of freedom? It's a crying shame that there's not as much as a plaque. Really the house ought to have been kept as it was in Mr Pringle's day. With your influence, Sir Nicholas, we could campaign for it. A museum, like the house of Sherlock Holmes, that's what I'd like to see. Alas, there is not a remaining scrap of the man's possessions, no papers to leaf through. Mary thinks that we should knock at the door and ask to be shown around all the same. The current owners will surely be pleased to discover that an illustrious poet and activist once lived here.

Nick stamps his feet impatiently; he does not see his way clear to such vulgar intrusion. It is no more than a house of brick and mortar, one in which he will have no difficulty imagining our man storming about, his head buzzing with grievances. There is absolutely no need to see the interior.

Mary is late, but Hinza, leaning over the railings from where the house can be seen, is pleased to linger for a while. Claremont Square may not be at its best at this time of year, but imagine this, he says, after the hot, parched colony, the houses all but newly built, the square bright green with grass, and the garden borders bellowing in summer their blood-red roses and blue hydrangeas. I for one had never seen such exuberant flowers, such splashes of colour. Ma'am, Mrs P, was much taken with the modern housing, the clean lines and gentle light; overlooking the freshness of grass and the newly planted saplings, she declared herself quite the happiest of women. I had no idea how the desolate Eastern Cape had worn the poor woman down. Really, there could have been no room for her thoughts, as Mr P's Great Cause always took centre stage. Only once did I overhear Miss Susan express misgivings: had it been wise to antagonise Lord Somerset in that way? But Ma'am sternly hushed her sister, said that the colony was a viper's nest of spies and informers who took against Mr P's principled stand for freedom.

Nicholas is impatient. Mary is late, but he can no longer loiter. The gates turn out to be unlocked, and they saunter through the gardens to the terrace on the other side, stopping in front of the house. A large male figure appears in the parlour window, stares at them, and then disappears to open the front door to let out a small sausage dog that rushes to the garden gate, barking ferociously. Hinza, stooping with his hands on his knees, barks back at it, so convincingly that the creature retreats somewhat in consternation, but nevertheless valiantly keeps up the barking. Nick too retreats; dogs have always been suspicious of him and he has too many times in his youth been a victim.

Mary, just arrived, can barely be heard above the cacophony. Respect, she hollers with arms held aloft. Show some respect. Let's not have this brawling on Mr P's terrace.

Nick looks down his nose at her. Bloody bossy woman, he snorts quietly. Who does this … er? Who does she think she is?

Ms Prince to you, says Mary, and turning to Hinza, Cut it out, Bechuana Boy, and let's get down to business. We need to get into that house.

Nick flushes a shoe-leather red. Certainly not, I'll have nothing to do with this, he says, walking off. You'll find me in the nearest public house on the High Street.

Mary gesticulates to the man who stands with arms folded at the window, indicating the door, where the dog barks furiously. But the man waves them away, making it clear that he has no intention of opening the door. Instead, he opens the window and shouts that he has no money, that they should go and beg elsewhere.

69

Hinza tuts, says that this is where Sir Nicholas would have come in handy. Really it's his job to come and speak to these people, persuade the man to let them in and show them around the house. Hinza would not mind seeing the kitchen garden; he has a memory of helping Mrs P grow strelitzias against the shelter of a south-facing wall. He rather fancied that the bird of paradise would still be there.

Mary says no, it was she who lived there with the Pringles. She helped Mrs P in the garden, but for all the poor woman's efforts the strelitzias would not take root; besides, what did Hinza know? Was he not by then a wraith?

Hinza looks at her in amazement. I was always there, he says quietly.

Nick Greene, toasting his feet by the fender in the King's Arms, sips contentedly at a jar of ale. Oh, he has come a long way, with a mind that over the centuries has become infinitely adaptable, and so he welcomes the two with open arms as if indeed the pub were his very own home. He resists an I-told-you-so, says that he'll see the house on his own at another time, and proposes that they start by discussing genre; he can think of nothing more appropriate than a narrative in rhyming couplets.

Hinza says he believes that that has already been discussed, the argument in favour of prose already settled. Mary, beating her fist on the table, says that she'll have none of it. Madame, Nick replies in mock courtesy, it may be best to leave such matters to the experts, and he launches into a complicated story (one told by Kit Marlowe, he'd let her know) of which she can make neither head nor tale.

I may well be less ignorant than you think, Mary says quietly, so take it from me, rhyming couplets are for limericks. This is the beginning of the twenty-first century and it is prose, none other than straightforward, plain telling that will do the trick and get Mr Pringle's story told. She nudges Hinza to take up the cudgels.

Hinza is in fact partial to poetry. Mr P used to declaim his poems, all of which he knew by heart, and Hinza the child, delighting in the rhythm, would drum his hands on his thighs. Many a poem he has tried to fashion for himself, but, alas, it is too difficult. He would not mind seeing what old Nick came up with, but there's no chance of that with Mary at the helm; besides Mary is, of course, right: verse is out of the question, and so the matter is done and dusted.

Perhaps, says Nick, Hinza! (he involuntarily pronounces the name with an exclamation mark) should start by finding himself a decent Christian name. Why had the Scotsman given his own son such a heathenish name?

Hinza laughs, says that he is not actually Mr P's son. (He is alarmed; he has surely explained this before. Is the man's mind faltering?) But yes, he says, he could try a new name. How about Orlando, he teases; it would draw less attention.

Nick guffaws. Misguided homage, and effeminate to boot, he adds, reaching for a newspaper. Or, Hinza says, with so many émigré Africans claiming royal descent, he could be Duke Hinza. How well it goes with his collaborator, Mary Princess of Wales. What a fine team they'd make. The two of them fall about laughing.

As if I cared, Mary says, some name-calling that was. A good Moravian Reverend even suggested that I write my name as Mary Princess of Wales. That's how I signed a couple of copies of my *History*, and with a royal flourish too. From behind his *Daily Telegraph*, Nicholas pops up to say that Hinza! may sound like something one shouts at one's dog, but that it had better stay since the lad can't be trusted to choose something plain and respectable.

So, back to the project, Mary declares. Why not go to the farm at Blaiklaw on the Borders, Mr P's place of birth, and then on to Edinburgh, where he studied and started his working life? She could do with a jaunt, now that the light is returning.

Nick, who has no desire to leave London, least of all with Mary, lowers his paper once more to say a definitive No, not yet, and what's more, you'll find that Scotland's no place for the likes of you.

Oh please, I've already been, some years ago, which makes me more qualified to speak than you are. I made it my business to go to

Edinburgh when the learned gentleman Mr Frederick Douglass visited Scotland, and six days it took me to get there. A more handsome man I'd never seen. Such fine sculpted lips and wavy hair, and fine speeches he made too, but did any of those good Christians heed that black man's words? He ought, of course, to have pointed out that the Free Church had no business calling itself Free, or for that matter a church, but too much of a gentleman Mr Douglass was. Hark what he said to the elders who, of course, accepted donations from the Scottish slave-holders: 'Give the money back, send back the blood-stained money,' that's what Mr Douglass declaimed in his rich American voice, 'and free your souls from the fruits of slavery.' But there's the crux of the matter: just like the buckras, they simply couldn't cut themselves off from the slavers. When it came to money, the genteel, Christian folk were deaf to the logic of those words: Give it back! All addicted to wealth, no matter how nastily acquired, like the very effects of tobacco and sugar produced by their distant slaves. They might as well have been on their knees, slavering like dogs, for they simply couldn't do without it. All the grand ladies in their lace and frills and bonnie bonnets unable to heed Mr Douglass, who after all himself came from Scottish slave-owning blood. So there in Edinburgh he witnessed the scandal of white masters reduced to slaves by lucre, whilst thinking so well of themselves and their godliness. Precisely what Mr P said of the white folks of the Cape colony: all turned into slothful savages because of their addiction to slavery.

Mary, sitting comfortably with her legs tucked under, turns her back on old Nick. Oh, I owe everything to Mr P, may God bless him always, even if he did not have the strength to survive in this new world. We have to fight his corner for him, with the help of the Good Lord, for that dear man had given his all to the cause. If it were not for—

Hinza interrupts, his head in his hands. No more preaching please; I'm converted, I swear. And he intones in a squeaky voice: *I have been a slave – I have felt what a slave feels, and I know what a slave knows;*

and I would have all the good people in England to know it too, that they may break our chains, and set us free.

That's from Mary's book, he says, tapping at Nick's newspaper, you ought to read it. In spite of the brouhaha it caused amongst slavers, that *History* really shook up this island of yours. If only you'd now cut out the preaching, Mary.

You, Hinza, are a true kaffir, a bloody heathen. When last have you been to chapel? How can you expect to be up to the task, to be inspired, if you do not worship the Lord as you were taught to do by the good Pringles? You should be in charge of this great project, but where will you find the courage without loving God? I owe my life to the Moravians, the only true Christians, even if they refused to readmit me because of my so-called depravity that came to light in the court case. Still, for slaves, it was the only place where God could be found.

Hinza smiles affectionately at Mary's preaching and preening. Her chin is lifted jauntily, as she adjusts with both hands her floral headcloth. There is a spirited edge to her voice that he fears some may find flirtatious, even if she means nothing by it. It is, of course, the spirit that has driven her through her trials.

Nick pretends not to listen. He deftly uses a toothpick behind his newspaper; he will leave the two of them to bicker whilst he slips down another pint.

Mary deploys the edge in her voice for sermonising: Now, the very best thing, and she holds her fists up triumphantly, a gift, and only second to God—

Hallelujah, Hinza interrupts again, for he well knows the old praise song to reading and writing.

How else, and she fixes him with stern eyes, would she have found herself, her story told, her true self made whole if her life were not written down? First the Moravian ladies who sharpened up her letters, then the blessing of Mr P who listened to her story, took her in at the hour of her need, and found Miss Susanna the scrivener. It is unfortunate but true that Miss Susanna spiced a few things up and toned others down, according to her very own wishes and, of course, her Christian modesty, and what with Mary's own decent omissions, trouble was bound to come, the book bound to bite back at them; but look, the main thing was that the story of cruelty and suffering, all of it true as God, has since been available to be read by all and sundry. It was, she supposed, a story shared, belonging to both Miss Susanna and herself, and not wholly belonging to either.

Mary recounts the writing lessons before the Moravian ladies sharpened her up. Oh, she will never forget that darling child, Fanny, an angel, who so many years ago sat Mary, then a young slave girl, sat her down and played at being the schoolmistress after being released from her own lessons. Bustling about with her papers, parroting the teacher, she made Mary recite the alphabet, and was not above taking, with pursed lips, the stick to the slave girl's ankles for sounding out a word wrongly. At which Mary would suppress a smile for the darling angel, and plead, Please Miss, I shan't forget Miss, shan't get it wrong again, please Miss Teacher. Of course she was young then, hardly more than a child herself. And then their beautiful parrot would squawk after her, Please Miss, Please Miss. Her feathers, the jewel colours of sapphire, garnet and golden green, ruffled as she strutted about the cage. But in a cage all the same, parroting away, while she, Mary, wrote her ABCs.

Yeh! Yeh! sighs Hinza, and while you're at emoting, why don't you tell Sir Nick here the story of the Pig that you told to Miss Susanna. If only you had practised writing about the Pig – they say that writing is therapeutic, that it gets the bile out of your body. Had you penned an Ode to the Pig instead of lying to Miss Susannah, you would have saved us all much embarrassment. Imagine, confusing the name of your fancy man with that of Pig!

Nick's ears prick up. That's the kind of story he'd like to hear more about. A fancy man called Pig? he asks, shoving aside *The Telegraph*.

Oh yes, Hinza explains, Mr P was prosecuted for publishing Mary's lies, and our Mary was forced to retract, had to confess in court that the woman who supposedly accused her of stealing a pig, in fact, rightly accused our princess here of stealing her husband.

Nick's eyes twinkle with merriment, and Mary throws her head back in laughter. Well, the coward squealed like a pig, no wonder I misremembered, she splutters. That one certainly wasn't worth fighting over, but I couldn't just walk away when his wretched wench came at me with her fists. I fought back – a small matter of self-respect. Of course, had I known that Mr P would be so damaged by the tale, I would have tried harder to remember the facts or even to keep the pig out of my story. Then her face hardens. But what do you know, and she turns on Nick, what do you know about being a slave, of your owners pouncing on the least thing to have you punished and sent to gaol? No wonder the facts of the story clean escaped me when I sat behind bars for no bloody good reason. Besides, should you not wonder about the logistics of stealing a man? Could you, Sir Nicholas, be stolen? Or you? She points at Hinza, whose face clouds over, but Mary storms ahead. Would you men confess to having been stolen? No you wouldn't. So, a child can be stolen; a pig can be stolen; but not a man. Hence my story: a load of nonsense unworthy of clear explanation; small wonder I didn't bother to tell it as it was and so offend Miss Susanna's innocent ears. The point of it all was to tell of the vicious Mrs Woods who had the power to send me to gaol for the least little foolish thing. And that is the truth. Besides, Miss Susanna changed many a detail that she thought would give offence.

Still, Mary's dead famous for the pig story, Hinza says. Here in London Mr P was taken to court, which had the slavers like MacQueen gloating in the *Courier*, and in the colony it did much harm. There the pro-slavery lobby used it against Mr P, said that his defence of slaves was based on a loose woman's lies. Come on Mary, all your doing, so why not recite for Sir Nicholas the doggerel that Geddes Bain composed in honour of you? A great hit his satire was, on stage in the Eastern Cape.

Mary purses her lips in sorrow and disgust. I know only too well that the pig story caused harm, but I can't be held responsible for the rest. That Geddes Bain attacked Mr P so viciously, she explains to Nick, while the rest of the settlers thought it a hoot, this dum-dee-

dee-da about a foolish native woman called Kaatje Kekkelbek. She was supposedly like me, all the rage (which I certainly wasn't), and strutting her disgraceful doings on stage was meant to show that Mr P's defence of slaves and natives and Dr Philip's mission station, his fight for native rights, were a travesty. A disgusting lot, those colonists, and fellow Scots to boot. Can you imagine how it saddened Mr Pringle?

Oh, let's hear the verse, Nicholas chuckles. Mary says she doesn't know their Afric tongue, but will see what she can remember. By way of encouragement, Hinza hums the tune of 'Calder Fair', and Mary recites in what she imagines a Khoesan accent might have been:

Next morn dy put me in blackhole
For one rix-dollar stealing,
And knocking down a vrouw dat had
Met myn sweat heart some dealing;
But I'll go to the Gov'nor self,
And tell him in plain lingo,
I've as much right to steal and fight
As Kaffir has or Fingo.

Plain vicious to put my story to such dishonest use. No decent person would find it entertaining, Mary says, holding her bowed head in her hands. It fair broke my heart, she mumbles, to have so unwittingly disgraced Mr P and the good missionaries at the Cape, and all because of the Pig. How could I have known that the story would be exaggerated and satirised to show abolitionists to be unreliable, making fun of the cause? Who would have thought that it would travel as far as Africa to show that natives do not deserve freedom, that they'd rather whore and thieve than lead the decent Christian lives that the missionary, Dr Philip, tried to secure for them through the Ordinance 50 law? That saucy so-and-so, making fun of me; just you wait till I get my hands on that besom.

Kaatje ended her song by wagging her ample behind at the audience, Hinza teases. Mary tells him to shut up, to behave, or she would have to box his ears until he squeals like a pig. Wait till she gets her hands on that disgusting Kaatje …

Hinza laughs uproariously. She's not real, Mary, just a person on stage devised by Geddes Bain. It's not possible to get your hands on a man-made character, and of another century to boot.

Not real? Mary squeals, well, you can talk, Hinza, you who've hardly had a life, but it was for sure a real bloody Hottentot woman, I mean Khoesan woman, who shook her behind on stage.

Time to go, Sir Nicholas announces, retrieving his paper and reaching for his stick. You two have got the entire bloody bar staring at us.

Another day, and once again the London skies are dark and heavy, threatening rain. Nicholas feels the dampness creep like a malevolent vapour into his joints; his arthritis feels as old as the city itself. It may not be wise to go traipsing about the streets, but sitting at his desk with pen and foolscap paper has proved unproductive. Hence he is with Hinza, having waited for Mary to leave before suggesting that they go out in search of Pringle material.

Surely your man was eminent enough to have been painted, he suggests, so how about a trip to the National Gallery, all nicely heated and with a fine café?

Hinza is tempted to agree, although he knows full well that the gallery does not have a painting of Mr P. Wonderful to spend a wet day at the National, but he has the sense that Nick would not want to linger over the treasures, would steer him through the various halls without as much as stopping to pull up his hose, so that there would be no point. He casts a sidelong glance at the old man. No visual sensibility at all, no wonder he had no truck with Orlando's oak tree, never mind a representation of it.

Why don't we try the National Portrait Gallery instead, Hinza suggests, for there had once been a rumour that the Finden portrait had ended up there. He knows that Mr Pringle sat for William Finden, who produced a fine stipple-and-line engraving. An unseasonably warm day in October it was when the picture was delivered at the house in Portman Square, to a Mrs P who was fairly overcome. How handsome and healthy he looks, she whispered, tears rolling soundlessly down her cheeks, as she clutched the portrait. He, Hinza, given his own shadowy state, was in no position to console her, but how good to see an image of the brave Mr P without the shadow of death that hovered about his actual person. By then the poor man, consumed with tuberculosis, was wasted, nothing like the former self who'd been the subject of Mr Finden's engraving; the illness had crept up on him so suddenly, and the artist had taken an inordinately long time over the picture.

The portrait is not on display, but Hinza is right. They consult the holdings, which shows the Finden engraving of 1834, published by faithful Mr Moxon, to be there. The lady at the desk says what a shame, but it's not available for viewing; and so Sir Nicholas, drawing himself up to his full height, adjusts his voice and introduces himself. He explains that having come all the way from South Africa, he and his man (Hinza cannot believe his ears) are happy to wait until she finds someone to make the portrait available. Which indeed, it turns out, is perfectly possible.

Mr P looks so much more distinguished than Hinza remembers. Here he sits with his elbow resting on a table, his head tilted slightly towards the hand against which his right temple rests. He wears the high white stock and frilled cravat of the times. His chin is neatly pointed, an elfin look with a girlish mouth of full, bowed lips. Altogether calm his expression, and still so youthful looking, even though pain must already have been nibbling at his lungs. His hairline was by now considerably receded, something to which he appears not to be reconciled, since a lock at the left temple has been dragged across to cover the beginning of baldness; his hand involuntarily pats the covered spot.

Hinza feels the tears prick; he swallows hard. He is grateful that the gallery had not been given the other portrait that he knows of, painted by he cannot remember whom, but one that they all loathed.

That was done some years before when Mr P, with a full head of hair, was young and healthy. But how foolish that artist made him look, with hair perched absurdly on his head like an ill-fitting windswept wig, and with his cheek resting on a poorly painted hand, the fingers fat as doughnuts. Whilst the pose was meant to be contemplative, there was no intelligence in that painted face.

Nick, stooping over the Finden portrait, and turning his head knowingly hither and thither, says that this engraving is not up to much either, that the sitter lacks gravitas. I pride myself as one who can read character from physiognomy, and really this is not at all the image of a man who can stand his own against authority, one who would fight for his beliefs, indeed one who could fight back at all. This Thomas Pringle, he says, is a girlish, simpering coward, and what's more, what I see from the cast of his eye, one who easily takes offence. Didn't you say that he fell out with all and sundry, even in his youth in Edinburgh?

Hinza guffaws, offended. Simply wrong, he says, a gross misreading. Just as well Mary is not with us. She would lunge at you, claw out your eyes, so do remember never to slander the good man in her presence, he warns.

Nick is undoubtedly being malicious, which does not bode well for the project. Hinza has thus far chosen to believe the man's skepticism to be healthy, that playing devil's advocate is no bad thing and can only lead to a more objective rendering of the subject. Now he has his doubts.

Nick declines the invitation to have a look around at other portraits. How about moving on to Soho, to a house of pleasure, he says with theatrical purple gestures. Just the thing for a wet afternoon, lazing on velvet chaise longue under soft pink lamplight, savouring the attention lavished on them by plump ladies.

Hinza laughs, shakes his head; he doesn't know where such ladies could be found, but a bordello is not for him. He will linger for a while in the gallery.

Surely you're not tied to Mary's apron strings, Nicholas jeers.

From what I gather, that one has not been known for abstinence; in fact, I believe the word 'voracious' was routinely used.

Hinza leaves without a word. That's what Mary explained, right from the start, when he asked about the court case. Don't you believe what those enemies of freedom had to say about me. Voracious indeed! I had the sexual appetite of any healthy woman who need not pretend otherwise. But look how all that malice and maligning cost me my husband, driven, they said into the arms of another on hearing lies about my so-called escapades in London. Of course, I didn't believe them, but how could I return when there was no guarantee of my freedom? All indecent, slanderous talk by those filthy-minded bastards. Oh, the very name of MacQueen makes me sick. What kind of top-drawer is that? With such a grand name, one would have thought that man to be of noble origins. My, how he's let himself down with the disgusting headlines in his newspaper, defending slavers and slandering Mr P with lewd suggestions about me. Gentlefolk, my foot, mired as they were in lies and hypocrisy, with men and women toiling for them far away across the ocean, slaves kept well out of sight and out of mind, whilst they built their empires, built their grand civic buildings and churches and private estates back home, their cities grown grand and prosperous. All pious Christians, capable of vulgar aspersions about me that had the poor Mrs P blush to her roots with shame. The least they could have done is to keep mum like that Sir Bertram-in-a-book, even when asked direct questions about his Antiguan slaves. Silence is more decent than broadcasting such filth. But see, all water under the bridge, so let's get cracking on with the task ahead.

III

Ke ... ke ... I am

I wanted to swallow, but all was parched, and my tongue like a flap of leather moved with difficulty.

Ke nosi mo ... le fat sheng, I tried to say.

Ik ben ... Ik ben ... hier ...

... in de wêreld

here ... in the world.

And the world is wide, wider than this land of stone. It sweeps far into the Highlands, to the old country where we have left behind the smoke-heavy air, our homes burnt down by the invaders. The terror of Mfecane all around as we Batswana refugees fled across the many faces of the land. Or so it says, for I remember nothing.

Finally the words fired out with a ra-ta-ta-tat: *Ik ben-al-leen-ig-in-de-wê-reld.*

I have to agree with Mary that it is strange how these came to be uttered in my new tongue, the Boer language of Baas Karel, but as the poem says, they truly were. There were two false starts: first a rustle of dry leaves in my throat, then the sound amplified, like goggas beating their wings into words. We heard, both of us, those sounds that sprang from my tongue as I looked up into the eyes of the white man leaning on a stick. Bright eyes, soft like a springbok's, even if they were of an unnatural bluish green colour. But I cannot help feeling that there was no actual springbok involved in the meeting. Would I not have remembered such a friend? Besides, I could not have said those words about being alone if I had been attached to a little pet bokkie. Or would I?

Ik ben alleenig in de wereld.

I am alone in the world.

It would seem that they were mine, the first words spoken by me in so very many days and nights of the full moon shrinking to a sickle and plumping up once more, and I having thought that I'd never speak again, that the veld, the plants and animals would not require the useless sounds of words. I had tried at first to hum, but to no avail. Then that miracle of words, like a fountain spraying over smooth white pebbles around which to wrap the tongue, though they were mine for the short seconds only that it took to utter. Small wonder that I remember them with difficulty, that they remain a dim echo. For no sooner were the words formed than they were no longer mine, and there lies the rub, their strangeness. Speaking *to* him, I gave those words – freely. So, having entered the world creakily, having tumbled out all helter-skelter, they somersaulted into another voice, to be shaped once again by him, by the poet's reporting tongue. Thus tangled in translation, the words, as any schoolboy knows, were fixed once and for all in the anthology favourite, Mr P's famous 'The Bechuana Boy'. That is the story of my origins, my beginning: in the warm heart and the creative mind of Mr Pringle.

So who am I?

I am born of a poem, born in words. Before that moment there is a blank, an absence, only part of which is filled in by the poet.

It is possible that the words of contact may have been different. In fact, how could they not have been, fixed as they were by another: inverted, following the demands of rhyme, exclamatory, translated from our common Boer language, and what's more, curiously addressed, a politeness that the actual moment of encounter surely would not have allowed.

Stranger – I'm in the world alone!

Thus is our meeting immortalised by Mr P, the stranger. The poem may suggest that you imagine me holding up my right hand whilst beating the left against my chest. I have no memory of hands with which to emote; in fact, do I remember anything at all?

Stranger! I do wonder how I, a black boy, could have thought it prudent to address a white man in that manner, to remind him that he does not belong here, on land from which natives had been driven. Yes, I appealed to his kindness, but at best I would have expected the variety of kindness bestowed on animals. (Was that why Mr P attached me to a springbok in the poem?) I knew that white men had guns, and felt contempt and hatred and also fear for people of this land. So perhaps I assured him that I was alone in the hope of stemming his natural antipathy. Not his fear, for I was a child of who knows how many years. That Mr P thought of himself as a stranger, rather than the colonial assumption of owning and belonging, is, of course, testimony to his difference.

The man's faltering speech came as a surprise. Clearly the guttural tongue of Baas Karel, from whom I had escaped, was not native to him. Ja, the strange white man said in the harsh language we shared so imperfectly, the Boèr language new to both of us, Ja-nee dat zien ik. Zo. Maar, ik vraagt, wat is jou naam?

What is your name?

Hinza, I replied, soothed into using my native tongue. Leina la me ke Hinza, I said, before I remembered that he was a white man. So I translated: Myn naam heeft Hinza. His voice bounced back in my own tongue as he repeated in Setswana: Leina la me ke … Hinza, and then having chewed and savoured the sounds, he said smiling, tapping his chest: Leina la me ke … Thomas. Mister, Mijnheer

Pringle. I looked again into his eyes, the strange blue-green irises, and found that my words had indeed stirred up something akin to kindness.

He shifted his walking stick from right to left, and as we walked off to retrieve his horse, I noted that he limped, his right hip being slow. A broken white man. Was that why he understood, why he spoke kindly? The horse was held by a San boy who stared with hostility and ignored my greeting, none other than he who often rode with Mr P afar in the desert, a boy who from the start saw me as competition. But much as I try, I cannot conjure the memory of Mr P's tents in the veld. Given that I was alone in the world, there could not have been, as the poem would have it, a Bushman who brought tidings of the tents. Would I not rather have taken to my heels on hearing such news?

Here, so many years, or rather centuries later, in the low light of a London tavern as he calls it – he will have nothing of the modern, bright, and noisy bars – Nicholas Greene and I discuss our origins. We are both born of texts, but he will not engage with my difference, the different or equivocal levels of the real. Nothing to compare, my boy, the old man says companionably, between a metropolitan birth and one in the colonial veld. Chalk and cheese, all so long ago, and such a strain on the unreliable memory, perhaps those old times are best forgotten. Besides, is this not a redundant exercise? You say it's all here in 'The Bechuana Boy', written by the man himself, so why the need to pore over it line by line? Why are you questioning the text? You don't by any chance doubt this daddy of yours?

Of course not, I remonstrate. But I cannot let go when so much has been erased, so many gaps remain to be filled, even if allowance has to be made for poetic licence. Yes, I am, or rather was, the eponymous Bechuana Boy found in the veld by Mr P, naked and unshod, although I must insist that the poem wrongly has a tame springbok accompanying me. What a foolish figure, a boy with a bokkie! I believe I really do have some memory of that meeting, strange and uncanny, as I saw my destiny unfold before me, not only inescapable, but one that I felt urged to embrace. Instead of caressing a gentle springbok invented by Mr P, my hands clenched and unclenched involuntarily as I said, keeping my eyes fixed on his own: I will come with you. Much later, Mr P teased me about that boldness that I could not recognise in myself, words that I surely would not have uttered without invitation? Mr P had no doubt asked if I would, or perhaps just said that I should go with him to Eildon.

Oh, *I* do, all right. *I* recognise the boldness, interrupts Sir Nick, whose smile carries more than a trace of incredulity. Uncanny eh, he croaks. These modern ideas about memory and the unconscious are best left alone, taken with a pinch of salt; they can only lead to unhappiness. It's not uncommon for lost souls to imagine memories, or see the uncanny in retrospect. I'm in the world a-lo-one, he intones in what he believes to be my voice. Fine words for a boy of the veld.

Then he tilts his head attentively. Why, I believe they ring a bell. For sure, it's Orlando! And Nicholas, known for his power of mimicry that could bring the dead to life, grows misty-eyed, and declaims in an aristocratic voice, fluty and feminine: *'I am alone,' he breathed at last, opening his lips for the first time in this record. He had walked very quickly uphill through ferns and hawthorn bushes, startling deer and wild birds, to a place crowned by a single oak.*

What have ferns and hawthorn, or an oak, to do with the Cape? I must not be influenced by this man who cannot think beyond his own world, his own culture. I remind him that we are speaking of Mr P.

Ah, yes, the illustrious poet of whom no one has heard, he says; in his own country a failed man of letters. Father of South African English Poetry, I remind him, but he sneers at the epithet, settling the matter with a dismissive, Of course, the colonial rhymester – and citing a twentieth-century critic, adds: So soothing, the familiar trot of iambic tetrameters. It is not surprising that Nicholas Greene, known throughout the literary world as a failed poet turned critic, turns out to be jealous of Mr P's reputation.

I hold aloft placatory hands. Okay, I concede, but for all the ring-ing of your bell, I have no idea what you're talking about, so let's drop the uncanny. I'll put up with ferns and hawthorn for now, but please hear me out on that meeting that starts my life, that lays bare my origins. It has to be unpacked. See, I would have liked to say to Mr P, whom I instinctively trusted: I will be your helper, I am strong enough to lend a shoulder, to help you off a horse, to carry you across a river, even if I am only a boy. But that would have been a foolish boast. Besides, he would already have had many boys, even men, to help him, work for him. So I said again, and that to a white man, I will come with you, and he nodded, Ja, as I knew he would. Earnestly, abstractedly, as if it were a given, as if he too knew that, destined, there could be no other way.

I had, of course, seen a white man before. Strictly speaking, I belonged to one, although the actual trading of slaves had already become illegal. I was not one of those, the people from Madagascar or the Malayas, but we native serfs were no more than slaves. The Bergenaars who preyed on Batswana refugees had sold me cheaply to Baas Karel, in ignominious exchange for the greatcoat he was wearing against the winter chill. Him, I refused to look at. While the transaction took place, I kept my eyes fixed on the stain, the grimy patch of sheep fat on the left pocket of the coat. Then my captor, the trousered Bergenaar as Mr P sometimes called him, slipped his own arms into the coat sleeves, and it must have been the play of light, for the stain seemed to spread slowly, evenly, across the worsted fabric, turning the entire garment into a darker shade, almost black. Voilà! he said, spinning round to the admiration of his folks, and I was handed over. But how I came to be wandering in the Eastern Cape where they found me, I cannot say for sure.

Baas Karel waved the Bergenaars on – Weg nou met julle. Loop – and he cracked his buffalo-hide sjambok so that it echoed through the valley. He saw them off his land, even though it was dusk and they would rather have overnighted with his Khoekhoe serfs, from whom they begged a karbonaadje before leaving. Hungry as I was, I could not bring myself to eat anything. Later, in preparation for my escape from Baas Karel, I searched the veld for edible tubers, a number of them unfamiliar to me, but in my hunger I took risks with veldkos, sniffed the leaves, gingerly rolled the roots in my mouth and waited a while for warning convulsions before consuming the whole. Thus I learned what was edible in that strange land of the south – kambroo, koekemakranka, and also eintjies, delicious but so meagre, barely worth the trouble of clawing out of the earth.

So wide and stony and still was the land, without any people of my own, that its silence invaded me. I could not speak. Baas Karel's commands failed to lodge in me. Not only did I not know his tongue, my own had dried to leather, immovable and silent. It was as if I had never heard a word, nor spoken one, so that my new master flicked his furious whip at my person, across my shoulders and legs. Verdomt! he wailed and stamped his feet in rage. Deaf and dumb and stupid, I was not worth the greatcoat; he had been cheated, he shouted. He named me Domkop. That I heard and understood all right. Indeed, it was not long before I understood much of what they said, but my tongue refused, and I remained dumb. Even at night in our compound I uttered not a word to the others, the Khoekhoe peons and the Mozambican slaves; nevertheless, I learned a good deal of their common language, which varied only slightly from Baas Karel's Dutch.

I pause to check on old Nick, who has sunk deeper into an armchair. The venerable monoglot, fast asleep, jerks as a snore escapes. Perhaps it is not so diverting, this story dragged out of the gaps and shadows of a poem for schoolboys. But how else discover who I am? How else uncover the past, if not by working my way through the poem? Nick should be asking helpful questions; it is his task to write up Mr P's history. He may not think my origins to be relevant, but Mr P after all became a father to me, became my father.

I help the old man out of the chair, steer him out into the bracing air, so that he shudders and says, It doesn't add up, you know; for one, one can't learn a language without speaking it, and that's not all …

Then he yawns. A carriage, he must have a carriage, he's had enough of this long day.

Nonsense, wrong century, there are no carriages left in the world, I say. Neither are there any black cabs around; we have to take the Underground. I point Nicholas to his westbound escalator, then dart back out into the street. I'd rather walk home than suffocate in that underworld so redolent of limbo.

So who am I? Born of a poem, I developed in a warm amnion of words, and before that a blank ... well, not quite. If part of the absence is filled in by the poem, a history that I do not recall telling – of a mother surviving the hoarse-roaring Gareep River only to be bought by Christians and taken from me – I also have a memory of her head held aloft, her mouth open in a soundless scream before she drowns in roiling waters. The time before Eildon remains swathed in mists, in which conflicting images surface and recede like so many heads bobbing in a turbid stream. Could it be that sitting with Mr P under the wittegat tree, where he read his verse out loud, I heard various versions of my story? Which is to say various drafts of the poem?

Yet it is with clarity that I remember us sailing away from Cape Town on 16 April 1826, Mr P having been persecuted and driven out penniless by the arrogant governor, Lord Charles Somerset, even if that gentleman had himself just left the colony. A few days before, as autumnal winds swept through the town, I strolled through the Company Gardens and came upon a clump of early crane flowers, both wonderful and terrible, for it reminded me that I would be leaving for a cold country inhabited by pale people, where no such wonders were to be found. Like a sunbird drawn to the nectar I knelt down by the crane and tried to fix its shape in my mind. I twisted my wrist and fanned out my fingers to resemble the orange and blue sepals springing at a right angle, a startled gift, out of their green sheath. Back at Eildon, the servant girl Vytje would drop crane seeds into cow's milk so that, delicately infused with that flavour of orange and blue strelitzia, the milk fermented more quickly and the curds remained edible for so much longer.

I knew that it was wrong, but I wrenched off a tough stem, and once home offered it to Mrs P, who scolded me thoroughly before putting the flower in a jug of water. I could tell how much its elegant structure pleased her. Mrs P explained that the plant was named after Queen Charlotte of Mecklenburg-Strelitz, a German lady who no doubt had been as frightened as I was about going to England. Her flared nose and thick lips spoke clearly of her African ancestry, Mrs P said. So you see, African blood has always found its way into Europe; you will not be such a stranger there.

I liked to think that the strelitzia Queen's unknown black tata came from the Camdeboo in the Eastern Cape, a Khoesan name that I have always savoured and loved to say out loud, even though I supposedly came from much further north. Might that not be a name I could take on in faraway England? Hinza Camdeboo? A shocking thought. Was my name not Marossi? Why did I think of exchanging it?

All through the long sea voyage, I saw that splendid bank of crane-shaped strelitzias, staunchly holding their own against the Easterly wind, even though only one in fact had been in flower. For nearly two centuries it has lodged in my mind's eye as a mascot, and still the bird of paradise structure, its brilliant blue and yellow colours, remain unfaded, imposing themselves on the stems I occasionally indulge in, strelitzias nowadays being imported to this cold island. Mrs P thoughtfully tried to grow one against a south-facing wall, but at which of the many London houses we lived in, I can't be sure.

Our small family paced about the deck, mouthing to each other the mantra of 'Alles sal regkom', which Mr P had picked up from the Boer neighbours in the Zuurveld, although rather than allaying the tension and unspoken anxieties that hung over our unit like fog, I believe that, as is so often the case with reassuring utterances, it did nothing of the kind. Nicholas may question my use of the word 'family', but I have no doubt that they thought of me as their son, and they were no less than parents to me. They did not speak of their troubles, but I knew that Mr P, having exposed the governor's autocratic misrule – his neglect of the settlers, the ill-treatment of native people, and the infamous commandos sent out to wreak havoc in the Eastern Cape – was financially ruined through Somerset's retaliation, and thus was banking on justice and compensation. No doubt, I thought, the Pringles also harboured fears about how London would suit me, which was to say how I would suit London. And indeed it was the unhomeliness of the great city – as I sat motionless, as was my wont, in that dark parlour in Finsbury Square, my feet shod and planted on a threadbare Persian carpet, my eyes tracing over and over the intricate pattern – that so many years later moved me to recall the day of my arrival in the Pringles' lives.

Feeling the permanently grey skies bear down upon my spirits and seep into my lungs, the pea-soup fog stealing into each bronchiole, I tried to find – via the poem, via entering Mr P's imagination – my entry into this new world of London. Whilst my temperature soared and my chest tightened with every breath, I heeded the good man's injunction that illness should be considered God-given time for thought and introspection. And, above all, for poetry, although I would have fancied that greater clarity of mind might be required for that. But I forgot how busy he was, how hard he worked on the noble cause of emancipation, and how limited were his hours for writing poems. Mrs P, Margaret, Ma'am concurred: We must gain something from adversity; that is how life becomes endurable, how we see light gleaming beyond the darkness, and thus find it easier to understand the ways of God and to praise Him. Alles sal regkom, it turned out, was secular shorthand for this complex divine process. Mr P's 'Letter from South Africa: Slavery' was indeed a ray of light. It was a firsthand account of the miseries of slavery and a commentary on its debasing effects upon the hearts of its practitioners and abettors, a tract that rightly earned him an office in the Anti-Slavery Society and a welcome source of income.

If Ma'am was a patient, unassuming woman, I found few fissures in the glowering skies; the little light that seeped in was of a sickly, sulphurous hue. Ma'am plumped my pillow and brought me Messrs Coleridge and Wordsworth's *Lyrical Ballads*, a volume that I did not find half as diverting as Mr P's African poems, which he has been feverishly reworking since our arrival in London. I have an idea that Mr Coleridge had a hand in the latest draft of these poems.

Mr P was too fastidious, Ma'am thought, but no, he remonstrated, revision is the essence of a poet's labour. Not only will there always be a better, a clearer way to say something, but the very underlying idea itself must remain open to revision. Resting on the day bed, I pondered a draft of 'The Bechuana Boy', and perhaps I found it lovely because it was about me, and being about me, it taught me to read and think, to love poetry. Although, even then, I could not help being uneasy about the need for a springbok in the narrative, or 'fawn' as Mr P also called it, to usher me into the world. However, I then thought it churlish to question him, and more's the pity, for there would surely have been a plausible explanation. (I hope to be forgiven for harping on about the springbok.) It is, of course, not a matter of mendacity; I know too well that art demands invention, that it translates the world in novel and revealing ways, and yet I am troubled by the presence of the beast. Where does it come from? Why do I have to enter his world with a pet springbok in tow? What is its function in the picture of my arrival?

Well, he could have translated you into a feast for hyenas, half eaten before his very eyes, before he hobbled to your rescue and fashioned out of words new ears and a left leg for you, Sir Nicholas says spitefully, guffawing. I have learned to ignore his snide reading of the poem as a fiction.

More troubling than the springbok itself is Mr P's strange translation of the beast into a fawn, as if through ferns and hawthorn we had been traversing the dales of England. If only there were not also the verb to fawn, to cringe obsequiously, which I would like to think has absolutely nothing to do with me, but it was as hard then to let go of that meaning in London, when often the only safe way out of white people's wrath, out of the vicious gangs of uncouth, marauding youths, was to hang my head, eat humble pie and sorrily slink off into the shadows. I did, of course, not tell the Pringles of such encounters with the natives; they would have found it distressing, and there was in any case nothing they could do about it.

Am I being foolish about minding the fawn? Or touchy, as Nick calls us? Mr P was after all a stranger in the Cape, a foreigner from across the seas who naturally remained bound to that world, to its flora and fauna. No sensible person could expect him to have cast aside his past, its history and influences. Such was his impact, his commitment to justice, his extraordinary influence, that we all forget that he spent a mere six years in the colony, forget that he was driven out prematurely by the vindictive Somerset. The kind of information over which Sir Nicholas lingers, the facts he claims to extract from new sources and from which he draws unpleasant inferences, constructs a very different man from the one I knew.

Oh come off it, Nick protests. You were a child, a savage, a wild cub rescued in who knows what manner by the man – or, and this you will have to consider: possibly gifted or sold to him as a slave. Unable to tell nobility from plebeian sentimentality, what choice did you have but to fawn at the white man's feet?

I cannot help laughing out loud. Old Nick tries to goad me into seeing Mr P in a nasty light, as someone who would stoop to buy a child. Look, he says, not unkindly, I'm sorry but one has to consider the facts: the man spent ten years as a humble clerk at the General Register House in Edinburgh, where he transcribed the claims of heirs to landed property for Chancery. Any mind would wander from such tedium to fantasise about his own aristocratic values; no wonder that he developed airs and graces, tied to a desk as he was. Like any upstart, he no doubt thought of enhancing his image with a black boy in tow. Then follows a story of so many failed projects, of antagonising his betters. He had failed to learn a lesson from his editorship of *Blackwood's*, where he ended up being reviled and the laughing stock of the Edinburgh literati. Being leader of the Scots party of emigrants to the

Cape ought to have settled him, but no, look what follows: an Academy at the Cape that had to be abandoned; a job as librarian, no, *sub*-librarian of the Government Library in Cape Town; and his friend Fairbairn, brought out to the colony to help launch a newspaper that, not surprisingly, was brought down by Charles Somerset for its seditious content. Note that all was achieved through the intervention of Sir Walter Scott and the kindness of Lord Charles. Then Thomas's high mind did not object to privilege and nepotism, yet he was ready all the same to devour the hand that fed. Why did he not go home to Scotland? No, there he had long since burned his boats, so to London to upset the apple cart here, to make up for his own failure by incriminating respectable folk with nonsense about slavery, making enemies even amongst his fellow Scots. And as for the writing, there is little evidence as far as I can see of his knowing the first thing about the divine spirit of La Gloire that infuses all great poetry. But go ahead, laddie, I'm listening. As you know, I keep as always an open mind.

I can't expect Nicholas to be interested in the literary story of my origins, and given his own history as a minor poet, it is easy to dismiss his reading of Mr P as envy. It ought to be as easy to dismiss his dismissal of me as a found beast, a fawn who slavishly continues to admire a flawed master. I ease my shoulders and stretch nonchalantly in my chair; I will not let on that I'm rattled, neither by him nor by Mr P's use of the word 'fawn'.

Let me return to our meeting, Mr P and I, by which I mean the event represented in the poem. Embedded in it is a precursor story – of the springbok, first persecuted, then rescued by a kind human, which is to say me, and its subsequent devotion to the rescuer, which is to say a mimicking of human gratitude – that neatly mirrors my own narrative of being rescued by the poet himself. Writing is ever a business of doubling, which is no doubt why Mr P employed this image of my own situation. But I still find it troubling, the story of oppression, persecution, rescue and gratitude, reiterated in this manner. Could it be that I was indeed no more than a pet to him?

As a child at Eildon, I was charmed by the story of the springbok.

So what happened to it? I asked. Seeing you in safe hands, it bounded off into the veld; the springbok too wanted to be free, Mr P said. In my sickbed in London, shielded from the terrors of the streets, I recited 'The Bechuana Boy' to myself. As my temperature soared and my voice failed, I felt myself to be in a hall of mirrors, of multiple reflections. With eyes shut I tried to empty my mind and think of Mr P's pride in the poem, but, slithering in and out of my consciousness, an argument tried to take root:

Mr P is to me as I am to the springbok.

The springbok is an animal, a fawning animal.

Therefore …

Nowadays, rethinking the poem, I lay out the incidents as I once did on the patchwork counterpane, designed and sewn by the frugal Mrs P herself. Look, she said, here and here and here, stroking in turn each of the squares of yellow fabric designed with a greyish fir sprig – Douglas fir, sure it is. With the other squares of plain fabric in green and grey, they formed an artful pattern, pleasing to the eye, and contained within an inner border of strips of the same yellow, sprigged stuff. All salvaged from the frock, she said, her best and favourite, that she had donned on that magical day. The day that God sent you to me; the day I received you. What better excuse for the indulgence of best wear? God's gift, she smiled, and stroked my head. And my heart flooded with love for her.

My mind leaps as it did then from square to square, to the patterned configurations of yellow grey and green, to the incidents or accidents of the story:

The Bechuana Boy (Hinza) is oppressed by Baas Karel, to whom he had been sold.

He finds solace in a springbok that he rescues from persecution by wild dogs.

The springbok loves him like a child.

Baas Karel covets the springbok and takes it away from him.

The boy recovers the springbok and escapes the tyrant by fleeing into the desert.

The boy is in turn rescued by Mr P ... (I pluck out the wicked thought planted by Nick: ... *to whom he has been sold*.)

The springbok that Mr P found so fruitful a cipher offers an explanation: just as Baas Karel took the springbok away from the boy, Mr P must have felt a threat to our relationship, the fear that a tyrannical enemy would separate him from me. Did he fear that the Governor would not allow me to travel to London? That I would be separated from them? I was after all their son.

I am no sooner soothed than a problem that I choose not to disclose to Nick arises. If I had been found by accident in the veld, how did Mrs P know to expect me, and so wear her favourite frock in which to receive me as God's gift? And why had I not thought of this before? I must dismiss Ma'am's words as being an expression of her piety, a fanciful affirmation of her regard for me and therefore not an inconsistency. It is with no little pleasure that I remember that I was loved as a child (as the fictitious springbok loved me?). That Mr P, having experienced Somerset's malice, so feared losing me that he would flee, escape with me. What else could the homology suggest? The poem was written well after he found me; in other words, it encompasses the poet's fear. I would not have known or understood the perils of a Motswana child belonging to the Pringles. Is that what happened: the Pringles fleeing to England in order to protect me?

What a fool this exercise has turned me into! I say this out loud, and Nicholas yawns, says that preposition-stranding at the end of a sentence is the only fault he could find with Joe Addison's otherwise exquisite prose style. If only the man had heeded his advice.

So many deaths in so short a time. Unjust death wreaked its havoc, and there were several poppycock rumours of my own death, touching stories of my black arms clinging to Ma'am's white neck as I rasped my last breath. Balderdash. No. After Mrs P's death there was for me at the time only a brief sojourn in the spirit world, or rather several sojourns as I escaped from the wrath of the native English. Ma'am followed hard on the heels of Mr P. For all her concern for

my weak constitution, it was I who kept guard through her brief illness, along with her devoted sister, Miss Susan Brown, who lived
with us in London and of course stayed by her side.

For weeks – Miss Susan having returned to Edinburgh – I would
not leave the silent house, stripped by death. Oh, Miss Susan did the
right thing, invited me to live with her for a while until I found my
feet and returned to Africa, but I discerned from the handkerchief
that she clutched and twisted in her hands that it would not be a
good idea. Quite apart from the work he was committed to in London, Mr P had not thought it prudent for us to live in Scotland, and
there was no need for him to elaborate. What a disappointment, our
visit to Edinburgh – where, using the bad weather as an excuse, Mrs
P insisted I mostly stay indoors. For reasons that I was not privy to,
Mr P returned downhearted, defeated really, even after seeing his
many dear friends, including Nanny Potts, so that it took some chiv-
vying by Mrs P to lift his spirits. There had been no talk of a second
visit.

No doubt you would find Scotland difficult, Miss Brown conceded, especially after the business with Mary Prince and the court
cases, but we'll manage, she said. I owe it to my sister and Thomas to
resist the prejudice in my native land. I'll protect you, she bravely
insisted. I smiled at the thought of the retiring woman defending
me on the cobbled streets of Auld Reekie, but Scotland was out of
the question. I would never forget how Mr P was persecuted and
pilloried by MacQueen and his supporters. Or Lockhart's malicious
review of his *African Sketches*, calling Mr P a parochial schoolmaster
who assumed grand airs. So I declined; besides, I thought she too
would be better off in London. Absolutely not, she explained. It was
only for her sister's sake that she had tolerated the arrogance of
London folk, their contempt for her Scottish tongue and silly jibes
about imagined stinginess.

Well, the winding ways of prejudice are ever foggy, but I promised
that if ever I felt strong enough I would one day visit her in Edinburgh. Difficult as London was, I knew how to negotiate my way

around, but could not think of managing fresh ways of being ridiculed in Scotland. Besides, Mary and I were putting our heads together, devising our plans for survival in the city.

Miss Brown protested that Mary was kind and competent, but that her reputation could hardly do me any good. I tried to explain that Mary's battles in London precisely equipped us with the means for living there, that I could be left in no more capable hands, and that Mary would best know how to manage the small annuity from the house that Mrs P had left me. Mary was adept at cutting through the taunts, I continued, and it was she who encouraged me in my desire to be an artist, finding me the apprenticeship in Mr Holland's studio.

Miss Brown wrung her hands in distress. But do you not remember, Hinza, that Mr Pringle educated you so that you would return to the Eastern Cape as a missionary? He discussed it with Dr Philip who, as you know, has been working tirelessly at the mission to convert indigenous people, and how wonderful that he's managed to get Ordinance 50 passed, a Magna Carta for the natives. That's where you are needed, at the Kat River Settlement, the lovely fertile land that Dr Philip secured for your people, and where dear Thomas himself had hoped to return. An astounding success the settlement is turning out to be. Thomas thought it only correct that you should contribute as a missionary and a schoolmaster.

I prevaricated, saying I did not feel equipped as yet; besides, was the ministry not a vocation that literarily required a calling? And would further experience and education in the mother country not stand me in good stead? Miss Brown agreed, but she urged me not to worry about a calling since, contrary to popular belief, a calling can brook delay. There was also a great thirst for knowledge amongst the Khoekhoe and the Bergenaars (she too refused to call them Bastaards), who surprised the authorities by collecting their own money to pay for teachers. But teachers were hard to come by and that was where I would be invaluable. I recognised the pleading in her voice, her desire to carry out Mr P's wishes, which indeed I was not averse to, so I thought of a compromise. Perhaps missionary stations have room for artists? I asked. That quite confused the poor woman, who blushed and frowned, and stuttered that that was not what the mission stations were about. The poor, ignorant people of South Africa were in need of far more urgent and useful help than the smocks, easels, canvasses and dubious values offered by artists. You should read Mr Brougham's *Penny Magazine*, she recommended. That good man, another Scotsman committed to uplifting the uncouth English working classes, has started the Society for the Diffusion of Useful Knowledge, and speaks most elegantly on the need for it amongst the newly literate here at home. I do not believe he would allow for art being useful for those who pursue knowledge under difficulties.

At this point Mary, who had come in earlier, interrupted. Oh, she knew all about that society. Mr Bonnington, for whom she did washing in St John's Wood, had warned against Brougham's 'useful knowledge' of science and engineering. It was no more than a ruse to lead working people away from radical politics, he said.

Miss Brown fairly gasped in disbelief, so that her voice rose an octave. That was nothing short of slander, she said; ignorant accounts of the Society for Useful Knowledge caused needless harm, and Mary herself would most certainly benefit by expanding her mind via the *Penny Magazine*, indeed it was incumbent on working people to better themselves in that manner. Mr Brougham was after all a beneficiary of the broad and universal Scottish education that brought light and civilisation to every corner of that country, a state of affairs that he magnanimously wished for England as well.

Mary promised to alert Mr Bonnington to that fact, and having soothed Miss Brown with a cup of lime-flower tea, she gathered her skirts and departed.

Mary was often out and about doing God knows what, and I knew better than to ask, for she was fiercely protective of going about as she pleased and not accounting for her movements. For some time after the publication of her *History*, she trudged around meeting houses to testify to the truth of her account, but proud as she was of the book she soon tired of that, and after Mr P's death freed herself of that obligation. Quite redundant they were. Why could she not do as she pleased and choose for herself topics to discuss with the good English folk? Was she forever doomed to speaking of the atrocities of slavers and of the abuse of her body? Oh no, she'd had enough after those court cases; she could no longer go about helping white people's souls out of the misery of their ill-gotten gains, for remember, she averred, no one could escape the benefits of economic growth based on slavery. These people would have to learn to stand on their own feet and help themselves. It was only to the Pringles that she owed anything, and they were sadly departed. Besides, they would surely have absolved her of that responsibility had there been a chance to explain her abhorrence of the crazy workings of English guilt and the Society's eternal demands for gratitude. Really, it was out of that discussion that Mary and I put our heads together and arrived at the project of having Mr Pringle's life written from our point of view.

I left the tedious business of managing money in Mary's competent hands. For a while she had taken a job as housekeeper in a grand villa in the new district of St John's Wood. A veritable holiday, she called it, after those days in the salt pans of Turk's Island. Besides, there were two young drudges to do heavy work, thus nothing arduous for her. She lived in, and arranged for my lodgings close by in Bayswater where she often visited, putting up her feet and fishing from her bag a bottle of ale. Accustomed as I was to genteel manners, it took some time to get used to Mary's loud laughter and abrupt speech, but I soon came to find that for all her apparent difference her heart was soft, and that beneath the roughness she was as refined as any lady. Only, she never spoke of her husband, and I knew better than to probe.

That is as much as I can summon; I have no recollection of our tumble into the spirit world, just as I have little understanding of our return, except that it is in cahoots with a woman whom Mary had enlisted.

Mary calls this re-existence our 'rejuvenation'; little wonder that she is sprightlier than ever. Hallelujah, no more drudgery, she squeals, joyfully throwing her arms aloft, but mind that we do not forget our responsibility, our grand project of honouring Mr P. It is to him that we owe this return, although I always feared that he'd be too frail to participate.

How will we live? I ask, mindful of the limited funds, the fact that our few guineas will go nowhere in this century. Really, she scolds, call yourself an artist, and you so banally tied to the real. Here is an opportunity for us to abandon convention, throw caution to the wind, forget all parochial concerns as we wade our way through ugly truths and sweet-smelling lies, so once and for all: forget the business of realist operators; they are for writers and readers of fiction, not for the likes of us.

Nevertheless, I have found an artist's housing association in the East End, behind the Mile End Road, with a studio upstairs and limited living space below. It was not with any great enthusiasm that I invited Mary to share with me the cramped quarters, the ground floor of a small terraced house, but she was delighted, said that really we have no choice, given that we're in this mission together. I am wary of living so intimately with anyone, but she has no patience with what she calls my pretensions. Namby-pamby nonsense, she says, do you think you're a gentleman? Had you not been found by Mr P, and escaped being a slave, you'd think this light and airy space the height of luxury. There's enough room for us to keep well out of each other's hair. Besides, this is how even gentlefolk have to live these days.

What about the small matter of explaining your presence to the Artists' Housing Association? I asked.

Oh hush, you are some screwed-up educated kaffir boy, she said. We're family, you and I; even artists have families, so no explanation needed. No need either to explain that you're working on an urgent project with me, although who knows what passes as a legitimate art project these days, in which case I'm your collaborator. This borrowed time too will run out shortly, so let's get on with the task of honouring Mr P, of getting his life written, of rescuing him from the pampered over-educated toffs with their crazy theories.

Why she persists in thinking of me in the modern terms of being screwed up, I do not know. For that matter, I am no longer a boy either, but I know better than to contradict her.

It was Mary who first met with Sir Nicholas Greene, a snooty old man who sounded like a West Indian Polonius risen from who knows where, offering his services. He said that the writer woman had recruited him. I believe you're quite illustrious, my dear, he simpered; it will be a pleasure to work with you, I'm sure. All delivered in a fake Jamaican accent, but her single word, Enough! accompanied by a hand signal and pursed lips, silenced the foolish voice. New century, new times. We have all to learn the tricky new tenets for getting along with one another, she warned, and promised to consult with me.

Well versed in modernism as I nowadays am, I recognised him instantly, and tickled by the piquancy of his origins, it was I who had to persuade Mary that he would do. Without a literary toff, our book simply wouldn't see the light of day; besides, Mary was not one for dismissing coincidences. Here old Nick turned up just as she was beginning to doubt that the woman who was meant to restore Mr P's reputation would manage. Then there was the felicitous coincidence of Sir Nicholas being a Bloomsbury man, in a sense born out of Bloomsbury, and Bloomsbury, where Mary herself lived when she first came to this country, was dear to her heart, the place where she will forever be remembered.

It turned out that Sir Nicholas, who had so many more centuries under his belt, found it hard to adjust to the times. He imagined that his contempt for us was disguised, and in his absence we rolled about laughing at his folly. A matter of keeping up pretences on both sides. Nicholas may have been renowned as an arch-mimic, but Mary too was proficient in that field. With a saucepan on her head she strutted about the room, drawling in the old man's voice his legendary litany of complaints: oh but for his palsy, the engorged heart, split spleen, and leaking liver! Not to mention his unrivalled sensitivity and the sensation in his spine that speak unequivocally of greatness – the variety of greatness marked by genius and infused with La Gloire.

Och, he is well connected and will do better than most, I soothed, as long as we keep our own heads level, keep a keen eye on him. It is after all a puzzling new century where people like us—

Speak for yourself! Mary shrieked, and then she gave up her secret. Her plaque in Bloomsbury was about to be unveiled, and Mary whooped with pleasure at her plan of attending the ceremony incognito. I would have to come along, she insisted, and indeed we had no difficulty passing ourselves off as bona fide guests. Mary, relying on British reserve, chose random people to embrace and, after fashionable air-kissing, thanked them for coming, before swiftly moving off. True to expectation, nobody questioned her. She looked, after all, nothing like the images that had been used to represent her. How bloody marvellous, she crowed, nudging me as the veil came down. And hark at this, she whispered, reading from the plaque:

Mary Prince
1788 —1833 *(what a lark!)*
Abolitionist and Author
lived in a house
near this site
1829.

If only she were the real, sole author of her *History*, she added wistfully, then it would have been larded with one or two jolly events, for a reader sure deserves a break from the misery, but she supposed Miss Strickland did what was within her means. No one could ask for more than that.

Only later did I discover that a descendant of Mary's slavemaster had arranged for the plaque by way of compensation; that, she kept under her hat. I fantasised about splashing out on more roomy accommodation, perhaps somewhere in Brixton, where Mary could reveal herself and be celebrated. Are you crazy? she scolded. How could I possibly have a plaque and be alive at the same time? We have to somehow or other meet the challenge of contradictions that magical realism heaps upon us, so an East End studio is what you'll have to put up with.

To Nick Greene, on the other hand, she boasted of having independent means, as she bought the skinflint yet another drink. He laughed uproariously. And where, pray, is this market for ancient flabby flesh to be found? Mary rose to her full height, tugged at her skirts, slowly retied her head-rag into an elaborate knot and, still staring at him, declared that the old man was dismissed.

It was I who yet again had to broker peace between the two.

For all her interest in life-writing, her belief in sorting out events of the past, Mary is impatient with what she calls Hinza's unhealthy obsession with origins – the nonsense of middle-class upstarts who must mimic the aristocracy. You're no more than the spoilt child from a comfortable, bourgeois home. Literary origins, she scoffs, get real laddie! What about the poor woman who laboured in your birth? Hinza stops her, reminds her that with everyone cruelly slaughtered or drowned, with no survivor but himself, there's no point in speculating about the birth mother he cannot remember at all. Well, she insists, it is no less than an insult to that woman to replace her with an author, and a white man to boot. If it were not for Mr P's indomitable fight against slavery, I'd say, let him rest in peace, because the whole story has made you ill.

By no means ill, just curious. Can't you see, Hinza explains, my investigation goes hand in hand with our project, and my literary origins have to stand in, cap in hand, for the biological past that is lost, so no disrespect to my birth mother. Mary has after all, more or less, had her say – for all and sundry to read. Mistress of her own story, arranged by Mr P to be spoken out loud to Miss Strickland, sifted, sorted out, and patted into shape, into a book, nicely produced, so why she begrudges his musings on 'The Bechuana Boy' he fails to understand. He persists; he must consider all the accusations against Mr P, all the stuff that Nicholas now claims to have gathered: that Mr P dissimulated, pumped up his concern for oppressed native peoples to get at Lord Somerset, revised his writings to fit in with newly acquired beliefs. They have to get to the bottom of things, but Mr P's story is bound up with his. It can't be written up without attending to his, Hinza insists, and Nick cannot be given carte blanche on that. Mr P's relation to him has to be clarified before the full picture can be seen.

Mary fixes him with her eyes. She comes round and nods. Okay, but let's bear in mind that your obsession is also plain vanity. If once upon a time you were the Bechuana Boy, you no longer are, she says briskly. You live in London; you're an artist who makes a buck when necessary as a model in art schools. Now listen carefully. All this peeking into a poem, it can't take priority over the task you took on: to help Sir Nick with the history. Talk sense into him and make sure he does a decent job. We may need an establishment figure but we sure as hell can't trust him.

Hinza is relieved; he cannot bear conflict between them. Mary is all he has. Earlier he had feared that she would make her way to Antigua, but no, she promised, there is nothing to return to; besides, she would not abandon him. Might as well banish her to darkest Africa, she shuddered, and he rolled his eyes and explained for the umpteenth time that there was no call for bandying about the colonial language she had imbibed in another century. Mary laughed, Just keeping you on your toes, laddie; you've got to lighten up.

Hinza knows that for all her commitment, Mary is wary of him and what she imagines to be his needs. From the very start, when they were sitting companionably by the just-lit fire, waiting for the warmth, he tried to take her frozen hand in his own. She withdrew as if from a red-hot coal, and did not hesitate to spell out the limits of her care. No point in trying to make a mother of me, she said baldly. She had spent enough of her long life caring for others, would herself like to be a suckling at the buxom bosom of Mother Nature, but that bitch of a lady had consistently turned her back, withheld her milk. No, sirrah, she may be old enough to be his mother, but she declines, thank you very much, especially now that they have time firmly in their pockets. They would be friends, adults who cared for each other. His regression into childhood, with that she would have no truck, besides, she herself had had to do without a mother – that poor woman grown mad with grief – and survived all the same.

Mary's speech is quite unnecessary. Hinza does not think that he has ever, even centuries ago, pined for a mother, certainly nothing as specific as that. Mrs P he supposed was his mother. Or something of a mother. Certainly she was kind and gentle, and her affection grew by the day. Still, he is grateful for Mary's friendship. In bygone days she defended him as fiercely as an old hen, beating off the impudent natives who tried to touch his hair; spewing a malodorous mouthful at those who insulted them, drawing him close as she walked off, cursing loudly. But the story of him being found by Mr P she did not want to hear. No thanks, not over and over again.

Let me start again: At Eildon I was raised as the Pringles' son.

Or was I?

There is what Nick calls the damning evidence: in Mr P's letter to Plasket, the Colonial Secretary, asking permission to take me to England, he promises to bring me up as a servant. Yes, a servant! And this after I had been part of the family for some time. There is the possibility that calling me their son would have further outraged the colonial administrators, Somerset and his ilk, that they would not have agreed to my removal from the frontier or perhaps entry to England. Spitefully so, for it was the case that all and sundry arrived from the plantations with their slaves in conspicuous tow. Mr P was no doubt pressed into using the racial discourse of his peers. Hence the word, servant, and hence also the promise in the letter to educate me to the best of his ability, so that in adulthood I might return to the Cape Colony. In my youthful ardour I had indeed expressed an interest in being a missionary, of all things, although that may well have been about wanting to meet their expectations, to please them. The idea of it! Me, Hinza, arriving in the Eastern Cape in the 1830s, scorned in a place run by bigoted settlers who had made the dear man's life such a misery. The swaggering, vulgar colonists, the mockery of Geddes Baines and his supporters – how could anyone have endured that? But that was precisely what Mr P had hoped to return to, believing he could persuade his fellow colonists to civilised behaviour, or that he might at least fight for the rights of natives. To that purpose we had tickets for our return to the Cape – and then poor Mr P passed away.

It was especially in company that Ma'am delighted in announcing that I was destined to return to serve my people. But who were my people? Were the Pringles not my people? I do ponder the notion of nameless folk I do not know as my people. So the question remains. Was I their son or their servant? Or something in between, a new category of relationship generated by the colonial condition? Surely the childless couple embraced me as their son, the child found wandering naked in the veld, bestowed upon them by Providence?

Mary hoots with laughter at this notion. It is not that she doubts the integrity of the Pringles; she too is grateful that they have rescued her from pernicious slavers. But no, she says, that's not how white people work. I am outraged by this formulation, but she has been a slave too long to see as I do people without their race.

You do? Really? Oh please, she says in disbelief and shakes her head.

No doubt the answer is governed by so much else in Mr P's life. The beliefs he started out with, those shaped and hallowed by his race and class, revealed themselves to be too limited for a thoughtful, intelligent person, and thus they had to be revised. Is that not what all poets do? For instance, is it not what Mr Wordsworth's life's work is all about – casting off the old self in order to recreate and rewrite a new self?

Mary agrees that there can be nothing wrong with that. Look, she says, the sun in the colonies has ever struck the heads of decent people from Europe, whipping their passions and turning them into monsters. Why else did they invent the pith helmet and line it with red flannel to protect themselves (a business we now know to have had quite the opposite effect as their brains boiled over into bad behaviour)? Happily, our Mr P never stooped to the pith helmet, and so his head, thankfully, was turned in quite another direction.

The Pringles were not above donning excessive clothing, I say, but it is the case that once they got to London, the poet was positively evangelical about revision. Forget, he urged, what you have always known, those dearly held beliefs, fed to you in your mother's milk (an unfortunate metaphor, I thought); instead, look carefully at the world around you and try to think afresh, following also your heart. That is the poet's holy task. So, Mary interjects, if his beliefs were melted in the southern sun and then remoulded, it must, of course, follow that he revised the poems. Cannae fault that, as Mrs P used to say.

Indeed, I agree, but that is not to say that Mr P ever held reprehensible views, although nowadays he is lambasted and lampooned for such rewriting. If only more were open to new influences, willing to assess each new phenomenon without recourse to received views, and be unapologetic about modifying their beliefs and preconceptions, the world would surely be a better place, as Mr P insisted. At the time, Ma'am remonstrated that that was easier said than done, but as always he was gentle with her. Your warm heart, Margaret, has and will continue to light the way, he said.

Mary sighs, says that such piety could only wear a woman down.

I return to the poem once more, to the line where the vexed question lurks: 'We took him for "our own"'. Why the scare quotes? Would that not have been acceptable to their fellow settlers, or for that matter to their Scottish family on the surrounding farms? No, more damning are the words in the previous stanza, of which they are an echo, the invented words that I, the child who by his own account had already had enough of servitude, could never, never have uttered:

'Then let me serve thee, as thine own.'

How odd that these words are attributed to me in the poem, but

I see that the reiteration, the reply, 'We took him for "our own"', complies with my stated wish to serve. In other words – and now it pierces my heart – they took me to serve them, according to my own wishes, or so the poem claims.

To serve them as a slave? False, false, false, I shout in the dark room, and fling a plate against the wall, shocking myself with the violence of the act. It is a fine Wedgwood plate, with admittedly a small chip underneath the rim, that Ma'am had given to Mary. How will I explain the plate to Mary who cringes like a child at any physical display of violence? We have, no had, only four plates. (Better to have four beautiful chipped plates than four ugly ones, Mary believed.) Chastened by the china shards about me, the scarred wall, I calm down, start again. I will clear up the mess in a moment, before she gets back.

Mary objects more to my dwelling on the poem than to the broken plate. The business of reading closely, over and over again, is ridiculous, she says. I retort that there is no other kind of reading, but she shakes her head disapprovingly. No activity that requires such slow perusal, over and over, going round and round in circles, can be good or healthy; in fact, I rest my case, it's downright dangerous, she says, pointing at the shards I have swept up. Mr Wedgwood, she says pensively, had also designed a bracelet with an image of a kneeling slave and a fine text below, *Am I not a Man and a Brother?* Miss Strickland wore one with pride, and generous as ever tried to give it to her, but really Mary could see no sense in such a thing, certainly no sense in any woman wearing it.

I may have to accept the proposition: Hinza the Motswana child, no more than a little tame springbok, was taken in as a servant, a pet for Mrs P. The truth is that I barely remember those first days of plenty to eat and drink, and the warmth of strangers. I certainly did not ponder my status in the Pringle household, so pleased was I with the balm of kindness, the quiet, soothing voices, the excitement of learning so many new things, best of all reading and writing. Perhaps they themselves were surprised to find that, as time passed, they viewed me in a different light. I cannot accept that love gushed forth as the poem would have it; instead, it was more likely that the childless couple came to love their little pet springbok quite as they would a human child, that they came to think of me as their very own offspring – an imperceptible shift that matched my own slow settling into filial affection. For whilst Miss Brown was there as part of our family, it was undoubtedly Ma'am who became … well, a mother. My mother.

I read the poem once more and examine my heart all over again. Bitterness and resentment persist, but I must try to nurse the thread of love that winds through and surfaces from time to time, prevailing in a blinding flash. The Pringles may not initially have conceived of a strange Motswana child as their own, but they took me in – whether at my own request or not, whether I offered myself as servant or not. No, it was I, Hinza Marossi, my ways that in time won them over. It was I who eclipsed the springbok of the poet's imagination, who posed questions about a culture, their culture, that equated a black child with a springbok; it was I, my winning ways, that taught them to see me as I was: a boy like any other, in need of the love of caring parents.

I present this case to Mary, who dismisses it out of hand as bullshit, a twenty-first century response. Why then, she asks cruelly, did you not call them Mother and Father, Mummy and Daddy? Ah, but I remember how Mr P abhorred the practice at the Cape of slaves having to call their owners mother and father, no doubt as false proof of the benign nature of that slavery. Reasonable, therefore, that I called them Ma'am and Mr Pringle. This cuts no ice with Mary. According to her I'm in a muddle of time, but it pleases me to think that they were not interested in displaying tolerance of my difference; there was, thank God, no pretence, no notion of ostentatious liberalism at play. Dear God, as if I had not struggled with these arguments all those years ago! But pondering the events, more and more details, whether significant or not, creep into memory, and who knows how these may link up one day, or fill in further gaps.

——

It is 1822. The searing heat of summer has gone as the sun mellows into kindness. How wonderful the milder days of late March, when white clouds billow and tumble in the sky! I watch a strange green spear burrowing its way out of the earth, with no annunciating leaves in sight. The miracle of the March lily. Lying on my stomach on the warm, stone-studded ground, I watch it for minutes on end, hoping to witness the lengthening of the green wand. But it grows in mystery, forges ahead and lengthens invisibly in spite of my watch. Ma'am says that it will not do to invigilate, that it is God's secret doings, on which we must not spy. Daily, I check the thrusting spear as it grows tall, thickening at the helm into a fist of folded petal from which, days later, the huge pink flower unfurls in secret and presents its corkscrew curls to the sun. I shriek and rush to find Ma'am and Miss Janet Brown, who are measured in their delight. I would so like to bury my face in the cupped hand of the fragrant lily, much as I know that that would destroy it. Is this my first lesson in love?

Ma'am says how she'd love to take me to Scotland in May. There we'll stride through a fresh green meadow with wild hyacinth and a blue haze of forget-me-not. Or, later, buttercup with stems so slender that the yellow petals float above the grass. And the flowering currant, she remembers, that's a bush that loves its leaves being brushed; it will thank you with a waft of holy incense. Even rain will release its perfume, so no need to bury your face in the currant, she says.

Nowadays, arrested in a London shrubbery where the incense of currant stops me in mid stride, its scented hallelujah perversely transports me to the Zuurveld, where it does not grow, but where Ma'am's head tilts forever with nostalgia. How sad their return to London, and sad the weeks in Scotland where, as nigger-lovers, they no longer belonged.

Quite the little linguist you are, Mr Pringle says at the end of our language lesson at Eildon. He draws up his injured leg and rubs the bad knee; he has been sitting for too long. Now you must earn your keep, he jests, as he pushes back the chair and strides back and forth, at first hobbling, until the slow blood returns to his bad leg.

I teach him a sentence in Setswana. Say after me, The days are getting shorter – and how well he says! He too is quite the linguist, having already so admirably mastered the Dutch tongue. Which is an unusual accomplishment, since the British settlers claim to find the language savage, especially the Boer version, and pride themselves on not being able to discourse in it. I too am reluctant to speak in Baas Karel's Dutch, but for a while it is our common tongue, and Mr P says that a language should not be equated with the folly of its speakers, that being also the language of the bonded servants we must not dismiss it.

Hinza, he probes, do you think of the mountains where you were born? I shake my head slowly, trying to conjure the place. You must try, he says, concentrate, think of the land, and his voice slows down as if to conjure in me a place. A river? A tree? Some rocks? A mountain? It is healthy, he says, to remember, to summon the salve of pictures in your mind.

It is not that I disagree; I simply cannot find such pictures, and the attempt to think them is far from healthy as it brings numbness into my arms and legs, and I believe also into my heart.

But the next day, as I enter the shade beneath the branches of Mr P's tree, the mottled pattern on the earth sends a shiver of recognition; something stirs, and prods at my heart. My lessons are held in the late afternoons before we tend the animals, and the breeze has started up. Holding the edges of a book, I note the shadows of my thumbs on the page as purple smudges that I shift this way and that, watching the colour grow a paler blue then once again deepen into a mesmerising violet. Why have I not seen this before? A few leaves at my feet stir in the breeze and seem to spell out a wobbly word. I take a deep breath but cannot say it out loud: motlôpi tree. I am sitting propped against the white bark of the tree. A figure leans over me, cups my face in her hands. Then in a light gust the leaves skitter, the blue shadow on the white page fades and a half-formed memory scuttles off. Only the word remains: motlôpi, for the wittegat tree. Can that really be all I remember?

I know that Mr P wanted me to speak of my family – of whom I remembered nothing at all, so I do not know where the information in the poem came from. As a boy in London I was much affected by the verse, the image of my mother and sisters flailing in the waters of the broad Gareep, of their screams as we were parted. As for having been bought and sold by Christian slavers, well, in the poem its force as oxymoron makes for a nice enough couplet – I do appreciate a neat rhyme – but I don't understand why the good man, who would rather die than tell a lie, arranged my story in this way. The truth is that I have no memory at all of my family, unless … I do not remember … unless in that early intoxication with speech, such words came willy-nilly. But no, it cannot be, for the words for wounds do not take shape so easily.

Ma'am and Mr Pringle. That is what I call them. Hand in hand, that is how I see them in the doorway of the beehive house on the ridge. That is where we live – well, strictly speaking I sleep at its entrance on my burlap, for being indoors is too stiflingly hot. Behind the beehive house is the circular kitchen shelter, and beyond, further away across the dry riverbed, the daub-and-wattle or hardebiesie huts of the servants. Fine boned and delicate as he is, Mr Pringle had constructed the beehive house with his own hands, and a very good house it was too. The site had been carefully selected with the steep mountain behind, the panorama of the winding river before us, and in the distance the semi-circle of picturesque hills as far as the eye can see. It is a land of stone; even the river is really a bed of stones gathered over time, huge slabs of rock dragged down the hills by the giants of yore that Ma'am speaks of. They are honed smooth by centuries of friction and water, although nowadays there is barely a trickle, except during the rainy season. Between outcrops of rock, candelabras of orange and yellow aloes grow; they are the first plants that Ma'am taught me to sketch.

There are other homesteads in the valley: in Glen-Lynden, more Pringle relatives, who urge me to be quiet, and some who keep apart special tin mugs and enamel plates for our use, the Khoe servants and me. They believe that I do not speak English, but they are not impolite, and it is not difficult to keep out of their way. Ma'am pretends that she does not note their inability to converse with me, but it is she who has taught me the intricacies of manners, the ways of civility, so how could she fail to see that they are not my friends?

I suspect she wants me to think of them as I've come to think of Baas Karel. When I wince at his name, she makes me say after her: I have no hatred of Baas Karel. We have never been friends, so I need not think of him with bitterness, need not dwell on the days at Weltevreden. Baas Karel too belongs to God, who will cleanse all our hearts and save us. It is true that the saying takes away the rancour, that soon I can say his name without shuddering.

Mr P puts me through the paces of reading and writing, and teaches me new English words, which I practise the following day as I go through my chores with Ma'am. Not long, he says, before you'll be reading the wonderful works of my great friend, Sir Walter. Mr P sets much store on friendship and loyalty, and often reels off the names of his dearly missed companions, always starting with his bosom friend John Fairbairn, whom he has persuaded to emigrate, and who indeed will soon be on his way to the Cape to start with Mr P a newspaper and a school. And you, Hinza, Mr P said, I am your friend. Margaret, Ma'am, she too is your friend.

It is not altogether clear to me, this business of giving and receiving friendship, so I ask if I am *their* friend. Mr Pringle says that this is necessarily the case; with his stick he draws the word 'reciprocal' in the sand. Mr P, I then assume, is also Fairbairn's friend. But who decides first? Is it a matter of declaring: I am your friend; or does one pose a question, Will you be my friend?

Mr P laughs. Oh no, friendship is something that shows itself. Like any plant that has living cells, it will simply grow, so declarations are not necessary. Both parties will feel the lure.

But I know in my bones that something is missing in that explanation. The San boy Dugal does not want to be my friend; indeed,
none of the servants, the Khoe boys or the girl Vytje, will befriend
me, in spite of my many overtures.

I like to think that I am useful to the Pringles. Ma'am has taken
to rubbing her left hand across my head, whilst with her right arm
she draws me close. She is a little woman; my head reaches the cushion of her soft bosom. She speaks much of God, says I am a gift from
God. A responsibility indeed, so that I search for tasks beyond the
given ones, in order to make of myself a worthy gift. In the vlei I have
secretly, over the past weeks, cut down tall reeds for drying. Today I
brought home a sheaf in order to refurbish the roof thatch, which
will not withstand the rains this year. Well done, she says, and prais-
ing my initiative, she pinches my cheek. It is perhaps vain of me to
say so, but I believe that she is well pleased with me.

I do remember the day I arrived, breathless from trotting alongside Mr Pringle on horseback, dog tired and covered in dust. Ma'am,
frowning, was undoubtedly perturbed. Oh dear, Thomas, she sighed
with dismay, och dearie me. There was sadness in her eyes, and I
wondered if in their distant land she had seen her own people flail
helplessly in the roiling waters, the mighty Tweed that Mr Pringle
speaks of with such awe.

But, pleased as punch, he announced to Ma'am, Yes, a gift for you,
my dear, a boy of your own. Or something of the kind, I imagined
from his gestures.

But she drew a deep breath and looked away until he spoke rather fast and firmly in their language. She visibly composed herself and
shook my hand. But I saw that the distress did not altogether shift,
that it took a good few days for her to shed the burden that my presence evidently had brought.

Today I carved the word *eildon* on a bit of wood for Ma'am to
hang on the tree. Mr Pringle is disappointed that I have not used a
capital E, as in the Paps of Eildon on the Scottish Borders. He does
not understand my love of the lower case 'e' and also 'c', letters that

are able to rock on their curved bottoms but are not closed off, as is the 'o'. A fine, sheltered shape too is 'e', one in which to hide, in which Ma'am would surely take comfort; besides, I do not like the idea of a capital bossing it over the rest. But to please him, I will do another. I have also reproduced from memory the map that Mr P drew of Africa and Europe, putting in the boundaries as best I could. What a tiny little place their beloved Scotland is; no wonder the Pringles have ventured out into the wider world.

Mr Pringle is a wizard with his instruments, with his pen, yes, but also with saw and plane; he has made some excellent items of furniture. On the farm he is masterful. I may not have been bred to farming, he boasts, but I come from a long line of proud farmers. Ma'am soothes: You will return to a life of letters and civilisation, my dear. She has the skill of hearing the sighs between his words.

There is not much I can teach Mr P, who can turn his hand to just about anything. But he does not know how to cure an animal's hide. It may be easy to skin a beast and salt the hide, but you have to judge correctly how to air it, when to shift it from morning sunlight to shade in the afternoon, how dry it should be before the arduous business of daily kneading and scrunching, until the skin is perfectly soft, pliant and sweet smelling. I have made a fine rug of hartebeest for Ma'am, having shot the animal myself, choosing the skin for its lovely markings, singular patches of white across the brown neck and shoulders, although much of the white skin is wasted as I shaped the rug into a rough oval, cutting away the suggestions of head and legs that others prize. Her heart is soft. Much as she loves the wild sounds of animals by night, she does not want to be reminded of the shape of a living beast underfoot.

Mr Pringle is proud of my workmanship, but he does so love probing, will not let things be. Who taught you to cure skins? he asks.

It is not that I am concealing things; I simply don't know. A man, I say, a strong man with large black hands. I remember how to do it, but that is all I know, I insist so that Mr P gives up.

The rug has given him the idea of sending his friend the Great Sir

Walter a present. The skin of a lion, King of the Animal World, for the King of Letters, he pronounced.

I promised it would be the finest, best-worked skin, soft and pliable as that of a living animal, with much display of neck and legs that would carry the echo of its roar and the shadow of its lithe movement.

Mr Pringle confessed that he had sent a lion skin before, but that it was shrunken, not having been well enough worked by Dugal, the lazy Bushboy who had made extravagant claims of his skill. Thus, to Mr P's shame, it arrived in Scotland in a sorry state of stench and decay, no less than an offence to Sir Walter.

There has been much roaring of lions at night in the glen, many of our sheep stolen by the beasts, so a hunt was sorely needed. I was allowed to choose the skin for Sir Walter. But I need not tell of the lion hunt, since Mr Pringle has written it up and with all the other fragments will publish it in the *Narrative of a Residence in South Africa*. There will be many a lesson, he says, that the people in England might learn from such accounts.

Sir Nicholas Greene is much taken with Mr P's friendship with Sir Walter, he tells me. He regrets that he had not managed to meet the eminent Scotsman, or for that matter got round to reading his tales, but he hopes after the Pringle project to produce something on Sir Walter. In fact, rummaging in his pocket last week, he dropped a page, which I found and read with interest, surprised that he had actually read Mr P's *Narrative*.

Nicholas has not as yet shown us his writing on Mr P's Life; he is waiting to complete a section. I do believe he left the page on Sir Walter deliberately, but I returned it without comment. I'm not sure why I kept it from Mary or why I thought it prudent to copy the text.

Allow me to direct you, dear reader, to the National Portrait Gallery, where Sir Walter Scott, gentleman and novelist, sits in his study at Abbotsford. Taking a well-deserved break

*from the demands of fiction, he all but reclines with a jour-
nal. Under his feet is the Cape lion skin, which catches the
light, as does the illuminated dog with whom the great man
shares the rug.*

*The Gallery is, of course, not in Abbotsford; it is in Lon-
don. There – being at the same time in London and in Abbotsford too – the great man is also transported to the Cape,
or Land of Lion as he calls it. It is hardly a relaxing moment.
He is disturbed by the article in the journal,* Friendship's
Offering, *a tract about slavery written by the indefatigable
Pringle. A good fellow, and not without talent, but he so does
have the propensity for stirring things, of getting his betters'
backs up, the people he really should be cultivating if he wants
to prosper. A dash of humility – that would help, for the fellow surely knows that he needs support. And here in the fa-
therland everyone knows that slavery at the Cape is benign;
it is nothing like the atrocious business in the Americas, so
really, why not let sleeping dogs lie? The chaps in Edinburgh
will not like this at all.* Friendship's Offering *indeed. Really, Pringle should not have taken on the editorship. Bah, a
bloody rag for lachrymose women who do little more than lie
and lactate.*

*It should be noted that Sir Walter, who received gifts from
all over the world, or rather, the pink-colonised world, did not
keep track of the donors. The lion's skull that had pride of place
on the mantle of his study at Abbotsford has clean disappeared;
the horns of kudu and hartebeest as well as a bushbuck head he
wrongly attributed to Mungo Park, when they were undoubtedly sent by Pringle, alongside various native artefacts. As for
the Tswana karos of wild cat pelt that Pringle had sent for
Mrs Scott, it was regrettably a case of sensible men losing their
ways in the wilderness of Africa. Worn by Tswana royalty indeed! As if that could compensate for the rough savagery that
inheres in such an item of clothing. Certainly Mrs Scott only*

touched it gingerly before waving it off to the chambermaid
whose man, given to theatrics, pranced about in it wielding a
kitchen knife, much to the delight of the working folk.

Nicholas has drawn my attention to Mr P's most celebrated poem, 'Afar in the Desert' where the poet rides alone in the desert with the silent Bushboy by his side. He believes that subject also to be a representation of me. I assure him that since I found my voice on the day of our meeting (Nick cruelly calls it the day of my capture), when I joined Mr P's household, I have been neither silent nor invisible.

Nick does not note the inconsistency of the poet being alone in the desert whilst having the boy by his side, and I have no wish to draw his attention to it. Driven as Mr P sometimes was by melancholia, he naturally rode out alone into the veld as anyone would, although it was by no means a desert. Ma'am sometimes persuaded him to take along the San boy who worked as a servant. The sullen Dugal, as Mr P called him, for the boy would not say his name, was indeed silent, which no doubt suited Mr P on his excursions. Occasionally, Dugal would disappear into the wilds, before returning after a few days as if nothing untoward had happened, except that his skin and hair shone with foul-smelling grease. I tried to befriend Dugal but to no avail, and was comforted by the fact that he also kept aloof from the Khoe servants and mixed-race tenants. By the time we left South Africa, Mr P had come to express sympathy for the boy's forays into the wild. It is we who have ruined their lives, he said. I did not question the 'we'; I was after all their son.

I gathered from the Khoe servants that Dugal brewed honey beer to which he treated himself liberally, although it generally failed to cheer him up. But once, in an unusually cheery mood, he beckoned to me to follow him. Off we went over rough terrain, competing with each other in fleet-footedness, but since I had to follow there was no question of outstripping him. At an outcrop of rocks we came to a standstill and Dugal motioned with his hand across his mouth that we were to be silent. We squeezed our way through a fissure and entered the darkness of a cave. He sat himself down with outstretched legs and solemnly lifted his head to stare in silence at the stone roof of the cave.

I grew impatient and was about to break the silence when he rose and led me to the walls covered in painted stories. There men darted about chasing their quarry of wildebeest, or danced in celebration, or slept off their weariness. Marvellous antics and dramatic postures that made me laugh, even as the surly Dugal shook his head disapprovingly. I went close up to look at the painters' rendering of limbs and Dugal followed, holding out a protective hand as if I were capable of erasing the stone images. Mine, all mine, he boasted in broken Dutch, and I said that he was lucky to have his ancestors about. He said that they were my ancestors too and I chose not to correct him. He said I should not speak of the cave, but to my shame I found myself within a few short weeks betraying him to Mr P, not least because Dugal himself refused to speak with me after the visit. In my defence: I was a child.

A child who then, spitefully, told Dugal that Mr P had found the cave, and urged him to come and see the initials that Mr P had carved into the rock, but Dugal, who knew nothing of writing, would have none of it. No, he said, shaking his head emphatically, it is for people of this land alone. No, Baas Pringle cannot go there. I saw no way out but to hang my head in shame and nod my agreement.

Nicholas Greene and I while away an hour in a beer garden in Edinburgh. We have put off the visit to the National Library until now, when it is supposedly summer, and indeed exuberant blue clematis cascades over the wall, putting me in mind of the blue trumpets of morning glory that shaded our stoep on Kloof Street in Cape Town. August, the month of frolicking, says Nick, but we shiver in our woollens whilst deceptive sunlight filters through the foliage overhead. Nick looks ludicrous in his sleeveless doublet, which he claims to be entirely appropriate in the Athens of the North, at least during Festival season when minstrels and thespians of every kind parade the streets.

Festival indeed! he exclaims, looking about scathingly. Nowadays, people do not know how to be festive, how to carouse. Oh, he sighs, for the halcyon days when the frozen Thames hummed with festivities, with music, the peal of bells and the laughter of lassies ripe for the taking. Oh, to be once again the Abbot of Cockaigne, he intones, thumping his chest.

Please, I remonstrate, don't get yourself in a tangle. Nowadays Cockaigne, the land of roasted suckling pigs and streams of milk and honey, is known as Cuckooland, so do give it a rest. Let's be realistic and remember who did the revelling and who froze to death in her plaids and farthingales, a blue-lipped spectacle in the Thames with her lap full of apples, still busily at work.

Nick laughs, Indeed, but Cockaigne also puts me in mind of your Mr P, who fell for Castlereagh's promise that at the Cape Colony the rocks were all roast beef, the hailstones plum puddings and rain water strong as gin, or at least that's what Cruikshank reported in his cartoon.

Mr P was entirely realistic about the Cape; he had read a number of Travels, I object.

Talk about being realistic, young man, it's time you faced the truth and beat your way through this amnesia. I've been thinking: why did Mrs Pringle say that she chose you, and on the other hand that God had sent you? And why was she distressed at your arrival? You've got to probe these contradictions and stop relying on the text of your origins. Memory, my boy, is a shape-shifting thing; the truth lies in those fissures.

Nick may have a point, but I am not ready to discuss his spiteful idea of the truth. Fortunately he has an eye for the ladies and does not really want to pursue the question. A sad figure he cuts, unaware of the possibility that the fresh, scantily clad young women may have no interest in a wrinkled relic like himself. He fancies himself quite the gallant, and I have to nip in the bud his plan to pay his respects with a bottle of champagne to the young women at the next table.

This, I remind him, is a new century, and you'll be laughed out of the house for such behaviour, for your assumptions. Besides, you can't afford champagne.

It suits him to think that I am jealous of what he calls his full-bloodedness, but how infuriating when he resorts to stupid English constructions: Like your father, you're too much of a stingy Scotsman for champagne, he taunts, although it in fact suits his own pocket to heed my words. How could I expect anything else, he sighs. Bourgeois to your boots, that's what you are, riddled with all that middling, middle-of-the-road, mediocre, middle-middle class worrying about what others may think of you, the never-set–the-Thames-on-fire Presbyterianism of your people. After a short silence, he continues, by which I mean your adopted people.

I settle for an indulgent smile.

Right, he says decisively, downing his ale in one long gulp, this is all about you, so let me start with a question. Why fuss over these radicals, this Pringle poetaster, what do you call him, the Father of South African Poetry, whom no one in the civilised world has read? Really the man should have stuck to his rabble-rousing. My question is, Should you not be thinking of your own, biological parents? As I understand it, this is the age of identity obsession, of racial authenticity, of seeking out real roots. Should your own native people not be your concern?

Has he been discussing me with Mary? If Old Nick thinks that he has taken me by surprise, he is mistaken. In fact, he is likely to think that I'd be insulted by his question. But I do not wish to discuss these matters with him, so I prevaricate. We have come to know each other pretty well, and with our different worldviews, skirting about a subject is a familiar, even necessary practice.

Who is to judge the value of poetry? I ask. As the critics nowadays say, If it's thought in your circles to be no good, do at least ask the question, Not good for whom? I think you'll find that Samuel Coleridge was a great admirer of Mr P's poetry. Not to mention his friends Sir Walter Scott and James Hogg.

Nick guffaws. As far as I can see, Coleridge referred to one poem only, 'Afar in the Desert', the one you won't admit is about you, but frankly, Coleridge himself, as we all know, is not the most reliable of poets. Think of all that tosh about Kubla Khan and the person from Porlock that had friend and foe alike fall about with laughter.

What I'd like to know, I deflect, is why Mr P, who was so proud of being Scottish, refers to himself in a poem as an English chief rather than a Scottish one.

Chief indeed, Nick laughs. How these colonials gave themselves airs and graces once they'd left behind their lowly circumstances. But then, anyone in his right mind would have called himself English if he could get away with it; there was after all nothing to be gained by being known as a wild Scot.

The man is beyond redemption. I think you should send a bottle of champagne to the women after all, I say, but first, let me make my getaway, back to the library.

Nowadays there is open hostility between Nick and me. Nick reminds me that we are both at the mercy of the woman who has wantonly chosen to drag us into life, into the light, kidding herself that she is doing so at our bidding when in fact there is a murky mutuality to the affair. So we are thrown together willy-nilly, with no regard for the lack of affinity between us. Nick has extraordinary ideas about manhood, has made it clear that I am deficient; in fact, he has taken to calling me a pansy. Which I do not mind in the slightest; 'pansy' is the lovely name of a kitten-faced flower which, in the spirit of the times, ought to be reclaimed; but this offends him. He is, I sense, bored with the colonial project. Having always been aspirational, he is now on the lookout for something more important than the life of an unknown poet and activist.

Bored, too, with me. If only I were able to fit in with his carousing. Not unlike the slave owners of yore, he fancies the piquancy of entering his stuffy gentleman's club with a young black man in tow, but there I do draw the line. Chalk and cheese we are, and besides, I find such places distasteful.

Why am I surprised to find that Sir Nicholas Greene would stoop to malice? It is after all the very clay out of which he had been fashioned. He wants to put me in my place, which is to say the place that he has allotted to me. My interest, for instance, in the visual arts irks him, possibly because his own understanding in that respect is deficient. This kind of work, he says, by which he means almost anything contemporary, is by charlatans for the consumption of gullible people like you. He refuses to think of me as an artist. All unprofitable pretence, dear boy, he says, not the kind of thing that ought to interest you. But asked about the Renaissance artists he may have known, he becomes proprietorial. Well, you really have to be steeped in European culture to fully appreciate such timeless, priceless works.

I tell him about the woman, a friend of Mr P's from Edinburgh, who painted a lovely portrait of me. I was so young, and it was torture having to keep still for such long periods of time. Miss Boyle was taciturn, concentrated, barely moving her lips to say sternly, repeatedly, Dinnae fidget boy, but after the sittings she was kind, and would give me a boiled sweet.

Of course, at the time I did not wonder about the Persian carpet and the oriental drapings in which I was all but swathed. I marvelled at the intricacy of the patterns rendered so beautifully by Miss Boyle, although my own colouring was rather too bluish for my liking. Mr P thought it an accomplished piece of work, and so effusive was he in his praise that she gave it to us, and indeed it had a prominent place in the parlour. If only I knew what had happened to the portrait. Miss Brown thought that Miss Boyle reclaimed it for herself. But it may well have been sold at auction after Mr P's death, when poor Ma'am was in a state of confused dithering and sick with worry about how we would survive.

Nicholas's ears prick up. Very fashionable, such Orientalist paintings once were, and if he's not mistaken a portrait very much like that hung in one of the houses he frequented in bygone days, a bluish-black fellow richly draped, in one of the great houses, but alas, he can't quite recollect …

IV

Sir Nicholas Greene is sick of life, sick as a parrot, he says, and this is not rhetorical; he is also sick of rhetoric. And strangely, he must admit, sick of himself, this self, derivative as it may sound. And yet, if many selves are available to us as they say these days, would that not court disaster? Is there not the danger of a pile of selves, like plates toppling down, smashing into each other, and where would that leave one?

Life, life, life, he sighs audibly, stretching out on the worn chaise longue that creaks under his weight.

He had hoped for a new lease of life from the Pringle project, a rejuvenation of sorts, or at least a change of scene, but he can muster no enthusiasm for it. Well, if the truth be told, he had hoped for reinstatement as man of letters, a poet, a contributor to culture. Given the tedium of time passing, he had thought of the foray into colonial culture, even an actual journey to the barbarian fields of Africa if that were unavoidable, as a widening of the immensely long tunnel in which he had been travelling for hundreds of years, a pouring in of light. (He no longer knows whose words those are, does not know why he hears an echo of goatbells, or sees the ghost of a faithless girl in Russian trousers floating by.) He gropes for words, tries to snatch at an image of so many plates – piled, are they, on a waiter's hand? – he doesn't know; he's been cast adrift. And the old self, it has slowly dawned on him, won't do, is hopelessly inadequate in this new world. Why has he allowed himself to be lured into this? Life has gone on for so very, very long, he all but blubbers.

Trouble is, he simply cannot get the hang of Mary and Hinza, subjects or collaborators; there appears to be no telling. He has lost the knack of sliding effortlessly through time, through history; he cannot comfortably adjust to the twenty-first century.

The know-all Hinza says it's a problem of translation, that an excess of sixteenth-century aura clings to him, will not allow its strangeness to be turned into the new. It's not been a problem before, Nicholas protests, but Hinza says he's never before been called upon to comment on Nick's strangeness.

Well, so be it, he sighs wearily; at least the memory of those halcyon days – of discovery, of Empire, and of England bright and great – could be buoyed up by the tenacious aura of the past. But no, he must prepare to acknowledge defeat. Oh, how he longs to lie down in a hidden nook of this green and pleasant land – somewhere far away from the new, unfathomable London teeming with all sorts – on a mossy bank beneath a great oak tree, and hear in the distance the sound of the twelfth stroke of midnight.

Yes, Sir Nicholas has had enough of this fraught world. How could he have known what a minefield he was entering: explosions all about him, kabaah! kabaah! – and he takes his head in his hands for protection, as if another kabaah! were readying itself for attack – with no indication of where terrains of safety might lie. Did Pringle have any idea, could he have foreseen what so-called humanitarian beliefs would unleash in the world? Which one of his selves could have anticipated such a bouleversement? He cannot help feeling that the old adage of *give them a pinkie and they'll grab the whole hand* holds as true as ever. It is one thing, he concedes, for everyone to be liberated from slavery or serfdom, no decent human being could argue against that, but quite another for people to take liberties, to go on and on about their rights, to go about sniffing out discrimination and tracing inequalities, to demand and demand. Were these native people born without a sense of humour? Above all, where is their gratitude? Here they are in the great city of London and not a sign of appreciation, let alone counting their blessings. And how the deuce can he raise these concerns with his close associates, Mary and Hinza, who themselves appear to have little by way of humour or gratitude? Or rather, their gratitude is misdirected towards Pringle. No wonder he's made little progress with the man's story.

Well, he has had enough of this fraught life, this tiptoeing through minefields. This twenty-first century is more troublesome than all his long life wrapped up together. He has failed to make advantageous connections with men of note; people take a wide berth, as if he is somehow contaminated; the descendants of his old associates are not prepared to receive him. They behave as if he is a ghost, or deranged, so that Mary and Hinza turn out to be all he has. He is sick of it, of the globe spinning so dizzily, throwing everything anyone has held sacred off kilter, up in the air. And it turns out that he is also sick of the old Sir Nicholas, that a brand-new self is what's required, is what he has to conjure out of this murky air, but the very thought is exhausting. Never before have both the past and the future seemed so out of reach; he cannot escape the clutches of a bullying present, the sense of having to walk on eggshells. And he is sick of being reprimanded, of being brought to order when he has something humorous to say about all the strange people in London, especially the females. How can the boy deny that the West Indian women waddle about like stuffed bin bags, and that the Mussulman women peering out of the letter-box slits in their veils are sinister? Does the twenty-first century not claim freedom of speech as a measure of this new enlightenment?

No one would want to curb your freedom to speak your mind, said Hinza, and it would be pointless to object to your holding unpleasant views, but such freedom has to be measured against civility, the code of politeness that ought to govern the ways in which people relate to one another. Do you and your kind not insist that civility is a timeless aristocratic value? So I question your right to say to Mary that she looks like a stuffed black garbage bag. Just as I ought not to say to you that you look like a stuffed white garbage bag, for the simple reason that it is not polite, that it gives offence. There is nothing new or arcane about contemporary manners.

For all Hinza's misguided notions, he has grown a little fond of the boy. Perhaps he should fight inertia, embrace adventure, and go with Hinza to Africa after all. There is nothing for him in London, and he has a terrible fear that the young man will not return, which is to say leave him to the mercy of that scold, Mary.

Nicholas knows that the rot set in after he had gone to see Mary's plaque in Bloomsbury. What, he wonders, would the bohemian Group have made of it? Mary Prince, Abolitionist and Author! Pah! And that when the wench had not actually written a single word herself. As if any fool can't talk and parrot the views of their betters, which is exactly what the great Scottish philosopher David Hume pointed out about black people's so-called learning. That plaque was the last straw. Nicholas could not have imagined how it would stick in his craw, how it would reveal to him that his efforts with the Pringle history are unlikely to make the grade, not in this world where the actual fine art and hard work of writing are not appreciated. There clearly won't be room for belle lettres if every sad person will rattle off her story. Not that he doesn't believe Mary's tales about slave owners, no doubt the upstarts in the colonies had no idea how to comport themselves, but he does have doubts about the suitability of such grotesque material in print. He for one would not read such accounts, although he does admire Mary's spirit, her determination to throw off that yoke. And a fine cook she is too.

Nicholas rises from his couch. Buoyed up by the thought of food, he makes his way over to the East End. Hinza and Mary are all the companions he has, so he ought to be more tolerant, make do; besides, perhaps argy-bargying with the young man over a glass of ale will do the trick.

The idea of it! Hinza will not come down from his studio until dinner time, Mary announces, but she makes a pot of coffee. He eyes the bitter, black liquid balefully, shaking his head. I want to die, he mutters, his eyes sorrowful as a spaniel's, misty with pity, not only for himself, but also for this last opportunity, the project in which he now has little confidence. If only the woman would sit down by him, allow him to rest his head in her lap. Truly, that is all he is after: to snuggle up against a goose-down bosom, his thumb lodged in his mouth. She surely had once upon a time been a mother, damn it.

Mary does sit down. She pats his hand abstractedly. You have the gift of time, the glory of eternal life, she tries to soothe. Don't give up, the good lord will give you guidance. Nicholas has no truck with her Moravian chapel discourse, delivered, as it happens, without conviction. If this century has taught him anything it is that his creator, having unleashed him in this world, has taken no further responsibility. In which case he can take his leave with impunity, take his life in his own hands whenever he wishes.

Mary fixes him with her defective eyes, but her voice does soften. I know, I know, it's not easy, she agrees, so tiring at times, this blessed new life we've been blessed with, so very trying. I too have had many a wicked thought, have at times longed for earthquakes and tsunamis, although today I can't say I'm ready. But nowadays there are pills, you know, even for us, I'm sure; I've done my homework. I could certainly come by a suppository. Two a penny they are in the Sodom and Gomorrah called Amsterdam.

Sir Nick sits up, shudders squeamishly. Not actually by my own hand, no, never, and he holds up his hands, shows her the near transparent, paper-white palms. Unthinkable. Someone will have to administer the death draught.

Well, says Mary, you're in fine fettle, so I don't know where you'll find such a person, such an accommodating doctor. In bygone days you could have given a slave the task of shoving up the suppository, and no doubt there are destitute migrants around nowadays who'd do the job at a pretty price.

She stands up, rubs her palms on her hips, and takes her leave with what seems to Nick to be an unkind swagger. Why don't you have a nap right here, she advises, pointing to an uncomfortable, stuffed chair. I'll fix something to eat, and Hinza'll soon be down.

*

> But here comes dinner (the best bill of fare),
> Drest by that 'Nut-Brown Maiden', Vytjé Vaal.
> [To the Hottentot Girl.] Meid, roep de Juffrouwen naar't middagmaal:
> [To F.] Which means – 'The ladies in to dinner call.'

Pringle, 'The Emigrant's Cabin'

I, Vytje, am the one who's been skulking at the back, still somewhat confused, not comfortable with this lot, and not sure how I landed here, except for a vague memory of cajoling, no, actual coercion, on the part of a plucky woman. I kept my mouth shut while the others raved, although I did not turn my back snootily like the old white man, whom I suspect does not want to be here at all. I know the English, but am shy to speak it out loud; besides, the woman – Mary – has much to say, even if her tongue is strange, hardly intelligible. She turns out to be bossy and controlling, and for all her insistence that I be in this strange place, has no time for me. I may be a minor character, a latecomer, a country woman, ignorant of their fancy ways, but I will stand my ground and not be bullied by these people, certainly not by her. Their project having stalled, they've seen fit to drag me here to give witness, so the least I expect of them is to listen, not to interrupt, even if Mary claims that it's all Hinza's idea, that she cannot see the point since I am of a different order, a mere mention in a poem. I refuse to respond to such a foolish insult.

Mary, admittedly, is the author of a book chock-a-block with first-class atrocities, but if she's a reader, as I am, she'd know that slavery at the Cape was as harsh as that in the West Indian islands. Baas Pringle often quoted Mr Barrow on the spectacular ill-treatment of native people, enslaved by white farmers, but distinguished from the imported slaves by being given the name of serfs. Also his letters from Africa, on slavery as well as on what he called Caffer Campaigns, couldn't be clearer on the savagery of colonialism. The old white man may snigger or raise a comic eyebrow when I as much as mention Baas Pringle, but there is no question that his accounts of barbaric punishments – hangings, flaying with sjamboks, shots fired into buttocks and thighs – these were witnessed by him, and are all true, so help me God. My people, the Khoekhoe, could with impunity be tortured to death, for unlike the actual slaves from the East Indies and the African coast, who thanks to the new law could no longer be imported, we serfs were easily replaced in the land of our birth. But let me not be drawn into ugly competition with Mary.

Yes, our family and other Khoe people worked at Glen-Lynden for the Pringles, who were kind Christian folk, quiet-spoken too, and certainly we never feared ill-treatment. We in turn were obedient servants. Our people, all Gonaqua-Khoe, hailed from across the Gamtoos river where, for all our resistance and warring against the colonists, we were driven off the land with gunfire. Tata had worked for a while on a Boer farm, but from there we managed to escape to the missionaries at Bethelsdorp, an altogether better situation since you could hire yourself to a farmer for a wage and, when you so wished, return to the mission station. It was there that Baas Pringle found us and persuaded us to trek to the new Scottish settlement at Glen-Lynden, where there was so much work to be done. They surely could not manage to make the place habitable without our help, and Baas Pringle was scrupulous about paying us for our labour, although he did rather go on about the natural laziness of Hottentots as he called us, which he said would not be tolerated. As if we were not daily proof of diligence; but people will be wedded to the stories they've heard, and will not change their minds, although he, at least, eventually did.

It is, of course, unseemly to compete on matters of torture, suffering and endurance, but that does not mean I have to remain silent, so let us see who has more knowledge of Mr P and his ways, his customs and manners. Mary is after all no better than I; we were both servants, but I am the one born and bred at the Cape. It is the Khoekhoe who waited on the strand at Table Bay all those centuries ago, expecting the Europeans in their funny clothes to be humble visitors, until they produced their guns and beads and bibles. And it is I who am best placed to transport this motley group of investigators, as they grandly call themselves, back to the 1820s, take them on a fact-finding trip to the Eastern Cape where the Scottish party settled on the land of the San, who still lurked about in the veld, helping themselves by night to livestock. Bushmen they were called, as if there were no women.

It comes as no surprise that Hinza, that person from nowhere, barely mentions me. It is clear that he has no intention of consulting me on this story – too screwed up, he of the original identity crisis. Really, with all of us now claiming attention, all wanting to be acknowledged as having known Baas Pringle (I at least do not claim friendship), of having been of interest to him, all of us clamouring to fill in his story (which is also to say our own stories), to have a go at stirring the broth, I have every expectation that the story will be spoilt. This beehive house of fiction bursts at the seams, buzzes with our competitive spirits; it was not made for so many people. But that is no reason for Hinza to behave as if he had been the only one. And it is not only me whom he overlooks. What about Nooi Janet Brown, the spinster sister-in-law, who had much to do with the day-to-day organisation of the homestead? A stern, rustling sort of woman with longing in her eyes, but a good woman all the same, and deep to boot. Quite forgotten, she is. No one seems to want to hear about that Scotswoman, who after all would have stories from her sister that none could imagine, for we all know of the darkness of men hidden deep down in their souls that only wives have the misfortune of glimpsing.

Actually there is no room for any of us in Hinza's world. Imagine: I'm in the world alo-one. What pretentious nonsense, and I fear an effect of so much lounging about with Baas Pringle, speaking the poetry, and fancying himself quite the little gentleman. My backside! That boy should have been given more to do, should have been trained in the real world of work, of drawing water and hewing wood; I doubt whether he could as much as swing an axe. Poetry is not real, not about the real world. Hinza and Baas Pringle themselves, speaking the words out loud, did not even try to make it sound like real words – no, always in the droning, dreary, old-man's voice of a preacher. No wonder it turned into improbable stuff about being alone, alone, alone, when in fact the two of them, with their heads together under the wittegat tree, speaking in rhyme, were anything but alone. It would seem that people become unhinged by poetry, that aloneness perversely is one of its favoured conditions. Which also explains the strangeness of the hoary white man, the papery old poet, Sir Thingummy, who mostly turns his back on us, rustling and muttering to himself in verse, smacking his lips and shaking his head.

As a youngster, Hinza certainly thought himself a poet. I may know nothing of such matters, but what I do know is that poetry should last, should be arranged in neat black lines on white pages, bound into books. And where is his poetry to be found?

Indeed, where was Hinza to be found? Pronounced dead, when I could have sworn that it was he at the Kat River Settlement, a young man strutting like a bobbejaan in glasses, with a polished wood cane of all things, smarter than the crutches Baas Pringle used, and speaking the grand English of glass marbles rolling about his tongue. Ever like a preening parrot, that boy. He screwed up his narrow eyes, as he did all those years ago as a child, and I knew him instantly. More of that later, so do not for one minute think that this is his first resurrection; no, he is the kind of rootless Khoesan / Motswana / who-knows-what who endlessly has to reinvent himself. Now it suits him to waft about as Mary's sidekick, *the* authority on Baas Pringle, but see, he too had to wait for the stranger to release him from the pondok; in other words, his position is no different from mine.

For all Mary's branding me as a name in a poem, I am as real as Hinza, which is to say that we exist in books, although not in words of our own. In that sense I concede that Mary, whose story has by and large been dictated by her, has the edge over us. I was, of course, not privy to Hinza's conversations with Baas P, but I am surprised at what the man has to say about me. And especially what he omits. So the old Sir Thingummy has a point when he lifts a bushy eyebrow in mockery. (Europeans may mock our behinds, but don't seem to mind the vegetal tufts of hair that sprout all over their bodies.)

The beehive house at Eildon where the Pringles lived for nine short months before they went to Cape Town was indeed designed by Baas P himself, based on the huts that we Khoekhoe people have built for generations: the bent saplings, the daub and wattle, the floors fashioned from abandoned antheaps and pounded down with cowdung. But, of course, he did not do the actual work himself. That was left to Tata and some of the other men who laboured at his command. Indeed, they had also built the big house at Glen-Lynden, where the larger Pringle family settled on their arrival. Baas P called the beehive house a hut, the strangest affectation, since it was really quite a spacious house, even if it was bursting at the seams since Hinza came to stay. Strange, how that boy seemed to take up so much space. I, of course, did not sleep there. Our Khoekhoe huts were across the stream where the large flat stones were swept clean by the wind, and where we were at liberty to toast in the smoke of our fires.

What do these people have against woodsmoke? They do not understand its medicinal properties, its ability to gather together all the people smells, smoke them out, and ward off the sickness. I explained to Ounooi Pringle how we do not suffer the sick heads that so often bring down the white ladies, but she did not get my meaning. You have to concentrate, Vytje, she said, and by that she meant on the needlework, the fine stitching she was teaching me, which she said all women, including the white mistresses, had to excel in. I could, of course, not mention the monthly sickness to her, how that especially needs the medicine of a smoking fire and its lulling heat, even in the hot season.

If only the Ounooi had had a child of her own, then that Hinza would not have imagined himself to be one of them. And I must admit that the Ounooi in particular came to treat him as her child.

The Nooiens were strangely silent, quite unlike the Boer women who roar with laughter and scold loudly and do not bottle up their grievances. Although the Pringles were not easy to understand, we were fortunate to belong to them, Amanglezi or English folk, whose gentle manners and civility were a comfort after the terrible white farms where we had been slaves. Oh, we knew that at Eildon we had fallen with our bums in the butter. Mama once worked for Amanglezi at Grahamstown where workers were whipped for the least offence, let alone some of the Boers who delighted in actual torture.

At Eildon we were expected to follow God's word. Which was not so strange for us since Oupa Tatie had already had his head turned by Boezak, the mulatto preacher in a worn black outfit who travelled all over the Eastern Cape, mad for the Christian story and happy to do the missionaries' work for them. Baas Pringle conducted a weekly service, right there under the wittegat tree, but later, under his supervision, our men built a large hall that was kept solely for speaking about God, and also *to* Him, not that He ever got round to answering our prayers. We thought it wasteful, a building left unused all week; besides, we soon came to see that God is not partial to the Khoekhoe, even when we spoke carefully in the Dutch language, perhaps because our ancestors had not paid him any heed. But Baas P said we had to persist; that He would come round in the end.

Tata thought that sitting in the back row huddled together perhaps meant that we could not be heard, but that was churlish, since Baas P had to fight with others to allow us in the church at all for the monthly Communion. For the rest, we continued more comfortably under the tree at home. And we loved God for his love of Sundays, which meant that we too got some rest, especially dozing in the back row, and waking to lift a lovely hymn to the rafters.

Baas P had learned to speak Dutch in no time at all. Mama said that no other Amanglezi were capable of that, that they would not even try to twist their tongues around Dutch words, never mind our own Khoe language. We giggled at the comic way he said some words, although he could say the Gs for God quite comfortably, because of being from Scotland, a country, he said, that surpassed all others in beauty and bounty. Which begged the question of why they came here to this bitter land, but it would not have been polite to ask.

Tata wondered if Baas P would manage our Gonaqua tongue, and indeed he delighted in saying after us some words with spectacular clicks, but really there was no point when our people spoke the Dutch anyway. I was embarrassed when Tata, having turned the hymn *Laat ons God Verheerlijk* into our language, had without a by-your-leave launched into singing it at the end of the service under the tree. But the Pringles clapped enthusiastically, and praised the clicks that Tata exaggerated for their entertainment. Only Hinza sat po-faced, unmoved by Tata's achievement, and knitting his brow, presumably in the hope of sprouting hairy eyebrows.

How I loved singing the lovely hymns – like honey from the buchu bushes, they soothed and brought comfort. Even Hinza listened in admiration when I reached the high trilling notes with ease, or harmonised effortlessly to smooth over the croaking of old folks' voices.

Baas Pringle may not have known that not so long ago it would have been illegal to teach Tata to read, but he chose a couple of our men who in no time learned their letters and read the Bible. Which was just as well because before we knew it the Pringles upped and left. Oupa Tatie had already replaced our Heitsi-eibib with the white God, and according to the demands of the missionaries cast out the violin as the devil's instrument, so my Tata was proud to read for himself from the Book.

Things in this land are not right, Baas Pringle came to say when he returned from Cape Town; we will all have to put our shoulders to the wheel to bring about a better world, to live more closely to God's teachings.

He was a strict man, with great expectations of all of us, but over the months, as he learned more about this land and about our people, his heart grew bigger, softer, even if it didn't occur to him that girls too might like to read. Still, we were so very lucky to be at Eildon. In winter the service was held in Baas Pringle's beehive house; he did not mind us at all, and after the many Amens and Glories to God we feasted on meat, bread and suurmelk. Sometimes they asked me to sing a hymn and I always chose one with a high warbling refrain that never failed to bring applause.

The world was changing, for sure, although I wondered if it was not only a matter of saying so. We were servants, not slaves, and that was supposed to be better, but there were some for sure who did not know the difference. The Van Jaarsvelds from Warmpan and Bezuidenhouts from Zuidenkraal used to come over on Sunday afternoons to have biscuits and coffee with the Pringles, even if we would rather have our Sabbath rest than entertain the nosey neighbours. The Bezuidenhouts were particularly keen to visit since it was their dead cousin's land that the Pringles had been given by the Amanglezi rulers, who never acknowledged that it actually belonged to the native San.

But how we split our sides on the occasion when Baas P took a funny turn: he was ready for the service there and then, and his neighbours would have to partake. First, he asked Gert Jaarsveld to read the Bible story, and that young Boer turned redder and redder as he stuttered through the Good Book, so Tata, who had only now-now learned to read, had to do the second reading. Then Baas P invited the visitors to join us, servants and all, in the Lord's Prayer, to form a circle of hands for the Our Father, and only thereafter would coffee and biscuits be served. Having held our hands gingerly, with distaste, the Boers galloped off like heathens in the blinding heat, without having had as much as a mug of water. Phew! Baas P surely must have known that they were incapable of learning anything new, that they would never be able to stomach a circle of prayer with Hottentots, as they called us. We laughed at their discomfort, but deep down I knew that it was those people who did not know the difference between servant and slave who had the last laugh.

Baas P just shook his head at our Friday-night feasts over on the slope of the hill, when we roasted kudu and danced until the rise of the morning star to Oom Kabo's tickling of the tin guitar, his voice trilling high above the roar of lions and howling of hyenas. Such a pity, Oom Kabo wailed, that God had taken against the violin, that he did not have Heitsi-eibib's feel for the strings. I could tell that Baas P wanted to know what we did at our celebrations under the stars, what we ate, what our songs were about. Indeed, what we were celebrating, as if there had to be a reason for eating and singing when we were released from labour.

What a time you people had last night, hey? he would smile with questions in his eyes, but the Ounooi looked sternly at him. Vytje, please could you take the ashes away, she'd say; she didn't want to hear of our song and laughter. Always nicely: Vytje please, Vytje thank you, but all the same the tasks mounted up as they forgot how to do things for themselves.

No, feasting was not something the settlers were familiar with, not even when the moon was fully swollen or blood red. Unlike the Boers, who at least knew how to be merry, even if their vastrap dance was a dreary affair of turning first this way and then that way, strictly, with a stiff bend of the knee and barely a twirl. With the Amanglezi, everything was equally sedate, no difference at all that I could tell between partying and daily toil. There was lifting of eyebrows, nodding, and silent passing of dishes to and fro, and even talk of God when they were supposedly celebrating. I don't think they had ever drunk honey beer, let alone dance. The *Kaapse wijn* doled out on special occasions in frugal glasses for all to see how much was being drunk, was an acrid, sour brew, no less than a punishment that I for one couldn't stomach.

That stuck-up Hinza would have done well to come over of a Friday night and learn how to suck bones clean of the marrow, down a mug of honey beer and twist his bony frame in the snake dance or pound the earth with the kabarra. But I would have been the last to bother him with such suggestions. He was being groomed into a white boy, in spite of that ugly face they said was Tswana, and had even taken to walking strangely upright, his arse held high and rigid. Heitse! That boy. Pity I didn't know his language or the song of his land; that would have been the only way of getting to the person who came from his mother's womb. Oom Kabo said that in the land of the Batswana, the segaba is a fine instrument, but I feared Hinza had long forgotten the plucking of those strings. Did he not think that he ought to have remembered his people and his land? No, he sat there overdressed in clownish clothes and with pen and paper; always the writing, which brooked no interruption, even when I asked a necessary question like, When would he saddle Bleskop? Or when were the shearers expected? Things I needed to know in order to do my chores and keep the house in order. But no, that young master Hinza was too busy to speak to the likes of me.

Ag, I smiled to myself at his supercilious silence. What he didn't know was that Tata had in turn been teaching me to read and write, that I had already spelled out all of the Exodus story and puzzled over the strange behaviour of Moses and God alike. The business of letters turned out to be not half as difficult as we were led to believe; it was certainly more pleasant than emptying pisspots. We children sang the ABC together around the fire, and Tata said that in order to write we needed no more than a stick and the earth God had given us for the sewing of seeds, that writing was no less than cultivation and growth – the more you wrote, the more there was to write, as if the words themselves came bursting through the earth like so many seedlings. Whilst the others didn't care to practise their ABCs, I marked out and smoothed a stride of mud bank on which to draw my letters with a sharp stick, and the beauty of it was that the crooked ones could be smoothed over; they need not live to mock me. One sweep with a stick or even by hand and all was erased, ready once more for an attempt at healthy, firm letters.

Like any garden the writing patch had to be maintained. You poured water oh so slowly over it, avoiding rivulets, whilst smoothing with a flat stone, so that the muddy earth hardened evenly in the sun for a clean scoring of lines. I marked out my page by setting wee white stones all around a vast rectangle, prettily, with a line of even tinier stones down the centre to signify the spine of a book. But that was a temporary thing. The stone borders had to go as I came to fill up the whole bank; soon the whole Zuurveld would be covered in my writing. When my hand grew steadier and I no longer made mistakes, I also used the large flat stones and etched with a piece of flint the words I wanted to shout out to the world, declare them forever and ever to all and sundry who should pass by these parts. And Hinza knew nothing of me, the writer.

Careful not to betray my own efforts, I asked Baas P about writing on stone, but he said that that would be quite the wrong thing to do. Much given to sermonising, he said that except for glory to God and the law written by Moses, everything, however surely and solemnly declared, grows wobbly and faint, that we needed to check constantly whether what we once thought of as truths remained true. Our words would always need to be adjusted, and writing on stone does not allow for that. Ideas themselves, he said, dance about as we wade through the world; they shift their angles in your head, turn as the sunflower with the sun, and throw new shadows where once there had been light. Etching into stone was a vainglorious thing that would come back to haunt and taunt you when new ideas tilted the world, and your thoughts no longer matched those words.

So I came to see that it was best to keep writing on the earth, where words could easily be erased. But what about the eager wind, whose help I had not asked for? What was the point if writing turned out like the house I cleaned, or the food I cooked, all gone in a trice without a trace of my labour? I did not like Baas P's idea one bit, but I supposed that he spoke from experience, having come from a land of strange dark views that could not survive in the bright light of Africa. I repeat this for the benefit of old Sir Nicholas Thingummy, who has no truck with Baas P. But I too had my doubts. If such teaching made sense, why then, I asked myself, did Baas P do the black writing on white paper? Or did poetry not count? And what did Hinza think of this inconsistent behaviour, I wondered.

Hinza could turn up his flat nose all he wished; he didn't know of my secret writing. But I must confess that it would have been better if we had been friends. With whom could I talk about the truths that would surely not shift their shapes, of which there were always more to be added, and which ought not to be erased? I whispered the words, those letters that were not finely enough drawn to set in stone. I had whispered them before, after the long awaited rainfall, standing under the buttery yellow, full-faced moon overhead, with my feet firm in the gurgling stream and the murmur of water at my toes. The stars winked and beckoned, and then I knew, as my bones filled with air and grew light as a bird's – and still I know –that I will never revise those words: *to be free to live and do as I please without the bidding of a master, whether he be good or bad.* I knew that one day, when my letters were perfect, I would score that in stone.

It was on a Sunday afternoon, the dinner dishes all cleared, that I came upon Hinza in the Baviaans cave, and for once he spoke without mockery, even though he kept his eyes averted. Thank heavens he did not suspect that I had followed him. He showed me where Baas P had, in fact, written in stone. His own name, TPringle, for all to see, for ever more, that he had been there, as the date below his name declared. Hinza said that they had been out together for his geography lesson, exploring the Baviaans crags where long ago the San painted their stories; that Baas P invited him too to write his name, HMarossi, right there beside his own.

Admittedly, the name was well above the picture of a huntsman on the large red eland's back, and well away from the line of stick-figured men. Still, surprisingly, Hinza had the good sense to refuse, he didn't know why, he said, but felt that he couldn't. Perhaps that was the only time ever that he said to the master that he would rather not, and I imagine it could have been no easy thing to say, which is perhaps why he wanted to tell me about it. Did he speak firmly? hesitantly? That I don't know. But it pleased him that Baas P let him be, that he did not remonstrate or insist as a master would, even though Hinza offered no reason for refusing. He ought to have explained that the krans with its cave paintings was sacred, filled with spirit of the San, with the powers of healing, that it ought not to be defaced with the marks of strangers. But he kept silent.

Tata had taken us there some time ago, before Baas P scored his name into the rock. There he read to us children the stories of the elongated people and their animals, drawn in white, ochre and black, for the San, he said, were also our ancestors. What I liked best was the line of dots that followed the contours of the rocks, disappearing into crags and reappearing on the next rock. There were those who had escaped across the line, men and kwagga, but Tata did not know what to make of that.

After Baas P had desecrated the cave, written his name in stone, I wondered if that meant that the rocks with all their pictures then belonged to him. Hinza laughed out loud. Did I not know, he boasted, that Mr P had written his name on a piece of paper when he arrived in the country, so that much of the Zuurveld territory, including the cave and rock paintings, now belonged to the Pringles anyway? How extraordinary, I thought, that a piece of paper covered in writing, with not as much as an eland drawn on it, could have such power, and that the people who have always lived here knew nothing of it. That was reason enough for me to beaver away at writing, that which could bring such strange meanings into the world.

After Hinza showed me Baas P's name carved in the cave, I visited the paintings again, on my own. A strange, unmelodious, echoing sound, like a distant gora perhaps, swirled about the rocks, and I tried not to be afraid. I wondered if the dotted lines that I had thought of as escapees were a more recent addition to the paintings. What if they spoke of the San's revenge, of how they would kill the settlers and take back their land? Perhaps that was why Baas Pringle had to carve his name: to assert his own magic, and so ward off disaster.

It is a long while since the San lived in these parts, writing their stories on rocks, long before the white people came and drove them away. Except they had not actually been driven away; rather, they grew adept at disguising themselves. They scurried about in the undergrowth and came by night to help themselves to mealies and to make off with sheep or horses, and then all hell broke loose as our men were commanded to pursue them with rifles. Oh, it was continuous skirmish all right, also with the amaXhosa across the border, and not so many years after Baas Pringle left, the whole of the territory was not surprisingly awash in blood.

Baas P had asked the governor for a commando to help defend the settlers against the San inroads. That was also why the Bastaards, as Mama called them, had been drafted in and had set up homes at the foot of the hill. I for one did not mind having more people, more young men around, even if they were snooty and thought themselves too high and mighty to eat and dance with us. One could have sworn that they were not ashamed, as Mama thought they ought to be, of the white blood that had stolen into their veins. I reminded Mama that Baas P would not have us use the Boer name of Bastaards. We were to call them 'mulattoes'.

I used to be quite the favourite with the Nooiens, even if they did not think me capable of reading and writing, but that was before the arrival of Hinza out of nowhere. Then it became Hinza this and Hinza that, quite their little hanslam with his wagging tail and foolish bleating in English. The Pringles clean forgot about me, so yes, I was surprised that Baas P even remembered to mention me in his poem, even if things were not quite as they are in his account. He did not, of course, imagine that I would be able to read it. And that was just as well, since it did not occur to him that when I squatted by the bank, lingering around Hinza's lessons, I looked and listened, and practised when I got back to my earth-book. Already I had outstripped Tata's learning.

Mama and the younger children fell about laughing when I spoke the English at them, but I promised them that they too would learn to shape their letters. Little did I know that I would have to leave well before that promise was fulfilled, but that I would later teach many a child to read at the Kat River where we ended up.

Once Mama found a page blown against a thorn bush deep-deep in a gulley. It had been beautifully covered in letters that had started to fade, and I could just imagine one of the Nooiens in the cool of an evening, sitting pen in hand on a rock, her long, full, unwieldy skirts neatly tucked under, and looking wistfully at the tumbling sun and the wisps of gold-rimmed clouds. Then whilst she was drumming her fingers, waiting to continue with just the right word, a gust of wind would have whipped the page clean away. How distressing that must have been. I could not read every single word, and besides, the fading work of sun and wind rendered them difficult, unfamiliar; but I gathered it to be the work of poor Nooi Janet. She would have been distraught; no doubt she comforted herself that the page had been shredded in the wind, or carried off high into a treetop, where it would be washed clean when the rain finally came. Mama stood waiting. What does it tell? she asked eagerly, but I said that it had lost too much meaning to the sun, that I could make neither head nor tail of it.

It would not have been right to say, or for that matter to return it to Nooi Janet, to make her blush with shame for the heart so splayed open on the page. She may have believed that I couldn't read, but I could not trust myself to keep an ignorant face whilst I handed it over. There was no water in the riverbed so I pounded the page to shreds between two stones. No one could foresee the trouble of winged words and their wayward flight into the wrong hands. There is no trapping them, no chance of sealing them back into the heart. I will, of course, not betray Juffrouw Janet here, will keep it all to my-self, for I read the page also as a lesson to be learned by me. With my own eyes I saw the danger that lurks in writing. Indeed, is this not the source of this hullaballoo about who Baas P really was, what he really thought, how he really behaved? All because of things he had written himself in various letters, the words in black and white.

Thus I came to see that it is after all best to keep your writing on the earth, where the wind will sweep up the words and smudge them, and the rain drive them back into the earth. It was there on my earth page that I scored the name of Plaatje the mulatto boy into the winter clay, where it aired for no more than a day, by which time the letters had already buckled out of shape. Then the rain erased his name. But I remembered; the writing kept it burned into my memory, even after I left and ended up at Dr Philip's mission school. I liked to think that Plaatje knew of my writing, for he started smiling shyly at me, and once complained that he did not want to be called a Bastaard.

It is question of setting straight the record. Of all these people, I am the one who was longest at Eildon and, as far as I understand, our task is to give a truthful account of Baas P now that the sincerity of his writing is being questioned by clever folk who are able not only to read between the lines, but to hold a verse upside down and examine its weft, woof, waft and all.

I must remember that if Baas Pringle had initially taken on the Boer practice of Baas this and Baas that, and also Ounooi and Nooi Janet, he no longer wanted to be called Baas when he returned from the long stay in Cape Town, though what difference that was supposed to make, I for one couldn't tell, for he had always been kind and softly spoken. I have no idea what brought about his decision. Mama joked that he had come face to face with a baboon in the Winterberg, that he shat himself in terror, so that the fastidious baboon let him go, but on condition he drop the bad ways of the Pale Beasts. I have no truck with Mama's fanciful stories. Still, I must remember from now on not to refer to the Pringles as Baas and Nooiens. No, it should be Mr or Mijnheer Pringle and the Juffrouwens, for what that's worth, for I can testify that everything else at Eildon remained unchanged.

Vytje, what kind of heathen name is that? Mary asks, by way of getting her own back.

My name Vytje is short for Sofia, I explain, a way of saying Fia-tje, but saying it fast so that -ia slips into -ay; a diminutive that Hinza as a child wilfully chose to misconstrue as one for vy, the Dutch for fig.

He used to hail me cheekily, even if I was older: Turksvy! Miss Prickly Pear! he would shout to annoy me, but I'd lunge at him and clip him round the ear. As it happens, I am rather partial to a prickly pear, and can barely wait for the month of March when the large show-off yellow flower fades and the fruits begin to swell, perched on the edge of the leaf blade, where they balance pertly. Of course, no such thing to be found here in this cold northern world.

You, I said, with your silly name of Hinza, you're jealous. You've heard Mr P say that Sofia is the name of a wise girl. And even if my name were from fig or prickly pear, there is plenty to admire about that. Think of its fruit, bursting with sunshine and honey and the crunch of seeds, but only for the skilled hand and nimble fingers that can avoid the thorns.

Although Hinza was stronger, he allowed his ears to be boxed, but he carried on calling names as if I had not spoken.

Mr Pringle was certainly an odd white man. After all that time of fixing up the farm, clearing the land and finally getting a good harvest and a fine flock of fat-tailed sheep, he clapped his hands together and off they went to the big city, which I believed pleased the Nooiens. Mama was fearful that we would be turned out, but no, Baas William, that is Mr P's brother, took over. Being fresh from across the water he had no understanding of our people, and seemed to think we were all children, but at least there were no cruel floggings, so at first we let them be.

Then one summer, when our Pringles returned from Cape Town, I knew something terrible was brewing. Mr P stormed about in fury. He would gallop off for hours into the veld; his head, it turned out, was filled with the roar of the sea. There was sadness in his eyes as he chewed his poet's pencil under the wittegat tree, and the Juffrouwens as we now had to call them, were unusually quiet. Not a word did they say.

It was Hinza's strange, boastful behaviour that confirmed for me that they would sail away to the white man's land far across the oceans. We have no choice, he said, the governor Somerset will never give up persecuting us; he has ruined us financially too.

Haai goetsega! Imagine 'we' this and 'we' that, from Hinza who thought he was white because he could read and write and had been to the city! I knew that that boy would get his comeuppance, sure as God is good. And when that day came, I would make up a song in which to tell the story. In the Gonaqua tongue too, so that he would have to beg for a translation.

Our family had in the past stayed at the mission station at Bethelsdorp, and that was where we hoped to return, since Ordinance 50 had not yet been passed and the Kat River land ceded to us. At first the other Pringles vied for my services, which had been talked up by the Juffrouwens – but my, what a business that turned out to be. Only goes to show that blood relationships cannot be relied on; in fact, it shows how dear Mr Thomas and the Juffrouwens had opened their minds and hearts to our world, especially after they returned from the city. Speak of chalk and cheese! How could these people be so stupid as to imagine that one would not cheat and lie when not treated as well as we had been by Mr Thomas. As if I had no self-respect! Of course I helped myself to whatever I thought necessary to take. How else could I show my contempt for them? Not fit to wear Mr P's old boots!

As soon as the Kat River became available we left, as did the mulatto families, and kept our ears open for news of Mr P's return. Because he promised Dr Philip that he'd be back, that he would be returning a smartly educated Hinza to work for the good of our people. The idea of it! But such was Mr P's misplaced optimism and belief in that boy.

Sir Nicholas Greene is not happy about being summoned, and especially not by that pair. They have no idea, although the boy who thinks of himself as an artist ought to know that creativity does not brook directives. For all his reputation as a critic, Nicholas is still a poet; he is at the glorious mercy of the muse.

Mary evinces patience, Yes, yes, of course, inspiration is necessary, but could it not be injected at a later date to improve an existing text? There has been no progress; they have waited long enough, and now they insist on helping him get the first chapter off the ground, or at least sketch out the bare bones. They could start with the ordinary, the flat work-a-day stuff that the poet could flesh out later, ready for leavening when inspiration arrives. All change, Mary announces: collaboration is the name of the game. She knows that Nick's bias and snobbery will at some stage have to be redacted, but right now she'd be happy to see anything at all.

Café Cherubini on Junction Road has a convenient, secluded nook where they meet. Nick has spruced himself up for the occasion. Brought somewhat up to date, he sports a lively constructivist tie, and his signature carnation, shamelessly taken from the mean bouquet at his usual table at Café Rouge, adorns the buttonhole of a well-worn grey morning suit. From his jacket pocket he pulls out a volume of Tennyson. For Hinza, who should read the Victorians, he wheezes, turning his back to Mary; there's nothing nowadays to beat the gloire of Victorians. Without a word, he also returns the folder of Mr P's African Poems.

Hinza refrains from asking if he has another copy. He is pleased to note that Nick's fingernails for once are spotlessly clean, but is alarmed by the old man's heaving chest, the laborious breathing that sets the carnation aquiver.

Mary announces that they'll start with the 1820 settlers, the departure of the Scottish party for the Cape, and not bother with Mr P's earlier writings.

Sir Nicholas has never been on a sea voyage, has never left the shores of England, but he has, of course, read the work of the celebrated John Mandeville, the most erudite of travel writers. Although he lived through the astounding era of travels and explorations, had felt ecstatically the expansion of his own mind as geographical boundaries melted away, and pondered the wonders of Mandeville's discoveries – of men with second heads grown out of their armpits and women with pendulous labia that could be slung over their shoulders – actual travel to foreign climes has never held an allure. Having pulled himself up by his own bootstraps, having suffered the indignities of clambering up rickety social ladders and being trapped precariously on various rungs for far too long, Nicholas has for some time felt settled in a comfortable social niche. Sheer folly it would be to pursue the instability of travel by sea and seek out the rough ways of uncivilised nations. Hence he shrugs indifferently when Hinza, who remembers the excitement of the slow journey from Africa, says how sorry he is that ships have been replaced by aeroplanes.

Nicholas all but collapses under a coughing fit. What have they done to this planet? he pants. You have no idea how strange, how toxic the atmosphere is, what a far cry from what we used to think of as air. The pea-soup pollution that old Charlie Dickens banged on about has nothing on these poisonously clear blue skies; Nicholas fears that his lungs will not manage for much longer.

Mary, impatient for the story to get started, gets him a shot of whisky, the best thing for emphysema, she insists. Come now, let's focus. It's 1820, the first days of February, still dark and bitterly cold, though there are signs of the light returning, a glimmer of hope.

Nick screws up his eyes. It is by no means easy to visualise a party of anxious Scots on the quay, so Mary, by way of encouragement, orders another shot.

Ah, tartans! He turns to Hinza, What were the colours of the Pringle plaids? There's no better way to start than with the sartorial. Surely, Hinza remonstrates, you've had enough time to research your subject. Why rely on me? He has to admit that he too doesn't know the clan tartan. He had never heard Mr P as much as mention tartans. Besides, who in their right minds would have worn a kilt in the Zuurveld?

Nick tuts. Most remiss of your poet, and not very patriotic either.

Actually I have tried to find out, but it's all a muddle you know, so many different tartans it would seem for the same clan.

Mary fears that this nonsense will go on all day, Nick being the master of slow deliberation. The Pringles, she says briskly, were Border folk, who would not have dressed in Highland plaids. Besides, in the United Britain the ban against Highland dress held for many decades, really until just before Mr P's birth, and Mr P being enthusiastic about the Union would most probably have supported the ban. Only much later did Lowlanders take to the kilt; no wonder they felt free to take on any pattern they fancied. Let us not then bother with kilts that the good people of Blaiklaw would most likely not have worn. Tartan trews for best wear perhaps, but who knows in what colours? And who cares, she sighs.

In which case, how about the plain checkered black-and-white kilt, the stylish Border Reiver tweed, just the ticket for our dour Presbyterians, Nick says, and his eyes light up as the men and women of yore materialise before him in pleasing plaid.

Hinza thinks that Mr P, who was so fierce about reassessing his beliefs, would in time have given up his youthful distaste for Highland culture; he would have recognised the dissenting potential in wearing a kilt. Kilts have recently made it to the catwalk, and Hinza applauds Nick on the choice of the voguish houndstooth plaid. That settled, they need to get cracking.

What is there to say about the voyage of seventy-two long days on the *Brilliant*? It is the case that they dwelled on the tedium of time dragging its feet, as excitement about sea travel, anticipation of the new world and the new prosperous life ahead was first paused, then all but snuffed out with having to wait for the brig to sail.

A watched kettle never boils, old Mrs Beatrice Pringle, older than her forty-nine years, muttered repeatedly, so that others kept out of her way. How well they got to know the brig after a wearisome fortnight of waiting at Deptford. They watched as merchants thrashed about, plying their trades from sooty warehouses on the banks of the Thames. The flag of the East India Company fluttered in the westerly wind;

young boys, no more than children, pushed heavy barrows laden with turnips along the quay; refractory packhorses stamped their hooves, exhaling smoke; and women wearing ill repute brazenly on their brows strolled with intent. All whilst they, the emigrants, kicked their heels, with nothing to do but follow the travels of pregnant rain clouds scuttling across dreary English skies. Oh, for the golden days awaiting them in Africa – that was what they kept in the mind's eye, warding off impatience and boredom.

Sir Nicholas Greene cannot believe that the party of Scots were not diverted by so fine a dockyard as Deptford, where the magnificent spire of St Nicholas pierced the sky and surely filled any despairing heart with joy. Just a stone's throw from Greenwich (named for his very own ancestor) and the very port from where Oswald the Reeve started his Tale as he set off for Canterbury, an admirable man who clung to the salt of youth though his heart be mouldy. A model indeed, and Sir Nick boasts that, taking a leaf from the Reeve's book, he too wears his old age like a leek, sporting a green tail in spite of his head being white. Those were the days, and he slaps his thigh with merriment, when Deptford was a jolly sort of place to be savoured by anyone with spirit. Did Hinza know that Peter the Great, well in his cups, whizzed through the town in a wheelbarrow? And that Kit Marlowe found rest for his soul in the very churchyard of St Nicholas? Fair bursting with gloire, with history and poetry, that fine port of Deptford. No better place from which to embark on a new life in the colonies.

Enough, Mary interrupts, of your selective history. Let us please not dwell on the indecency of those docks where the noble African, Equiano, was sold from one captain to another; let us please get back to our emigrants.

Dear woman, you would not know what the loss of that incomparable Kit meant for our isles, or rather, for civilisation. How well I remember the day when the news reached the City of the playwright's needless accidental death in a drunken brawl, and how I saw myself …

Come, come, Hinza says, everyone knows that it was not accidental at all. That the system of spying, tale-bearing and conspiracies was firmly established, and Marlowe's death, if it actually came to that, was just a matter of time. For that matter no different from the hornet's nest that Mr P was about to enter at the Cape, where Lord Charles Somerset too had in place a network of espionage and tattle-telling that eventually led to Mr P's estrangement from the governor.

You are surely not comparing your man with the genius that was Kit Marlowe? Preposterous.

Mary groans, holding her head in her hands, so that Hinza concedes, Well not in that sense, but first things first – Mary is right; let's get on with the journey.

The muddy waters of the Thames slapped sluggishly at the sides of the brig, and Mr Thomas Pringle felt bearing down upon him, like the very leaden weight of time, the responsibility of being leader of his party, a brand-new role to which he had yet to become accustomed. After the long period of preparation in London, waiting for slow letters to and from the colony and from the tardy Home Office, what did their embarkation amount to when there was no movement besides that dreich surge and fall of tidal waters, the slap-slap against the sides of the brig that so easily could drive a thinking man to distraction? In the Edinburgh offices of *Blackwood's* he could never have imagined himself as cheerleader, but really there was no profit in thinking about that past life of humiliation when now the promise of the new stretched before him, though often as a long train of shimmering stuff to be snatched at awkwardly as it slipped through his fingers – all brilliant, insubstantial African sunlight.

Mr Pringle, mindful of *The Reeve's Tale*, did not think that his fellow Scots would appreciate the bawdy narratives of Canterbury pilgrims. Instead, he rallied the weary and dejected party with tales of colonial prosperity, bucked up their spirits with poetic visions of the veld. From Burchell's *Cape of Good Hope* he recycled images of abundance: the diverse scenery of the Zuurveld with its herbage, wood and water, a world of rugged natural beauty, not so unlike the Scottish Lallans, images that offered prosperity to hardworking men. There they would find, albeit in a different key, the wild crags, the sweep of the valleys and the dear music of burns bounding into the Tweed, the Lammermuir peaks, the Eildon Hills, the ancient lands of Earlston. Certainly in paler, sun-bleached hues, but God's earth was everywhere sand, clay or rock, out of which men must shape their lives and feed the imagination.

Whilst the brig tarried on the Thames, Thomas managed to turn around the impatience of the men rearing to go. The scattered Pringle family, brought together once more, as well as Margaret's people, the Browns and Rennies, were readily transported to the colony by his tales. Easy does it: a slow and steady acclimatisation to life on the stationary brig was no bad thing; settling in and getting to know each other in new ways. After all, that was what would make or break the settlement – the ability to endure, and to work together. Mr Pringle surprised himself. How easily it came after all, story generating further stories, and Margaret for one marvelled at his ability to placate, to talk up the dreariness of waiting that is outwith one's control, to conjure up the Mediterranean brightness of the promised land, the call of the wild. Oh, her dear Tam all but roared like a lion and growled like a leopard.

If the group of ungodly English farmers, the traders and artisans and low-bred mechanicals, quarreled rudely, Thomas believed that their Scottish party – people who had lived for and loved the wild cliffs and cloughs, the rugged peaks of highlands and lowlands – would keep faith. But how to manage his own legitimate impatience? He watched with anxiety the days draining away on the Thames, days that ought to be spent tilling the land of the South, for how would they survive if they did not arrive in time to sow their cereals?

Margaret and her sister Janet allowed themselves a giggle at the long wait on the *Brilliant*. No question there of missing the boat, a phrase that had inspired hilarity in their more youthful days on the farm, when a neighbour brought the news that spinsters were needed in the colonies, that there was yet hope of a boat for ferrying them into that wilderness. Janet thought it brave of Margaret to enter marriage, mild as her Thomas seemed to be; she, on the other hand, having gingerly peered into the possibility, having scanned the bland faces of bachelors loitering on the deck, felt relief that the boat was no more than that – a vessel of transport to a new country.

At long last old Mrs Beatrice Pringle heard the hiss of a kettle about to boil. On 15 February 1820, under glowering skies and driving rain – the English winter having settled in anew – the *Brilliant* finally set sail from Gravesend.

After such tarrying, the vast, endless blue of the ocean came as a relief, even as stomachs heaved and folk old and young stumbled about drunkenly, clinging to the railings and licking the salt from their cracked lips. Thomas paced the deck, pronouncing out loud the guttural sounds from a well-thumbed Dutch grammar. My dear Tam, Margaret smiled, as he took to addressing her as *my geliebde*, which made her tilt her head with admiration. How lovely, the plain beauty of her face at that angle, and Thomas, much encouraged, for once did not mind at all being called Tam by the good woman.

The energy of movement, the power of mountain-high waves parting before the bow of the brig whipped up their courage. With misgivings blown off in the hearty gale, he penned the lines:

Better to launch than sink forlorn
To vile dependence in our native land.

Proudly leading their clan, Thomas saw his defeated sire lift his head once more, his brothers peer brightly into the horizon, and with Margaret's strong hand in his own, he knew that all would be well in the colony. The Scottish families could put behind them poverty and adversity; if they were not gentlefolk, they were after all of sound agriculturist stock. Good fortune would undoubtedly await them at the Cape.

The older Rennie lad with flaming hair had brought his reel pipe and led them in song: Thomas the Rhymer, Sir Walter's ballad, surely written in honour of their own party leader. Pringle's heart was ever warmed by Sir Walter's lyrics, charmed by the vision of the Rhymer under Eildon's thorn tree, he of the tongue that can never lie, bowing gallantly to the silver bells of the fairy queen in her grass-green silk. How appropriate that Sir Walter should transcribe the fairy queen's gift as harp *and* carp, rather than a choice between harp *or* carp, as some of the older versions of the ballad would have it. Poetry after all cannot be separated from music, just as it cannot be separated from truth, or the Rhymer's gift of prophecy. So Tam Pringle saluted young Rennie; he too would keep faith, he solemnly promised, to his valiant people, the Scots transporting their history and culture to the wild land waiting to be civilised. But he explained to the young farmers that Sir Walter's *Border Minstrelsy*, published when he Thomas was but a laddie, in no way referred to him, and they cheered his modesty, for his was ever the tongue that could never lie.

Thomas had looked forward to the seventy-five long days on the ocean as a time for composing a long poem, starting with the lines that had come so effortlessly on the deck. But no, he must focus on the future, on what awaits them:

A land of climate fair and fertile soil,
Teeming with milk and wine and waving corn,
Invites from far the venturous Briton's toil:
And thousands, long by fruitless cares foreworn,
Are now across the wide Atlantic borne,
To seek new homes on Afric's southern strand.

With hard work ahead, the ship was a space for dreaming, a fruitful time for feeding the imagination. He would write a long poem, 'The Emigrants', which with the fragment 'Glen-Lyden' and some of his much-praised juvenile verse would constitute a modest volume. For all the responsibilities that lay ahead in the country that needed settlers, he would not cast off the role of poet, never give up the literary life.

Alas, Thomas paced the deck disconsolately as the muse kept out of sight. He cursed aloud, and raised his voice at Margaret for asking anxiously how 'The Emigrants' was coming along, as if he were in the clutches of a bout of constipation. Then it took some time to beg her pardon; he fell on his knees, promising that he would never again shout or use vulgar language, that he would ever be an example in the uncouth African veld.

How exasperating, the business of poetry that demanded of conditions to be just so. Impossible to compose with the rolling agitation of the ship, the uncertainly ahead, and he had to admit to trepidation about what the Zuurveld held in store, for as his new knowledge of Dutch revealed, the name of the region did not bode well. How would they till a land already branded as acidic? Whilst Thomas smiled at his fellow travellers, Margaret learned to keep out of his way, especially when he sat down with pen and paper, and thunder on his brow. He turned his gaze resolutely back to the old country and, resorting to exclamation, produced but a couple of stanzas of a farewell hymn, a fit conclusion to 'The Emigrants'. The body of the poem would be composed in more tranquil times.

Our native Land – our native Vale –
A long and last adieu!
Farewell to bonny Lynden-dale
And Cheviot-mountains blue!
Home of our hearts! Our father's home!
Land of the brave and free!
The keel is flashing through the foam
That bears us far from thee.

Of the voyage, the time in interim, Thomas Pringle would later say no more than that it was 'pleasant and prosperous'. Fish flew out of the ocean in shimmering arcs; whales bellowed and spouted seawater into bright sunlight; and without incident, the *Brilliant* arrived at Simon's Bay on 30 April 1820. Once more the migrants, not yet settlers, had to remain on board and endure again the dull thud of water against the vessel whilst Mr Pringle and the English party leaders went ashore.

Thomas lost no time in finding a horse on which to gallop to Cape Town, where he was all but struck dumb by its beauty. The town, bathed in glorious autumnal sunlight, nestled at the foot of the majestic Table Mountain, elegantly flanked by Lion's Head and Devil's Peak and covered in the misty gauze of the legendary tablecloth. Right on the Table Bay coast was the Castle of Good Hope, and trotting about the stone fortress he pronounced out loud in flawless Dutch the names of the five bastions: Leerdam, Buuren, Katzenellenbogen, Nassau, Oranje. Its grand belltower solemnly struck the twelve hours, and Pringle dismounted, hat in hand, his Presbyterian soul thrilling to the call. Oh, it would do, would do very nicely for a literary life.

But where was the governor to whom his letter of introduction was addressed? Lord Charles Somerset, he learned to his dismay, was on leave in England. Their ships had passed each other in the night, somewhere about the equator, Thomas reckoned; the letter remained sealed. No chance then, of an appointment in government service or, more importantly, of taking up a literary life in Cape Town. Well, not as yet. And as Margaret later pointed out, the delay was of no consequence. They would after all have to make sure that things in the settlement went according to plan; the success of the crops and the prosperity of their clansmen had to be secured before they could leave the Zuurveld for the city. Yet again the victim of slow time, Thomas brushed aside impatience; urban life must necessarily be put on hold, and the letters of introduction to the governor could happily wait.

Meanwhile, in the blushful English spring, Lord Charles was in no hurry to return to the colony. Courtship took time, and he would not think of resuming his position without acquiring at home a new Lady Charles. His first marriage had been exciting, a hasty affair of eloping with the lovely Lady Elizabeth, whose liveliness, alas, did not last, so that now in middle age and after the social aridity of the rude

Cape he savoured dallying with eligible females in the elegance of English drawing rooms. Besides, there was the coronation of King George the following year which he would not miss for anything in the world. Thus Lord Charles allowed whole afternoons for lingering on the ancestral lawns of the spirited Lady Mary Poulett, an admirable horsewoman, and one whose firm, broad shoulders showed her best able to endure the African heat, to stamp her sturdy feet on parched land. For her he would refurbish the hunting lodge in the woods of Camps Bay, and in the evenings they would bathe in the refreshing chill of the Atlantic. Lady Mary would not be one to tolerate nonsense from a rebellious governing board, and thus the Cape could be happily shaped to their design.

Pringle? Thomas Pringle? Can't say that he'd ever come across the name; he had never heard of such a person; it didn't ring a bell. Lord Charles frowned at the sealed letter of introduction that had been forwarded by Colonel Bird. Damned foolish of the man to regard the mark of 'Private' so scrupulously; he ought to have dealt with the mundane business of settlers himself. With a frown and a shrug he tossed it aside. He had done his duty; he had no thoughts to spare for the people whose passage he had organised so meticulously and at such exorbitant cost. Of course, he had done his best, had apportioned land for them on the colony's border where the marauding savages had been driven off and the rough Boers brought to justice – advantageous really to all concerned. The letter could wait.

With a jolly fanfare at Simon's Town, where the Royal Navy boasted a spick-and-span village, with its own brand-new mast house, boathouse and sail loft, the *Brilliant* sailed away to Lord Charles's land of promise. Not much longer would they have to tolerate on board the excitable English mechanicals, sadly lacking in manners and unfortunately prone to fighting amongst themselves. Thomas wondered how on earth that lot could be relied on to tame the wild land.

They reached Algoa Bay without incident, except it was yet again the same old story of waiting once they docked. Having just found their wobbly feet on terra firma, having straightened their sea legs and disembarked with the English settlers for barely two hours, the Scottish party, destined for the far-flung Baviaan's River Valley, were herded back on to the *Brilliant*. Had they not finally, after months of tossing on the wild seas, arrived? Was this not their destination? No, Mr Pringle patiently explained, their actual arrival was dependent on the arrival of another, no less than the Acting Governor. There was no room in the settlement camps on the seafront where the English whooped around their fires, and the Scots would have to wait three more weeks on board until Sir Rufane Donkin finally arrived. Affable, sympathetic and helpful he may well be, but why had he not managed to get there sooner?

Cooped up in their cabins, the Scots could not hide their disappointment. From the dreary deck of the brig they watched the party of ill-bred English folk embark on their short journey inland. Long trains of wagons carried them off to plots in the comfortable environs of the Bay. Thomas insisted that they who awaited welcome by Sir Rufane were the favoured ones, but the feisty young farm lads thought otherwise. Same old story of English settlers being privileged and the Scots having to put up with discrimination, they grumbled, and as for Mr Pringle's protestations, well it was fine for him as party leader, for he was allowed to disembark. A cripple he may be, but there was no stopping the man, who once again managed as if by miracle to conjure a horse and a tame Hottentot in no time at all, and to gallop off into the wide veld whilst their view ahead was no more than barren sandhills rising from the coast.

Guided by the Hottentot boy, who trotted alongside his horse in leather trews and sheepskin karos, the indefatigable Mr Pringle found his way to the Bethelsdorp Mission Station some nine miles away.

Amen and of course, says Mary, a visit to God's own settlement is entirely to be applauded. And what did he find? What did he do there? Sir Nick, exhausted by the narration, stares at her blankly. He frightened a little mouse under a chair, Hinza says in a sing-song voice. Oh spare us. It's all there, written up in the *Narrative* by Mr P himself, so no need for twice-told tales, he sighs.

They are at the Turk's Head in Islington. Nick has read the piece about the sea journey out loud, having made Mary promise that all questions would wait until he had finished. He would brook no interruptions. It had been irksome enough having to narrate from the Scots' point of view, as Hinza insisted. Exhausted, Nick slumps in his chair, but then sits up sharply at Hinza's words. He couldn't agree more; there certainly is no need to repeat, to translate what had already been written by the man himself, but for the moment he chooses to hold his tongue. Nick is not in the mood for an argument; he knows exactly what Mary would say. That the point of their project is to introduce Mr Pringle to the wider world, to exhume and burnish those words buried under the woodpile of history, to show their man freshly polished to the troubled Britain of today. No, he would hold his tongue. What did he care about the so-called poet and his wild countrymen?

All the same, a crying shame what those people had to endure, Mary offers. That's what needs to be told, what Mr P so delicately refrained from telling. Imagine, the English sacrificing the Scots as a buffer against the amaXhosa.

Nonsense, Sir Nicholas sighs, waving both his hands dismissively. The buffer theory has long since been discredited. No evidence whatsoever, and note how the Scottish immigrants themselves did not think of themselves as buffers.

Ah yes, Hinza says, Lord Charles had earlier proposed to bring thousands of settlers to keep the natives at bay, and yes, it is the case that the Colonial Office did not approve of such a human shield against the amaXhosa, so there is indeed no evidence in the Colonial Office papers, in parliamentary debates, or in the authoritative works of Barrow and Burchell of such a plan being carried out. But when, I ask you, has your Lord Charles ever been stopped by democratic decisions that didn't suit him? The English migrants were indeed not strategically settled, but the fact remains that the Scots *were* placed on the Albany border, and all credit to them for flourishing in the harsh conditions, unlike the English, I might add. Somerset, see, followed his original plan regardless of approved policy, and the Scots, stoically, gratefully buckled down to their role on the frontier. So I for one have no truck with the buffer theory falling for lack of evidence. Somerset was autocratic and more corrupt than the new South African politicians who, they say, succumb to the old South African financiers.

Sir Nick protests. Perking up, he straightens his back indignantly. He won't have such slander. He had not lived through the centuries without influence, without meeting people of stature. And indeed he had come across Lord Somerset, an imposing figure of a man, a gentleman of the first order, at the grand house of Poulett who for a while, Nick is pleased to report, floated the idea of commissioning a poem about the very house by no less than his own illustrious self. Somerset thought it a first-class plan, but, alas, Poulett cravenly withdrew and what's more, left Nick weary and out of pocket vis-à-vis the travel. So, he'll not tolerate an ill word against Lord Charles. If the Scots were settled on the frontier, they no doubt in ignorance claimed the territory themselves. Or stoically, yes, simply accepted the circumstances they encountered, circumstances which after all were a vast improvement on their miserable lives back home.

Hinza is outraged. You forget that I was raised by Mr P, and I too won't have such slander; I may not have been there, but their lives on the Scottish Borders were certainly not miserable. True, there was no wealth, but they were respectable farmers nonetheless. It is the case that Mr P was given a choice by Sir Rufane Donkin – no friend, incidentally, of Somerset – who promised that the frontier zone would also later be occupied by 500 Highlanders, serving as a local militia, an attractive enough proposition. The Zuurveld, unsuitable as its name suggests, was presented as a beacon of civilisation, with the promise of a church, a magistrate, and a town called New Edinburgh, and so the Scots agreed to settle there rather than nearer the coast with the English. As it happens, New Edinburgh didn't come about. The Scottish ship foundered near the Equator, went up in flames, and Mr P's party found themselves isolated on the Border.

Now we'll have to address the other story, one the settlers chose not to hear, or disregarded: the story of those they replaced on the frontier. The rebel Boers, whose very farms they occupied, could be dismissed for their inhuman treatment of natives, and in the foreshortened British version of history the native people, originally driven off by white expansion, were conveniently forgotten. And remember, your colonial names for native peoples too will have to be replaced.

Sir Nick sighs, presses his palms into his ears and begs for a break. He had hoped to cheer things up by bending events in the direction of Lord Charles; the rough colonial story could do with some uplifting gentility. Now they expect him to summon the energy for stories about displaced savages. No! he lifts his head, explodes, What's with all this talk of black and white? Are you lot not supposed to turn your backs on such racial branding? Is this not meant to be the post-racial era? Typical, the two of you just want to carp, harp on about your own histories, your suffering of which we'll never ever hear the end. Mr P's history, my foot. This is just putting salt on the man's tail; it's an excuse for your endless lamentations, and I for one have had enough.

Old Nick has had too much to drink, and Mary, drained, is happy to call it a day. There's no point in responding to Nick's post-race nonsense, and even Hinza with his talk of sea journeys has no idea of the restraint such talk of the wide salt sea requires of her. How it brings to life her poor old mam, singing sweetly, madly, in a foreign tongue of the salt water and the stench of the ship, before tearing at her clothes, her matted hair, and howling with the cry of the osprey. She will not rise to Sir Nick's bait; besides, what does the pampered old fellow know, other than the salt that cures and heals and preserves? He has, of course, not deigned to read her story of slaving in the salt pans of Turk's Island, of the salt biting like so many fingerlings into her flesh, leaving her with scarred stumps for feet and hands. Oh, she's had enough, and Mary wanders off without a word, so that it is left to Hinza to get Nicholas another wee dram of Highland Park.

Fortunately, as far as Hinza can remember, although he hasn't read it since it was published, and that under Mr P's supervision, there is nothing in *Narrative of a Residence* of the salt pans of Bethelsdorp, for that would certainly have upset Mary, he says.

Nick cackles. The glittering wonder of salt was of course outstripped by the delicious scandals of the London Missionary Station that everyone at home had already heard of. No doubt it was well worth going native for fresh young virgins. Given the success of the old missionaries Van der Kemp and Read with savage wenches, it's small wonder that your poet hotfooted it to Bethelsdorp, wouldn't you say? He certainly makes no mention of the old men converting the lassies to Christianity in order to fuck …

Do stop, that's disgusting. Mr P was not one for gossip, and it was entirely to his credit that he'd done his homework on the mission station and went to pay his respects. Bethelsdorp was bitterly resented by both Boer and Brits precisely because it was a haven for the sorry remnants of Khoesan people who escaped violence on the farms. He would have known of the attempts to shut down the mission station, as well as the assassination attempts on Read and Van der Kemp. He knew of their marriages to Khoesan women, but his sympathy remained with the missionaries who at least protected native people against white violence. And if nowadays we see that they exploited the Khoe, destroyed their culture and colonised their minds, let's remember that the only other position in the colony then was elimination or enslavement of indigenous people. So, far from aligning himself with the ruling class, we have here proof positive: from the very start, Mr P's sympathies were with the oppressed. And not, as our learned historians nowadays say, purely because he was rebuffed by Somerset.

Yeh, yeh, my friend, of course, Nick slurs, holding out his drained glass for another wee dram. Nothing restores like your Scottish eau de vie; makes the salt rise in the blood, and he winks at Hinza. What I meant to say is that the struggle with poetry ... and in between loud hiccupping he disgorges an idea about Sir Walter Scott's Thomas the Rhymer languishing under his thorn tree. Like Lord Orlando all those centuries ago lolling under his own majestic oak, and now your Thomas, versifying under an African tree. How is one supposed to write poetry these days when things are so damned confusing, figures blending into each other, and the trees, ah the trees, the oaks all felled, he all but sobs, so that Hinza reassures him that they'll somehow manage, that a brisk walk on the Green will set all to right.

V

Vytje is back and Nicholas, who has found a new seam to follow, is only too happy to withdraw. The woman insists that she has been cut short, that she has barely begun, and he has no desire to engage with first-hand Africans. Or with women's stories. Hinza and Mary must hear her out. These days black women's stories are all the rage; anything they have to say is legitimate, publishable, he complains.

Mary nods sympathetically, says Nick must be right; why else is there a dearth of books by buckras? White writing is being swamped by these female upstarts.

Hinza doubles up with laughter. Yes, Nick's country has gone to the dogs, so they might as well hear Vytje out, he adds.

Juffrouw Margaret had instructed me not only in fine needlework, but also on fine feeling and good manners. My my, well done Vytje! she exclaimed with pride at my delicate stitching of white daisies on white lawn, her birthday gift for Juffrouw Janet. I had taken a chance, had tested her by insisting that the daisy centres too should be white – why stick to the real world? Surprisingly, she was not angry at my impudence; rather, she tilted her head thoughtfully and nodded, yes, go ahead. A risk it was, but together we admired the finished work, which really was exquisite.

Always remember, Vytje, she said, that you are capable of delicacy also in matters of thought and feeling. Shush! Shush! she had cried, red with distress, when I told her of how Tata had been tied to Baas Cloete's ox wagon, dragged along, and thereafter flogged to within an inch of his life, of how we had to wrap his flayed flesh in buchu leaves for ... Stop right now Vytje, she interrupted, actually raising her voice angrily to drown me out. It is not nice, neither civil nor polite; such ... such things must never, under no circumstances, be spoken of. Her palms, poor woman, were pressed against her delicate ears. Her heart was soft as the silk thread between my fingers.

I don't believe that my earlier account of Hinza will be thought vulgar. I had been taught that nice people do not sympathise with stories of ill-treatment, or even of slights and insults, and I don't mean to complain, but the question of my name is one that I must return to. Besides, such vulgarity is only a problem for white people, whose ears are not in line with real life. Vytje: it is there in black and white in Baas Pringle's poem, in print, and that, incidentally, as far as I can see, is all the dealing I need have with the old pale beast Nicholas Greene who shares with us this pondok of fiction. It is pleasing to be mentioned by Mr Pringle – I will remember not to call him Baas, nor the ladies Nooiens – but it is the case that he took licence with the facts. 'The Emigrant's Cabin', they say, is still read by thousands of schoolchildren, so it is only right that the record be set straight, that readers hear the truth from my own self. For instance, the surname of Vaal that Mr P has dreamed up for me is a piece of nonsense that irks, for how many readers would bother to read his note that declares my real name to be Dragoener? And there lies another story to which I will return. Vaal may well serve a pleasing rhythm, but what a liberty, for who in the world would answer to such a name? Vaal is a *colour* for God's sake, greyish brown, as if there were not enough dull greyness all around the Zuurveld. Since the farm is peopled with native servants, why does my skin colour have a place in this story? Mr P explains in a note that vaal is pale reddish like a faded leaf, which for all his knowledge is simply wrong; besides, I cannot be nut brown and vaal at the same time; I am simply brown like everyone else – we come in all shades of brownness, for even if we are Goniqua, our blood has flown in many directions since the world has been stirred up by the settlers. But I have yet to see a people who are grey.

Our family name was Windvogel, Dutch for the original Khoe word for bird-of-the-wind, and I have no reason to believe that there is anything to be ashamed of in such a name. Rather, I fancy it tells of times when the master hunters, our great-tatas, all but flew through the veld, skimming the ghannabush like birds driven by a powerful wind, not touching ground until they'd pinioned their prey. Windvogel may not be an easy name for a rhyming poem in English, but that is hardly our concern. Why Mr P should say in his note that my name in fact was Dragoener, I have no idea. It is true that Jantje Dragoener too once worked at Eildon, but that poor man was no blood relation of mine. In fact, Jantje was ashamed of his tata, who had been pressed into fighting for the English, given a gun and told to shoot at his own people, and so came to be called Dragoener. Mr P, of course, approved of the dragoons, relied on them for protection against the marauding natives and runaway slaves who stole, or rather laid claim to, the Pringles' livestock. But he also knew that Jantje Dragoener, whom he called a tame Bushman and leader of the banditti raiders, eventually turned against the settlers and was killed by their commandos. It all goes to show that the poem was written long after Mr P had left South Africa, when he had all but forgotten us, had got our families all mixed up, and that is why I am of the opinion that the poem should be burned, notes and all.

Mr P does not explain in his rhymes how I am the one who kept the floors sealed with a weekly smear of mud and cowdung, otherwise they would all have suffocated with dust. Even the oven of which he boasts was fashioned by us. Which is not to say that he is a liar; it is simply the way in which settler folk see and manage the world that they command. True, he had admired the anthill, but would no doubt have stopped at a useless sonnet were it not for our knowledge of outdoor cooking. It was I who hollowed it out and, admittedly with Mr P's help, mainly his voluble enthusiasm, built it up as an oven, with mud-bricks that Tata had baked in the sun so that they soaked up the fire without cracking. And allow me to state here that nothing, or I should say very little, was achieved with Hinza's help. As for the poem about that boy surviving by himself in the veld, well that was a miracle indeed, a story of which I have always been suspicious.

On the question of being called a Nut-Brown Maiden, I have nothing to say, except that at one point Hinza took to capering in a strange, wooden manner, flinging his arms about, lifting his legs and stamping each foot in turn. Then he would twirl stiffly, hilariously, as he sang in a mocking tone:

There blooms my Highland Mary
Like wild rose 'neath the ben.
Ho-ro my nut-brown maiden
Hee-ree my nut-brown maiden
For she's the maid for me.

The other servants would fall about laughing, especially when he condescended to hail me with a Ho-ro or a Hee-ree, but I would not be baited into replying. He was no more than a foolish boy, and could not mean anything by calling me *his* maid, his girl. I understood well enough that the crafty boy had turned the word against me, that with the English word sounding the same, he gave himself licence to call me 'meid', a Boer word for servant girl. It is one thing Baas P calling me meid as white people do (except that having at first adopted the Boer way of speaking, he returned from Cape Town with new ideas of politeness towards natives), but why a foundling boy like Hinza should imagine himself as my baas is beyond me. These Hee-ree Ho-ree words had no doubt migrated from English poems. I could only hope that they would not settle here to belittle us, and make fools of us Khoe women.

When we Windvogels first found our way to Glen-Lynden, Tata thought it bad luck – the white man who flew about with crutches, always in a hurry, even whilst dragging his right leg, but I could hear right away from his speech that the lame man was also a good man. Just a kle'meidjie I was then, but I could tell that his heart was large and open like his hands – unusually large for such a small man, they were. Baas Pringle promised that I, the apple of Tata's eye, would be happy as their housemaid. Imagine then how sad we all were on discovering that Mr P and the ladies would leave the Zuurveld for good. They did not actually speak of the trouble he had run into in town, but it was clear to us that things had changed. Tata said it was not our concern if the white people fought each other, that the rumours about Mr P defending our people in his newspaper was a smoke-screen best dismissed. The Juffrouwens did not always remember that I understood much of the English language I heard daily; sometimes they spoke as if I were not present, or could not make simple inferences. Heitse, it was amusing to think that they believed their plans to be secret, but how we worried about what would become of us, when we had got so used to their kindness.

Mary interrupts to say she believes Mr P to have made that last visit to Glen-Lynden on his own, the ladies having remained in Cape Town; besides, his sister-in-law Janet was by then running her own school for young ladies in the city. Precisely my point, I explain. Having written up his travels and poems well after he'd left, Mr P did not always remember correctly, perhaps was already too ill by the time he got down to writing. As for Juffrouw Janet taking a holiday from school, well, I can't account for that.

For all his claims of not being interested, the nasty Sir Nick has slipped into the room and meddles with his penny's worth. These are digressions that do not concern the project, he says, rolling his right index finger in small circles about his huge hairy ear. So on you go with events in the poem, 'The Emigrant's Cabin'.

As if I don't know the name of a poem in which I'm founded. Mostly inaccurate, I say. For one, it is the case that Mr P's bosom friend Fairbairn, although he had been on a couple of occasions expected at Eildon, never in fact managed to visit, so the entire conversation which is the poem is no more than a made-up story, wishful thinking on the part of Baas P.

And that, Hinza interrupts, is scarcely a problem. Poems are about different kinds of truth, and the poet may choose any device he wishes. A conversation with Lucifer is as valid as one with Fairbairn or with God himself.

I suppose I am ignorant of the business of poetry, but it is, as Sir Thingummy says, important to establish what really happened, for beneath all the fine words lies a kernel of truth, so I am happy to testify. Of course, I know that the poem is meant to be a letter to Fairbairn in which Mr P imagines his friend to be there. So he shows him round, shows him why he emigrated from Scotland, and shows how perfectly civilised their lives are in the Eastern Cape. But it is just as well to get the record straight. On how many occasions did we thrash about, having to scrub and cook in preparation for the man who never arrived? The way our people saw it, that no-show Fairbairn was not a loyal friend or decent person at all –how anxiously Mr P used to wait for his no-show letters as well! He did not deserve to be addressed in the poem. But then, as Hinza says, I was no confidante of the Pringles and do not know enough about the fine art of poetry.

It is Mary this time who interrupts, and who for once comes to my defence. Vytje is right; there's no question that the man was a cad. Let's remember that if it were not for his carelessness, we would not be in this pickle of having to write Mr P's story, of putting him in his rightful place in history. Mrs Pringle, trusting soul that she was, sent Fairbairn all the papers. I was the one who parcelled it up for her, and what I'd like to know is how a grown-up man loses papers entrusted to him. Imagine Mrs P's loss, too: ten love sonnets written for her when Mr P was laid up, thrown off his horse, delirious with pain and buchu brandy, and stuck in Genadendal with nothing better to do. And where are those sonnets now? Lost to the world. Oh, there is no question that Fairbairn was a faithless, treacherous scoundrel who must have been jealous of Mr P's achievements, and did not want him immortalised.

Sir Nicholas says there are other ways of looking at the situation. Firstly, Pringle may have imagined that his feelings for Fairbairn were reciprocated, so sheer insensitivity prevented him from making the obvious inference from his friend's silence. Secondly, only in the colony is Pringle celebrated as a poet, and even there not everyone is convinced of his stature or indeed of his history of humanitarianism. Was he not at the time reviewed in the colony as an ungrateful viper? In which case, a perspicacious Fairbairn may well have realised that a biography could do his friend's reputation no good at all.

Really, the man is impossible. How many times do I have to remind him that South Africa is not a colony? It's a re-pub-lic, governed by Africans, I spell out. Ever heard of Nelson Mandela? And since it's all speculation about Fairbairn, I'll carry on with what actually happened, with my account of the poem in which Mr P chose to call me Vytje Vaal. Remember how it ends with a visit from the abaThembu chief whom he calls Powana? Now I do not remember Chief Bawana and his Lady visiting us at Eildon; I do not think they would have been received; they certainly were not lavishly entertained by the Pringles, as claimed in the poem. It is true that there were rumours on a couple of occasions that the Chief was planning to negotiate with Mr P over disputed land. And yes, it was the herdboy Flink who brought the news of the ambassadors, at which Mr P laughed heartily, not thinking that the abaThembu would have the temerity. But like Fairbairn himself, they never arrived, so one could say that the poem was inspired by the absence of its chief players.

Every time we were expecting Fairbairn, there were feverish preparations: the airing of the best woven mats and animal skins, the cooking of festive foods – although Mr P does so exaggerate the number of dishes, food I have never even heard of, when really we mostly ate mutton and some game with sweet potatoes and wild cabbage. By that stage, Mr P had heeded Tata's warning not to eat the sacred eland.

The first time Mr P shot an eland, Tata took a chance, refusing to skin the animal; he flailed about wildly on the ground as if possessed by its spirit. I had to bite my lip and try not to laugh, but Mr P bowed his head and agreed that he and Hinza would work the carcass, since the animal was already dead. Civil as Mr P had become in his dealings with us at Eildon, he said that they would never again kill eland.

Actually, there was one incident, a small group of abaThembu who stopped by, a few of Bawana's people, but I didn't know the purpose of the visit. I remember sending Flink to fetch Mama, who would have wanted to hear the news from the abaThembu. Although we all understood each other – our blood and languages having been for some time co-mingled – Mama's mother was abaThembu, so she knew the language well, and never tired of talking the talk with those people. Mama loved to tell us stories about her abaThembu family. Actually, I did not think much of those vain people who predicted that their chief would one day rule over vast areas of this land, also over the north from where the mfecane had come raging down. He certainly was the angriest of the Angry Men, who ought to have remembered that we, the Khoekhoe, gave them that name, which they were so proud of. So vain had they become, these aba-Thembu, that they would not acknowledge that we were all men of men, that even the San, who happened to be the real people of the eland, were part of us.

Mama would laugh drily and say that none of the real world mattered any longer, not since the People of Another House arrived from over the seas. When they did not behave like decent guests and tried to turn us into slaves, we renamed them Pale Beasts, for that is what they earned with their firing of guns.

Mama treasured all the old stories. As for me – well, they no longer held water; those stories were of another time, and it was clear that

the new time of writing had come, the time of the People of Another House who ruled the roost. That is what I still called our Pringles, who had not become Beasts like the rest of them. Mama said,
Just give them time, and mark my words: if they keep living here and
carry on slaughtering animals for meat alone, they'll turn into Pale
Beasts. She had come across many who, fresh off the ocean, behaved
half decently, but soon turned into cruel savages in the sun. So perhaps it was a good thing, for the Pringles at least, that they left, that
from across the water they could see things more clearly, keep their
hands and their minds clean and keep the settlers back home in
check. Juffrouw Margaret assured us that they would fight for our
rights on the other side of the ocean, that they would return trium-
phant, but sadly that was not to be.

The abaThembu told Mama of the latest white incursions into
their land – Beasts of Prey, they said, that's what the people from over
the seas had now become in the hot sun. Not here at Eildon, I said,
impatient with the proliferation of names. The abaThembu had made
themselves at home without as much as a by your leave, squatting in
the cooking shelter where they ate and drank too much, cackled and
sneered, and called us slaves. One of them said that we were fooled
by the Englishman into thinking so well of ourselves – the people
who had enough to eat – that soon we would wake up and find ourselves transformed. We would be the creatures they had turned us
into. He spat out the word: *slaves*. That is the dolos that the Pale
Beasts throw: they cast their bones to name you Not Slaves, and you,
more fools, believe that the ancestors have spoken. Impostors, with
their guns and their magic, he raged. And all that talk whilst they
were gorging on our vetkoek and sosaties and honey beer that Mama
provided, licking their lips and patting their taut bellies. For us, they
proudly handed round cured strips of kudu meat, as if they had not
learned these very skills from us, the Khoekhoe. Oh no, all that had
been long forgotten now that they too lorded it over us, even if they
clicked away with the borrowings from our tongue.

All hell broke loose as Baas P arrived on his horse from the border, where there had been yet another raid of sheep. He cracked his whip and without dismounting spoke briskly: that he had nothing to say to them, that he wanted them off his land. He ordered Flink to fetch tin mugs and a bucket of water for the visitors to refresh themselves, but thereafter they had to leave. Which they did, but at their leisure, whilst the horse stamped about and Baas P cracked his whip impatiently. The last to gather her karos and leave was a stick-thin woman who drew herself slowly up to her full height and looked Mr P in the eye, gesticulating fearlessly and speaking angrily in her own tongue about their right to the land. She promised that her chief Bawana would himself be coming soon to show him what's what, none of which Mr P understood, but he did not deign to ask us for a translation. If she most definitely was not the jolly and gay Queen Moya that he invented in the poem, she certainly wore her rich beads with pride and arrogance, and held her haughty head high.

When they left, I said to Hinza that I did not trust these kaffirs, that I found their manners crass and uncivilised. Little did I suspect that he would tell tales. To my shame, Mr P later upbraided me, said that I was wrong to call them by the rude name of kaffir, and that all people have their own civilisations, which I concede is the correct way to look at world.

Let us not these simple folk despise / Just such our *sires appeared in Caesar's eye*, he intoned. Thus I'm not surprised that Mr P took the opportunity to use those previously honed words in the poem. Many a story we'd heard about Mr P's own country being invaded by Romans so many, many years ago, Romans who looked down upon his ancestors. He says it's called history, and that everybody has done it, this history thing, invading other people's countries and spitting contempt at the conquered. I ventured to say that that was exactly what I had in mind about the abaThembu, although I didn't mention their name-calling. Would the Khoekhoe's time for taking over and looking down upon others also come, I wondered to myself. Having observed my masters at close quarters, I did not think it so desirable, and hoped that we would guard against being bullies.

Mr P shook his head thoughtfully. The Roman story, he must have realised, was just a way of excusing his people for having taken over the Zuurveld that not so long ago belonged to the San, then the amaXhosa, and then was taken by the Boers, before the Amanglezi came along to bully the Boers and lord it over all of us. But it did seem as if Mr P was growing more and more troubled by this making of history from which he could not extricate himself. And I felt sorry for the helplessness of this white man who found himself in such a pickle, such a tangle of beliefs. I don't know if Hinza had any idea what the man was going through. But Mr P was clever and no doubt came to see that if he arrived in Africa with certainties, the new mix-up was no bad thing. That was no doubt why he rattled on like a child about drawing up grants of land for some of our respectable families at Eildon – but, as Tata said, Mr P did not have the government on his side, thus it was the idle talk of one who felt guilt about occupying our native land. It was only when Dr Philip's Ordinance 50 finally gave us the freedom to own land at the Kat River, some three years after the Pringles had left, that we happily removed to that settlement and set about working for ourselves.

The Scots settlers at Glen-Lynden were not happy about losing their workers to the Kat River, and I wondered how Mr P would have felt, had he still been there, given how reliant he was on us. Things were so very different in those days, and I for one would not like to be judged by the fact that we cared not one bit about the government having taken the Kat River land from the amaXhosa, or 'kaffirs' as many of our people had now learned to call the unconverted, for at the mission station we were all Christian. The amaXhosa, of course, fought back, and at first our people readily took muskets from the Colonial Office to defend the land that so conveniently buffered the white people. Mama said that Mr P had foreseen it all, that the name of Dragoener he had given me in the poem turned out to be prophetic.

At the Kat River, we finally came across Mr P's so-called friend, Fairbairn, who by now had married into the missionary family. A distant, puffed up, arrogant man who particularly disliked the ama-Xhosa, not least because they would have nothing to do with the Christians, whom they called Beasts of Prey. Frankly, none of us took to him, and how right we were, for it was not much later that I came across his ideas about how the colony ought to encourage civilisation because it is more profitable to have friendly native customers than to kill or enslave us. That, then, was the function of Christianity, to profit from our land. Certainly it helped us Kat River people to understand that the colony was and had always been the enemy, even if the missionaries had brought education and relief from slavery, and so we later joined forces with the amaXhosa in the bloodiest Frontier Wars against the colonists. Oh, then we too became irredeemable savages to the likes of Fairbairn, of no use to the colony after all, and that brought an end to the Kat River idyll. Just as well Mr P died and was spared the confusion and terror of those days.

It was after the abaThembu visit to Eildon, when I was hunkering down by the dry stream to scour soot off the pots with coarse sand, that I heard Hinza question Mr P about the Scots and the English. Why, he wanted to know, did the settlers call themselves English? Mr P disagreed, Oh no, they were all proud to be Scots, but Hinza corrected him. He was right to do so: I too had heard Mr P call himself Amanglezi.

It was just a matter of their common language, he said, a way of differentiating themselves from the Boers. Besides, he explained, Scotland had united with England into Britain, which was the greatest country of all, a nation at the very head of history. But Mr P was no doubt confused about Britain, for on his return from Cape Town he declared himself a full-blooded Scot, an altogether separate nation who were not oppressors or prone to prejudice like the English ruling class. I had to stop myself from laughing out loud. Did he really have no idea how other members of his party treated their servants? Or what they said about us in our very presence?

As I later said to Hinza, either the Scots people are all mixed up in their minds, or perhaps there is no difference at all, perhaps Scotland and England are one and the same place, all parcelled up into each other. But my opinion has never counted for anything. Hinza laughed his ho-ro, hee-ree laugh, and said that I knew nothing of geography, of the big, wide world and the ways in which it is carved up. There's the great river Tweed separating the two countries, and even a Roman wall, he explained, more or less right across. People will ever think of building walls, and I wondered if the abaThembu had thought of that. Their idle, round-bellied men could've been usefully employed building a good dry-stone wall to keep the Beasts of Prey out. But, of course, they wouldn't have wanted to be contained behind a wall, not when they planned to eventually drive the Pale Beasts into the sea.

I would dearly like to report that Mr Pringle was ever truthful, but poetry is a beast of another kind, and I fear that we cannot bank on finding truth in the poems. It is as if poems are meant to bamboozle, but I can tell the difference between the real things that happened and those which did not. If Chief Bawana's portrait was based on the visit of his ambassadors, then 'His Maker's image radiant in his face' is a line, which for all its loveliness, stretches the truth, for the men were anything but comely. And if the tall woman brought beauty to her speech, she was nothing but a bag of bones, which showed that the abaThembu were sorely deprived of victuals. But for that matter, neither was Mr Pringle a man of beauty, although he was comelier than the Englishmen, who have huge noses and ears. Hinza said it's because they are Scots, altogether smaller, neater people with nicer noses. Such casting is all confusion, all nonsense, for other members of their party of settlers match neither Mr P's manners nor his neat features.

So much for men and their poetry. I am glad that we were not called upon to confect poems. The ladies were much more sensible and did not bother themselves with verse. Of an afternoon they would get out their sketchbooks and with pencil or ink draw the world around them. Juffrouw Brown was especially accomplished in her rendering of hills and crags and even the shape-shifting clouds that occasionally drifted across the sky. Before they left, I took them to the krans to see the old San drawings in the cave. The ladies were thoroughly exhausted and parched by the climb. If only there were water, they complained, and chastised themselves for not having brought along something to quench their thirst. Which is to say that I would have had to carry the canvas bag of water. I tried to cheer them up by pointing out that Miss Brown's pictures were better likenesses than the rock paintings. And very nice too to see that lady's face crease into an indulgent smile. Thus must we carry on fooling one another, I thought. There was, it would seem, no other way.

After Mr P's return from Cape Town, when all was packed, the freshly baked bread, biltong and dried fruit, the Juffrouwens helped up on to the boxed seat of the cart, and the horses tossing their heads impatiently, I howled and tore off my doek, waving it with sorrow. Little did I know that a life of knowledge and learning and freedom awaited me at the Kat River, even if that did not last. Could not last, given the settlers' greed for land.

Hinza shouted, Goodbye Miss Turksvy! See you in another country, another century.

What a seer you were, hey Hinza?

I am pleased to see that Hinza is much improved in body and mind. Quite transformed he is, stretched out, elongated like a !Xung rockfigure – the strange English diet, I imagine. In the olden days, believing him to be Motswana, I'd have sworn that he would take on the taut round belly of a braggart. But no, he strolls about quite the dandy in a Panama hat with a drawl to match, tall like the amaXhosa, and always accompanied by that impertinent woman, Mary Prince, who is as brisk as he is measured. Ga! She can't speak a word of our language, so I have to struggle with hers, and what a peculiar, indecipherable kind of English it is.

Mary asks if I knew Kaatje Kekkelbek at the Kat River. It seems she has some score to settle with Kaatje who has, of course, already departed from this world after her fleeting appearance on the stage, something that Mary has difficulty in understanding, as if she expects everyone to live forever. I do wish she would give up talking with her hands on her hips – that is exactly the stance that young Kaatje so readily adopted. Prince sneers and swears she'll root Kaatje out, even while I assure her that the woman is dead from the devilish drink, the witblits that white people paid as wages once labour was no longer meant to be free. She lies buried with not so much as an aloe or a kanniedood to decorate the grave, though if I were the missionary Dr Philip, I would not have allowed the treacherous meid in my churchyard at all. Not after her performance that harmed their struggle to free the Khoesan and mixed-race peoples. Being illiterate, Kaatje may not have known that her author, Geddes Bain, had dedicated the scandalous doggerel to Dr Philip, and may not have understood the mockery; nevertheless, it was foolish of her to throw in her lot with Bain and his bigoted Pale Beast comrades, and perform the horrible piece on stage. All for no more than a bottle of Witblits.

Hinza says that we are mistaken, that Kaatje is a character imagined by Andrew Geddes Bain and not a real person at all. He believes that it was a white man who played the part. But what does he know about the shows that were actually performed in Grahamstown, where at times, at least when she was sober enough, Kaatje played herself and shook her own behind at the white audiences? True to her name, Kaatje was a veritable kekkelbek, a gossip, a cackler, a yackety-yack in cahoots with her paymaster – the despicable Bain – really no more than his creature, whom he kept pickled in cheap brandy. I hate to think what he promised her, but it must have been pretty irresistible, more than drink, to allow herself and all our people to be so lampooned by him. Luckily for her, her behind was not as splendid as she thought it to be, otherwise she too would have found herself on the stage in Europe.

All the hard-working, sober people of the Kat River knew that Bain and his band, angry about the rights for native people that Dr Philip – with the help of Mr P's campaigning in London – had secured, would tell any lie to discredit us. I have no doubt that he did not even fulfil his promise to Kaatje, which would explain why she gave up the ghost, for how else could she have lived with herself, having betrayed the philanthropists who had secured the land for us and protected our people from the tyranny of colonists? After Bain, I imagine Mr P would have had to revise his view of the Scots as a decent, egalitarian people, but then having to change his mind was what that poor man was all about. Barely would his feet touch new ground than he had to somersault once again as new horrors on the part of the Pale Beasts assaulted his ears.

It is one thing calling people names out loud, nicknames, but why did Kaatje allow herself to be called Kekkelbek in writing? How could she have been proud of being likened to a hen who cackles and proudly announces to the world that she's laid an egg? Now there's a stupid boast: where are the hens that do not lay eggs? Misled she was, by Bain. Of course his bigoted doggerel had nothing in common with Mr Pringle's poetry, flawed as the fine people nowadays may find it to be, but that stupid Kaatje had no way of telling. Some said that she may have been sick of her baptised name of Kaatje Geduld, and so happily took on the name Bain gave her, and there could be something in that. Many a Khoe name was seen not to suit the fussy Christian God, but how could her ancestor have allowed the settlers to call him 'Geduld'? Even the fancy English version, 'Patience', would make anyone vomit. Patience requires of a person the stillness of a statue, such effort in doing nothing while she waits for something that will never happen of its own accord, that it must drive any sensible person crazy. It can only speak of the wishes of a Christian immigrant who relies on the patience of a pining slave.

Mary says the name is no excuse. Still smarting, she is incensed. Kaatje has to be taught a lesson; she must be knocked down for mimicking Mary in her infamous show. Not that she, Mary, had ever been so vulgar as to lift her skirts and wiggle her posterior at anyone, she declares.

Upon which I correct her: there is no call for exaggeration. At the end of her show, there was no question of flesh on display – Kaatjie simply turned her back on her audience and twitched each fully clothed buttock, up and down in turn, a trick unknown to white people. Bain's point was to make fun of Khoekhoe women, whose bottoms were meant to indicate that they were dissolute, lazy, and immoral – as in the case of Saartjie Baartman, who came a cropper in London and Paris.

Instead of soothing Mary or talking sense into her, Hinza struts up and down, twirling the old man's cane, and starts declaiming in a high-pitched voice:

My name is Kaatjie Kekkelbek
I come from Katrivier
Daar is van water geen gebrek
But scarce of wine and beer
Myn ABC *at Philip's school*
I learned a kleine beetje
But left it just as great a fool
As gekke Tante Mietje.

At least, says Mary pursing her lips, I have never spoken in crazy pidgin Dutch.

No, sighs Hinza, but it was not actually about you, Mary. The show was designed by Geddes Bain to make fun of the anti-slavery movement, of missionaries and Mr P, whom they believed to be misguided in their defence of native peoples. We've been through this before: everyone knew from your court case, Mary, that you had lied about the Pig, so the Kekkelbek ballad and performance were used by Bain to show that the campaign for rights was fuelled by liars and bamboozlers, and that Khoesan people could not be cured of drunkenness and debauchery.

It is only fair that I should come to Mary's defence. I lived at the Kat River from the start, and I know how our place was hated by the white people, and not only by the Boers, as so many Amanglezi claimed. The English and Scots settlers too objected to fertile land being given to us. Nothing will come of it, they predicted. They would

181

have used anything to prove that the missionaries' education was wasted on us, that we were incapable of learning anything, except to hone our native skills of stealing and cheating and drinking. No one spoke of how successful and self-sufficient the settlement was, how hard we worked on the land that was our own. We had our own school and council; and I, for instance, had become a teacher, paid by our people themselves. So thrilled were we at first to escape serfdom and slavery that we didn't realise that our settlement, too, was designed as a buffer zone between the expelled amaXhosa and the settlers. Only later, when things became clear, did we join forces with the amaXhosa in the Frontier Wars. So really, even Kaatje could be excused, exploited as she was by colonists. Although she had no business mocking Ta' Mietjie; that poor old woman lost her marbles years before, when her children were shot for sport.

Mary thanked me most graciously and conceded that there was no point in pursuing old Kaatje, who as I said had snuffed it more than a century ago.

I am sorry to harp on about poetry, of which I freely admit my ignorance, but how do you explain the fact, I ask Hinza, that so many clever types, the so-called 'expert readers', misled people for so long about Geddes Bain's nonsensical rhyme? Oh yes, he was claimed as a well-meaning liberal who gave the spirited and humorous black woman her own voice. Many critics praised Kaatjie as an independent spirit who defied the strait-laced missionaries.

Hinza agrees that I have a point. But we shouldn't be surprised, he says. Expert readers the world over read only in the interests of their own groups; that has been and will always be part of their expertise.

I am pleased to say that this new Hinza is altogether a finer, a more sensible person than the snooty boy I knew so long ago at Eildon.

After several days of avoiding us, Nick turns up in high spirits. He has done some fruitful homework, tracking down letters written by Mr P to John Fairbairn – something that had never occurred to me,

Hinza, possibly because the friendship with Fairbairn had always seemed distinctly one sided. Heartbreaking it was here in London, watching Mr P pace up and down, wondering why the bosom friend yet again had not got round to replying to his urgent enquiries about frontier matters, and attributing his silence to the unreliable mail boats. Thus I had not imagined Fairbairn to have valued or kept any communication from Mr P. He had after all lost all the original documents that Ma'am had sent him after Mr P's death, and that negligence hastened Ma'am to her grave; she thought herself to have failed by letting the papers out of her hands. Little wonder that I did not expect to learn anything from that gentleman's archive.

Nick is as pleased as punch with his success, especially since his information focuses primarily on me. 'The Bechuana Boy', it turns out, had been adapted for common readers; the simple story was meant to move such undeveloped minds to sympathy for my plight, that is to say the plight of the Batswana, persecuted as they were by Griquas, or Bergenaars, or Bastaards as they were more often called. Mary, who turns out to be more literate than I thought, has immersed herself in the frontier histories that the helpful librarian ordered for me.

She'd be the last person to criticise Mr P, but should he not have concerned himself, she asks, with the colonists waging continuous war against indigenous people rather than with natives persecuting one another? The Bastaards were after all a minor issue in the larger picture of bloodshed at the frontier, where gun-wielding settlers drove indigenous people from the land and then claimed it for themselves.

I suggest that we should follow Mr P's example and refuse to use the despicable name of 'Bastaards'. Mary says yes, it can't be nice to be known by such a name, but the shame of it lies squarely with the Europeans, who so distanced themselves from the people they coupled with that they named their own offspring bastards.

Nick nods impatiently. High-minded of you lot, he says, but do you want to hear this or not? What do you make of the fact that

Pringle did not want to be known as the author of the 'Bechuana Boy' poem? He actually says that he hopes people will think it written by Dr Philip. Intriguing, eh? How rich: the man who would not countenance the name 'Bastaard' fathers the 'Bechuana Boy' and then denies his fatherhood. Abandons his 'Bechuana Boy' to a missionary and bastardy. And what does it tell us about the man's professionalism? Old do-gooder Dr Philip – who, incidentally, was no doctor at all, my investigation reveals; your missionaries were not the most trustworthy folk – godly Philip was hardly known for his versification, so did your man believe any old Christian could knock off a poem?

If Nick thinks that I'd wince at these blows, he is mistaken; besides, how trustworthy is he? And what do I care about the missionaries of yore? I lift my chin in preparation for the next barb and look him coolly in the eye.

So, my dear fellow, he continues, it would seem that your origin myth, your story, and I emphasise *story*, was conceived as an object lesson. Your history was shaped for didactic purposes, a homily, in Pringle's own words, for rough folk, women and children. And therefore, I would venture, untrustworthy as a document of your origins. No doubt your poet was following the fashion set by the misguided Messrs Wordsworth and Coleridge, who composed ballads about down-and-outs that no gentleman could possibly read, as I explained at the time to that pious William – another one, by the way, to father a bastard …

Perhaps women saw the sense in such ballads, Mary interrupts, but I shush her. The blood has rushed to my head. My heart pounds. I must stay calm. I must remain sitting, and to that purpose grip the sides of my chair.

We--ll, I'm glad, so very glad, I say slowly, to have been of service. If your not-so-gentle folk were in need of civilisation, of homilies, then I am happy that my story did the trick, that it was of help, and that I relieved the true-blue gentlefolk of that burden.

I can take no more of this, and leaping up I all but shout, Please excuse me, I have an appointment – and surprise myself by trying to snatch Nick's notebook out of his hands. I rush out into the night, ignoring the old man's indignant Whoaa! as I keep running, my ancient heart swollen and drumming against my ribcage. I keep running, I don't know for how long, until I find myself at the Embankment, and exhausted, sit down on a low concrete wall.

A dark shape behind me, on the other side of the wall, stirs and only then do I register a strong smell of urine. A phlegmy throat is cleared and a raspy cough escapes as a man tries to sit up. Like a mummy, he is neatly, too tightly perhaps, parcelled up in what looks like bands of polythene against the cold, presumably by someone else, so that he struggles to bend and balance on his behind. Spare change mate, he rattles through the phlegm, before turning his head away to spit.

A demon inside me explodes, atomises into anger so that I have to sit on my balled fists. I'd thank you to ask nicely; can't you say please? There's no excuse for impoliteness, even …

You're so right, the man interrupts mockingly, I do apologise. Then he fires off: Look, why don't you fuck off mate? Who do you think you are? There's every fucking excuse, you little toffee-nosed arsehole. My name's not Lucky, and manners are the last thing on my mind, encumbered as it is with wondering how to get out of these feathery bedclothes to biff you one on the fucking nose. There's no excuse for impoliteness? he mocks in a voice that's nothing like mine, and twitching his torso once again to get some leverage, he rasps, Allow me to give you an excuse … But he loses his balance and topples over, the parcelled legs at a precarious angle.

Okay, I say, drawing my legs over the wall to help him up, I am an arse and I'm sorry. Dunno what came over me.

But he beats off my hands. Gerroff, he rattles, rolling over on to his front with a muffled Don't-touch-me.

Here, I say, rifling through my wallet for a small note, here's a fiver, and try to hand it to him, but he turns his head. Fuck off, off you go, I want nothing from you. I tuck the note under his shoulder, and he shouts after me bitterly, So now you can feel better about yourself, nig-nog? Off you go then, see who else you can take advantage of.

Shall I retrieve the fiver, then get my hands around his filthy neck and squeeze the life out of him? Would that not make me feel better? Jesus, what a thought. What a night. I run and run, making no attempt to check my bearings, until the light drizzle turns into hard rain and I am driven into an underground station and somehow make my way home. Pray God that Mary leave me alone. I slam my door shut, strip hastily, wet clothes scattered on the floor, and scramble into bed.

Much of the next day is taken up staring at a beautifully stretched blank canvas. I potter about, stretch and prime another canvas, clean brushes, tidy the space. I have no idea what to do with the canvasses; in fact, I cannot imagine these rectangles looking any better than in their current pristine state. I drag a rickety bentwood chair out onto the little patio that leads from the studio door. I do feel guilty about this space being exclusively for my use: Mary does not come upstairs to my studio, that is the rule. My eyes follow the deep cracks in the concrete floor, the highways where ants scurry in pursuit of their invisible quarry. The summer sky is grey as usual. Soon it will rain. My agitated mind whirls around Nick's revelation, will not let go. I come to a decision: I need to hear the whole of Mr P's letter; fragments cannot carry the full story. Besides, Nick is known for his malicious half-truths.

It is early evening by the time I go out in search of Nick and indeed find him at The Turk's Head. The old fool has not photocopied the letter; no, he hadn't thought or known of that. Instead, he copied out the relevant passage in fine, if somewhat shaky, copperplate. No snatching, you need only ask, he says prissily, taking a sheet of paper from his pocket.

I can no longer look to context for an amended meaning. There can be no sugaring the pill, as Mr P plainly states that he turned my history into a nursery rhyme for educating what he calls 'rough folk', for the benefit of very common readers such as women, children, counting-house clerks, country functionaries, aides-de-camp etc. I should hold my sides with laughter at the idea of such a motley collection of people – who knows what comprises the etceteras – eagerly sitting in a row, tracing with their fingers and spelling out loud the lines of improving rhymes.

Instead I'm overcome with weariness, saddened by my own folly. The moment of meeting ('the mode of my falling in with him') that I had so meticulously gone over, over and over again, is in Mr P's own words 'pure fiction' – and on my part, shockingly, a false memory induced by the poem. Can I trust nothing that I remember? Why can I not recollect the actual meeting? Or should I say, how Mr P actually acquired me? There is also the new question of why Mr P later, having got to know me (even loved me, for that I surely remember correctly), should have devised such an improbable scene, used such improbable words. And what are the 'several reasons' he mentions to Fairbairn for not wanting the poem to be traced to him? Why could he not give these reasons? Is it not cowardly to hope that readers would attribute the poem to Dr Philip, whom he presumes to be immune to criticism? Mr P says that it wouldn't matter, since the missionary 'has a broad back'.

Then it strikes me. Perhaps the very aspects I find problematic in the poem are included precisely because they are objectionable, a ruse to prevent the authorship from being traced to Mr P. This I explain to Sir Nicholas, who stares at me in disbelief.

Right, he says briskly, let's hear these objections, and consider them in turn.

I start with the fact that Mr P knew only too well how I suffered under bondage to Baas Karel, and yet according to the poet I have no thoughts of escape and freeing myself until the Baas takes away my pet springbok. Only at this point, finding the loss of the animal unbearable, I steal back my pet and escape into the veld. This misguided sentimentality shows a failure to understand the human desire to be free, shows a flawed notion of slavery. But see, it's encoded in the poem where I address Mr P:

Oh, Englishman! thou ne'er canst know
The injured bondsman's bitter woe.

So the poet is being ironic. All and sundry know of Pringle's exposition of slavery, hence the poem could easily be attributed to someone else. Oh yes, Mr P is redeemed.

Nick rises, Enough, we need more drink to wash this down. At least you need no longer puzzle over the springbok. All fabricated for purely poetic reasons.

I down a pint of Guinness rather too fast. Surely Mr P could have told me himself. Why did he persist in the fiction, as if I were incapable of understanding anything other than a nursery rhyme? Nick reminds me that I was a child, and then from an inner pocket he draws another sheet of paper and reads out:

So much for poor Hinza Marossi. He was altogether a most interesting child.

Words from the horse's mouth, he says.

I have been too hasty in redeeming Mr P. Nick had planned to withhold this second page of notes, but now explains that he does not after all want to see me deluded.

... a most interesting child: so ends Mr P's letter about me to Leith Ritchie, a gentleman writer who had read the poem. He may not qualify as the 'etcetera' cited earlier to Fairbairn, but the story had indeed made him weep.

Not exactly a reliable test for good poetry, Nick mutters.

I look up at his lowered head, note that his eyes are clouded with a disconcerting sympathy, and quickly look away. It is to Ritchie that Mr P confesses his poetical aims for condensation and simplicity of expression, tried out in the poem about me where the facts of our meeting are sacrificed to this loftier demand. Simplicity of expression is indeed laudable, I say, and Nick adds, And not as easy as people might think. But I have my doubts about the value of condensation. What purpose could that serve other than for the famous *Reader's Digest* series?

I must try not to think of the concluding words about me, *poor Hinza Marossi*, so devoid of regard, of love. One cannot absolutely rule out the possibility that Mr P may have known something about Ritchie that dictated so detached a tone, I opine.

Really? Nick looks up sharply. You've had a rough time, lad. How about giving this a rest for now, get yourself a good night's sleep.

Can it be that a note of kindness has crept into the old man's tone?

I remember my childish love of curved letters, of the shelter I believed them to offer. Nowadays I prefer to write my name in the straight lines of the upper case. I use a ruler and set square to lightly draw the lines of my name just below the centre of the primed blank canvas, then quickly score the letters HINZA with a razor-sharp Stanley knife. I watch the sagging of the taut, pristine surface and wait for a while, for I know not what. A layer of paint, I decide, will hold the cut-outs more rigidly. There is nothing more to be done, or for that matter to be undone. It is not a pleasing sight. I turn the canvas over: gobbledygook. Then hold it upside down so that at least the first two letters remain sound.

Hinza may not be my name. Having been cut adrift by the mfecane, having seen my people slaughtered, having been captured and sold into white service, I chose, when the chance to escape came, to live, to be made anew. A new name: Hinza. How true is that? I have an idea that when I first met the white man, I was indeed of foot unshod and naked limb, as the poem says. I also have an idea of having been out of breath, as if I had run across the veld. But that is not in the poem. What could I have been running from? A man waiting on a horse?

Hintsa, the name of a Xhosa chief – or Hinza, as Mr P taught me to write it – was as good as any for a boy clad in plaid trews and buttoned shirt. We had long discussions of what it means to be civilised, and Mr P agreed that trews and shirt and shoes were more suitable for the colder climes. But, he said, it would not do to be naked, now that things had changed. I understood that he could not say, Now that the white people have taken over the land. Poor man, he was horribly torn between acknowledging the rights of the people whose land it originally was, and condemning the San who stole our live-stock, and whom he therefore had no qualms about shooting. He was at pains to explain that he respected African dress, that there was no call for despising people who were different, but conquest, as history showed, was inevitable. Even England was conquered by Caesar …

I refused the discomfort of shoes, or rather, I begged to be ex-cused, and when I was alone in the veld, or at least not within Ma'am's vision, I tied the shirt round my waist and felt the caress of sunlight, of air, on my chest and back. Why the Christian God should so fa-vour unsuitable clothing and take against bare feet was puzzling, but I believed that in time I'd get round Ma'am. The Khoekhoe servants did not wear shirts, but my different position in the household, she said, had to be marked by this dress. Surely there had to be another way of showing my difference?

With foot unshod and naked limb – for sure. But what I do not un-derstand is the unlikely words attributed to me in the poem. Bold as it may seem, I may well have said that I would go with the white man; no doubt I was emboldened by my escape. Or it may have been a reply to the question I read in his eyes: Will you come with me? But how in heaven's name could I have said, *Then let me serve thee, as thy own*? Being a servant, a slave – for that is what I must have learned to be at Weltevreden – was precisely what I had run away from. Even allowing for the words to be shaped into another language, Mr Pringle surely knew that I could never have uttered such words, would not have offered myself as a chattel to be owned by him.

Having churned these thoughts, I conclude that the discrepancy lies with the interference of Coleridge, a man much given to ro-mance and fantasy, and what's more, one too fond of drugs, as every-one knows. Taken as he was with Mr P's 'Afar in the Desert', he saw fit to offer advice and suggest revisions, and that as a man who knew nothing of the veld, for whom travel was a question of boarding a coach, or later taking a fashionable train ride, but mainly following on foot his friend William, climbing the green hills of their small island. What does the romantic, so trusting of his own invention, know of the wider world and its peoples? Of relations between different nations? Of the complexities of slavery? Nothing, I fear, except what he reads in books confected by other romantics. And since we know for sure that Coleridge has put in his oar with other poems, I see his interference as the only explanation for my amended words in 'The Bechuana Boy'. We will surely find such a letter to confirm my hunch.

This at least is beyond doubt, for my memory of the time after my arrival at Glen-Lynden is unsullied. On the last visit to Eildon, just before we were to leave for England, we sat in the cool evening under the wheeling stars, the moving constellations for which Mr Pringle had strangely unsuitable names. Thought, he said, was to be prized above any other faculty, but being thoughtful does not mean that you know everything. What we know and believe are like the stars in motion, and we must never rest in the belief that we know once and for all. I raised my head, having leaned against the comfort of Ma'am's bony knee. But, I protested, he knew so much, so many things that surely are good and right and fixed.

My dear Hinza, he said, before I came to this land of yours I thought I knew an awful lot about it – I had read the travels of Burchell and John Campbell; but it turns out that I was mostly wrong. You see, there are things I had not considered, things I knew nothing of until I saw for myself and took the time to mull them over; for instance, the difference between servitude and slavery, or the fact that we Europeans, decent Christians, are necessarily dehumanised by slavery. For all our belief in enlightenment, for all the thinking and talking with men greater than myself in the city of learning and cultivation, the beautiful city of Edinburgh, I do not recollect such matters being raised or having crossed our minds. It is only by being here and seeing so many new and different peoples that I came to realise how brand-new ethical demands are made on us. And we cannot blame the powers that be for realising that domination is a burden that corrupts. Without having come here, having seen this with my own eyes, I too would have dwelled in European darkness. The sad truth, my boy, is that if we remain here, as we must, for evangelism too has its demands – and there is the conundrum – we cannot ignore the rights of people whose land ... who were here before us ...

How imperfect the idea of love is in the places of cultivation, Ma'am interjected. For all the hardships here, Africa brings the richness of posing new problems and therefore of new thinking.

It was on the tip of my tongue to say that it has not brought new thinking to Baas Karel and his people at Weltevreden, but that would have been churlish. And Ma'am, with no other defence, would have had to resort to Jesus. For whom, under that lovely star-studded sky, I did not always have the stomach. No doubt I would get round in time to adoring Him, as the lovely hymn bids us do.

The sky pulsed with sparkling clusters, the large full moon a portentous red, the Milky Way an arc of brightness, and across the drift the Khoekhoe celebrated with loud crowing and whooping that Ma'am tried to erase by making me recite the names of constellations: the Southern Cross, Sagittarius, Scorpio, Libra – stars, she said, that have whirled themselves into new places on this side of the world. Which explained why the constellations looked nothing like their names, and that was a lesson I have ever found useful: not to trust appearances, since almost everything turns out to be a man-made construct and needs to be turned upside down. Such insights under the stars were, of course, not available for the likes of Coleridge in his parish, and more's the pity. As for his interference: I rest my case.

I was small, but not as young as they thought. I reckon to have been about ten years old when I arrived, rather than seven, as Mr P told people. The Pringles did not agree, in spite of what I said. Ma'am taught me a childish rhyme about a girl called Mary who had a little lamb that was sure to follow wherever Mary went. I think that Mr

Pringle had Mary in mind when he wrote of the tame springbokkie that followed me. How laughable the idea of me as a pinafored white girl with her pet, when in fact I had already stalked many a springbok, shot clean through their heads with my bow and arrow. Why superimpose such an image on a boy of the veld?

I had also been taught 'Humpty Dumpty sat on a wall', a rhyme that made perfect sense to me, although there was nothing at all desirable about putting Humpty together again, and I did not know why Ma'am should hold such faith in the king's horses and the king's men. After a great fall, there is no virtue in being restored to an old self, and besides, no one else can do it for you. After a fall it is a brand-new person who rises from the broken pieces. Ma'am spoke of God's Garden of Eden and the great Fall from which we will never recover. I looked into her sad eyes and nodded in agreement and sympathy; it would not do to suggest that it might be more interesting to roam freely, to have left the confines of the garden.

The Pringles, I think, believed me to be younger in order to avoid a discussion about initiation. It was Plaatje the mulatto boy who teased me about the bush. I would never go to the bush, which meant that I would never grow up, he said. Living with the Pringles would turn me into a savage, a baboon, because they knew nothing of initiation.

I asked Ma'am about the bush, but she affected such alarm, that I knew I had said something profane. Her voice was pained. My dear boy, she said, drawing me close, her hand gripping my shoulder, we do not approve of heathen practices; you'll have to abandon all thoughts of the terrible bush. You are my son and must be christened in the name of God and his beloved son Jesus Christ. That will be your initiation into everlasting life.

That was the first time she said it: *You are my son*. Really she meant, *my beloved son*. And my heart flooded with love, warm and red as the gushing blood from a sheep, slaughtered and finally at peace. Hush now, Ma'am said, not another word about initiation in the bush.

Only much later did I think of the adventures that the Khoe boys speculated about, a party of boys-becoming-men from which I was forever excluded. I promised myself that christening too would be an adventure.

The next time, months later in Edinburgh, the words came differently, hissed from behind a closed door: *He is my son.* Her voice was raised in anger, and her hurt rushed into mine as I tiptoed away.

I am ungrateful, and worse, I know myself to be so. Instead of loving these good people without question, my rebellious heart twists and turns viciously, demanding and demanding answers, explanations.

I have now read the letter to Sir Richard Plasket, dated 14 March 1826, in which Mr P asks permission to take me to London. It is puzzling, and I have to accept that neither Coleridge nor any other poet could have amended those words. They are from the horse's mouth. Why does he say that I am seven or eight years old? My intention, Mr P writes, is to bring up the boy as a servant.

Have I not all that time been a son to them? That is what Ma'am said: You are my beloved son. Had Mr P not declared his friendship? Nick says that one can be both friend and servant, and it is with no little irritation that I explain to him why that is an impossible liberal fantasy. Must I think of myself as a pet, beyond the category of either friend or servant? My heart clenches in pain.

The truth is that I would rather have slept with the boys in their kookskerm, but they would not have wanted me. Plaatje, Klonkie and Apie, who herded the cattle, did not disguise their mirth at my breeches and shirt; they fell about laughing and would have nothing to do with my overtures. Neither did Vytje bother to hide her contempt for me. Only the pipsqueak Kleinpiet, who was so much younger, would speak with me, ask me to play, which of course I would not. They did not know how I envied them sleeping under the stars and going shirtless. They tried to mimic me by walking on tippy toes and turning their heads this way and that in a girlish fashion, cackling to each other in gibberish that was meant to be English. Nothing at all like me, and yet without recognising myself, I knew that it was I who was being laughed at.

I had been nameless, speechless for some time. There had been the name of Domkop, which I understood to be insulting, but I neither spoke nor answered to that name. Could it be that the months with Baas Karel were a fiction? I was indeed alone in the world, had surfaced from a long darkness, and no one knew who I was. Free then to name myself, I chose one right there in the kloof where the white man with kind eyes slid off his horse towards me (I did not see his limp until later) and spoke. Nothing could have been easier, even though I have never before thought of naming myself. Speech itself may have been creaking new, but the name came to me instantly. Hinza, the name of the amaGcaleka king, the bravest of warriors, whose fame echoes throughout this land. Even the fearless Mnanthatisi, spreading mfecane all around, would stop in her tracks at the sound of his drums, would quake at the very mention of his name. Encroaching white farmers may cock their guns, but Hinza would be sure to take his revenge. The cowardly Griquas, or Bergenaars as Mr P then called them, spoke of him with awe, and for me that was enough to recommend the name of Hinza.

Mr Pringle said that I was a Bechuana boy, so he surely suspected that Hinza was not my true name. Could it be that he knew? That out of delicacy the man would not probe? There are so many questions I ought to have asked him. Later, when he lay pale and drained on his deathbed, his bony hands on the counterpane, well, that was not the time for questions.

When, as a child, I asked Ma'am where I came from, she said, You belong to us and need not bother about an unknown past. She cannot mean that, I thought, for at other times she said that we belong to Jesus. Whilst I understood the business of God, I never managed to get the hang of Jesus. And not through want of trying.

Mary is incensed by Nicholas, who makes an unexpected visit just as we are about to retire. He is well in his cups. Shame on you, she says, you ought to be home, at work on the history. A sobering cup of coffee, and then off with you.

Nicholas hiccups. He's been hard at it all day, making good enough progress, but really it is now up to me, Hinza, to make a greater effort at remembering. How could I possibly claim to have been alone in the world when the poet found me?

Hinza's been struggling long enough with that damned story, so let him be, Mary says.

Ignoring her, Nick splutters, Alone! When a horde of your people descended on the Zuurveld! Surrounded by your folks, Hinza, you must have known where you came from, how you lot came to be there.

I stare at him, speechless.

Well, he explains, it's there in your man the poet's letter to Fairbairn. Did I not say? That there were some five or six hundred strangers – and he pauses to emphasise the word –*distributed* in that part of the Colony, no doubt a euphemism for God alone knows what. Your Mr P does not actually say that he, er, took you, but then, there is always the gentlemanly delicacy and coyness, the poet's huggermugger in the different accounts of finding his Bechuana boy. No wonder he became muddled and even told conflicting stories to his best friend. Nicholas struggles to draw out of his pocket a half-jack of whisky, and takes an ungentlemanly gulp.

It will not do to show myself affected by this news. I say breezily that he'll no doubt turn up tomorrow with another dribble of information, and walk him out to hail a taxi.

VI

Hinza does not have much of a sense of direction; thus he was pleased to discover in advance of the trip that Cape Town is a city in which you can't get lost. Nicholas gave him a book, a guide to Cape Town, he said, summarising it as a city with a Table Mountain, a Devil's Peak and a Lion's Head – all visible from every which way, so that you cannot fail to find your bearings. But the cover was not inviting and, having dipped into the book, Hinza left it behind. Nicholas could surely have found something contemporary; the book was written in another century, though Hinza himself, being of another century, would be the last person to applaud the present day.

Still, he ought not to have so resisted this journey, ought to have made more careful preparations for this flitting across the skies. No point in lamenting the sea voyage of yore, the nowhere in which to adjust at your leisure to the idea of the new, the elsewhere. If he fails to achieve anything here, he will perhaps write his own guide to the city, bring the book bang up to date. Mary and Nicholas set great store by this trip, and he, suspecting that the inconsistencies around his origins will never be cleared, ought at least to embrace the new experience.

The old man was surprised at Hinza's fear of flying. What, anxious about travelling? And you so up to date, a man of the modern world! True, we've largely kept to these parts of London, but all will be well once you reach Heathrow, just at the end of the tube line, he wheezed.

Hinza was not amused by the London Underground map that Nick casually thrust into his hands as he set off for the airport. It was only at King's Cross station, flustered in the luridly lit bowels of the city with its insistent merchandise and by the busker with no voice to boast of, that he discovered the map to be some kind of artwork, with Vasco da Gama and Christopher Columbus stations south of the river, at the end of the Victoria line. Where Heathrow ought to be, in the far west, was the perplexity of St Anthony and St Augustine stations, the creator not having made up his mind on an appropriate brand of piety. *The Great Bear* is what the artist called his Underground map, which Hinza may have appreciated at a less stressful time. (Mr P had spoken of Ursa Major, a constellation that could not be seen at Eildon, but once in London, there had been no time for stargazing.) Nicholas the poet no doubt found it piquant, but he should have known that levity at such a time was indelicate. Hinza was after all setting off for the Cape after an absence of aeons; no wonder that the thought of tears, girlish floods of tears, crossed his mind, and the busker's strained 'No Woman No Cry' set his teeth on edge.

And now he has arrived at Cape Town International, left the arrivals hall and is hanging around in the delicious sunshine. He hopes to find a Zimbabwean taxi driver without a licence. Nicholas, who had done his homework, assured Hinza that such a person is always available, that he would be overeducated and would undercharge for the journey. And indeed such a person in a woollen hat boasting a rainbow row of pompoms sidles up to him, offering a ride to the city for a mere ninety-nine rand.

In the jalopy Hinza sits up front with the man, who asks if he would mind a personal question. Is he a Bushman? No, and bloody no again. He is sick of it; since childhood he's been mistaken for a Bushboy, with people referring to Mr Pringle's famous poem as if he were the model. Summoning his poorly maintained Edinburgh accent, he assures the driver that he is not Khoesan at all. The man looks at him askance, expectantly, but Hinza declines to elaborate. Glad as he is for not being thought a tourist, he will not explain himself to this ... this coxcomb. Instead, he turns away, then gasps loudly. All along the road, and appearing to stretch endlessly over the dunes, are miles and miles of shacks on which satellite dishes perch precariously. Informal housing, the taxi driver offers. Informal housing, Hinza repeats, and tells himself to watch the echolalia that horror so often induces. But are these higgledy-piggledy sheets of corrugated tin and cardboard really houses? Do people actually live in them? he asks.

The driver looks at him in the mirror. Welcome to the Mother City, he shrugs.

From the car whooshing by, Hinza can indeed see a show of stick figures going about their business in what seems to be dramatic slow motion. He would like to avert his eyes, but he can't. Why would people erect their shacks right up against the motorway if not to insist on their presence? If not to remind travellers driving to and from the airport that they are there, that they too belong to Cape Town? That passage to the city cannot be granted without the rite of passing the shacks? Besides, there is nothing else to see. He supposes that they are still some way from the city, but really he expected the solidity of a giant granite table, also the devil's peak and the lion's head to be there, visible, and offering guidance. The mass of mountain ahead does not hold these fabled shapes, looks nothing like its images, offers little by way of relief from the spectre of 'informal housing', or for that matter orientation to travellers who have lost their way.

Wrong approach, the taxi driver says curtly. Not the classic view of the mountain that met Jan van Riebeeck as he sailed into the bay with his guns and his beads and bibles. The man drives like a maniac but so does everyone else, all frantic to get away from the shacks that accuse in their skew-whiff, wobbly ways, lurid in the sharp light. Suffused with shame, Hinza gulps repeatedly.

Anachronistic, the man continues, to take this business of informal black housing so … so personally. This is the face of modernity. People would rather live in shacks on the edge of the city than be unemployed in the old Homelands.

After miles of spectacular shacks, informal housing gives way to sturdy structures in bright colours that alternate strictly between blue, red, yellow and green. Coloured housing, the driver explains with a snigger. Coloureds are really proud of these, as they are of everything coloured, proud in fact of just being coloured, so they have no time for people from Zim.

Hinza says that surely people cannot be generalised in that way. Good point, the man concedes; there must be some who're ashamed of being coloured, but I can't say I've heard of anyone who simply *is* coloured.

Hinza would like to point out to the man that he would, of course, not know of such a person, since simply being coloured means not having to assert or discuss it. But he must not encourage the driver's foolish talk; instead, he ought to focus on this strange world that Mary persists in calling his home. Nicholas will demand a detailed account of the trip, starting here with the journey to the city, so what will he say? That there is a motorway with miles of shacks, brightly painted coloured housing and thereafter the web of highways and the affluence of the modern city. Could this not be gleaned from any tourist brochure? Does the city promote its shacks as picturesque? Has it become a place where supermodels strut 'ethnic' haute couture? Unlikely that the driver, in his rustling sports clothes, would know.

Hinza wants to go directly to Berg Street, or rather St George's Mall as it later became, to the site of the old newspaper offices, where Mr P and Fairbairn's struggle for freedom of expression started. Freedoms, it would seem, just come and go, arrive all dressed up in grandiose style, until they grow tired, give up and disrobe, unceremoniously, shamelessly, and what's more, in public. The shack dwellers have the freedom to erect their houses right there, on the edge, the threshold of the city, claiming their brief moments on the motorway. That freedom does not look like it's ready to disrobe; for all the wobbliness of the houses, it looks like it's there to stay.

Would the taxi wait for him whilst he makes his visit? Berg Street was also the site of Miss Janet's Seminary for Young Ladies, a place Hinza must have visited as a child. The driver says no, he can't oblige. It's now St George's Mall, all shops and stalls, possibly some establishments selling diamonds. In any case, it's for pedestrians, so there's nowhere for him to wait. Besides, this is the day of the Indigenous People's march on Parliament, and he does not wish to be caught up in terrible traffic. This city, he explains, gets completely snarled up, and with the world's tourists wanting to decant into Cape Town, the traffic barely moves at all, so a march means major trouble. The driver can, however, recommend a shop on St George's that sells all kinds of authentic seventeenth-century Khoesan gear made of animal skins, ostrich shells, feathers, beads and other ethnic accessories. Hinza as an unidentified and deracinated African may well find it diverting, may even like to buy a bow 'n' arrow, but please, don't ask him to wait; he has no time today.

Before Hinza finds a barbed reply, the man rolls down his window and shouts, Fucking hell, what the fuck are they up to? Do these seventeenth-century people not know their way around town? This is not the route to Parliament, he calls above the screeching brakes.

Advancing towards them is a motley group of marchers in various items of fancy dress. Some in loincloths adorned with feathers, shells and beads, their faces daubed with white and ochre paint. Others, sporting colourful blankets, carry either bows and arrows or what look like metal staffs that could easily convert into weapons; indeed, a few are brandished at the taxi driver, who swiftly rolls up the window. Marching in stiff-legged gait are a couple of men in faded military uniform, one of them surely a blue-eyed white man with shaggy, unkempt hair who, brandishing a staff, shouts at the driver, Jou ma se poes! He is summarily restrained by a clutch of women in huge frilled Boer bonnets and, presumably for balance, bustled behinds. They march to the mournful sound of a hymn to God, or so Hinza infers, since he doesn't understand the words.

These are the more-indigenous-than-thou who call themselves the leaders of the original Khoesan people, the Zimbabwean explains; the men I mean, in original dress as you can see, demanding their rights. In other words, the coloureds who are not proud of being coloured. But beautifully turned out, hey! We Zimbabweans just don a plain old white sheet, toga-style, over our normal clothes, and that only in England, on special occasions like poetry readings or music festivals. Just in case people mistake us for Windrush folk.

What's the language? Hinza asks.

Oh, we speak very good English when we're in England. Or do you mean these Cape people? Afrikaans, that's what they're singing in, but some ginger up their lines with the authentic clicking sounds of the original Khoe peoples. Does Hinza by any chance know any click language? Nelson Mandela identified only eleven national languages, an oversight on his part, but the taxi driver happens to know that the Honourable Julius Malema of the Economic Freedom Fighters – themselves beautifully turned out in Parliament in red boiler suits and woollen berets from China – has pledged to make the Khoe language official. Then no one need any longer be ashamed of speaking the -qua-qua clicks, he says pointedly.

Hinza gives him a filthy look, and now borrowing Nicholas's pompous English voice asks to be taken to his Airbnb flat in Vredehoek.

A modest place it is, on the slope of Table Mountain with a good view of Lion's Head and its mane of trees along the ridge of the lion's back. He sets about making himself comfortable, firstly by turning around the hideous pictures on the wall, fortunately hung from hooks, so that, instead, there is the inoffensive uniformity of their backs in buff brown card. A small brown sticker on each declares that the paintings are original works by nameless people who paint with their feet, which he supposes ought to give him pause. He makes a cup of rooibos tea from the welcome pack that contains also a bottle of cheap wine and a miscellany of sauce sachets and miniature lotions scooped up from various eateries and hotels.

With his tea on the little balcony, savouring the late summer sun, Hinza should be comfortable, but he is oppressed by the task ahead, or rather by its vagueness. Why is he in Cape Town? How valid is it to visit the modern city in order to capture something of Mr P? They do after all have the necessary information, so what precisely is he supposed to capture? He feels like a toddler chasing flies with a fishing net in the park. Mary and Nicholas managed to excuse themselves, but thought it fit that he, the indigene, should come. The feel of the place, Mary insisted, that's what's important; then sternly: You're a bloody artist, so just do your thing.

Are they not his collaborators? Protesting that he was taken away as a child cut no ice with those two, who for once stood united. Nonsense, Mary said, you are South African; languishing in a sick bed in London doesn't count. Nicholas was confident. Faith, that's the key. Once there, you'll know why you came, feel in your bones if not in your soul the spirit of the 1820s hovering like an angel over the city. History can't be wiped out, no matter how hard politicians try to do so. If you keep vigilant, receptive to the soul, the lifeblood of the place, you'll find your subject. Find yourself. Hinza shook his head; never before has he heard such bunkum.

At least he does not have to get himself up in fancy dress, though he is surely more entitled than those marchers who, like himself he supposes, are stumbling about in indelible history. Christ, he hopes for their sakes that they've not been resurrected by some desperate author, lifted out of some forgotten work of nasty colonial fiction.

Hinza tries one of the beds, and, succumbing to the heat, falls asleep, only to be woken up far too soon by a rap on the front door. Nicholas warned that the very many hungry people knock even on modest doors asking for food, sometimes wielding threatening knives. They would have to make do with the welcome pack, Hinza supposes, and opens the door to find the Zimbabwean taxi driver smiling broadly and carrying a parcel. He appears to be without a knife.

The traffic is impossibly hellish out there man, so I brought us an early lunch, the best fish 'n' chips in Cape Town, and then you'll probably want to get down to some sightseeing, so I'm right here at your service. Good idea or what? Oh, and my name is Joshua – as he settles himself contentedly in a chair with the *Cape Times*.

Hinza cannot but laugh at the effrontery; they both laugh uproariously. For sure, he agrees, finds plates and cutlery, and fishes sachets of tomato sauce and mayonnaise from the welcome pack. Joshua eyes the courtesy bottle of wine longingly but Hinza reminds him that he'll be driving. For courtesy's sake, the man pleads, besides, in this town a glass or two is generally known to improve one's driving; but his host without further ado puts the bottle in a cupboard and serves tepid tap water. The fish and chips are surprisingly palatable; the sun shines directly into the kitchen-diner, and Joshua yawns. It might be an idea to keep off the road for a bit longer. He wouldn't mind stretching out on the sofa, catch forty winks, while Hinza clears up. And indeed, by the time the dishes are washed and the newspaper wrapping is bundled into the bin, the man is snoring gently.

Hinza flicks through the *Cape Times*, through its many articles about state corruption with scare quotes around the oft-repeated phrase, 'white monopoly capital'. He allows the man twenty minutes, but calling his name gently has no effect.

It is no mean feat waking Joshua up. He bellows and shudders as if in the grip of a nightmare, and holding his arms defensively aloft, stares wild-eyed at Hinza, who sees no way out but to take him firmly by the shoulders and coo in motherly fashion there-there-it's-all right, over and over, until the noise subsides.

Joshua giggles, embarrassed. Man, he explains, you never know who's going to knife you in this town for the sake of five rand. A cup of coffee, that would fix them up nicely, but Hinza says no, the sachets of Ricoffy are not worth having. They should be off to the South African Library before the evening traffic starts up – then, ashamed of his bullying tone, adds that they'll get a coffee afterwards, somewhere nice.

Joshua seems to think of the day as something of a holiday. He has never been to the grand Library, so if Hinza doesn't mind, he'll just hang out with him, check out for himself the hallowed halls of knowledge and learning. It is not often that he gets to meet interesting natives who have lived abroad; besides, Hinza would be surprised to hear how crass and monstrous the average tourist turns out to be, horribly lacking in culture and manners. Mostly they want to be driven to shop at the Waterfront and get drunk in Irish pubs, although the kilted bagpipers at the Waterfront are not to be sniffed at; he for one wouldn't mind winding up the day there with a coffee and ice-cream.

Hinza lets it pass. He tells Joshua something about his mission, about the Library where Mr P came to work, a job well suited to his scholarly bent and love of books.

He does not say how intimidating at the time the city was for a country child, how awestruck he was at the buildings, the carriages, the throngs of people going about their business, even by the slaves rushing about cobbled streets, and how he loved the attention that the Pringles lavished on him in town. He remembers Ma'am in her fine muslin frock taking his hand firmly in hers, not caring a tuppenny about those who stared or laughed outright. Gone were the Eildon days when he hated being clothed. From the drapers in Strand Street he was allowed to choose a fine cambric shirt that he loved wearing as they strolled together in the Company Gardens. They were, after all, about to leave for London.

There are ignorant folk who know no better than to titter, Ma'am said, shameless people who think nothing of displaying and abusing their slaves, and she held on to his hand as if he were precious. Now he wonders if he too had been taken for a slave, albeit a pampered one. A light sea breeze capered about them and the air was heady with brine that Hinza fancies he can once more smell here, centuries later, in Strand Street.

They stand across the road to admire the grand Athenaeum-styled building, then the pride of the colony. Lord Charles Somerset, whom Mr P at the time thought to be a fine gentleman, had levied a wine tax to pay for the Cape Public Library. Joshua thinks that given the amount of wine consumed these days, a tax would certainly cover an overhaul of South Africa's education system; he has heard that standards here are plummeting to British levels.

Joshua is excited about going inside; he has never thought of entering the place, and to tell the truth, he has never been in a proper library. His old university in Harare with its handful of dog-eared books really did not count. A good percentage had been eviscerated by needy students, so that the shelves housed no more than lines of slack book-covers with Dewey-numbered spines. He slaps Hinza on the back, Let's go, bro.

But Hinza hesitates; he will have to gird his loins. Libraries, he has believed ever since being thrown out of the municipal library in Islington, are not for the likes of him. It turned out that a group of youths had been noisy, and when a librarian found him perusing the shelves, he insisted that Hinza was one of the culprits. Besides, Hinza had found it to be a place of arcane rules and systems, of invisible barriers, a place designed to keep you out, or to have you tremble with ignorance whilst a headmasterish librarian stares scornfully at your fumbling.

But Joshua takes him firmly by the elbow and steers him through the imposing doors as if there were nothing to stop them, and before he can say Thomas Pringle Joshua has introduced him to a stern-looking librarian, whose hand Joshua pumps is if she were a long-lost friend. Oh, he is sure that the lady would help them with information on Thomas Pringle, whom he glosses as the Father of Scottish Poetry; he and his friend here from London are particularly interested in spaces that Pringle may have occupied, a desk perhaps?

Shame, all that way? The woman smiles, of course, she's there to help. Really they were just after the man's aura, Joshua says, the actual research having already been completed. Hinza, amazed, keeps mum. Also, since it's a place of knowledge and enlightenment, Joshua wouldn't mind flicking through any books they may have on Nelson Mandela. Now there's a man whose head he simply can't figure out; perhaps the new Letters will give some idea of how he arrived at that place of forgiveness, because as far as he, Joshua, can see, that brand of forgiveness may well have been a mistake. The librarian says, Oh no, the man was a saint; Joshua will soon see that from the letters, and she takes him off, leaving Hinza to look through papers that, in the main, Nicholas already had copies of. When they return the woman smiles warmly and assures Joshua that he is most welcome to pop in whenever he likes; she is usually there between nine and five and would be happy to show him other collections.

My, what a fine time we're having, Joshua says as they walk towards the car, but shame, man, how can you be so timid, frightened of librarians of all people? And you the British sophisticat with your fancy speech. This is Africa, man; the country belongs to us – well, so to speak, if you ignore for a moment government corruption, neocolonialism and white monopoly capital. In the manner of the *Cape Times*, he hooks his index fingers around the latter phrase, and laughs, Shame, now that's a term wealthy people do not like at all.

Why don't you tell me about this word 'shame' that people here use in such a strange manner?

Joshua nods thoughtfully. Yip, it's infectious, hey, and such a useful word too. Clever really, because its meaning of disgrace is completely wiped out, stripped of its sting, so no nastiness and guilt in this society, because, shame, everything is nice and cosy and sympathetic in this town. But you, a man from London, you really ought to buck up.

Well, there you are, Hinza says, lucky enough to have grown up in a country that belongs to you. As for me, I'm pooped; got to get some rest, he yawns, forgetting that he had promised coffee. And no, he is interested in neither dinner, nor the nightlife that Joshua describes with a clicking of fingers and a twist of his slender hips. He needs some time on his own.

Joshua drops him off, but not without extracting his mobile number and a promise that Hinza will avail himself of his services tomorrow. Since the man has no qualms about turning up announced, it may well be more convenient to have a call instead.

By the time Hinza arrives at the gate the next morning, Joshua is there with a large zipped plastic bag. The taxi driver had noted the washer-drier in the kitchen and wondered if a few things could be laundered while they are out; he has brought his own detergent.

Hinza tries not to laugh, stops himself from saying yes, although why should the man not use available resources instead of wasting time and money at the laundry? No, he ought to be more cautious with this guy, who is surely overstepping the mark, even if the mark is a bourgeois piece of nonsense. Nope, too late to go back indoors, he says cravenly, you can do it tomorrow. This morning he has an appointment with a Professor Ritchie at Cape Town University, and no, Joshua need not wait for him; he has not decided what to do for the rest of the day.

Phyllida Ritchie does not respond to his knock, so that he waits, wanders down the corridor and knocks again before she calls Come in.

A tiny woman with dreadlocks and glossy red lipstick behind a large desk strewn with papers, she motions him to sit on an uncomfortable chair facing her. Hinza tries not to think of himself as a student collecting a failed essay. But how can he fail to feel uncomfortable, going as he does by the name of Nicholas Greene?

It was Nick himself who pointed out that a woman who has published articles on Mr P and who is shortly to bring out a major monograph would find the name of Hinza Marossi suspicious, or at best, diverting. But Nick balked when Mary suggested Hinza take his name. Given his own eminence as a poet, he objected, his name might well raise questions for a scholar in the field of English poetry, even if her specialism is the colonial stuff.

Academics, as far as Hinza knew, took pride in their chosen field of knowledge, in Prof. Ritchie's case Mr P's work and life, which would include scribbled scraps of paper like shopping lists and notes on minor ailments, but in the name of specialism and expertise would know nothing beyond their subjects; the name of Nicholas Greene was unlikely to mean anything to her. In politeness and to prevent a sulk, Hinza falsely promised to think of another.

Professor Ritchie does not let down her guard, for which Hinza is grateful. Her formality will help him to concentrate, to remember his pseudonym.

Let's face it, Mr Greene, she says, Thomas Pringle was an immigrant who riled the governor with his articles about the hardships of British settlers that were all but ignored by the colonial office. And Somerset retaliated by insulting and persecuting him – his newspaper, his academy, his job at the Library. In response, the outraged, out-of-pocket poet turned to humanitarianism. As for the poetry itself, of little consequence, but well meaning, as in his sonnets on *The* Hottentot, *The* Caffer, *The* Bushman (she stresses the articles), where their dispossession is lamented, even as timeless characteristics for entire groups are pinned down in verse. De-dum-de-dum-de-dum, she taps her fingers mockingly on the desk, the familiar iambic trot, as one of our laureates calls it. It is the case that his letters from South Africa on slavery and the Caffer Campaigns are fine essays that persuasively, elegantly even, present the injustice of colonial rule, but really these were written once he had left the colony. Our celebrated figure is no more than a cipher, constructed by liberal English South Africans intent on distinguishing their polite racism from the crass Afrikaner version. Pringle came in handy by way of establishing their credentials via an early colonial forefather, defender of the free press and of native rights. As an icon, he embodied their ambivalence, as people who both displaced natives and at the same time were defenders of the people they dispossessed. South Africans are no longer taken in by such hogwash, if ever we were, and she stares at him sternly.

Hinza cannot remember the wording of his introductory letter, but he must have said something that drives her to such gleeful gall. Does she expect him to object? Nodding his head in appreciation, he says How fascinating, and scribbles furiously in his notebook. His throat is dry. It is clear that she will deliver her lecture with no regard for anything he might have to say or ask. When she stops to catch her breath, Hinza notes the kettle on the counter and wonders if she'll offer tea. Instead she wants to know why he doesn't use a tape recorder, but does not wait for a reply. Accuracy is important, she admonishes; she would not like to be misquoted.

The history of Pringle's work is so transparent, Professor Ritchie continues, that one wonders how the benign reputation of humanitarianism came to be. The man, typical of his times, saw natives as commodities to further the interests of settlers, and he was perfectly happy to shoot at San marauders in defence of the land usurped by the Brits.

So, what does she make of Pringle's work for the Anti-Slavery Society in London? Hinza asks.

Well, if the ethical did not come to him naturally, the man nevertheless was not without decent feeling, at least not without the kind of thought and feeling, shaped by the Enlightenment, that saw no problem with the oppression of people thought to be inferior. Which is to say that in his defence of freedom of the press and in campaigning for the rights of white settlers, he came up against the autocracy of Lord Charles Somerset, who was determined to crush the upstart. So what does the injured guy do? He adopts the mantle of radicalism, pumps up his defence of natives, his abhorrence of slavery, and gives the aristocrat good reason to persecute him. No more than a stance, which he then pursues more fully in London. But it comes belatedly, and so there's the task of having to rewrite the liberal observations, the stuff he had composed before the volte-face. She drums her fingertips on the desk: de-dum-de-dum-de-dum, all over again. Note how his radicalism does not stretch to denouncing the colonial project and returning the land.

No, it's purely textual, all in the writing. And for all our theories of ethics supporting the aesthetic, Pringle's injection of humanitarianism does little for the quality of his verse. Now, writing poetry is necessarily about revision, but how does one excuse the rewriting of his *Narrative of a Residence in South Africa*, where events themselves are recast, filtered through the new radicalism? What, one wonders, did Pringle actually see or experience? Did he believe that alerting Europe to the plight of native people and slaves would enhance his reputation as a poet?

Hinza struggles with the idea of a natural ethics, but he is too craven to raise it. But his, er, his heart, he stammers instead, is the condition of his heart not the key? Can literary criticism not show that he wrote from the heart?

Professor Ritchie stares at him, amazed. Well, Mr Greene, I am no physician, so perhaps you'd like to elaborate. Hinza says that there is no reason to suspect dissimulation, knowing as we do how Pringle immersed himself in humanitarian work in London. His heart was in it, so no reason to doubt his conversion. Why not embrace the convert as all cultures surely do? Besides, is the growth of a poet's mind, as we see also in Wordsworth's 'Prelude', not necessarily about recreating the self?

Professor Ritchie leans back in her chair and fixes her gaze on Hinza. I do not say he was dishonest; no doubt there was much gentle remodelling of the delicate self. But how is that to be squared with colonial violence, dispossession, genocide? And would it not have been better for the poet to speak openly of his Damascus and come clean about his conversion?

Hinza hears the sound of her voice, but not what she has to say. The woman clearly thinks him foolish and naïve. The churning in his stomach grows thunderous, and there is a strange buzzing in his ears that makes it difficult to absorb her words. The very shape and form of Mr P shivers before his eyes, dissolving as it were in moving liquid. Nothing is stable … he grips the sides of his chair, summons rapid words of thanks and stumbles out.

Ritchie calls after him to shut the door, but Hinza, now sprinting down the corridor, is deaf to anything other than the thunder in his head.

Hinza has been away for only eight days, but already it feels like a month. Nicholas Greene misses the young man more than he thought possible; he is at a loose end, and from Mary's pacing about and plumping of cushions he suspects that she is too. Neither of them finds it strange that with Hinza gone they spend more and more time together – what else would they do? – even as they continue to rub each other up the wrong way. But more playfully so.

This evening they have again dined together. Nick had requested what he calls Mary's heart-warming steak-and-kidney pudding; he supposed there was no point in yearning for the halcyon days of sumptuous peacock pie; besides, there was nothing to celebrate. At your service, Sir Nicholas, Mary said with a curtsey, which was anything but respectful or, for that matter, amusing. Why does she persist in treating him so scornfully? He thought that they had become more tolerant of each other, that they have a tentative friendship of sorts.

My dear, Nick, plain Nick, will do. I wish you'd stop calling me Sir Nicholas. No one else does, or for that matter even recognises the name. Commonplace, these knighthoods are, mushrooming here, there and everywhere. The bloody title gets one nowhere in this so-called democratic age, opens no doors, or worse, one gets mistaken for some shopkeeper made good. Yes, titles, my dear, turn out to be two a penny nowadays, he sighs.

Mary is alarmed by this revelation. What, then is the point of him? But she bridles her tongue, does not even say that she'd rather not be called My Dear; better to get through the evenings with as little friction as possible.

Unlike Hinza, whose zestful embrace of modernity he finds disturbing, Nicholas does not see television as an option. He believes that such an assault, such an onslaught, the floods of news and views, could be of no help; rather, it would only hinder one's managing of the contemporary world, contradictory as that may seem.

Mary agrees. She suspects that it would get in the way of their project – how on earth do people these days manage to focus on anything?

Tonight, however, a strange discomfort pervades the air, making Nicholas long for distraction. Mary refuses to go to the public house, urges him to go on his own; she does not have the stomach tonight for being stared at as a relic, or mistaken for a luvvie. So Nick settles for staying put. Why don't you make a fire, she suggests; at least we can look into the flames when we run out of things to say.

Nick stares at her in disbelief. Me? Build a fire? But how? he frowns, sucking at a cold pipe. Then, since Mary makes no move to leave the table, he goes to the grate and eyes it dolefully before sinking, not without difficulty, to his knees. He fumbles with paper and gingerly arranges kindling, and indeed after much puffing and blowing and fanning conjures out of the construction a joyful burst of flames.

Ah, the Promethean gene! (He is much taken with the modern idea of genes.) How naturally it comes after all. It's a triumph, he declares, drawing up two armchairs and patting the cushions. Do come and sit down, Madam, he beams. His heart sinks when Madam ungraciously leaves the room without a word, but she soon returns to take her place, bearing glasses and bottles of ale. Which would have gone down very nicely with the steak-and-kidney pudding, but he must let it pass.

No word from Hinza, eh? he says again. No doubt he'll be immersed in that strange world, exercised by its goings on, and with all youth's propensity for the Manichean, will see things starkly in black and white. Take it from me, who's been around for so many centuries: that good and evil feed off each other, and in the end, well, I no longer know what I meant to say, in the end, well there's no telling how one will leach into t'other. Do you not now, my dear, in retrospect think that we ought to have gone with Hinza to Africa? I can't even remember why we didn't. Do you?

Truth is, I can't decide what I feel nowadays about that continent where my Mam, then a wee lassie, was caught by slavers and transported to hell, but I guess one should let bygones be bygones. Perhaps it would've been the healthy thing, to gird my loins and leave this small island. I would be interested to see with my own eyes what's happening in that remade country after all their rainbow talk-talk, but I thought the boy had to be on his own. It's his country, and he needs to come to terms with whatever he finds in Africa, or finds out about his people, all on his tod – even if it pains me not to be there to offer comfort, or for that matter share his joy, for surely there must be something of that kind to be found in such a place, such a past? It will be warm down there. Late summer, the beginning of autumn. At least Hinza will return to spring in London.

How thoughtful of Mary. Nicholas feels a surprising, burning stab of jealousy, so that he moves his chair back a tad from the fire. Does he really wish it were he, comforted in those strong arms? He casts a sidelong glance at her, so serene, and with her head held high, so, well, regal … but Mary meets his eye and frowns.

That was the very moment, he decides only a couple of days later, when he fell in love with her, head over heels as they so accurately say, for in the very slight turn back to the fire his head spun, as if recovering from a somersault. Nicholas fumbles in his pocket for a handkerchief and mops the sweat on his brow. Why, only this very afternoon he thought of her at best with indifference, and now, what to do?

What would you say, Nicholas ventures, if I went in search of a peacock. It is not beyond my means to wring the creature's neck, and let's see, if I can summon the taste, my memory will surely come up with the ingredients for peacock pie. A festive dinner in celebration of … of our dear Hinza. How about it, my dear, both of us trying our hands at peacock pie, improvised with your Indie spices? And this place decked out for the boy's return with the sumptuous jewel colours of its feathers, stirred festively by the fire? Ah, there was a time when fine ladies wore peacock feathers in their hair, he muses; then enthusiastically: and you, Mary, were made for it – a swathe of feathers lodged in your hair, there, in the braid just above the left ear, imagine it drooping elegantly over to the right, brushing your cheek. He leans over to demonstrate, but Mary ducks deftly out of his reach. A veritable princess, he says – oh, we'll step out and paint the town red, so we will.

Mary laughs heartily. It's best to ignore Nick's nonsense. Peacock pie! she exclaims. Don't be ridiculous. I'll make a marrow-bone stew with barley and greens, and we'll eat it right here. If the cold persists you could try your hand at another fire. And now I'd like you to take your leave. Turning her back on him, she retreats to the little kitchen where she does her bustling and calls a good night so that he sees himself out.

Damn, has he misunderstood, Mary wonders, for it is not yet eleven o'clock when Nicholas arrives at her door the following morning, stamping his feet with the cold.

Don't stir. I'll make us some coffee, he says as she shuts the door.

Mary frowns: What do you mean? She is after all in her coat and gloves, about to leave. There's no knowing what old Nick has up his sleeve. No, she says, before he replies, no time for sitting around with coffee. For all the cold it's a lovely bright day, and I've got to see to the allotment.

Allotment? Pray, have you come into an inheritance, my dear? What have you been allotted and by whom, may I ask?

Mary laughs, explains. The allotment is from Tower Hamlets Council. A little handkerchief-sized patch of brownfield land, over towards Hackney, on which to grow things. You wouldn't know, she says quietly, pinching her eyes shut for a moment, what it means, how precious to be able to rake the earth for your own pleasure and profit. Then briskly, I reckon it's about time to get the soil turned over, prepare it for planting in the next week or so.

Nick says that that sounds fascinating, that bucolic pursuits are not to be sniffed at, even if he has never understood the business of sowing and reaping. All too predictable for his liking. You'll reap whatsoe'er you sow – now there's a maxim for a bourgeois dullard. But he would be very happy to accompany her, offer his help in tending the earth, for whilst he has no practical experience he has after all a wealth of knowledge accumulated over the centuries. Actually, he has just remembered his very own 'Ode to the Ripe Wheat Ear' commissioned by the Earl of, of, damn, can't recall the name, on the tip of his tongue; anyway, an innovator the gentleman was, way back in the 1700s when the man had his fenlands drained and introduced a clover crop for rotating with the wheat. A marvellous summer it was on that estate where he watched wheat ears grow uncommonly plump and golden, waving in the sunlight, so that the ode came effortlessly, as if Ceres herself warbled the song of fully-fledged stanzas that needed no revision. Fascinating business, the daily bread we break; for instance, does Mary happen to know that the first cultivars of wheat …

Mary sighs, holds up a cautionary hand. Yes, he's welcome to come along to the allotment, no need to take off his coat, but since she doesn't plan on growing wheat she'd rather not be burdened with its history.

They are about to leave when Nick, whilst knotting his scarf, grips her arm. Look, he whispers, pointing. On the white skirting board, the cold bright sun refracted through the windowpane has painted multiple bands of perfect prismatic light, from glowing red to glorious violet. Mary kneels down; her fingers hover over the wood, wanting to touch, but the colour flits off. But there, and there again, the light catches on the edge of the table, a chair, a glass, where ribbons of incandescent colour settle fleetingly before moving on with the sun. They wait in silence until all has evanesced.

We should go, Mary says, buoyed by light, and tosses to Nick Hinza's woolly tartan hat, which he briefly examines before shoving into his pocket. No need to court ridicule in the street, but not wanting to cross Mary, he says that it may well come in handy.

And indeed it does, as they struggle against an icy breeze and weave their way through busy streets. With the hat pulled well over his ears, Nick keeps up a steady flow of talk, whilst Mary keeps silent.

What a perfect haven, he exclaims as they reach what once was a bombsite, then poorly constructed mobile houses gone derelict, before being cleared by the council to satisfy the new demand for allotments. Hedges of mixed shrubs – box, cherry laurel, red robin, and also beech that holds on bravely to some burnished leaves – mark off these gardens in their various shades of greens, reds and browns; their rain-spangled leaves sparkle in the icy sunlight.

They collect each a spade and fork from the lean-to, and with much difficulty set about turning the resistant soil. Nicholas, quite out of breath from the fruitless exertion, ventures that it may well be an idea to wait for the earth to thaw. Mary glares angrily for a moment and then, deflated, agrees. She has always made this mistake. Impatient for summer, she cannot believe that spring drags its heels in this way, that the sun, so dastardly, fools her with a brightness that carries not a molecule of heat. But she'll try again in a week or two.

From her rucksack she draws a flask of tea, the Cape rooibos that is Hinza's favoured brew, and they settle down on the rickety, damp bench. She has forgotten to bring mugs, so they pass the flask-top to each other, blowing at the scalding tea. Nick finds himself watching her, quite as if he has not seen her before. He watches the hands cupping the plastic container for its warmth, sees for the first time an abrupt shift in colour from the chocolate-brown skin of her upper hand to the dusky pink of her palm, the pale ovals of nails; his eyes follow her full lips as they pout in anticipation of the raised cup, of its heat, and again a glimpse of pink inner flesh of her mouth before the eager lips meet the rim from which she blow-sips the hot liquid. How delicately she does it. Nick, entranced, all but feels the tea rolling through the cavity of her mouth, and down her throat with a soft swallow. When she refills the cup and passes it to him, he knows precisely how far to turn it so that his own lips come to rest on the hot plastic where the shadow of hers still lingers. Feverishly he swallows the horrible redbush tea.

In the sunlight, everything blazes numinous and new, all aglow. All seems unfamiliar, and Mary has become a hallowed stranger to him. Nicholas, in a state of disbelief, asks in a gruff voice that he does not recognise, whether the redbush herb is meant to have magical qualities. Next time he will bring along a dash of brandy to make it palatable, he adds hurriedly. Upon which Mary snatches the cup out of his hand. If he doesn't like it, she'd be happy to down the lot.

Now what has he done? He cannot very well wrestle the cup off her. Transfixed against his will by her lips, his thirsty eyes follow the warm liquid into her mouth. Brand-new blood bounds through his veins, a strange surge of health and youthfulness that urges him to lean somewhat towards her. Can she feel the heat? Dare he look at her? But Mary's gaze is distant; she stalls, speaks of time, of the winter, year after year, that will not let go of its grip, but my oh my, when spring finally manages to elbow her way in, how fast it all happens. The merciful thaw and the sunlight palpably warm on one's skin, then the green shoots that pierce their way through cold clods of earth. She pushes her palms together, her elbows reclaiming the space around her.

Hinza will be loading up on sunlight and heat, Nick offers lamely. Talk of Hinza is what will draw her in, bind them, words to supply a single source of warmth into which they could lean together. How long will he have to settle for the slippered comfort of mama-and-papa talk even as youthful ardour fountains in his breast, and Mary oblivious to the blazing newness of his interest in her, his new understanding of her?

Or so he thinks. Mary has felt the centimetre of movement towards her person and cannot decide whether she imagines the heat of his gaze. It is all too puzzling. Nick is a sly one and she'll have to keep on her toes, will not be tricked into anything, although she must say that it is altogether more companionable to have Nicholas in so strange, so pliant a mood. She rises, beats dust from the rear of her coat, and declares the day over. Look how the clouds are creeping up, darkening, how the day like so many English days is simply giving up on itself. She has things to do, must head back, and will see him tomorrow perhaps.

Nick sighs, oh, for the good old days when one could grip a woman by the shoulders and grind … but such thoughts will get him nowhere. Mindful of Hinza's little lecture on modern women, and remembering that a sharp tongue lodges in Mary's luscious mouth, he must find a sensible way of detaining her. She has clearly not forgiven him for not finding a peacock, he declares, so he would like to make amends. Might she be willing to be taken to lunch at The Peacock's Tail in Bloomsbury? Then, worrying about chauvinism in such an invitation, he hypercorrects: They could go Dutch if she does not want to be taken … er … for granted.

Not at all, says Mary, who thinks of Nick as a skinflint. She'd be happy to be his guest, but it will have to wait for another time; she would not be comfortable dressed in her old gardening clothes. And then Nicholas slips up, surprises himself. He splutters that Mary looks wonderful, lovelier than the sun … more precious than … loveliness itself … will always be, that there is no woman in Bloomsbury fit to tie her shoelaces. Fortunately, the speech tumbles out in courtly French and, much relieved by that, he follows it with an idiotic English haw-haw.

Mary looks at him in horror. She can only imagine this strange volley to be one of mocking insults, although his face does appear to deny it, but one never can tell with Nicholas. Might he have found her blue plaque in Bloomsbury? I thank you, she says formally, hedging her bets, and turns sharply to go. She will no doubt see him once he has caught that peacock, she says over her shoulder. Mais oui, he quips, aujourd'hui, they'll sally forth to Bloomsbury and see what lies in store.

Frankly, Hinza wishes he were back home with Mary and Nicholas, his own kind as he now fondly thinks of them. He does not like being a tourist. Having seen some sights with Joshua in tow, Hinza has become heartily sick of the fellow. How different, for instance, might the District Six Museum not have been without Joshua's prejudiced commentary, humorous as it was? Hinza castigates himself for minding the man's pushiness – are his own bourgeois sensibilities not to blame? Is he simply a product of bloodless British manners? The solution is to bring forward his trip to the Eastern Cape and not to tell Joshua of his plans until the last minute, when he needs a taxi to the airport. And no, he hasn't booked a return flight, does not know how long he'll stay; he'll call before he returns to Cape Town. Joshua sniffs, hurt; he trusts he'll be available.

If only Mary were here in the Eastern Cape with him. He begged, but she was adamant. Oh no, she didn't have the stomach for Africa, where her ancestors had been taken in bondage, or sold to traders by greedy chiefs, which is all the same to her. No, Africa is no place for Mary, whereas he, Hinza the native, would be better placed to check on the world where Mr P had sojourned. She believes that he would benefit from the trip; it would be good for his restless soul. Resorting to her usual strategy for silencing him, she sang, humming between the lines, *Lay your troubles down ... down by the river ... Glory, glory hall-el-u-jah*. If only you believed, she sighed, the word 'hallelujah' would lap like a flame around your heart; if ever a single word could quieten you, it's the hallelujah that will lead your soul out of darkness.

Ah, I thought South Africa was meant to do that, and he tried once more to persuade her to come.

Too old, she sighed, too late, as if they who walked the night were subject to time.

He'd imagined that with Mary's experience of having travelled as a slave from island to island, she would have no difficulty coming to a new continent. But Hinza understood, and did not pester her with his misgivings.

Instead, she preached at him: cut out the feartie, she said; the sturdier your feet are planted on the ground, the easier it is to take off to strange places and land back on those feet, plant them wherever you choose to land.

Hinza was flustered by the metaphor of planting, but no, she said, he was misled by the idea of roots. A comparison is just that, a comparison; we are not actual plants – and she waved her arms about in the manner of branches swaying in the wind – these are arms, not branches; look, we have stability without roots. So there should be no problem moving about, anywhere in the world, *on*, and not *in* the earth. And it helps, Mary said, looking critically at his two-toned brogues, if you're not over-reliant on shoes. Even in the cold northern summer she kicks off her shoes at the least opportunity, and sighs contentedly, unperturbed by the obscenity of her ancient salt-nibbled toes trying to mount each other.

Mary would have helped to ease his way into this alien world. Why do men find simple things so difficult, she pontificated. How hard can it be, the skill of inserting yourself into the world of others? Brushing aside the umbrage he took at her gendered view, Mary said: Look, you know that this trip, for all its business with Mr P, is also about you, Hinza, so do as you see fit, but if you'll excuse me, I'll say no more; I'll stay put, be here for you when you return. Just speak to people, find out what they remember of that past, or rather, what was passed on by their ancestors.

This is precisely what Hinza cannot imagine himself doing. Speak to people? How intrusive, and why would they want to speak with him? Answer his questions? He knows that that's what people like Professor Ritchie do, that their research includes interviewing people, probing, and how could probing not be rude? What would they think if their subjects were to turn the tables and interview them? Certainly he would not entertain any questions about his life or his memories of the lives of others. Perhaps Mary would have known how to do this business of speaking with people, but he shudders at the idea. How repellent – the world of the real.

In spite of his protestations, he had at some level imagined that there would be a feeling of homecoming of sorts, a landing after a long-haul flight through the centuries. Instead, this alienation, being nothing more than a common tourist in the Eastern Cape, comes as a shock. Was there really nothing at all to prod a memory or awaken an inchoate sense of belonging? No, and no again. There is not as much as an imagined shadow of a birth mother, of siblings, of a grandparent on whose knee he could have been dandled. A blank that cannot be accounted for, a blank he must live with; indeed, surveying the poverty of the former Ciskei Homeland all around, a blank for which he ought perhaps to be grateful. He had checked on the current state of affairs, of the land claims by old inhabitants of the Kat River before apartheid evictions, and recognised some surnames of people who had once laboured as tenants at Glen-Lynden, but not a sliver of light did it shed on his own history.

· Allow him then, like any British tourist, to start with the weather. It is autumn, or the tail-end of summer, and he has chosen his rarely worn summer clothes with care. But apart from the deliciously warm, dry day of arrival in the Eastern Cape and the opportunity to wear a new butter-yellow shirt, it has since rained cats and dogs, stormed, in fact, and he is trapped on this mountain called Hogsback, only a few kilometres away from the old Kat River Settlement. Looking up at the vertiginous dolomite rock, Hinza does not feel himself. He chuckles wryly at the reflexive pronoun; like old Nick's, the self has become a burden, and he has spent much of today behind drawn chintz curtains, terrified of the rolling thunder, of the clashing spears of lightning and sheets of rain that pound the earth into hissing streams. The little car he had hired at East London airport would not survive such an assault, so he stays in his room and writes.

It was, I believe, a mistake coming to Hogsback, a mountain of lush vegetation turned into various recreational resorts. How do those who are presumably tired of life re-create themselves here? Through hiking and horse riding, fine dining and mountain cycling, and there is the verdant entrance to 'Fairyland' with a grotesque man-size gnome carved from wood, holding up a sign commanding the punters: ENJOY. (I think of Nick's objection to the command.) In Fairyland they will be transported to another world, one washed clean of the shameful, blood-drenched history of the Eastern Cape. No doubt · the revitalising power of water is key to cleansing. If the city of Cape

Town is drought stricken, parched in more ways than one, here old selves can be laved, cleansed, dissolved in exorbitant rainfall – and re-created. Here renewal winks at tourists who may gaze into roaring waterfalls, or stride through woods of luxuriant foliage from which water drips ceaselessly, or dart from car to holiday rondavel in lavish rain. Water everywhere.

This manner of re-creation is not for me; I have no need for a fresh start. Instead, I am strangely undone, drained, as I feel the phantom world of yore beckoning, feel the lure of oblivion. Hence the locked door and drawn curtains, a childish attempt at keeping both worlds at bay. If only I could speak to Mary, but that one, so critical of modernity, so protective of her resurrected status, will have nothing to do with a telephone. Thus I must manage without her life-giving voice. In order to *be* – this being that I have come by so unexpectedly and at the behest of another – I must rehearse the reasons for coming here. Who am I? If I came to in the Eastern Cape, why would I feel so unequivocally a stranger here? I may as well have driven through the old Glen-Lynden settlement with my eyes shut for all the sense of belonging it bestowed, and certainly I could not bear the thought of knocking on the doors of the descendants of the old Scottish settlers, trespassing on their estates. And still I'm inclined to believe that I am a native of the Eastern Cape rather than a refugee from the north. What did Mr P really know about the Bechuana boy?

There is no end to the questions. Also, why on earth have I chosen to stay at a resort for tourists? Hogsback was once the headquarters of the Xhosa Chief, Maqoma. I had hoped to explore the area, hoped to find some trace of that past. When Mr P enthused to me about the Kat River Settlement secured for displaced natives, Griquas, Batswana, Goniquas and various stray Khoesan peoples, a place where they could escape serfdom and ill-treatment by settlers, he said nothing of Maqoma, who had been expelled from that land. The Kat River was where he planned for me to work amongst what he called 'my own people'. A miracle and a model, he declared it. There the people, previously seen as dissolute, had converted into a successful, productive and God-fearing community, committed to education and the Protestant value of self-improvement. In those days in London, sitting at Mr P's feet by the fireplace, I too thrilled at the success story, and indeed saw myself as missionary in the land kindly ceded to native people. Imagine, my life spent preaching a gospel of fictions and flummeries. That, at least, was what Mr P's death saved me from. And, of course, death saved him from the rebellion of people who came to see the effrontery of being ceded land in their own country.

I flick through a copy of *Narrative of a Residence in South Africa*. Mr P read out passages to me in my youth, in another century. He writes admiringly of Maqoma as a chief of superior sense, talent and integrity, of how his people had been subjected to colonial aggression and treacherous disregard of verbal treaties. But he also suggests that natives could have been expelled from their land in a more just and amicable manner, or indeed according to some rational plan for their civilisation, instead of with Charles Somerset's insolence and violent measures. I had blocked my senses to Phyllida Ritchie's final rant on dissimulation, her précis of the *Narrative*, but here on the Hogsback I read, surely for the first time, Mr P's chapter on native tribes; a rant on Somerset, yes, but ending with this injunction:

Let us embrace them as MEN *and* BROTHERS. *Let us enter upon a new and nobler career of conquest. Let us subdue savage Africa by* JUSTICE, *by* KINDNESS, *by the talisman of* CHRISTIAN TRUTH. *Let us go forth under the blessing of God to extend the moral influence, and if it be thought desirable, the territorial boundary also of our Colony, until it shall become an empire ... to which even the equator shall prove no ultimate limit.*

It is the words in upper case that carry the weight of offence.

Maqoma's resistance had been legendary. Now, amongst the variety of entertainments for tourists, the municipality offers a Maqoma Heritage Route that includes attractions like a Martello tower with gun placements, by which means the nineteenth-century colonists defended themselves against native attacks. What kind of visitors do they have in mind? There are indeed no black tourists in this hotel.

In the dining room I eat on my own and shamelessly listen in on the conversations of others. I do not have to pretend otherwise: transparent, invisible to my fellow diners, it would seem that I've indeed faded into the phantom world of the past. Last night at a table close by there was a spirited discussion amongst local academics about the swift promotion of their black colleagues. From booming, lecture-theatre voices I discovered that it was not only a disgrace, but that the inevitable decline of standards will grind down the sorry remains of civilisation in this country. Then the voices receded, distorted as if they were channelled through water, and all around shapes slithered in and out of recognition. For the first time since my revival I felt myself drawn into a strange darkness, so that I stumbled out and dashed through the rain to my rondavel, where mercifully I fell into a deep sleep.

Hogsback is a place where people talk only amongst themselves. Whatever the conditions may have been for conversation with others, these have long since been stripped away, and for all the recreation and plenitude of water there seems to be no hope of recovery. Small wonder that I feel a dissolution at the edges of being, a sensation of fading, of my feet wanting to take off, like an exhausted, dispirited Angel of History. How would the indomitable Mary have fared in this? How would she have kept whole? What would she have made of this strange monochromatic, one-dimensional world where you feel yourself receding, longing for oblivion? Even Nicholas, I believe, would have lost his puff and floundered here.

I would like to leave this resort where the hostilities of the nineteenth century seem to be in place, but the electric storm shows no sign of abating. I fancy that the black men and women who work here snigger behind my back. To my face they keep a stony silence. I have never been any good at banter or bonhomie, but I tried all the same to engage the waiter, a fine-looking fellow, at dinner last night. Had he any idea where on this mountain Maqoma's headquarters were?

Yes, he said curtly, you could sign up for the heritage route that takes you to all Maqoma's homes, to his Great Place, but as he turned away he added that, as any native knows for certain, none of the homesteads was ever on the Hogsback. This mountain, he thinks, has always been shaped by white people in search of recreation; besides, he has no idea what heritage means.

Fortunately, before the storm, I had driven through the Kat River valley, heady with the fragrance of wild dagga and lingering orange blossom. In the midday heat I stood on a bridge and heard the cool cascade of water below in the ravine. A land of lushness, in which the dense green of citrus groves promised soon to sport their orange globes. Then the poverty-stricken villages, where bare-bummed toddlers scrabbled in the dirt and beggars in tattered clothes tried to wave me down.

I confess to a squeamish cowardice. I do not see a way of speaking with people who are so very poor. What could I possibly say? What to do about my shame of having so much more than they, and all thanks to the Pringles? Besides, what would be the point of enquiring after the people of the past, of searching for the mixed-race descendants of European colonists and Khoekhoe serfs? Mr P had welcomed such offspring as tenants at Glen-Lynden, where the strong young men cleared the bush for cultivation. What did he think at the time of their expulsion from their fathers' farms? Not surprisingly, such people readily gathered with other dispossessed natives at Fort Beaufort to trek into the Kat River valley, where they were allotted land of their own.

They would have been grateful for Ordinance 50, by which the British ceded to them territory where the People of the Eland once hunted and gathered. And once again they would have cleared the dense bush and dug irrigation furrows and ploughed the land. How could they not believe in demons that demanded a perpetual swing of the axe and bowing of the torso like a mechanical toy? How could they not believe in evil elves who re-rooted by night the trees that had been felled whilst they slept the dreamless sleep of exhaustion? Had they not already done this work on the farms of their fathers who disowned them? Then again at Glen-Lyden?

But no, they were grateful to the Brits; besides, after years of oppression, did they not deserve a green place by the clear water of the Kat? Here their troubles could be laid down; they would sing full-throated hallelujahs and toil for their own good. If bordering on the land of the amaXhosa, fighting off their incursions, and serving as buffer between black and white was the trade-off, so be it. God knew best – at least for the time being.

Their labour paid dividends, but the colonists, angered by the loss of fertile land, scoffed. That success story of diligence, morality and sobriety will necessarily come to a halt, will descend into degradation and poverty, they predicted. How right they were, in a sense: the bulwark strategy backfired, for borders are also places of gradual assimilation. The Bastaards, as their fathers named them, may have lorded it over the Khoe people of their mothers, and defended the colony against their black neighbours, but within two decades of shifting loyalties many of the Kat River people, exasperated by white suprematism, threw in their lot with the amaXhosa. The blood of rebellious people interfused, and bloody wars against the colonists laid all to waste. After nearly two centuries, there is little evidence of recovery.

I must confess to the failure of this fact-finding mission that the others have entrusted to me. I cannot see my way clear to engaging with the poverty of the Kat River villages, hence the holing up in my tourist's cottage to welcome the rainstorms. Not having the courage for another evening of invisibility in the dining room, I plead a migraine and ask for food to be delivered to my rondavel. A man arrives with a tray of tepid hog's flesh. This he leaves wordlessly on my table, where I have cleared a space, and I mumble my thanks, which he may or may not hear, since he leaves without as much as looking at me. Teetering on the limen of the living as I feel myself to be, I rush to the mirror to check that there is indeed enough of me to pass for the real, even though a grey, ashen film has settled on my brown skin.

My confinement in this tourist rondavel leads me to a book I acquired in Cape Town: I have not as yet had a chance to study Mr

Nunn's photographs. Now I push aside my half-eaten hog's belly, transfixed by an image of a church elder at Tambookiesvlei in the old Kat River Settlement – Tambookie being the name given to the abaThembu. I read with excitement the caption that identifies him as W. Pringle.

A model of respectability, he sits upright at the communion table of his Dutch Reformed Church. The formal dress of the elder, in white shirt and white tie and with receding white hair, echoes the lacy white tablecloth on which grand silverware is displayed – communion chalices, an ornate tall jug for consecrated wine, silver platters for the wafers. He poses for the photograph as if he has no idea that behind him things fall apart. There the silver candlesticks, flanking a fretwork bowl, sit on a shelf from which an ugly chintz curtain sags. At the far right of the shelf, the formality is further undermined by an aerosol can, then on a cupboard below, cardboard boxes that once contained Chappies chewing gum and Lemon Cream biscuits are crookedly stacked. What look like crumpled plastic bags spill from these unsightly containers. Perhaps the cupboard is, in fact, a safe in which the silver is kept, only to be brought out for sacramental service when faith and belief allow the grandeur of the communion table to eclipse the tawdry background. Putting his best foot forward, the man in the photograph does not acknowledge the tatty space behind him, on which he has turned his back. The elder's right hand rests on an open register (births, deaths, marriages?), and a padlock lying on the table confirms that all the grand silverware, donated, as the caption says, by a descendant of the founder of the mission church, is usually kept safe under lock and key.

W. Pringle does not smile, not quite; his facial expression, if not quite pleased with himself, could be called benign. He bears the glow of having that day officiated at and partaken of Holy Communion with God.

This is the kind of place that Mr P had in mind for me. It is there in black and white, in a letter to Leith Ritchie: a homecoming for me, Hinza, who would preach God's word amongst his people and educate the youth. Had he lived longer I would no doubt have ended up at such a Nagmaal table, encumbered with sacred vessels donated by the good, indefatigable Christians of Europe, a guardian and polisher of ornate silverware, my back turned on the sagging, faded chintz and the bounty of cardboard boxes overflowing with plastic bags. Of course, Mr P would have brought me himself, would have eased me into the motley society of various mixed peoples, all dulling their dispossession with the blood of Christ. I feel a constriction in my throat, as if the aerosol can in the photograph has released a toxic spurt of air freshener. Such a place would not have encouraged longevity. Exhausted from guarding chalices and candlesticks, and by the demands of nineteenth-century respectability, I would surely have embraced easeful death and resisted any resurrection.

It should not surprise me that it is once more a book rather than the real place that delivers the most fruitful revelation about the Kat River. I return to the pleasing figure of W. Pringle. W. Pringle is not a Scot. He is a black man.

Did Mr P know of his Bastaard family? He whose delicacy would not allow him to use the term. I thrust from my mind the thought that the elder is a direct descendant. Over and over I murder the image of Mr P pinning down a shell-eared native girl with slanted eyes, no more than a child – a Vytje, perhaps? No, it can't be; besides, the hostile settlers who so derided his abolitionist activities would have made a meal of such offspring; rumour and gossip after all were rife amongst bored colonists. Rather, the elder must descend from another Pringle, but to what extent was the mulatto family acknowledged as their own? Were they driven off Glen-Lynden, the family land that not so long before had belonged to the Khoesan, to the shell-eared peoples? Did Mr P know of his black relatives? I shrink from the thought of the terrible example of immoral European missionaries: Old Van der Kemp; and the Reverend Read, whose Bethelsdorp congregation were considered to be the most suitable as first occupants of the Kat River Settlement. These were Christians that Mr P himself applauded, who claimed to save people from exploitation, only there were so many nubile native girls to lead them astray. Again I try not to think of a rheumy-eyed Pringle pinioning a Khoesan girl in the veld.

The Kat River Settlement: a fertile land of many meanings; a buffer zone where God knew best, at least until the Rebellion, when more favourable versions of God took root; and cradle of coloured-ness, for the Rebellion was also when the Khoekhoe abandoned their name, certainly the derogatory name of Hottentot.

A black Mr Pringle is, of course, of no consequence; in these parts it is to be expected. Would Mary expect me to speak to the man? But I can't wait to leave, can't wait to get back to London. I am clearly useless as researcher; I cannot don the role of interviewer, prying into the lives of others. Joshua's words return about gingering up to the task, but truly I cannot imagine seeking out the elder, speaking to the man. Besides, why would he want to disclose his story to the likes of me, whom he does not know from Adam? Did the mulatto Pringles even know of Mr P's adoption of a Motswana boy, taken to London, whilst they, the blood relations, were packed off to the Settlement? I think of Vytje's flayed Tata wrapped in buchu leaves. What do I know of the wounds that may or may not have healed? The Kat River may be the home of grand dames such as Kaatje Kekkelbek and Sara Baartman and Vytje Windvogel, but crouching here behind chintz curtains against an apocalyptic storm, I must be content with what I do not know. Not having the stomach for the embarrassment of pov-erty, and born as I am out of a text, the printed word and the photo-graph must suffice, so that viewing an image of the elder, W Pringle, is all I can manage. I suppress the admonishing voices of Mary and Nicholas, and instead bow respectfully to Mr Nunn. I am happy to make do with his efforts, his considerable talent as a photographer.

VII

That night Nicholas Greene cannot sleep. Feverishly hot, he pushes off the covers. On Hinza's recommendation he has given up unbleached linen gowns for these ultra-modern pyjamas, and now believes its busy paisley pattern to be a source of agitation, let alone the fact that the fabric turns out not to be silk after all, but rather a slippery stuff that crackles with electricity. He turns this way and that, then with arms and legs stretched and joints straightened to the best of his ability, tries the various Vitruvian Man positions, keeping within its imagined square or circle. How well Nicholas knows that his bulk hardly represents the ideal human proportions, but lying in that circle, pondering his condition, his thoughts seem to settle into the cosmic symmetry of the universe.

Yes, yes, and yes again, as things fall peacefully into place – it *is* love, none other than elusive love, for all its evanescent glory, finally caught in his cupped hands. How many centuries has that trickster played loose and fast with him? Not that the various dalliances had not been blissful, the bounty of plump female flesh ever divine, but that had been no more than a tantalising shadow play, an imitation of the ideal whilst he remained chained in the darkest cave of ignorance. But this strange woman, this unsuitable sooty Mary to whom he has thus far paid scant attention, no, whom he viewed through a lens of distaste – for love presses him to be truthful – it is this black magic woman who has prised the scales from his eyes and invaded his heart now brimful with love. The marvel of it, the joy of being invaded, and for once a fortified Nicholas Greene is ready to face the century squarely. With Mary by his side he'll be invincible. He will slough off that old self, get to know her strangeness, her every cell, will pay attention to her movements, to every syllable breathed from that luscious mouth. Rejuvenated, he will tackle their writing project afresh, will come to understand more clearly her position, her interests and arguments, the urgency of her project. Tomorrow he must find her book, the *History* produced by Pringle, and get to know her voice – the sound that issued directly from the lips he has studied and now knows so well.

Refreshed by these new thoughts, he feels the stretched limbs finally settle into relaxation in spite of the slippery pyjama fabric. He retrieves the bedcovers and sleeps like a baby.

Some time ago, at the beginning, Hinza had held out to him the slim volume, and Nicholas had taken it in his right hand, briefly examined its cover, both back and front, and returned it to Hinza without a word. What was he meant to say? Now, as he steps out of Waterstone's as the owner of Mary's *History*, he takes the book out of the paper bag and presses it to his heart. He resisted the desire to hide the other copy in the bookshop, to prevent another from entering that life still sealed from him. As he did the desire to check in the poetry section for his own works, once upon a time so popular.

In the centrally heated library he settles in a comfortable leather chair at the end of the aisles, blocks out the horrible sound of computer keys clacking from the central tables – is everyone nowadays a writer? – and enters that history, immerses himself in the words, convinced that he can hear her strange, lovely island voice. Oh, he could weep for that suffering; the pain and indignity inflicted on her person make him wince with guilt and shame. He, Nicholas Greene, will make amends. He will gather her in his arms and draw from her body all memory of pain. He will lave her with healing, rejuvenating love.

And so transported, with his gout all but forgotten, Nicholas arrives at Mary's house, where he finds her hunkering before a just-lit fire, ready to blow life into the pyre. No, no, he urges, that is for me to do, but she cannot be persuaded to rise until flames leap from the wood.

There, she says, then notes with trepidation the book that Nick clutches in his hand. Strange how that book still induces anxiety as the memory of its reception returns. Can Nick be trusted? What in the world does he have in mind? He places the book on a chair and follows her to the kitchen, sniffing appreciatively at the stew, and insisting that he must contribute to the dinner; he cannot simply be served by her. Mary hands him a strange knobbly vegetable and a scrubbing brush with a brisk there-you-are, and sighs audibly as he cursorily brushes it under a running tap. I don't know how women manage these carbuncular growths, he complains. Tomorrow I'll take you out to dinner, at which she looks at him askance. Then she surprises herself, says that that would be lovely.

When they sit down to eat he speaks of the *History*, how moving it is and how he has found the story of Mary's early life to be so revealing, so different really from what he imagined, or from the woman he has thus far known. He finds her voice enchanting, he says, but how unbelievably shocking what she has been through. He is determined to make amends.

Mary would like to ask how, but refrains. How do you like the stew? she asks instead, and then, softening, says breezily that that story was all a long time ago and really there is no need to take on so, no reason for him to make amends. But she must thank him all the same for his interest, she says sincerely. The book, as he probably knows, is not entirely hers, not really her voice, well not all of it. Miss Susannah, to whom she dictated her life story, has left her own mark on it, taking out all the truths then considered too raunchy for England, and slanting a word or a notion here and there to suit the Anti-Slavery Society, but Mary is grateful all the same that her experience has been made available to educate British people about the savagery of slavery. She will never forget how hard, but ultimately healing, it was to speak of that life, to narrate it out loud, and that is why she will ever be grateful to Mr Pringle, who facilitated it all. It was he who found Miss Susannah to speak with her, to put her at her ease, so that each session left her with a lighter heart. Nicholas must understand that Mr Pringle was by no means wealthy, far from it; nevertheless, he paid from his own pocket to get the *History* published.

Nick nods appreciatively. He apologises for not having paid appropriate attention to her story; he will devote himself to reparation. He will put new energy into their project now that he has a clearer idea of the situation, for Pringle's words about slavery being the perversion of a person into a thing, contrary to the spirit of Christianity, have only just struck a chord. Really Hinza ought to have insisted that Mary's *History* was essential reading, but no, he corrects himself, it is entirely his own fault for resisting her work. Also, he has a few questions to ask, clarification on the matter of her husband …

Mary interrupts hurriedly. No, she does not wish to speak of him, of those times; she has been successful in shaping for herself a new life free of pain and strife, so how about a celebratory day out tomorrow? – to which he nods respectfully.

Mary cannot pretend that she is not pleased. Nick's will not be a Pauline conversion, but she is grateful all the same for this amiable new approach, really for the good manners that he has summoned from who knows where.

And so the evening passes companionably, and Mary feels free to throw back her head in raucous laughter that is unfailingly infectious. She produces the last of the ale, and Nick keeps feeding the fire so that the flames leap joyfully in the grate. In the warmth he notes that Mary is for once unguarded; she even encourages him to tell wicked tales of his earlier cavalier self, at which she slaps her thigh appreciatively. She confesses that having learned to read and write passably well, she regrets not having formal learning, and Nick assures her that it is not too late, that in this modern world that too is possible; indeed they would investigate tomorrow, on their day of celebration. Mary knows from Hinza that there is a wealth of pleasure to be had from learning, from music, art and poetry. But even without learning, Nick points out, she would be able to appreciate much of Will Shakespeare's works; his wife, after all an earthy country woman, understood only too well the love sonnets. Especially the ones not addressed to her, he adds. At which they laugh heartily.

Did he actually know the man? Mary asks. Nick admits that Shakespeare appeared not to care much for him, in fact pointedly avoided him; but then, he adds humbly, I was in those days quite a different person. Not without difficulty, Nicholas rises to his feet. He would be happy to recite for her Will's tribute to his wife: *Let me not to the marriage of true minds admit impediment*, he declaims. But he near falters at every mention of the word love, so that the recitation ends in a strangled ... *nor no man ever loved*, as he finally wrenches his eyes from Mary's mouth.

Mary declares it beautiful, but she is uneasy, and the concentration has exhausted her. She yawns extravagantly and asks Nick to go; she will need her beauty sleep for the morrow.

Which Nick, perking up, takes for encouragement. Christ, he upbraids himself, what a milksop all this has turned him into. He cannot see himself surviving on the textual, the cerebral love of Will's sagging marriage bed.

Mary has indeed had her beauty sleep and Nicholas is grateful for having picked up the demotic, My, you do scrub up nicely, to avoid gushing over her dapple-grey hair brushed out into a frizz and haloed around her face. He must be careful not to alienate her with enthusiastic appreciation – such he knows, is not the way of modernity, aspects of which Mary seems to have taken to with ease. Strange that it has never before occurred to him that it may well be in women's interest to do so; he will have to keep on his toes. It is with a trembling hand that Nicholas takes Mary's arm. Come along, my dear, he says gallantly, let us sally forth, first to the High Street where I've spied some peacock feathers in the window of a second-hand shop.

It is another day of joyous sunshine and bitter cold, so that Mary does not mind at all having a warm arm hooked into hers; in fact, it is a comfort. At Tammy's Treasure Trove they stop to enquire about the feathers. Oh no, the assistant says, that is part of their window dressing, and absolutely not for sale. Nick whispers to Mary that if she would wear the peacock feathers in her hair he'd make the woman an offer that she can't refuse, so that Mary squeezes his hand appreciatively, but no, much obliged as she is, she will not make a spectacle of herself in feathers. Instead she enquires about a woollen sweater in the window, of the loveliest hue of deep orange, with just a tinge perhaps of pink, a colour she has always adored. She would like to try it on.

The saleswoman frowns, says, Actually it's cashmere, and turns to another customer. Mary waits to repeat her request – the sweater in the window – upon which the woman repeats, not without irritation, that it's cashmere.

But I have nothing against cashmere, Mary says, why would I object to cashmere?

Nick intervenes. Could he trouble Madam to get the sweater out of the window, yes, the one worn by the mannequin, so that Mary could try it? Mary would look magnificent.

Persimmon, he believes – not only an exquisite colour, but also a fruit of exquisite slippery texture, a fruit to feed to a beloved.

Madam looks at him askance, obliges without a word, but as she tugs the sweater over the mannequin's head, hisses, It costs £40, I'll let you know.

Much as Mary would like to thwart the woman's assumptions, there is no way around it. The sweater, far too expensive really, is a tad too short, too fashionably boxy, even though Nick applauds enthusi-astically. So she hands it back to the assistant, who sighs audibly and tosses her chin in a *thought-so*.

Mary takes Nick's arm and steers him out of the shop; he must be prevented from making a scene, although she doubts that he under-stands the unspoken. You should have whipped away those peacock feathers while Madam was breathing fire over me, she laughs by way of distracting him.

Nick shakes his head. He ought to have told the woman to be more civil; he registers that Mary is flustered, but the irrational shop-girl discourse is quite beyond him. As is late dining. They won't be able to eat until 6.30, but whiling away an hour or so in a public house will suit them fine, and he bestows on Mary an intense puppy-dog look that she refuses to acknowledge.

Tonight the Vitruvian-Man position offers no comfort. Nicholas has thrown out the paisley pyjamas, found his old linen gown, but all to no avail. He believes that short of falling to his knees with an offer of marriage, he could not have made himself clearer, and yet Mary re-mains unaware of the new turn of events. While he burns with pas-sion, she coolly resists his meaning. On the way home she put her arm through his, companionably, so that there was no mistaking it as anything other than friendship, especially with her initiation of ma-ma-and-papa talk about Hinza, who should be returning within the week. How profoundly shocked Nicholas was that she turned him away at the door, would not let him come in for tea. Oh no, she was too tired. They have had a long day; besides, they agreed on meeting tomorrow to discuss aspects of the last section of the work that Mary thought needed revision. Their project has been neglected of late, and it would be good to show Hinza that they've made progress. And that they worked together so well, she added.

How he wanted to take her in his arms, enfold her with burning love, yes, make the amends he had promised, but so matter-of-factly did she speak, smile even, that his courage failed. Now, with love bounding, broiling through his veins, and with Mary's resplendent form conjured before him, he all but writhes in agony. He cannot bear it. Tomorrow he will declare himself.

The kitchen table has been cleared; Mary's notebooks and pencils are laid out; she is ready with coffee. You ought to cut out sugar, she admonishes, but smilingly stirs his cup all the same. Nicholas can hear his heart pounding. He cannot help himself. He lurches towards her; places his hands on her shoulders; fixes his eyes on hers and explodes. I love you. I'll do without sugar, salt, anything. And Pringle's Life too – I'll amend anything for you, anything to …

Mary, frozen in surprise and confusion, backs away, stutters, No, no, no, this won't do. This is not why we're here, not what our mission is about. Please stop. There isn't room for such … such stuff. This is not destined for us. You don't, you can't. Our hearts have not been renewed; besides, there is no script for love, no room for such a carry-on. We wouldn't know how to proceed. Please, we've become friends, haven't we? Good friends, so don't drag in difficulties, she says, and pats his hand gingerly.

Nicholas moves away, dazed. Can love generate itself unilaterally in this way? It is surely impossible without a morsel of interest on Mary's part – unconscious, perhaps, my dear?

But Mary shakes her head; she has had no part in it. Besides, he is fooling himself, because it simply can't be. There are constraints on their resurrection.

With bowed head, he shuffles towards the door. My stick, he whispers, I'll need a stick, and Mary finds him the stick he left behind some time ago.

She sinks into a chair as he shuts the door behind him. She does not know what to think.

The next morning, Mary is woken early by the squawking of seagulls. She does not know that Nicholas is standing across the road looking up at her window. He is wrapped in his coat and scarf, tugging at his gloves; he has been standing there for some time, keeping vigil, not knowing what else to do.

There is a sudden cacophony of seagulls whirling agitatedly about in the sunlight, white and grey in the true-blue sky. The birds squawk viciously, swoop down and rise repeatedly for no apparent rhyme or reason. Their shapes flit starkly across the whitewashed walls of the house, and Nicholas is transfixed by the strange shadow play. The gulls tumble over the chimney pots where the quarrelling grows louder, where something ominous seems to be happening just out of sight, then once more they tumble over the roof and swoop frantically about, flapping and crying.

Mary opens the window, sees him, and wordlessly disappears. Minutes later, she opens the door, fully dressed. Come in, she says sternly, but please, not another word of impossible love talk, and do have as much sugar in your coffee as you like.

I've come to present my suit more soberly, Nicholas says, shutting the door, so please listen to this plan. London is a huge city and we could simply disappear, adopt whatever disguise appeals to you. We may be here at the behest of a scheming writer, but it must be possible to escape her clutches. A half-hearted contrivance on her part I'd venture; she's played no part, paid no attention since recruiting me, and I wouldn't be surprised if she rather wishes us away, doesn't care, or indeed has forgotten all about us.

Mary stares at him, incredulous. No, she says firmly. We can't abandon Hinza, and besides, you've grown above yourself. We simply can't do as we please; we're bound by a moral contract. There is latitude to become friends and cooperate more efficiently, but that is all.

Madam, either you have a bosom of flint or cannot rise above being a slave. But let me …

With both hands Mary grabs him by the ends of his scarf. It is surprisingly easy to push Nicholas out of the door.

In spite of the horror of Heathrow, of being herded in queues, followed by aggressive interrogation, Hinza is engulfed by a warm sense of relief once he makes it to the Underground. It may be icy out there, but how wonderful to be in a familiar place where you do not have to ponder the business of belonging. It simply is where he wants to be, with his companions awaiting his arrival. Mary will be home with a steaming pot of beans and okra for an early lunch, anxious to hear of his travels, and as he boards the train he thinks fondly of Nicholas and the artist's Underground Map the old man had thrust into his hands after an awkward hug. Nick will be there, no doubt dressed up in his doublet, slouch hat and wilting carnation, ready to raise a glass for a jolly debriefing session.

Instead, Mary greets him anxiously, and Nicholas is not there. She insists that Hinza eat without herself partaking of the bland, hastily produced stew. Only when he finishes – and he fairly gulps his food – will she explain. Nicholas has neither answered his phone for three days, nor responded to messages. At first she attributed it to his hatred of mobile telephones, his reluctance to carry on his person the device that Hinza insisted on giving him.

The deal was that Nick would check it at the beginning and end of each day. How he'd objected: he had no inclination to struggle with the thing, whether in private or public, could not help thinking it vulgar, and would not be seen using it. Call it a phobia if you like, he'd said to Hinza's reproof that they could not rely on the hit-and-miss of vague plans to meet; that he, Hinza, was sick of time wasted in public houses while they waited. Then a clipped, Bugger off, let me be. How dare they speak to Nick about time when Greenwich itself was named after his illustrious ancestor? Besides, what was wrong with waiting when there was always ale and a pie to be had at the Turk's Head? That's how things have always been done. He would resist to the bitter end this urgency, this view of time constructed by modern technology.

Mary thought that he may have mislaid the phone – she too will have no truck with the thing – so she went over to his place yesterday, but her loud knock was not answered. There is a problem, she insists. Nicholas had so looked forward to Hinza's return, had been counting the days, so she'd felt sure that he would turn up well before lunch. Something is wrong, and they must go to his house immediately.

Neither of them has been to Nick's mews flat. He made it clear from the outset that guests were not welcome, but investigate they must. With no response to her banging on the door, Mary decides that they will have to break in, by which she means that Hinza should do it, should find his way through the locked door or window. Find a crowbar, she orders when he makes no move.

Hinza stares at her uncomprehendingly. A crowbar? How? Where?

You're a man, she says, that's what a man does – finds a crowbar when the need arises.

Hinza does not especially want to be like a man, would happily give up the dubious privilege, but this is clearly no time to prevaricate. I'll see what I can do, he says, whilst Mary sits down on the stone step, humming and hugging herself in the cold sunlight.

Nearly an hour passes before he finds on the High Street a desperate Syrian refugee, a man standing redundant alongside his mate who strums a guitar and sings listlessly. He struggles to understand Hinza at first but then, with no little persuasion, allows his palm to be greased, and walks off without a word. To Hinza's surprise he does turn up with a crowbar, takes a deep breath, grits his teeth and bashes in a window, then takes to his heels. Hinza helps to haul Mary through the broken glass. Cut, and not without a show of blood, they survey the kitchenette in which they land.

Filthy old bastard, Mary exclaims, shaking her head. Nicholas can't do without a daily, so where has the woman gone? And when? No doubt he hasn't paid her. Who does he think would clean this pigsty? The table, cluttered with dirty dishes, hosts a swarm of noisy flies, and columns of ants march across with their booty. Hideous effluvium rises from the sink, where encrusted porridge pots drift in sludge. They rush up the steep, narrow stairs, pinching their noses.

Sir Nicholas Greene, or rather what looks like his shadow, lies stiffly, immobile in his bed. They tiptoe in. Is he dead? In a grand four-poster with hand-made lace drapes, red velvet cover, and a starched embroidered sheet drawn neatly to his chin, he cuts an imposing if ghostly figure. He is lying on his back, hands raised on either side of his head to show his palms, and there is a spectral transparency to the form, like a hologram sliding in and out of visibility. Then it stabilises; the eyes flutter and appear to take in the pair leaning over him. Is it a smile that plays fleetingly on his lips?

Mary thinks it's the work of morphine. It won't take long, she whispers. Touch him, she orders Hinza, no one should die alone, die without being touched. Hinza squirms, squeamishly tries to pat a waxen palm that is barely visible on the white sheet, then swiftly withdraws. Mary tuts, places her hand on the papery white forehead, and leans down to press her lips on the icy cheek. Nicholas exhales his last with a slow, weak sigh, and she pulls the sheet that all but crackles with starch over his head. Come now, she instructs Hinza, straighten the other side, so that the scalloped edge is neatly folded over. Together they pull the sheet taut, and the bulge that was Sir Nicholas Greene's body collapses like a sigh and is no more. Mary plumps and smooths the pillow that seconds ago wore the crease of his head. The bed is pristinely made; there is no trace of a cadaver, only at each edge of the sheet a trace of blood from their injured hands has left the ghosts of red fingerprints.

Dead as a dodo, Mary says, crossing herself haphazardly. You've got to hand it to him, that man had resolve; he would stand his ground and take himself off, script or no script. Now we'd better take to our heels. The boys in blue will have to figure all this out by themselves. They will in any case not know what to do with a pair of spooks like us.

It is already early evening. They take themselves into the nearest pub and swiftly down double scotches. Mary is tearful, confesses to feeling guilty. She ought to have treated Nicholas more kindly. Why did she persist in calling him Sir Nicholas, when he had asked to be called Nick? Her unkindness has killed him. She sees no point in burdening Hinza with the business of the days they spent together, but she drops her head on to the table and sobs, so that Hinza puts a consoling arm about her, and says it is time to go home.

Mary stumbles; the St Anthony's fire in her left leg flares up as she rises; she can barely walk. With the unfamiliar flooding of her eyes – did she last cry as a child? – she can't see a thing and, panic stricken, has to be led, supported by Hinza's slight frame. Yes, her sight is vanishing with biblical retribution, a fit punishment for a murderer, she claims, and now tears stream unashamedly.

Hinza says Nonsense and helps her to bed. A shame, he says, about her eyes, but hopefully they'd be better tomorrow. He has brought some postcards from the Cape that Mary ought to see.

Barely has Sir Nicholas bowed out when I hear from Belinda. A postcard with an image by Vanessa Bell of Virginia Woolf wielding knitting needles, her eyes peculiarly smudged, or perhaps the knitting has put her to sleep. Belinda's departure from the Impressionists compels me to read it.

With ever so light a touch, Belinda makes no reference to Old Nick. This purports to be no more than a hello-how-are-you message; the weather has been hellish; do get in touch when you come up to London; let's do lunch. In a postscript she asks how the novel is getting on. Are the characters all on board? Any new characters she ought to meet?

A sly one, that Belinda.

Hinza is alarmed. Mary's sight has not recovered, and she clearly can muster no interest in hearing of his visit to the Cape, although she does exclaim Hallelujah! when he tells her that the word Bastaards is no longer used, the business of miscegenation being long forgotten. He describes one of the manifestations of this – the colourful march of people claiming original Khoesan blood.

You should be kinder, make concessions for people, Mary admonishes. The history of that word no doubt clings like an odour and would account for all kinds of bizarre behaviour.

They sit in silence until Hinza announces, This morning I threw out my Setswana dictionary and phrase book.

I didn't know you had them. Do you not know the language? Is it not your mother tongue? What did you need a phrase book for?

Quite. I no longer do. I got it to write about my meeting with Mr P, thinking that the writing would prompt the language to come back, but, well, it didn't. Turns out I can only speak English and a smattering of African-Dutch. Setswana cannot be my mother tongue, and I fear that Thomas Pringle knew that. In fact, Hinza is my name, for sure, because I chose it, the name of a Xhosa chief as Mr P also well knew, but I don't know what my surname is, and never will. What I strongly suspect, Mary, is that Pringle acquired me by means that he took pains to conceal. He needed people to work on the farm and there were plenty displaced natives that the Magistrate would have been happy to hand over as serfs to the settlers, who were after all more humane than the Dutch farmers. As for me being so young a child, well, he had hoped to find such a present for his Margaret. I, the little wild amnesiac, fitted the bill.

Mary says that he must be mistaken, that Mr P was an honourable man, that Hinza had been unduly influenced by Nicholas.

Oh yes, Thomas Pringle was an honourable man; he did remarkable work for the anti-slavery movement, was much loved and admired by many, but for all the kindness, I believe he deliberately misled me. There are too many unanswered questions about Mr P's life in Africa, which makes me believe that our project is impossible. I must withdraw. But not before checking with Vytje, whose role in Mr P's life may have been greater than we think. Not only is she mentioned in 'The Emigrant's Cabin', but there is also the idyll of miscegenation in 'The Forester of the Neutral Ground'. Ever keen on the notion of borders, Mr P gave that poem the subtitle of 'Border-ballad'. The protagonist, a young Afrikaner, speaks of his love for Brown Dinah, whom he pursues after his outraged family sells her off. He finds Dinah, and with their mixed-race children they live in harmony with indigenes in the Winterberg. I've cast out the thought so many times, but having seen the photograph of a brown Pringle, I do wonder about Vytje. Could it be that our man too broke the 'harsh fetters of Colour and Caste', as the poem has it, with vulnerable young Vytje?   .

Mary shakes her head balefully, Merciful heavens, rather a dead and forgotten white man than this! Breathing deeply, summoning her energy, she says that it can't be. No, absolutely not. Hinza should be ashamed of himself. Had they not been through this very discussion when she suspected Hinza himself of having been abused? As far as she understands, these poems offer no evidence of anything real at all, and that uppity Vytje, who spoke so critically of Mr P, would not have held back.

Besides, Mary has forgotten to tell him that Vytje has bowed out, taken herself off, claiming she's had enough of being a puppet. What kind of prurient world is this where everyone is suspect? She, Mary, will have no truck with such talk, and Hinza ought to hang his head in shame.

Hinza indeed hangs his head in a shame that burns with disgrace. Not the sanitised, Capetonian brand of shame, he notes sardonically – and then remembers his treatment of Joshua. Why had he neglected the taxi driver, and left without as much as a goodbye? He is a cad, and Mary is right. Such heinous thoughts have no place in a sane mind; he knows only too well that Mr P was not capable of such exploitation.

Not only has Hinza thrown out the Setswana dictionary; he has also brought back from Cape Town a modern edition of Mr P's *African Poems*. How foolish he had been! Given to romance, he had treasured the antiquated loose-leaf collection, imagined the imprint of Mr P's hands on the age-stained sheets, and thought it the poet's authentic voice recorded in those musty pages. The true, original 'Bechuana Boy' indeed! Foolish, when he knew that the man had been hard at revising his works in London. *That, my boy, is the very business of writing – revising and refining, polishing words that grow dull with everyday use.* Dulled soon enough, as northern light deflected old beliefs.

How foolish of him to eschew a modern edition of the poems, with notes collated by scholars. So much for being an autodidact! There is, as he now knows, no true story about his origins. Fallen accidentally under Mr P's protection, as the man says in his note: that is as close as he, Hinza, will come to the truth. Only, the word 'accident' is stretched to its fullest meanings, twisted into the tropes that the colony made available to one torn by its contradictions and dissimulations. There! That is the sum of his discoveries.

A pity, though, that Vytje has taken off. She would have liked to hear what the Professor had to say about Fairbairn. Hinza remembers that the terminally ill Mr P, concerned about his debt, had taken out life insurance for £200. This he put in the hands of Fairbairn, by then the son-in-law of Dr Philip, Mr P's main creditor. Stimulated by this forethought on his friend's part, Fairbairn the capitalist founded the Old Mutual Life Insurance Company, a money-spinner that still dominates in the Cape. The colony turned out to be far more profitable than this man, with his new fortune, could have dreamt. Mr P, who cared not a fig for money, was much mistaken about his lucre-loving friend.

And does Mary not find it distressing that Pringle offers not a single word of condemnation of the sexual atrocities of the missionaries? Could it be that he saw in miscegenation a solution for the colony, and so overlooked the abuse of young native girls? Van der Kemp was sixty years old when he bought an entire Khoesan family and married their fourteen-year-old daughter, allegedly in the interest of rescuing them all from slavery. And the scandal of Read, who impregnated the teenage daughter of one of his newly converted San deacons, was well known. For sure, these London Missionary Society men taught the people literacy and protected them from various kinds of European cruelty, but they certainly disregarded their own crimes. How *could* the kind, genteel Mr P view the missions as a civilising influence? Why did he not decry their foul deeds?

Mary says there's no getting round these horrible deeds, but in those days people did not know any better. And why brood over things the man has *not* said or done? She, Mary can testify to the fact that his behaviour was always gentlemanly, that he cared not a fig for money, and that she was not the only slave he supported. Remember also his campaign to free Stuurman, the Khoe resistance fighter, and return him from banishment in Australia – even if the man died before he reached home; but that so often was the way with Mr P's projects. Mary sits up, purses her lips. Still, if it were a case of Mr P turning to humanitarianism because of being slighted by Charles Somerset, if in the light of it he revised his writing to promote the rights of indigenous people, then I say, Well done Sir and congratulations on your conversion. Having had my history of slavery printed for all to read, I say, Three cheers for Thomas Pringle. His first-hand accounts of slavery at the Cape alerted the world to its wickedness, and if that also landed him a job at the Anti-Slavery Society, I say once more, Well done Sir.

Gonnae lay down your burden, as Mrs P used to say, down by the riverside my boy, lay down your troubles, Hinza, and sing Hallelujah for the end of slavery in the colony.

Hinza says yes, he has been selfish, thinking only of his disappointment, his own history; but the fact remains, they cannot carry on with a project that now is tinged with distaste. Much as he loves the man, there is no ambiguity about the Christian beliefs that underpinned colonialism – fraudulent to the core, as Mr P's own rhetoric shows.

It is also the case that not only has Nicholas gone, but his Gladstone bag of papers has clean disappeared, presumably destroyed by the man himself. There is nothing to show for all their work. Strange, the pattern of Mr P's papers being lost; it has ever been the man's fate.

Mary agrees that they've been defeated; besides, so painful is her leg and so fearful is she of the blindness that has fallen upon her, that she has no enthusiasm for anything. This new life is not what it's cracked up to be; lured into it by the writer woman, she believes that they've been misled, and frankly she's as sick as a parrot, as her dear friend Nicholas would have said.

What you ought to appreciate, Mary, Hinza explains, is that just as you freed yourself from bondage, slaves all over the islands unceasingly organised uprisings, for which they were brutally, savagely punished. The British back home, some revered writers included, condoned the brutality, but slaves carried on resisting. It was to such rebellions that right-minded western thinkers responded, and the anti-slavery movement gained momentum directly in relation to the slaves' own determination to resist. Ultimately, the whole enterprise became unmanageable. Of course, movements in Europe, like the French Revolution and the philosophies that underpinned it, also inspired the enslaved, but although abolition was hastened by the anti-slavery movement, it would be wrong to underestimate the role that slaves themselves played in gaining their freedom. Abolition was bound to happen precisely because the upsurge of rebellion threatened the profit margins.

Enough, Mary interrupts, says that lectures make her head spin; she waves away the glass of water that Hinza tries to place in her hand. Oh, they have tried, and seeing what this new world has thrown up has not been without interest, but all is topsy-turvy, scrambled, and she has lost her puff. Nothing left but to follow the example of the others and bow out.

Hinza says they should raise a glass to Mr P before calling it a day; he has brought a fine bottle of Kaapse Vonkel from the Cape. Mary insists that Hinza help her to the cemetery, to the empty grave where Thomas Pringle once lay for over a century before he was taken back to the Eastern Cape. There they'll pay their respects over a glass or two.

It is nearly dark. Mary, stone blind, refuses to wear shoes. Wrapped in coats and scarves, the pair stumble in the rain across London to the Barbican, to Bunhill Fields Burial Ground where Defoe and Blake among others still lie snug in their graves. In the gloaming they find their way into the grounds, across to the border – Mr P was ever fond of borders – where the empty grave lies. The city noise has subsided with the fading light and white hellebores nod their heads in the gentle rain that breathes through the oak tree, or might it even be a wittegat? Birds settle in its branches, murmuring their bedtime prayers.

Early next morning, Bill Bodwin, the barely awake warden, could have sworn that a couple of tramps huddled together, hugging each other, were just now sitting on the bank of wet earth, facing City Road. He hears a humming, something soft and sweet like a lullaby, but even as he approaches, the figures are gone. It is stone quiet, and lying in the grass is an empty bottle. Kaapse Vonkel, he reads from the label. Makes a change from Buckfast.

Belinda is in Glasgow to meet with her most lucrative writer, the prolific and reliable McGurn, with whom she'll have dinner. She summons me to lunch. I briefly toy with the idea of feigning illness, but suggest lunch at Eusebis, which is not to be sniffed at. Having in the past two weeks scraped by on beans and toast, and in spite of looking a tad better without the surplus weight, I'm haunted by hunger. It is possible that after my broken contract, supply teaching might still be available, that the education authority is desperate enough to employ me on a sink estate, but the truth is that I fear bumping into Annie, who is also on the supply circuit. That is how we met. Annie, the Caledonian beauty with pale skin and flaming red hair. And I a despicable coward, a cheat and a liar.

Belinda is, as usual, beautifully shod, and in the unexpected spring sunshine brims with enthusiasm. The lovely Giovanna comes over to say hello and recommends her new starter, creamy burrata with shavings of truffle on a bed of peppery rocket, which we both order. Belinda will drink only tap water – But do have whatever you fancy, she urges me. I order Prosecco; it may not be Kaapse Vonkel, but it comes in a beautiful glass, and I take courage from the bubbles winking at the brim. Fortification is needed for what I have in mind, and so I ignore her delicate raising of an eyebrow. I tear like a wolf at the delicious focaccia.

Belinda has abandoned her ever-so-light touch. Getting down to business, she asks outright what I've been doing. Which one are you now writing, *To Miss with Love* or *Thomas Pringle?*

I've had to abandon Pringle, or rather, the Pringle characters have abandoned me. She smiles. Well, she thinks the story set in a comprehensive school to be excellent, and as she's said before, worth pursuing.

It won't happen. Then I blurt, I can't write about the school without writing about Annie.

Who's Annie?

Of course, I haven't told her. I myself barely understand. Annie is the person I can't write about. I'm sick of stories with gaping holes, and the story of Annie must necessarily carry the hole of my shame. It can't be done, I explain. I may as well be sent to catch a falling star.

Belinda says that that's a shame, but that there are ways in which an absence in a story could be fashioned in an alluring manner. She'd be delighted to help me through, cast a veil, so to speak, over the holes.

I am not a woman true and fair. Cowardly, I resort to the prepared lie. I have just taken a job in a debt-collecting agency, full-time work that won't allow time for writing. By which I mean that I've already quit, that I renege on the contract, and would be happy to pay back the advance over the course of a year. Whilst Belinda sips her black coffee, I shamelessly binge on a tiramisu.

She washes her hands of me with customary delicacy. From her bag she fishes a bag of sweets. Your favourites, she says. And do look me up when you come to London, she says.

I leave the sweets on the table, under my napkin. I have no need of them.

ACKNOWLEDGEMENTS

My gratitude to my publishers, Diane Wachtell at The New Press and Fourie Botha at Penguin Random House, for their kind and longstanding faith in my work. Many thanks too to my meticulous editor, Henrietta Rose-Innes.

I am indebted to the STIAS Foundation for the generous award of a four-month residency at Stellenbosch.

Warmest thanks to my first reader, Neel Mukherjee, for his encouragement.

Thanks also to Hillary and Rick Rohde for a productive week of writing in their Edinburgh house; Jean Rafferty for access to her flat in Amble; Henrietta Dax for hospitality and help in Cape Town; and Patrick Flanery for his support.

Still Life could not have been written without Thomas Pringle's own works of prose and poetry; *The History of Mary Prince, a West Indian Slave;* and Virginia Woolf's *Orlando.* (However, as a work of fiction, it does not always adhere strictly to the facts: Hinza Marossi, for instance, enters the Pringles' lives some months earlier than was, in fact, the case.) Of the many works on Thomas Pringle that I consulted, the following have been invaluable:

Randolph Vigne, *The South African Letters of Thomas Pringle* and *Thomas Pringle: South African Pioneer, Poet & Abolitionist*; Matthew Shum's PhD thesis, 'Improvisations of Empire: Thomas Pringle in Scotland, the Cape Colony and London, 1789-1834', accessed on researchspace.ukzn.ac.za; Clifton C. Crais, *White Supremacy and Black Resistance in Pre-industrial South Africa*; and Robert Ross, *The Borders of Race in Colonial South Africa*.

I have also benefitted from the following: Andrew Geddes Bain, 'Kaatje Kekkelbek'; Damian Shaw, 'Two "Hottentots", Some Scots, and a West Indian Slave: the origins of Kaatje Kekkelbek'; and Cedric Nunn, *Unsettled: One Hundred Years War of Resistance by Xhosa against Boer and British*.

As always, special thanks to Roger Palmer for his invaluable patience, support and help in finding sites in the Eastern Cape.

Extracts from *Still Life* have appeared in *New Contrast*, Cape Town; *The Harvard Review*; *Gutter Magazine*, Glasgow, and in Dorothy Driver (ed.) *A Book of Friends: In Honour of J.M. Coetzee's 80th Birthday*.

ABOUT THE AUTHOR

Zoë Wicomb is a South African writer living in Glasgow, Scotland, where she is emeritus professor at the University of Strathclyde. She is the author of *October*, *The One That Got Away*, and *Playing in the Light*, all published by The New Press, as well as *David's Story*. She was an inaugural winner of the Windham-Campbell Prize in fiction.

Publishing in the Public Interest

Thank you for reading this book published by The New Press. The New Press is a nonprofit, public interest publisher. New Press books and authors play a crucial role in sparking conversations about the key political and social issues of our day.

We hope you enjoyed this book and that you will stay in touch with The New Press. Here are a few ways to stay up to date with our books, events, and the issues we cover:

- Sign up at www.thenewpress.com/subscribe to receive updates on New Press authors and issues and to be notified about local events
- Like us on Facebook: www.facebook.com/newpressbooks
- Follow us on Twitter: www.twitter.com/thenewpress
- Follow us on Instagram: www.instagram.com/thenewpress

Please consider buying New Press books for yourself; for friends and family; or to donate to schools, libraries, community centers, prison libraries, and other organizations involved with the issues our authors write about.

The New Press is a 501(c)(3) nonprofit organization. You can also support our work with a tax-deductible gift by visiting www.thenewpress.com/donate.